HERO'S ANGER

SONG OF PROPHECY
BOOK ELEVEN

P.E. PADILLA

OLIVER HEBERBOOKS

The Great Prophet predicted you would want to read his story

Tsosin Ruus, the most renowned mage during the Age of Magic, wrote the Song of Prophecy to aid the world of Dizhelim as it would exist thousands of years after his life ended. But who was the Great Prophet, and how did he come to be the most important person in history...up until the present time?

And what of Erent Caahs, the most famous of contemporary heroes?

Get these two full-length companion novels to the Song of Prophecy and Hero Academy series for free and find out the fascinating stories that transformed ordinary boys into figures idolized by millions.

To get your free books and find out about upcoming books, please visit my website at https://pepadilla.com (Newsletter menu item or the bottom of every page). Thank you!

PARTIAL MAP OF DIZHELIM

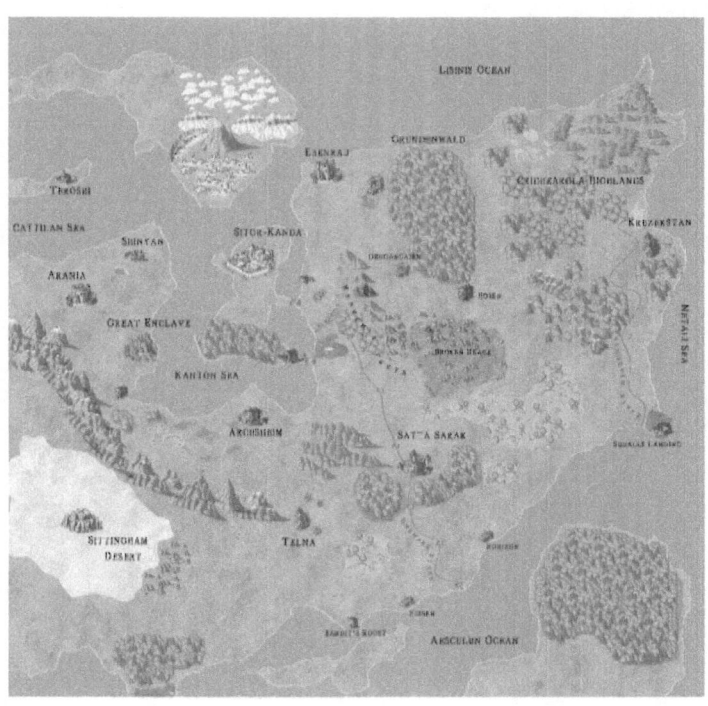

In my time, I have seen the righteous anger of men and I have seen foolish acts of rage. Much like fire, anger may be useful, if controlled. However, when the beast is set loose with no constraints, it has been my experience that no good has ever come of it. Alas, the result is quite often catastrophe.

Tsosin Ruus, on anger and warfare, from his personal journal.

PROLOGUE

Ten-year-old Marla Shrike yawned so hugely her jaw cracked. Her eyes darted toward the front of the lecture area to make sure it hadn't been noticed. She couldn't help it, though. The information they were being given was...well, it wasn't as exciting as she had thought the class would be.

Master Isegrith Palus stood in front of a group of fourteen students, lecturing. The master seemed so large to Marla. Not fat, not really, but just big. She always wore the same green master robes with the white fur trim and her posture was perfect at all times. Marla wondered sometimes if she had several sets of robes that looked exactly the same.

The master's nose was sharp, making her look like some kind of hawk, ready to swoop down on children not paying attention. She'd actually been known to do that, too.

Marla had mastered the School of Fundamental Magic, one of the schools all students were required to attend at the Hero Academy. Though today's lecture should have been on the subject of fire magic, with Master Ulrenod, he was not available, though the students were not told why. So, Master Isegrith, the Master of the School of Fundamental Magic, was taking his place.

"I know that each of you are well familiar with the techniques for gathering qozhel, the magical power of Dizhelim, and utilizing it for spells," the master said. "You also know how to manipulate it for a wide range of castings. I *know* you know this because I have taught you myself, some of you not very long ago."

Master Isegrith looked right at Marla—who was glad she'd decided to start paying attention—and nodded.

"Who can tell me how we effectively utilize the qozhel for fire magic, as opposed to, say, water magic?"

Several hands went up, Marla's not one of them. She'd found long ago that if she tried to answer every question, it not only made the other students dislike her, but at times irritated the masters as well.

One of the students answered the question and the master continued to drone on. Marla's eyelids drooped and she sat up straighter to keep from falling asleep.

It was a poor joke for class to be moved out to the edge of the magical combat field only to sit them down and talk at them. Marla's eyes scanned the field, trying to find something interesting to look at. Several groups of older students were sparring and practicing their spell work on magical training dummies. Marla wished she was one of them.

"I told you, stop irritating me," a voice said, drawing Marla's eyes. They settled on a tall, lanky man with dark brown hair. He seemed to be yelling at another student, this one with blond hair and maybe an inch shorter but thicker than the dark-haired man.

"What's the matter Ivel, you don't like it when I pronounce your name? Huh, Eevil?"

"It's Ivel, EYE-vil. I'm warning you, back off."

This wasn't the kind of interesting Marla had wanted, but she locked her eyes on the young men anyway. She recognized them, of course. The Academy didn't have *that* many students. She thought they were both somewhere near twenty years old. That meant they'd been in training for nearly a decade and a half. She wondered what they knew how to do.

"What are you going to do?" the yellow-haired student asked. A few other pupils—two girls and a boy—headed toward them to break up the argument.

Master Isegrith had paused in her lecture, but began speaking again when the other students reached the pair and their speech became softer. Marla continued to watch. She wasn't convinced the show was over yet.

Suddenly, the dark-haired student took a wide stance and held his arms out in front of him. Between his hands, a ball of roiling fire appeared. The other students backed away, all except the blond one who'd been taunting the other man.

"Do you think that can do any harm to—" the blond student started, but was cut off as the fireball blasted from Ivel's hands and slammed into his chest, full-force.

He must have cast a shield because, though he flew through the air to land on his back some ten feet away, he didn't seem to be burned. He scrambled to his feet and motioned with his hands to cast another spell.

He wasn't fast enough.

The dark-haired Ivel moved his hands more vigorously, muttering words of power as he pulled energy from his body and his surroundings. Marla could feel the draw and was surprised how powerful it felt, even as far away as she was.

What she witnessed next was something she was never likely to forget. Magic, in the form of light, fire, and wind in succession, rammed into the blond student, pelting him again and again. Each attack glowed briefly as it hit the shield protecting him, but the glow got weaker with each attack.

Finally, what looked like a lightning bolt, but straight as a pole weapon, punched through the shield and went completely through the blond student.

Ivel wasn't done, though, because several other magics were already on their way toward the downed student. Marla was afraid the victim would be disintegrated completely, but she was surprised again. A new shield sprung up, surrounding the blond student. It stopped all further magic from getting to him.

Then, a glowing orb surrounded Ivel and began to shrink. First his hands were restricted from the motions he was using to cast, then his arms were pinned to his sides. Within seconds, he looked like he was being squeezed by invisible ropes, his face even starting to turn red like he couldn't breathe. His head went limp and leaned to the side within the invisible bubble.

Marla tore her eyes away from the scene to find Master Isegrith standing halfway between her class and the conflict, her arms raised. As she motioned with them, Ivel's unconscious form floated toward her like he was lying on an invisible bed being carried by invisible people.

"Saria, please see to the class. Assign appropriate reading and dismiss them. I will be at the headmaster's office."

Marla wondered why the master hadn't done something to help the boy on the ground instead of taking away Ivel, but then a few of the students shifted out of the way and she saw the reason. The blond student had a hole as big as his fist blown through his chest. He was dead. Just like that. There was no healing a heart that no longer existed.

She stared at the corpse that had been living just a few moments before, wondering how such a thing could happen. *Why* it would happen.

Several days later, all Academy students were required to attend a meeting in a lecture hall large enough to hold all of them. When Marla got there, she sat down and waited for it to start.

Master Qydus Okvius took the stage and put his hands up. The hall went completely silent in an instant.

"I know each of you has probably heard rumors of what happened. The masters wanted to be clear on all the details before we addressed you about the sad situation that has befallen the school. I will explain briefly so that you will all have accurate information.

"Academy student Ivel Danson has attacked and killed another student of this institution. From witness reports, Sharan Kolga had persisted in taunting and provoking Student Ivel for some time. Three days ago, by all accounts, Ivel lost all sense of reason, due to the mocking and several other sources of tension in his life. He used his abilities learned as an Academy student to deal fatal damage to Sharan.

"I want to be clear on two things. First, if anyone feels that they are being targeted for taunts, physical attacks, or any other actions that are deleterious, you *must* report it to a master or to myself. Actions such as these will not be tolerated.

"Second, let me remind and caution every one of you. The only sanctioned use of your abilities and skills against another student or any member of the staff of this school is in sparring or demonstration. Any attack aside from an official school reason will be punished severely.

"That being said, I will inform you of the last piece of information in this most dire of situations. Mister Danson has had all his magical abilities and the knowledge of all martial skills magically wiped from his mind. He has also been expelled from this institution. Any further violent acts in the future, should they come to the attention of the masters, will result in his immediate execution.

"Losing one's temper and going into a rage is not a valid reason for harming another. Please take this unfortunate situation as a lesson. You are dismissed."

Marla walked back to her room in a daze. She knew Sharan had been killed; she'd been there. But the other things. Wiping things from Ivel's mind, putting him on notice that if he performed a violent act in the future, he'd be executed, it was a lot to digest.

One thing was for sure, she would never let her anger get away from her like that. Her fear of ending up like either one of the students involved would keep it from from happening.

ONE

Marla was mad enough to kill someone.

She stomped toward her room after a day of teaching classes and working on busy work that, honestly, she felt was far beneath her. Even that attitude in herself, the haughty entitled assurance, made her mad. Not quite enough to kill herself, but someone else? Definitely.

It had only been a few days since all of her friends were back at the Academy for the first time in...a while. She couldn't even think clearly enough to remember how long it had been. Everyone wanted to gather together for meals, of course. She loved her friends and family, but at the moment, she didn't feel like she was fit company. Better if she hid in her room for a while to cool down.

She kicked so hard at a leaf on the path she trod, she almost tripped herself. Great, as if the entire world being filled with idiots, greedy selfish bastards, and assholes wasn't enough, now she'd lost her coordination.

"Aaarrrgggghhh!" she growled, scaring a couple of girls walking the opposite way on the path. They both leaped onto the grass and skirted around her, giving her as wide a space as they could.

"Sorry," she said with a sigh, then took a deep breath and let it out. Home. She needed to get away from people and lock herself in her room.

The day hadn't started horribly, though the underlying anger and general disappointment was there as usual lately. Her own classes were fine. Not great, but not terrible, either.

Then she was subjected to two classes of younger students she had to teach artificing. Still, that wasn't a great tragedy, though it did move the needle on her bad mood for the day. It was a miracle of the gods that she hadn't used some of the many tools around them in the workshop to murder at least two or three of them. Had she been a bad student like the ones she seemed to get stuck with? Lazy, whiny, and unmotivated. How did they ever get into the Academy, let alone stay there?

No, she'd never been like them. She could remember students like that when she was younger. They were always there, the ones that maybe ended up mastering a school or two over twenty years. She and the only friends she had— Skril and Evon—were miles ahead of those other students.

Because they cared.

That was really the difference. Supposedly, each new student that entered the front gate of the Academy at Sitor-Kanda could possibly be the Malatirsay. It was the reason the school was founded. Somehow, though, the attitude developed that, though the Malatirsay would be found and trained at the Academy, there was plenty of room for others to learn valuable skills and gain outstanding abilities.

Now, in the time prophesied, the Dark Days, there was suddenly no desire to fulfill the original purpose of the school: to fight the animaru and save all of Dizhelim. It left Marla flabbergasted.

Though she thought seeing the attitude every day had inured her to it, this particular outlook was even more shocking. The general apathy and laziness of many of the students primed her for what she had witnessed only half an hour before, while she was gathering her things up after a class so she could escape and have some time to herself.

"That was really boring," one of the younger students had complained to his friend.

"I know," she responded. "Why can't we go to the field and practice magic instead of getting all this theory? Or at least, if we have to learn artificing, we should be able to work with materials instead of sitting next to them and being lectured at."

Marla almost chuckled at that. She could remember thinking the same way, before she realized that without the theory and the lectures, one could never really master casting spells, let alone anything else.

"I heard they're hiring mercenaries in Rhaltzheim," the boy had continued. "If I can hurry up and master three schools and graduate to become a *viro*, I can probably get a good job there and make lots of money."

"Rhaltzheim? What about this Malatirsay thing? Fighting the animaru?"

"Are you crazy? They already know who the Malatirsay is. That one that just lectured us and her brother, they're the ones. They're going to fight the animaru and the rest of us can do whatever we want."

"I don't think that's how it goes," the girl said. "I'm pretty sure the Malatirsay is supposed to be like the general or something, taking on the hardest enemies and everyone else doing what they can to help."

"No way. Where's the money in that? I mean, did you really think you were going to be the Malatirsay when you came here? I always knew I was going to get the training, then go and make my fortune from it. I was thinking I'd be a hero, but someone from the Academy as a mercenary? They make a lot of gold. That'll be good enough for me."

"Yeah, maybe. Anyway, it's going to be a while before you can master enough schools to leave here and be considered a graduate. You'll have time to figure it out."

"I guess. It won't be that long, though. How hard could it be? That Marla girl already mastered something like fifteen schools. I'll be out of here in no time."

Marla had almost gone back into the lecture hall and told the little pissant the truth of things. Luckily, the two students left as she was wrestling to get her irritation under control.

Mercenaries? Really? The survival of the entire world was at stake and the miserable little rat was thinking about ducking out and searching for gold?

She came upon another leaf in the path but wisely did not try to kick it into oblivion. It was enough to get to the safety of her room and throw herself on the bed. On second thought, she turned back, looked around her, and flashed the thing into oblivion with a fire pellet. *Take that.*

Two hours later, Marla gave in to her attack of conscience and headed over to Batido, the dormitory the Academy had allowed her friends to use as their home. She shook her head at the thought. Evon had already essentially moved there himself, taking up residence in one of the empty rooms so he could be with everyone else as much as possible. Especially Fahtin.

She came through the door into the common room, as busy and loud as it usually was. Tere Chizzit was the first one who spotted her, his bald head gleaming and his white eyes reflecting the lamplight and firelight fully. He nodded at her and she gave him a little wave, encompassing Lily, who was sitting next to him, with it. The statuesque archer waved back, her red mane shifting with the movement. Marla liked the woman. She kind of had to. They were red-hair sisters, after all.

Urun Chinowa, the scruffy-faced nature priest, lifted a cup to her as she walked past and Raki—seeming to materialize from nothingness near the priest—gave her another wave. Jia Toun, the black-clothed and constantly cheerful former assassin gave Marla a smile that almost made coming to the place worth it.

"Oooh," Fahtin squealed when she caught sight of Marla. "Marla. I'm so glad you came. Come and sit down." The Gypta beauty wrapped Marla up in a hug and squeezed hard enough to make her huff. The woman's long black hair, naturally wavy, tickled the side of Marla's face.

"Nice to see you, Fahtin."

She wasn't able to sit down because Aeden was suddenly right there, nudging Fahtin out of the way to hug Marla himself. He wasn't a hugger, and it showed in the awkward way he held her, but it was all the more comfortable because of it.

"Good to see you," Aeden said. "You haven't been around lately."

"A lot going on," Marla told her twin brother. "It's been hectic."

"I know. Come on. Sit down and relax. If you can do that with all this racket."

Marla snorted, the closest she had come to a genuine laugh in a while.

She took a seat next to where Aeden had been sitting, noticing Khrazhti as she did so. For a woman nearly seven feet tall, the animaru was adept at sitting unobtrusively and going unnoticed. It was especially incongruous because she was striking in every way, from her exotic features to her blue skin, of which a lot was showing. Khrazhti wasn't one for modesty in her dress. Marla guessed that went for most of the animaru, based on the hundreds she'd seen.

Khrazhti reached her hand out to Marla, who clasped it and tried hard to match the smile on the animaru's face. So strange to think that this woman, who had truly become a friend, had come to this world to destroy all life. But that was before Khrazhti understood that death was a permanent thing for people of Dizhelim.

"Hi, Khrazhti."

"Good evening, Marla. I am glad to see you."

"I'm glad to see you, too. I've been...busy."

Khrazhti's smile slipped fractionally, but she didn't press Marla. Everyone knew that it wasn't just her workload that had kept her from socializing. She'd snapped at enough people to make it clear she had been in a foul mood of late.

Aeden passed her a cup of ale and she sipped it while settling into the myriad conversations in the room. The noise of it seemed too much for the number of people there, but that's how it always was. It usually amused her, but this night it was all she could do to tolerate it.

12

As she scanned the room, she noticed Aila Ven. The diminutive woman was striking enough with her dark hair, angelic face, and fit form displayed attractively by the snug clothing she wore, but in her current situation, Marla was surprised she hadn't noticed the woman earlier. She sat less than ten feet away, the Clavian Knight Conren Gardner, who was her childhood friend and current protector at her elbow, and that peculiar creature she had brought back from her journey into the ancient magical area called Sintrovis.

Even now, Raki was leaning over, talking with the trebaxel, which Aila had named Scrapper. No one was certain how much he understood, but from the stories Aila, Tere, and Lily had told, he was intelligent. Scrapper, not Raki. Well, Raki, too.

Aila caught Marla's gaze and flashed her a smile.

"Princess Alevia Davenson of the Great Enclave," Marla said with a smirk. It had been quite a shock when Aila's real name and history had been revealed. The others still teased her relentlessly about it. From the look on Aila's face, they had done so recently.

Aila rolled her eyes. "Please. For my friends, even peasants such as you, I will always be simply Aila Ven."

"Simple is right," Marla quipped and Aila laughed. Bantering with her friends usually made her feel good, and she guessed it did cool the overlying anger she'd been feeling lately, but all she could think about was getting back to her room, pulling the blankets over her head, and getting some sleep.

She didn't stay long. Between the exhaustion in being in proximity to Fahtin's bubbly personality, trying to keep track of the conversations going on around her, and all the little things turning in the back of her mind pushing her mood back toward dark, she finished her ale, apologized that she needed some rest, and left.

As she strolled on the paths back to her dorm room, Marla took in the starry sky above her. She loved the Academy, the place she'd grown up in, but even that comforting feeling of home didn't dull the edge on her turmoil. How could she walk through the parklike setting, trees around her and the majesty of the night sky above, and still feel like she was at a low boil? It was as if anything at all could trigger her and she'd go into a full-blown rage.

She didn't like it. Not at all. And that, of course, made her angry.

When she got to her room, Marla threw herself into the chair at her desk. Though she'd looked forward to it all night, now she wasn't quite in the mood to go to sleep. Maybe she'd study. She had several more schools she was working on mastering, and one did not do so by slacking off with their efforts.

Her anger had cooled a little after meeting with her friends. It would have grown had she stayed longer, but she was in a better condition than before she'd left her room. That damn tugging, though. The sensation that something was pulling her toward the south sprung up inside her, as it had occasionally for the last week or two. She almost felt like she had to lean away to counteract it. It was, from start to finish, strange and inexplicable.

She sighed and opened the book closest to her. *On the Magic of Light*. Well, Master Saelihn would appreciate her opening the tome.

Marla hadn't read more than a few paragraphs before someone knocked at her door. It wasn't terribly late, but neither was it really a customary time for visiting someone.

Her irritation spiked and she tamped it down. Better to see who it was than to imagine an insult.

With a sigh, she opened the door to find a woman standing there. A woman she hadn't seen in many years, one she wasn't sure she'd ever see again. Her clothing was the same—or at least of an identical style—as she'd worn the last time they were face to face, though maybe it was a little more worn.

"Saria?" Marla said.

"Hi, Marla. Can I come in?"

TWO

S aria Gilwenys.

Marla nodded dumbly to the woman's question. "Yes, of course, please come in."

Marla's eyes swept over her guest. The woman was nearly identical in height with Marla and if pressed, she would have to say that Saria was maybe just a few pounds shorter, slender and elegant to Marla's slightly stronger-looking form. Then again, no one was a very good judge of their own appearance, so who knew?

The visitor's sand-colored hair was longer than the last time Marla had seen her. She still wore the high boots with the belted tunic that left her thighs bare, gathered tightly at her bust and with those loose sleeves that had fascinated Marla so when she was younger. Of course, her signature attire included the voluminous cloak, the current one a deep green and thick enough to use as a blanket.

It was the state her clothes were in that concerned Marla. Saria had always been so particular about her appearance. Even the slightly frayed edges or the shiny spots where the cloth had been worn thin were unlike the

Saria Marla remembered. The dust and stains from traveling she understood, but the evidence of combat concerned her.

"How?" Marla started, then changed her speech mid-thought. "Where? What happened?"

Saria's pretty face lightened up, delicate eyebrows raising over thin, mysterious eyes, the ice blue flashing as her lips curved into a smile. "Funny. I don't remember you being so inarticulate, Marla. How the time has changed us, eh?"

Saria's voice had a magical quality, still, like she was about to burst into song. Which, honestly, she sometimes did. Marla didn't miss the lute case hanging from the strap slung over her chest.

"It's a surprise, that's all. I haven't seen you in...five years? Six?"

"Something within that range. You've grown taller." Saria narrowed her eyes at Marla. "Fitter. More beautiful. Gods, Marla, you must utilize all that combat training every day to keep the men from hunting you."

Marla laughed. "You'd be surprised." She put her arms around Saria and embraced her in an awkward hug.

"Ugh. Perhaps I can shed my pack, my lute case, and then we can try this again?"

"Of course. Sorry. I don't even know what came over me. I think I've been hanging around my friends too much lately. Some of them might be rubbing off on me."

"That sounds nice." Saria set her lute on Marla's bed, her pack on the floor, and swung the slender sword in a scabbard at her hip to the side. "There, now come here and give me a proper hug."

Marla did so, and the anger she had been feeling slipped further away from her.

Saria released Marla and swept her hair back over her left ear, so the pointed tip could be seen easily. She had always taken special care to hide those ears when she had been at the Academy.

"May I sit for a moment."

Marla started. "Oh, sorry. Yes, of course. Please, sit. I don't have much in here, but I have a pitcher with some ale —though it's probably warm. I can get something to snack on, some wine, whatever you want."

"I'm fine for now. I do have a favor to ask you, though."

"Anything."

"May I stay here tonight?"

"Stay here?" Marla's gaze swept her small room. "Sure, but I think I might have a better option. The headmaster has allowed my friends to take over the old Southwest Dormitory Twelve. I just came from there, actually. There are several rooms left and you can take one as your own, if you wish. Not that I'm trying to keep you from staying with me, mind you. I figured you might be more comfortable with a place you can have for yourself. I don't know how long you'll be here. Are you back for good?"

"That remains to be seen. I'll speak with the head-master tomorrow. I tried to get a word earlier, but he was occupied. I got caught up with a few of the masters who spotted me and I'm just now trying to make arrangements for the night. The reason I'm here is because of his message sent out to all graduates. Something about returning for a historical event?"

"Yes, I know about it. Saria, are you well? I can't help but to notice you're looking a little bedraggled. For you, at least." Marla gestured to a rent in the side of her tunic that had been stitched skillfully so it was unnoticeable under casual inspection. Marla had developed the habit of looking carefully years ago. Which was why she also noticed some of the blood stain that had not come out in the cleaning, along the edges of the repaired cloth.

"Things have been a bit rough lately, but nothing to worry over. I'm fine." She stood, raised her arms, and turned in a circle to demonstrate.

"I'd love to hear all about it. First, though, tell me what you want to do about resting. You are welcome to stay here or at Batido. That's the name my friends have given the dormitory they're staying in."

"Second home, in Dantogyptain. Yes. I saw Evon earlier and he mentioned the place. Lovely."

"Oh, yeah. I almost forgot your obsession with language. Almost as strong as your obsession with song, and *the* Song."

Saria tapped her lute case. It gave back a hollow, musical vibration, like the strings on the instrument inside had reacted to the contact. "Of course."

Marla looked into Saria's eyes, something she hadn't done since she was a girl, and smiled. "I'll tell you what. Let's go to Batido. There's food and drink there and you can meet my friends. We'll take your stuff and if you decide you would like to stay there, you can do so. If not, we'll come back here. Hells, I'll even stay there with you if you decide you don't want to take a room with a dorm full of strangers. Sound good?"

Saria tilted her softly pointed chin up and her eyes twinkled. "It almost feels like you're trying to get rid of me by putting me into an uncomfortable position, Marla."

Marla barked a laugh. "It would take more than five or six years for me to develop the skills to make you uncomfortable, Saria. You are one of the coolest, most easygoing people I have ever met, even if you can also be one of the most intense when necessary. You could use a meal and a rest and I would love to introduce you to everyone. I know they'd enjoy meeting you, too, if they haven't already, though fair warning: they can be a little much sometimes. There may even be a surprise or two."

Saria put her pack back on, then slung her lute case across her back. "Well, why didn't you just say so. Let's go and meet these friends of yours."

"Uh, did you want to change first? Maybe into something that doesn't look like you've just come from losing a battle or rolling around on the road?"

Saria spread her arms wide. "This? Psht. The other clothes I have are in worse shape than these. What you see are my good clothes."

Marla shook her head and led Saria out the door. "Fair enough. Once you get settled in, we can see to your fashion. The Saria Gilwenys I knew would never attempt to woo all the men in such garments."

"This is all I need." She ran her hand over the lute case. As she did, Marla noticed that despite the ragged condition of her clothes, Saria's figure was just as fit and shapely as it had always been. Who was she kidding? With or without the lute, with or without clothes, Saria was gorgeous, and she knew one young man who had always thought so.

As soon as Marla walked back into the common room, all eyes went to her. All her friends were still there; it hadn't been long since she left. She counted in her mind. *One, two, three...there it is.* All eyes snapped to Saria, striding behind Marla, lute, pack, sword, and magnificent cloak entering through the door.

Conversation stopped immediately and Marla chuckled. Well, it would make introductions easier with the silence.

"Saria." Evon said, his voice cracking. "You decided to come see us. Did you finish talking with Master Qydus?"

"Hello again, Evon. I wasn't able to speak with the Headmaster, but some of the masters found me and talked until I thought my ears might fall off. I found Marla and she brought me here."

"Everybody," Marla said, "I want you to meet my friend Saria Gilwenys. She was kind of a mentor to me when I was younger here at the Academy. She graduated and left almost six years ago to seek her fortune. I'll go around the room and introduce each of you. I thought maybe she'd enjoy some food and company after being on the road."

While Marla was talking, Saria peeled off her lute, pack, and cloak. When she straightened and swept her hair back over an ear, a soft hiss escaped Urun's mouth.

Marla turned to find the priest half-standing. "Apologies. I was told, but...to see..." He sat down, his face flushing.

Marla decided it was best to address the obvious right from the start. "Yes, before we do the rounds, I'll tell you that Saria is one of the few living astridae."

"I'm not of pure blood," Saria said with a shrug.

"Astridae?" Raki repeated. "Like in the stories?"

"Yes, Raki, like in the stories," Marla said. She turned to Saria. "You'll like Raki. He is completely obsessed with stories of all kinds."

Saria flashed a smile that Marla would swear would make the young boy pass out on the spot. "Really? Me, too. I *love* stories. I might even know some that you haven't heard."

"Oh, stop it," Fahtin said. "You'll make him fall in love with you." She got up from her spot on the table and stepped in front of Saria. "I'm Fahtin. We didn't have time for a proper greeting before."

Saria smoothly bowed to the other woman. "*Mei sain avar, avar sai ik.*"

Fahtin's mouth widened into a gorgeous smile as she returned the bow. "*Jai avar sai ik, ais bhi mei sain ik.* How wonderful to greet you in the traditional Dantogyptain." She opened her arms to Saria. "It's great to meet you. Can you play the lute?"

Saria threw a glance at Marla, who shrugged. The astri smirked and stepped into Fahtin's arms and embraced her.

"She can play," Marla said. "She can do things with that instrument that shouldn't be possible. But then, she's mastered the School of Music and Voice Magic and, well, she astri."

"Ooh," Fahtin said into Saria's shoulder. "I'd love to hear you play."

"I'd expect nothing else from one of the People," Saria said.

The women released each other and Fahtin beamed at Marla. "Can we keep her?"

Marla shook her head. "I did try to warn you."

Marla took Saria around to each of her friends to introduce her. While she did, the others sat silently and watched instead of diving back into their own conversations. It was a bit eerie, Marla thought, but Saria took it all in stride.

Urun was nervous, as he'd already demonstrated. It got worse when Saria's eyes lit up as he was introduced as the priest of Osulin. His hand started to shake violently enough that he hid it under the table.

"Did you know that in the eight thousand years since Osulin was born, she has had only four other priests? You are quite the important person."

"I did not know how many, only that there were few," Urun said. "It is a great privilege to serve the goddess. She has great love for the astridae, as well as the arba."

When introduced to Aila, Saria bowed to the smaller woman. "Princess Alevia. I have always thought it would be a treat to meet you. Your attitude is...different than many of royal upbringing. I see by the expression on your young knight that he knows what I mean." Aila laughed and winked at Saria, caught up in the astri's charm.

"Gods, to meet Erent Caahs, decades after the world pronounced him dead," Saria said when Tere and Lily were introduced to her. "And his successor, no doubt. I recognize the calluses on your fingers, Lily. It's a great pleasure to meet both of you."

They made their way through Jia, Raki—who was so enamored of Saria he could hardly speak—and finally got around to where Fahtin had sat down again by Aeden.

"Evon told me about Skril." Saria said to Marla. The three of you were nearly inseparable when was here. I'm so sorry."

A stab of pain erupted in Marla's midsection. She barely managed to get out the "thank you."

"It's kind of a long story," Evon said, "but he was killed by Quentin Duzen. It was when everything started with the animaru and a lot of other problems. He was helping to track down the one who murdered Master Aeid. Turns out that Quentin did that, too. He's dead now. Marla and I made sure of that."

"I heard about the master, but oh, I'm sorry for your loss. I always liked Skril."

"Yeah, me too." Marla closed her eyes for a moment, then shook her head. "Uh, I would like you to meet the two people you haven't had a chance to get to know yet. This is

Khrazhti. She was the leader of the animaru who came to Dizhelim to destroy all life. She had been misled by her dark god S'ru and when she realized it, joined us and is now our most stalwart ally and one of my greatest friends."

Khrazhti emerged from the corner of the room where she had been trying to keep a low profile. She normally mixed freely with everyone, but when someone new arrived, she tended to fall back on her hiding. Marla understood it, but it made her sad to think about it. One day, Khrazhti would proudly place herself in the middle of the crowd, where she belonged.

Khrazhti put a hand out toward Saria. "It is a pleasure to meet you, Saria Gilwenys. I can sense the magic within you. It is a marvelous thing."

Saria reached and took Khrazhti's hand in both of hers. "Thank you, Khrazhti. Do all animaru have such honor? To disown your own people and your god is more than most heroes in history could manage."

"Sadly, no. There are animaru with honor of a sort, but none have decided to aid the world of life as I have, as far as I know."

"You are honorable and noble, and so exquisitely beautiful. Do all your people have your coloring?"

"Thank you. Again, no. I am...different. My mother was human. All other animaru are very dark; browns, greys, and black. I was ostracized for my lightness and for my color."

"I think it's fantastic. Your skin is so soft. I have trouble picturing you as a monster."

Khrazhti gave her a smile. "I thank you. I do not see myself as such."

"Except in combat," Aeden interjected. "The woman can fight, no doubt about that."

Khrazhti turned her smile to Aeden and it changed into a fond, thankful expression.

"And this, my final introduction for the evening," Marla said, "is Aeden Tannoch, of the Clan Tannoch of the highland Croagh. My twin brother."

For the first time Marla could remember, she saw Saria lose her composure, her eyes going wide and her mouth dropping open. "Come again?"

"Aeden is my twin brother. Sit down and have some food and drink and we'll tell you about it. It's a story of parental love, ancient traditions, tragedy, and angry provocation leading to an epic duel. You'll love it."

Saria sat in the chair next to Fahtin and Evon. "I can't wait to hear it."

CHAPTER

THREE

Saria sat in her chair at the table, leaning forward with her elbows firmly on the table's surface and her chin resting on her hands as Marla and Aeden—with additions by their friends when it seemed appropriate—recounted the tale of the last year. The astri was enthralled with the story. Marla thought she looked a lot like Raki did when hearing a story for the first time. Marla had forgotten just how much Saria loved all things related to language.

Like a master actress, Saria's pretty face went through a huge range of emotions, living the story as she heard it. In the times when Marla wasn't speaking, letting Aeden or one of the others take their turn, she considered the things that had happened to them, all in such a short time. It was no wonder Saria was so interested. It made for an impressive story.

"You should have seen Marla," Evon said as he recounted the fateful meeting between her and Aeden on the narrow road. "She was livid that he didn't bend over backward and act upon her every whim. Her face got as red as her hair and she did that thing where she growls in the back of her throat."

Saria barked a laugh. "Even as a young girl, she did that. I saw her get so frustrated once that she couldn't cast a spell on her first try that when she was able to manage it—after only three tries—she nearly burned down the classroom."

Marla didn't appreciate the exaggerations, but remained silent. Everyone else seemed to be enjoying the story, and she had been at least a little rude with Aeden upon their first meeting. She could remember the rage building in her when not only did he not cave to her blustering, but he ended up being too skilled for her to punish physically.

The story moved on to their hunt for Izhrod Benzal and then Quentin himself. The subject of the Wells of Power they skimmed over—far too much information to convey in a short telling—and they arrived at more recent events.

"The masters actually announced to everyone that you two are the Malatirsay together?" Saria asked with wide eyes.

"They did," Aeden said. "They revised their understanding of the Song, or rather, Evon figured it out and convinced them. They told everyone in a mandatory gathering and they've started to tell others outside the Academy, though I don't think it's common knowledge yet."

"It's definitely not," she said. "I keep up with things pretty well and it's the first I've heard of such a strong confirmation. It's...fantastic. To think, the Prophecy being fulfilled in our time. I mean, those dark creatures were probably as much of a hint as we needed, but still, for the Academy to make a proclamation..."

"Surreal, right?" Evon asked.

"Definitely." Saria's eyes flicked from Aeden to Marla. "And that Croagh magic, the Raibrech, it's based on the Bhagant?"

"It is," Aeden said.

"How closely?"

"Very. I've found that the different clans have slightly different ways of using it. For example, some use the Alaqotim words of power and may have movements that are not exactly the same. We're studying it. I only know for sure that the Tannoch Raibrech is the only one to use entirely the Dantogyptain words of power, taken directly from the Song itself."

"You know this?" Saria asked.

"He speaks Dantogyptain," Fahtin said proudly.

"Truly?"

"Not fluently," Aeden said, raising a hand. "Most of what I learned is from the Song itself."

"The Song? You have learned some of the Bhavisya-ganant in the original Dantogyptain?"

"He knows the entire thing," Fahtin interjected, "and when he sings it, it's like the gods themselves are gathering and throwing blessings on us."

"Please, Fahtin," Aeden begged. "Stop making it sound so magnificent. I learned the Song. So what? Jehira taught me and I practiced it."

"Sure, but even she can't sing it like you do. I've heard her do so many times, but when you sing it, I can see the images and feel what the Prophet must have experienced when he wrote it."

Aeden looked ready to hide under the table. Marla loved her brother and respected that if someone complimented him on things he accomplished, like through his combat training, he would gracefully accept praise, but it wasn't like that with the magic. No matter how many masters or famous heroes, or anyone else praised him for it, he became timid and shy when it was brought up. As far as she could tell, he really didn't see how exceptional his abilities were.

"I have always thought the Song was beautiful in the original language," Saria said. "The Alaqotim is pretty, but doesn't hold a candle to the Dantogyptain. My belief is that there is more power in it in its first form, though even singing it with the accompaniment of my lute and using all the magic I have, I can't seem to derive any power from it. Yet you have?"

"It's the Raibrech," Aeden said. "As I was taught as a child."

The astri tapped her chin. "Hmmm. Could I convince you to sing it for me? I could play my lute for you if it would help."

"I...I wouldn't know how to sing it with music. The melody doesn't come from me or any other source I can recognize. It springs from the Song itself."

"Now you're just teasing me, Aeden Tannoch. What can I do to convince you to sing the Song for me?"

"No, no. I'm not trying to negotiate. I'll sing it, if you want. I only wanted to make it clear that I'm not completely in control of it. No, that didn't come out right. I mean, the Song seems to come from within me and also from all the qozhel in my surroundings, maybe all of it in Dizhelim. That is, I...uh, no thank you, I don't need music. I'd like to hear you play the lute, but it's not necessary for the Song." He breathed harder than Marla had seen after a hard workout.

"Splendid. You sing the Song of Prophecy for me and I will play the lute and sing for you all after that. Is that fair?"

"Ooh, yes," Fahtin said.

Aeden looked at his adopted sister and gave her a half smile. "Okay, then. Just let me—" he took a drink from his cup, then cleared his throat "—prepare myself. Good. Ready?"

The others all nodded and many of them settled into their seats, knowing what was coming. Even Marla waited with anticipation. She'd heard him sing it before, but she thought she could hear it a hundred times and it would still be amazing.

She wasn't disappointed.

As Aeden's voice emitted pure, smooth notes that she'd never heard the like of in anyone else, Marla closed her eyes and let the sound and the magic wrap around her. As Fahtin had said, images appeared in her mind, things she knew the Song was describing, even though she was not familiar enough with the language to recognize the words.

In a blink that seemed to have stretched for eons, the last note carried around the otherwise silent common room. She opened her eyes to see Saria nearly fall out of her chair.

"Gods," the astri said, "that was the most beautiful thing I've ever felt. How? How can you generate magic like that?"

Aeden shrugged. "I don't. I invite it to come to me and it fills me, then spills out."

"It's getting stronger," Marla said. She hadn't even realized she'd spoken until everyone turned to look at her. "What? It has. Since the last time he sang it, it has definitely become stronger. Right, Evon?"

"Absolutely," Evon agreed. "Aeden, I think you're attuning even more to the magic of the Song."

"Huh," was all he had to say.

Saria blinked at Aeden, seeming in a daze. "Do others know about this? Have you sung for others?"

"He's sung for some of the masters," Fahtin said. "He's good about doing it when we ask him, even though he gets embarrassed for some reason. If I could sing like that, I wouldn't ever talk. I'd sing everything. All the time."

Saria laughed. "And everyone around you would appreciate it."

"It's not me," Aeden said. "It's the Song itself. I can't sing anything else that well. It's like it takes control of me and uses me as a conduit."

"It's amazing," Saria said. "I've spent most of my life studying music and language and sound. Especially as regards magic. But I've never heard anything like it. I almost feel embarrassed myself singing after that. It's an act that's hard to follow, as they say in theater. Still, a promise is a promise. Let me tune my lute and I'll play something for you."

Saria took her lute from its case and held it in her arms. It was a beautiful instrument, the dark wood smooth and flawless, the thrum as it moved promising the music to come. The workmanship was exquisite, as well, and Marla knew without asking that Saria had created it herself. She'd seen things the astri had made when in the Academy. It would be just like her to build her own lute.

In the few minutes it took her to fine tune the instrument, all of Marla's friends returned to the anticipatory mood they'd been in before the Song of Prophecy had thrown them into the pleasurable stupor it had a way of doing.

"The song I want to play is ancient. To allow you to experience it in its original form, I'll sing it in the language in which it was created. Coincidentally, that language was

31

Dantogyptain. The song is not magical. When I'm finished, I'll sing it again, this time translated into Ruthrin. You'll make the connection between the two languages when I do."

The astri strummed the melody and sang. The song was complex, with a meter unlike most songs Marla had ever heard, yet it also seemed at least a little familiar. She understood maybe one word in ten—and she wasn't completely sure about those—but the sound of it nearly brought tears to her eyes. The sound was not sad, though it wasn't a happy tune, either. In fact, she would have had trouble describing its mood. Maybe when she heard the translation...

Too soon, it ended and Saria placed a flat hand against the lute strings to stop the resonance of the final note. Applause erupted from the others and Marla joined in, not quite sure if it was expected or appropriate.

"Now, I'll sing it again so you can understand the words. I translated it myself and I took a few liberties so it makes more sense in Ruthrin. My primary goal was to stay true to the spirit of the song, not to make every piece of it literally accurate."

She started strumming the same tune and her pure, clear voice lifted up above the music of the lute. Though the original evoked more emotion, made Marla feel every single word even though she didn't understand it, the words in the common tongue of Ruthrin gave her another type of chill. It was no longer only the music and the sound of Saria's voice, but it was the story being told.

The Gypta, fair Gypta
Chosen of gods
Cherished of He

Of music and song

Alas, the loss
Their home taken thus
Their children to live
In wagons and tents

Undaunted, inspired
They traveled the world
Serving and helping
All whom they met

Betrayed and abandoned
Cast out for their goodness
Reviled and threatened
They homeless became

The way, the way
The People did follow
Their kindness and song
Shone light in the world

Agypten, the king
The power, the army
None could remove
Their honor and soul

All of Dizhelim
Tried to suppress
The kindness within
The family song

Betrayed and abandoned

Cast out for their goodness
Reviled and threatened
They homeless became

Ever they moved
To flee those who harm
The music within
Refused to be lost

Through epoch and age
Did the family thrive
Looking ahead
To when they would act

Song and tale
And magic abounding
Harp, lute, and fiddle
They weathered the storm

Betrayed and abandoned
Cast out for their goodness
Reviled and threatened
They all heroes became

"That," Fahtin said, tears in her eyes, "that was about the Gypta. About their trials and the way the world turned on them as a people. It was my people's history."

"It was," Saria said. "I've always loved that song, even if its ending is confusing. I thought you and Raki might like to hear it."

"It's beautiful. Thank you. I wish my mother and father could hear it, and Jehira. My whole family, really."

"Maybe I'll have an opportunity to sing it for them one day."

"I would like that."

The others watched Saria put her lute back into its case and close the latches. She took a drink of ale and looked around. Still no one spoke. She broke into a wide smile.

"That's the kind of reaction a minstrel loves to experience," she said. "But let's not get carried away. I didn't sing the song—twice—to stop your conversations."

Almost like it was a command to speak, voices sprang to life.

"Where have you been, Saria," Marla asked her as her friends discussed the song in pairs or threes. "You don't look like you've had an easy time of things. Is everything all right?"

The astri looked down at her ragged clothing. "It is now. Life's been a bit rough, but then, everyone has been having a hard time lately, eh?"

That struck a bit too close to home for Marla, but she didn't want to get into her own problems. "Tell me what you've done for the last five or six years."

"Very well. It's only fair, since you told me all about your exploits. My life hasn't been nearly as exciting as yours, though, so don't get your hopes up. I'd hate to disappoint you.

"The simple fact is when I left the Academy, I had dreams of traveling the world, or exploring the unexplorable, of doing great things. It turns out that it's harder to do than one would expect. I did travel for a year or so, using gold I'd saved up from selling things I made when I was at the Academy. I wasn't above playing songs in a tavern for room and board, either.

"Surviving takes money, though, and room and board is

not all one needs to live. Clothing, materials for the creation and repair of items, it all adds up, including this beauty here." She patted her lute case as she said it. "So, I looked for work.

"I have several skills that I learned while here, but most are not very marketable. I focused on sound and music magic, invocation, and a bit of combat."

"A bit," Marla said. "You're fantastic with that sword of yours."

"Ah, yes. So you bring me to the next part of my story. I was able to get work as a scholar. A traveling scholar. My job entailed journeying via caravan to remote parts of the world. The expeditions, while seeming scholarly on the surface, fulfilled a more pragmatic role. My employer, Noud Grissen, wanted me to find particular items, ones not only important to him, but valuable besides."

"Did you say Noud Grissen?" Tere asked.

"I did."

"As in the crime boss and magical artifact smuggler? The man with the most extensive pipeline of magical weapons in the world?"

"I see you've heard of him," Saria said. "Yes, the very one."

"Dangerous business, getting involved with that one. He was just coming into his own when I...took my leave. Since I've been back among civilization, I've heard that he's even more powerful now. Just the type of man I would have been hunting. Back when I was younger and more idealistic."

"Everything you've heard is likely correct. He didn't mistreat me, though he made it clear that once I joined him, I was truly part of his organization. Not something to easily leave. Some of the things he's done, though, they truly disgust me.

"I have been toying with fleeing for some time, but hadn't been sure I was willing to pay the price to do so. I would have to take another identity, or try to, and stop my music. It's hard enough to slip past the notice of others with ears so distinctive. My music would make me stand out even more.

"Then I read the call from the Academy for all graduates to return. It was the impetus I needed. I picked up and fled in the middle of the night and made my way back here. Of course, the journey wasn't that easy. They were watching me and I was pursued. I fought, but was afraid to kill anyone important in Noud's organization lest he put a priority on finding me. Leaving his employ is one thing; actively fighting against him is another.

"So, I was perhaps injured more than needed to be the case, but I don't believe I elevated my status to the highest priority. If I run into any old acquaintances, I'll have problems, but I don't believe he will go out of his way to search for me. In the meantime, I can help the masters and see some old friends I haven't had a chance to talk to in several years." She reached out and squeezed Marla's hand. "Happily, it also gave me the chance to perhaps meet some new ones."

"I'm sure the masters will be thrilled that you're back," Marla said. "As for that other part, everyone, I have offered Saria the use of one of the rooms in Batido until she figures things out with the masters. Are there any issues with that?"

"You're welcome to any room that's empty," Fahtin said immediately.

"She's right," Aeden said. "Any good friend of Marla's is

at least a friend of ours, if not family. Besides, though we've been allowed to take over this dormitory, it's still the Academy's, so if anyone has the authority here to offer you a room, it's Marla. She's practically Academy royalty." He winked at his sister.

"Not really so," Marla said, "but I am a big proponent of the philosophy that it's much easier to ask for forgiveness than to ask for permission."

Saria snorted. "Same old Marla. Even at fourteen years old, you had that attitude. I appreciate your offer and feel privileged to accept. It's great meeting all of you and I hope we can get to know each other better."

With her acceptance, Marla brought Saria to her new room and took her leave, promising to talk to the astri the next day. Marla was tired and, though her mood had definitely ticked up, she's still had enough of other people for the day. It was past time for her to go to bed.

CHAPTER
FOUR

M arla got up before the sun the next morning and was already one class into her busy schedule when Lucas Stewart found her preparing to teach a class on edged weapons.

"Hi Marla," Lucas greeted her.

"Hey, Lucas. Sorry, I can't talk right now. I've got a class to teach in a few minutes."

"Uh, that's what I'm here about. Master Yxna has assigned Ailuin Lufina to teach the class."

"What? Why? Did I do something wrong? Not that I'm complaining about not having to deal with it, but still."

"No. She and Master Qydus sent me to summon you to a meeting. They apologize about the short notice, but it was either now or they wait until the next space in their schedules, which is a few days from now."

"Oh. So the meeting is right now?"

"In twenty minutes. Sorry."

She tried to force a smile, for Lucas's sake. This early in the day, it was easier than if she'd already been through all the irritations a typical day brought lately. "Do you know what it's about?"

After all this time, the younger student still had trouble keeping eye contact with Marla for more than a few seconds at a time. He shuffled his feet, looking around them. "No, not really. I think all your friends are going to be there, though, and your brother. Saria, too." He bit his lip nervously. "Is it true that Saria Gilwenys is back? The astri with that magical voice?"

"Huh? Oh, Saria? Yes, she arrived last night. Do you remember her? It's been a long time."

"I remember hearing her sing and playing all those different instruments. I can't remember a lot of detail, but I do recall having the biggest crush on her. I moped around for weeks after I first saw and heard her."

Marla barked a laugh. "Don't be embarrassed about it. You're in good company. I would guess that more than half the students in the Academy were in love with her, male *and* female. She is a fantastic person, besides being gorgeous and exotic and all that musical stuff."

Lucas chuckled weakly. "Yeah, I guess so. Um, I'd better get going. I have more messages to deliver before my first class."

"Thanks, Lucas. Great job, as always. This place would probably shut down without you tying it all together with the messages you deliver."

The trademark blush she expected from him with his fair skin showed up, erasing some of the irritations she'd already been confronted with so far this early in the day. With a wave, she headed toward the administration section of the Academy grounds as he headed the opposite way, toward the Physical Training lycad.

When she got to the headmaster's office, she found his assistant, Aletris Meslar at her desk.

"They're in the big meeting room, number four. Too many people for the one next to Master Qydus's office."

"Thanks, Aletris. Did you get a chance to talk to Saria? She's back."

"I haven't, but I plan to. I always did have a soft spot for that one. Sort of like the little, red-haired troublemaker that scampered into this office so many years ago. Of course, Saria doesn't try my nerves as much as that one." She raised an eyebrow for a moment before her face collapsed in a smile.

"I'm better now," Marla said.

"Are you?"

"A little?"

Aletris put her finger and thumb an inch away from each other, then lessened the distance. "Maybe just a little. Now get to the meeting. I think you're already the last one. Troublemaker."

Marla did as she was told and found a not insignificant number of people already populating the seats in the large room. Master Yxna caught her eye and waved her over to a chair next to the master. Saria was on the other side. She'd always been a favorite of the Edged Weapons Master.

Master Qydus was at the head of the table, his pointed beard, pointed head, and stern visage a familiar feature of the room. Masters Isegrith Palus, Goren Adnan, Nasir Kelqen, and Beldroth Zinrora were also present. All of Marla's friends were scattered about as well, including Conren Gardner and —surprisingly—the trebaxel Aila had named Scrapper.

Master Qydus was chatting softly with that last one, the furry creature paying attention as if he could understand what the headmaster was saying. Apparently, he could. According to Aila, Scrapper understood Ruthrin well enough, though he didn't seem to have the faculties to speak himself. What a strange thing the world had become.

"That is all of us, I believe," Master Qydus said. "My apologies for the abrupt manner of the invitation, Marla. Thank you for arriving promptly."

Marla nodded, but the master was already moving on.

"There are several issues we must discuss. I have been remiss in establishing a regular meeting for the interchange of information, but in my defense, things are rather volatile at the moment. We must gather when we can.

"First, I would like to welcome back our graduated student Saria Gilwenys. Several former students have returned to answer the call we sent out and we appreciate every one. I have no need for presenting the masters to you, nor you to the masters, and my understanding is that you met everyone else last night, so we can dispense with the introductions.

"If there are no arguments, I would like to assign you to work with Aeden and Marla. I feel that your unique talents would be best utilized helping out the core group of the Malatirsay's support team rather than performing simple messenger work or emissary duties."

"I would be honored," Saria said.

"Good, good. Endeavor to learn what has transpired so that you are up to speed, so to speak. As for emissary work, I would like to report that we have sent out agents to contact all the major nations and kingdoms of the world, asking them to coordinate with us to gather in a concord. It is imperative that we gather as many troops as possible as quickly as we can.

"On that note, the first contingent of Clavian Knights

will arrive soon." The headmaster nodded his head toward Aila and she repeated the gesture. "They will be more of an advisory group than the backbone of our forces, and they will work closely with Master Goren in developing the overall campaign strategy against the animaru invasion."

"I would like to thank you once again, Princess Alevia," Master Goren said. The grizzled Master of the School of Military Strategy dipped his shaggy head at her. "A force of heavy cavalry will be invaluable in our cause, as will the experience of your commanders."

"Please, just Aila is fine," Aila said. "Princess Alevia is someone I used to be. Here, I'm plain old Aila Ven."

Marla almost choked. The way the woman flaunted her body and flirted shamelessly—mostly with Aeden—the term *plain* wasn't what usually came to mind. Aila seemed to sense what Marla was thinking and the smaller woman winked at her.

"Right," Master Qydus said. "Moving along, let us discuss the effects of the Wells of Power for a moment. The release of more magic into the world is beneficial, but not exclusively so."

"Release of magic into the world?" Saria said, shifting her gaze from the headmaster to Marla to the other masters.

"Marla will explain the wells to you later. Let us just establish that more magic is being introduced into the world, mostly due to the efforts of those in this room. As I said, it is mostly for the good, but there are issues as well. Isegrith, would you like to expand upon that statement?"

The Master of the School of Fundamental Magic straightened fractionally and addressed all in the room, as she would in a lecture. "Yes, Headmaster. Thank you. While the freeing of magic that has been bound up in the well is a boon to those who can cast, it is also causing some issues to arise. First, we are not able to control the types of magic that are released. For example, the wells that have been found so far released mental magic, nature magic, the magic of honor, darkness, knowledge, and strength. While most of these are helpful, their effects have been mixed.

"It seems obvious that we did not understand completely the interaction of different types of magic. If we consider the pure type of qozhel in the wells, the base categories of magical energy, what we are learning is general types of magic are not pure, but combinations of different types of those base magics. In other words, the fire magic we cast is a combination of several types of pure magics, not simply undiluted fire magic.

"The problem this causes is that as the balance of the world's magics is upset, a few types flooding back into Dizhelim, familiar spells do not act as predictably as previously. Rather, they do not act as we have previously predicted. I am confident once the effects have been studied sufficiently, magic will work as reliably as it always has. The problem is we must have to do the study.

"Even now, masters as well as students, are experiencing some unexpected effects of magic they attempt to cast."

"So," Evon said, "you're telling us that if we cast a particular spell, it may or may not work like we want it to."

Master Isegrith nodded. "Precisely. Within the structure of the Academy training, this is a minor issue. The higher-level magic can be used in a controlled environment with safeguards in place. However, those who can cast advanced magic and do so away from here, such as in a combat situation, may find...problems arise."

"Problems like spells not working or backfiring and injuring the caster or allies," Marla said.

"Just so."

"Are you suggesting we don't cast spells if we are fighting for our lives somewhere?"

"Of course not, child. We are saying that you should be wary and careful, that you should ensure the spells you use are behaving as expected. I would suggest that you practice the spells you frequently use in your missions prior to doing so in actual combat to ensure they work as expected. Then, if more wells are found and more magic released, repeat your studies to detect any changes with the new balance of magic in the world."

"Great," Marla huffed. "Now we have to relearn every spell with each well that's found and freed."

Master Yxna nudged Marla with her elbow.

"What Marla means," Evon said, "is that we'll select a handful of our most commonly used spells and try them out. We all have to recognize that there will be times, though, where a spell we've not tested will need to be used. Of course, we'll try to minimize the occurrences of this situation, but you never know what you might need to do when faced with enemies."

"Fair enough," Master Isegrith said, glaring at Marla. "Please use your discretion. As we discover what effects the different magics have on spells, we will communicate that to you as well as the entire student body.

"Now, for one particular magic, there is some concern. Raki Sinde, you released the Well of Dark Magic. Some of the masters fear this may have given the animaru more powerful weapons with which to combat us."

Khrazhti raised a hand from the edge of the room where she sat unobtrusively.

"Yes, Khrazhti," the headmaster said. "You have something to add?"

"Yes, Headmaster Qydus, I do. Thank you. I would like to point out that only a small fraction of animaru are actually able to wield magic. It is true that their magic is of the dark, and that each animaru is infused with dark magic that fuels their strength and individual abilities. But I do not believe the release of dark magic into the world will have a significant effect overall."

"You do not know this," Master Isegrith said. Marla sat up straighter in her seat and was going to call the master down for her rudeness, but Khrazhti spoke quickly.

"Who can know the complex ways of magic over the entire world or with an entire species? I do know that I am animaru and though I felt the magical shift, it has not increased my normal abilities, nor has it significantly increased the amount or power of magic I wield. I have tested it out, much as you described earlier, and have found that though the magic seems sharper and more readily accessed, it is still overwhelmingly my skill and experience that dictate what I can do magically."

"Thank you, Khrazhti," Master Qydus said. "Your input is invaluable in this matter."

"Regardless," Master Isegrith continued as if Khrazhti hadn't even spoken, "Master Beldroth would like to speak with you, Raki. She wants to test your attunement with dark magic, especially since you were the one at the point of release."

Beldroth Zinrora, the Master of the School of Dark Magic, added, "I would like to speak with you also, Khrazhti, if you would be willing. I have been meaning to ask you and perhaps now would be a good time to do so."

"Of course," Khrazhti said. "I will help in any way I can."

"Splendid," the headmaster said. "Now, I would like to hear your progress on all things having to do with the wells, as well as your progression on the books the Prophet left for you, Fahtin and Aeden."

Again, Saria looked around in confusion. They hadn't told her about the books specifically written for and addressed to Aeden and Fahtin the night before. It was funny, because Marla didn't even really consider the book for the Malatirsay to be for her. From what Aeden had told her, it primarily covered the magic that was tied to the Song itself. He had offered to let her take her turn reading it, but she'd been much too busy to do so, even if she had wanted to.

"I'll tell you about it after the meeting," Marla said to Saria, to the astri's relief.

Aeden and Fahtin glanced at each other. The Gypta gestured to him that he could go first and he acknowledged the movement with a nod.

CHAPTER
FIVE

"I have to apologize for how long it's taking me to digest the book the Prophet wrote for us," Aeden said. "Marla has been gracious enough to allow me to study for as long as I like, but it's slow going. My Alaqotim is getting better, but Tsosin Ruus uses a lot of words I don't know.

"The book is written informally, almost like a very long letter to a friend, and it gives me a feeling of how much he cared about people. I learn something with every page. I feel it's better to take my time and not miss any information than to rush through it."

"Of course," Master Qydus said. "It is your and Marla's decision on how to utilize the information. I know many others want to read the book, but like you describe, I see it as a communication between the Prophet and you and your sister. Please avail yourself of whatever aid the Academy and its personnel can provide, but do not feel pressured to use the book in a way you do not desire. Any suggestion that you do otherwise should be brought to my attention."

Marla recognized that statement for what it was. Some,

probably some of the masters, had been wanting to wrest the book from Aeden's hands so they could review it themselves. She was glad the headmaster was on their side.

Aeden nodded. "Thank you, Headmaster. It is my top priority. Some of the delay is that Tsosin Ruus provided exercises within the book to help me attune to the Song. I have been practicing them carefully before moving on, as he suggested I do. I'll be sure to inform you all when anything significant happens."

"What of you, Fahtin?" the headmaster asked. "Have you found the book the Prophet wrote for you to be helpful?"

"Oh, yes, Headmaster," the Gypta said. "Evon has helped me when I get stuck with the Alaqotim, but like Aeden, I'm learning fast. The book covers several general things about prophecy and visions. He also included exercises for me to practice. They seem to be helping me to come closer to controlling my abilities. I can occasionally force myself to have flashes of visions when I want, but they're so fleeting, they don't mean much. I think with more practice and Evon's guidance, I might be able to actually look for things or have visions when I want to. I hope so. I think it would be very helpful."

Master Yxna leaned forward in her seat. "Have you had any of these fleeting visions you could share with us?"

"I..." Fahtin worried her bottom lip in her teeth, as Marla had seen her do before when she got uncomfortable. Master Yxna was observant enough to realize what was happening.

"It's not a problem if you don't. I was only wondering about the nature of the things you've seen. We can wait until you have more fully-formed images."

"It's all right. I have had a few in the last week. I tell

Evon about them each time and he writes them down in the book he uses to record them. I can describe them to you, but they don't seem to mean anything."

"If you're not too uncomfortable to do so, we would appreciate it."

"Okay. Well, they're not in any real order and, like I said, they're only flashes. I plan on meditating on each of them and I hope that will give me more information or extend the images.

"I saw a great flash of power, strong enough to burn my eyes if I had been watching them with my real body. I don't know how, but I recognized it as the creative power of Surus himself. When the blinding light dimmed, I saw things start to move across vast green areas. They were all different shapes, but I could sense that they were now alive, where they hadn't been moments before.

"A dark splotch was in front of me, too shadowy to see into. An even murkier hole opened up within it and expanded. Then, a shape that was even blacker than the hole clawed its way through, coming directly at me. I didn't recognize what it was, not even what the shape was, but it was the single scariest thing I had ever seen in my life. My heart felt like it was going to burst if it came any closer. Thankfully, another fraction of a vision took its place.

"In this one, Marla stood before me, only a few feet away. As I watched, her hair burst into flame, crackling like a bonfire. It didn't seem to harm her, but it did send her into a rage. She cursed as she stomped around, squashing things beneath her feet that I could not see.

"A bright light shone from the west. It was like a light-house had trained its beam on me and I had to hold up my hand to shade my eyes. Even as I did, the light turned to liquid darkness, sweeping out like it did before, but this time painting all it touched with blackness, like it was spraying ink all over everything. When the umbra covered me, the world spun and the vision disappeared.

"A great fish, as big as an inn, leaped up from the depths of the ocean, sweeping up several smaller fish that were standing on their tails on dry land, swallowing them whole. I don't know how, but I knew that those fish on land were me and my friends. The fish lived inside the huge fish for several days, learning things that made them wish they could die.

"The last image I saw involved the Academy. I saw the entire grounds from above. In addition to the buildings, I saw swirling colors throughout the entire area. Something told me that the colors represented plots and schemes within plots and schemes. Some of the colors came in contact with other colors, tainted by them, while other colors resisted, became brighter, and burst through the colors coming in contact with them. The swirling of dozens of hues continued until a massive wave of darkness came and swept them all away.

"That's all I've seen lately. I don't know what any of it means, other than what I described."

Evon sat back, tapping his lips with his finger. He'd already heard them before, Marla figured, and had written them in his little book. She wasn't thrilled with the vision about her and her hair catching fire. The anger Fahtin described sounded far too much like what she'd been feeling lately.

"Disturbing images," the headmaster said. "Thank you for sharing them with us. Please keep us apprised of any clarification you receive."

"I will, Headmaster."

"Do you think any of it involves more Wells of Power?" Master Nasir asked. It was the first time the Master of the School of Research and Investigation has spoken in the meeting.

"I don't know, Master. It's all so jumbled. It could be pointing toward a well or it could be dangers that face us. For all I know, they could be telling me about minor matters. Maybe they're telling me we'll all have fish for dinner." She chuckled weakly, but it trailed off within a couple of seconds.

"If I may?" Saria said. "I would like to try to use some voice and music magic to help Fahtin relax and be more receptive to her abilities. There are several fine works on the efficacy of soothing magic being used to help inexperienced mages settle into their power. It seems to work especially well with prophetic abilities."

"Really?" Fahtin said. "You'll sing for me to help me with my visions?"

Saria gave the Gypta a wide smile. "Of course. We can try. The worst that can happen is I waste your time, but you'll get a private concert for your troubles."

"Ooh."

"That is a solid idea," Master Qydus said. "Thank you, Saria. If Miss Achaya is willing, I think it would be a worthwhile endeavor."

"I'll coordinate with Fahtin, then."

The conversation dwindled and Master Qydus pronounced the meeting finished. As soon as he did, Marla got up and was the first one out the door. She had a host of things still to do before the day ended and waiting around chatting wasn't going to get them done. She noticed a few people raising their hands to her to get her attention, but she continued out the door without acknowledging them. If they had something important to tell her, they would find another time to do so.

⁓

IT HAD BEEN some time since Saria Gilwenys had been in a meeting with the masters. She had done a few tasks for them as an agent of the Academy before she left for good, and the meeting she had just been a part of was similar to those, though larger. More important. Weightier. It seemed strange to her that even Master Qydus showed the group of Marla's friends the respect due full-fledged Academy graduates.

She definitely needed to learn more about what had been happening. Such treatment was not given lightly, so there was obviously more to the group than an acquaintance with Marla or the things they'd told her briefly the night before.

As Master Qydus ended the meeting, Saria turned to Fahtin to speak with her about helping with her prophetic ability when she spotted Marla shoot up out of her chair and make a beeline for the door. Before she or anyone else could say a word to her, she was gone.

Saria met eyes with Master Yxna, sitting next to her. She raised an eyebrow.

"Marla has been having a rough time lately," the master said. Saria knew the edged weapons master was fond of Marla, had been even when Saria was still a student. She felt a little pang of jealousy, like Marla had supplanted her in the master's affections, but she dismissed it quickly. It was a ridiculous notion.

"The pressure seems to be getting to her," Master Yxna

continued. "She's been tense and irritable. It's understand-able, with the weight of the world riding on her shoulders." She jerked her head toward Aeden. "It's evident with her twin, also, though he shows it differently. With him, it's throwing himself heart and soul into preparing himself, training and making himself better able to face the chal-lenges. He's wearing himself thin, though I haven't seen his moods turn dark or him deflecting his troubles onto anyone else.

"Give her a bit of time to settle down. I plan on talking to her, but you know enough about Marla to recognize that if someone confronts her about something that might look like weakness, she digs in and can out-stubborn anyone."

Saria let out a long breath. "I understand. I can't imagine what it would be like to have to live up to a millen-nia-old prophecy like that. I'm glad she has you to look out for her."

"Not just me. Her friends see it. I know Evon has talked to her and I believe Aeden has tried to get her to talk about things. We're all trying. Someone will get through, eventu-ally. She has to be the one who wants to make things better, though."

"I haven't been in Marla's life for a long time, but please let me know if I can do anything to help. It's not just because she's the Malatirsay. I've always thought Marla Shrike was special."

"I will let you know if you can help out. Thank you, Saria. I'm glad you're back. I've missed you."

Saria smiled at Master Yxna and realized that she didn't look different at all from when the astri had left the Acad-emy. Not one more line on the master's face, not one thing that would demonstrate that almost another six years had passed. She wondered at that, but relegated it to the back of her mind. For now, she had a budding prophetess to help with song and music.

It was good to be back.

CHAPTER
SIX

A few days after the meeting with the masters, Marla stretched her muscles after warming them up with a few exercises she'd stolen from her brother. The martial movements he did every morning were great for preparing for heavy exercise or combat.

She looked over at Aeden, a few feet away from her and stretching out his own shoulders. It was early yet and the training grounds at the Lycad of Magic was not too crowded.

Aeden jerked his chin toward a group of younger students that had gathered and were watching the twins closely. "What's that about?"

Marla frowned toward the gathering. "Gawkers."

"Gawkers?"

"Yeah, that's what we—Evon and Skril and I—call them. They're watching to see if anything miraculous happens. Or something."

"Does this happen a lot?"

She rolled her eyes. "Oh, yeah. It'll probably happen

even more now. With everyone knowing what the situation is, the chance to see both halves of the Malatirsay together is a big deal. Even more so if we were to spar. I think that's what they're waiting for."

"So, this happens to you all the time? It's like you're some kind of hero or visiting dignitary or something."

"It is. You should get used to it. With me, it's always been that I had mastered more schools than anyone. With the Malatirsay thing, we've got thousands of years of prophecy to shine a light on us. It's usually harmless. Occasionally someone gets really obsessed, though, and they crowd in on me. I've had to be stern with a few, to keep them from getting too close as I was practicing or sparring. I don't want to be responsible for some idiot getting injured by walking into my weapon while trying to get too close as I practice."

"I had no idea," Aeden said, dropping into splits to stretch out his legs.

"Just another damn thing," Marla said. "Ready?"

"I am. I almost want to suggest sparring. I think our audience will be disappointed when all we do is practice the Raibrech."

"Percipius take them. I stopped trying to figure out how to live for everyone else a long time ago. That's how you go crazy and flip out."

Aeden laughed, but cut it short when he realized she wasn't trying to be funny.

"Okay," he said. "Let's work on Ice in Spring. It's from the third quatrain of the Song and it can freeze or slow a target. Done with slightly different motions and order of the words of power, it can also heat, or even make something catch fire, but we'll just focus on the cold part of it."

"Fine."

"Oh, I haven't told you yet. I read in the book the Prophet left for us something about esoteric magical systems. I don't think he knew about the Raibrech, though he did nudge things a little bit to have it developed. The explanation he gave seems to fit the magic, though. He knew there was power in the words of the Song and he said that if a magical system based on the Song was used, he felt certain it would have some interesting characteristics.

"One of those would be that it was magically perfect, so he predicted there would be three levels of power that could be utilized. The first, the basic level, was what was readily apparent. The second was something that required a deeper understanding of the way the magic flowed. He didn't call it enhancing the spells, like I do, but his description sounds like what I've been trying to accomplish with enhancing each of the spells. The third he called the final form. That requires the most intimate understanding of the magic and the Song and creates the most powerful effects. He wrote that some might even be unrelated to the effects of the first two levels, something new and more powerful."

"So not only do you have to figure out the enhanced spells," Marla said, "but now you have an entire third level of spells to learn to use?"

"Uh, yeah." The look on his face almost made her feel sorry to point out that he'd just received more work he needed to do.

"Well, good luck with that."

"Right. Okay, Ice in Spring. The movements of the basic spell are pretty...basic. I'll demonstrate."

He adopted an upright stance, one that at first glance looked to be unbalanced. As with many stances in the martial arts from Shinyan and Teroshi, however, upon closer examination, they proved to be perfectly balanced, if the practitioner was doing them right. Aeden was, as always.

He pointed his right hand toward the practice dummy several feet away, index finger extended and pointing. His left hand he rolled at the wrist from back to front while holding it out to the side. Marla could sense the collection of the qozhel from the surroundings even before he spoke the words of power.

"*Vasant. Parat. Ushma.*"

An almost invisible stream of magic flew from his hand and struck the dummy, coating it with ice.

"The main thing to watch out for is the stance and keeping your wrist loose to draw in the power. At the first level, an even meter when speaking the words work best. The choreography with the movements and the words is more important with the second level. Did you get it or do you want me to demonstrate again?"

"I've got it," she said. The familiar irritation at wasting time bubbled up from her belly, but she pushed it down. Aeden had been wanting her to learn the Raibrech for some time now. It was important to him, even if she didn't really see it as a good use of time.

She adopted the same stance he had been in, the duplicated the hand motions. When she spoke the words, a thin layer of rime coated part of the dummy.

"Wow," Aeden said. "That was very good for the first time trying it. I think the pronunciation of the words was probably why it wasn't as strong as it could be. You almost sounded like you were pronouncing it half in Alaqotim and half Dantogyptain."

For some reason, that statement rushed heat into her

middle. Why was she wasting time dealing with these obviously inferior spells?

"Are you okay, Marla?" Aeden asked, narrowing his eyes at her.

"I'm...I'm...oh!" She cast an ice magic spell and a dozen sharpened ice pellets flew from her hand, blowing the top off the training dummy. "I can't really justify spending time learning these weaker spells when I can already cast ones so much more powerful. I'm sorry, Aeden, but I don't have time to work my way through three levels of the same spells when I can use that time to practice spells that have proven reliable. I need to go."

She turned and walked back toward her dorm. The surprised and disappointed look on her brother's face shot needles of disappointment at herself through her, but even if it was harsh, what she said was true. Dabbling in those weak spells was all well and good for him, but she had better things to do. More things than it was humanly possible to complete.

She'd apologize to him for being so abrupt later. For now, she wanted to get busy crossing things off her list of things to do.

Back safely in her room, Marla threw herself onto her bed. She chastised herself. What about all the things she had to do? Here she was, lying down, being lazy, when her whole excuse for snubbing her brother was that she didn't have time to deal with his inferior spells.

Even thinking of it that way made her wince. It wasn't really that his spells were inferior. They did well enough when she first met Aeden and fought that duel. Still, she had magic that was more powerful, at least for her, and to learn an entire new system from scratch? It seemed like a colossal waste of time.

Hands behind her head, Marla lay on her bed staring up at the ceiling. Her moods, the impending sense of anger building within her, were getting worse. She'd developed a thin skin over the last several years, a certain regrettable intolerance for things—small and large—that irritated her. Sometimes it felt like she was losing herself to it.

Less than two months before, she'd discussed it with Master Yxna. She had stopped by to chat with the master in between other appointments that were themselves sandwiched in the empty spots when she was out on missions that seemed more and more prevalent.

"Sometimes, it seems like I'm angry all the time," she admitted.

"It's the way you react to the incredible pressure put upon you," the master said. "Everyone has their own way of dealing with tension in their lives. Some resort to food, some to exercise, others become emotional and weep often. For you, anger is how it is expressed."

"While I'm glad I don't try to eat it away, doubling my weight and getting fat, I can't help but to hate that my natural tendency is toward anger."

Master Yxna patted Marla's arm. "I know. Some things we have no control over. Even with thousands of years of study, both magical and mundane, we understand so little about how the mind works. All we can do is our best with what we've been given."

"I know, but I can't stop thinking about Ivel Danson."

"Ah, Ivel. I remember."

"He let his anger affect him. He let it build until it blinded him to all reason, to the point where he attacked other students. Killing Sharan Kolga. Every time something irritates me and sets me off, I think of that day. The only way I'm going to be able to win over this is if I gain complete control by pushing all anger away and never letting it take root. I can't let any anger in at all. If I won't allow irritations to affect me, then there will be nothing to build up into the blind rage that could make me like Ivel."

"Marla, we've discussed before how everything can be either beneficial or detrimental. Anything can be utilized for good or can be a path to bad things. The trick is not to try to cut parts of ourselves out and fight a doomed battle against what will occur naturally. The key is to harness things that may on the surface seem to be liabilities and use them in a positive way."

Marla hadn't wanted to directly disagree with Master Yxna, but neither did she want to discuss the matter further. She had taken the coward's way out.

"Oh, I better get going or I'll be late for my appointment with Master Videric. Thank you for chatting with me, Master. I'm sorry I have to cut it short."

Master Yxna's neutral expression, her default, didn't betray what she was thinking or feeling, but Marla was certain she hadn't fooled the master. It made her feel even worse about the almost-lie. She did have an appointment.

"Busy, busy," Master Yxna said. "Very well, off with you. I will see you when your schedule allows. Think about taking some time to yourself to relieve some of the tension on you. As with any pressure vessel, you need to come to equilibrium occasionally or you will burst from the mounting force."

"I'll try to fit something in."

She had waved and left the master in apparently good spirits, but it was one more thing weighing on her. She did need to learn how to eliminate her tendency to become irritated. If she was able to let things slide over and around her without it affecting her, then she could be controlled at all times.

The only problem was that she didn't have the first idea of how to do it. Even thinking about trying triggered her temper. She shook her head and closed her eyes, hoping something would come to her before she blew apart like the proverbial pressure vessel.

CHAPTER
SEVEN

For two days, Marla was able to keep herself busy enough that she could truthfully say she didn't have time to stop by Batido and chat with her friends and her brother. She felt a little bad about it after storming off from Aeden, but he'd understand. She could explain it all to him when she was in a better mood.

Marla woke up, as she had most of the time recently, with a sensation that someone—or something—was trying to get her attention. It was the same tugging, like someone had hold of her sleeve and was pulling it so she would acknowledge them. It seemed the slightest bit more insistent this morning than it had been, but the feeling was still easily ignored. She had things to do and didn't have time for flights of fancy.

First up was an early appointment with Master Videric Dewitte. The Master of the School of Magical Healing had been very accommodating toward her as she worked through the requirements for his school, allowing her to miss normal classes and meet with him for one-on-one instruction and help. She hoped he knew how much she appreciated it.

She'd already learned so much. It would be a while before she could master the school, but that wasn't the most important thing to her. After so long with only mundane healing skills, she had decided to learn as much about magical healing as possible. She had already learned a handful of spells and she worked hard to progress even faster than Master Videric's already-inflated expectations of her.

After a quick breakfast, she headed to the master's office. He was there, already at work. He was very conscientious, which she guessed was what one really wanted in the man responsible for the Medica and all of the healing at the Academy.

"Good morning, Marla," he greeted her, pushing his spectacles up on his face. He looked as he always did, his narrow face drawing in whoever he spoke to, kindness radiating from him. His robes, thinner and closer to the body than some of the other masters, were spotless and unwrinkled. His dark hair, combed into some semblance of order, had only the familiar flaw: the large cowlick on the back of his head.

"Good morning, Master Videric. What do we have in store this morning? Will you teach me some more of the intermediate healing spells?"

"Perhaps, if we have time. What I want to accomplish first is to test you on the spells I showed you last time and asked you to practice last week."

"Test?" Marla asked.

The master chuckled. "It's nice to know that even the Academy's star student is wary of surprise tests. I'm sure the other students would take great solace in that."

Marla tried to smile, but she was not feeling happy or particularly amused at the moment.

"First," the master said, "I would like to measure your grasp on the Medium Cure spell. Just let me—" he quaffed a sickly green liquid in a vial he held in his hand "—and there. I'm ready now."

"Master Videric?"

"Yes, Marla?"

"What was that?"

"Ah. I just drank a poison I will not identify for you. Your test is to cure me of the poison. Preferably before it kills me, of course. As the cure spell I want to test is of the intermediate rank, the poison is rather potent. I would ask you to do your work speedily so that I do not suffer any deleterious effects.

"P-poison? Master!"

"Oh," the master said, swooning a little. "That *is* powerful. If you please, Marla. The spell. I can feel it moving through my body. I imagine the pain will be excruciating in a moment. I may black out. That will make it difficult for me to assess you properly. Please hurry."

Marla stared at the master, her mouth open. Had he really just downed a vial of poison to test her? The master was not one to play practical jokes. He did look like his eyes were starting to lose focus and he was sweating like he was fighting something painful.

Her mind was a blank. The spell, which she had practiced, didn't seem to be there. She had planned on repeating the spell over and over, but she'd been so busy...

Master Videric grunted and doubled over.

No, no, no, she repeated in her mind. The master wouldn't have actually risked death like that just to test her, would he?

She found herself literally pounding her palms against her head, like that would shake the information loose. It seemed to work because she did recall the words of power and the gestures. She performed them, directing the magic toward the master, who seemed to be in a great amount of pain.

"It didn't work," the master gasped. "Again."

She tried it again, but it still didn't seem to take.

"Again."

By the time she finished the third casting, Marla was frantic. She was scared, mad, and on the verge of tears.

"Master Videric?"

The master opened a drawer in his desk and pulled out another vial, this one a pale blue color. He fumbled with the stopper, but his hands didn't seem to be working correctly. Marla reached over to help, but Master Videric put the top of the vial in his mouth and bit down on it, crushing the glass between his teeth. He spit the shards out of lips that were already bleeding and downed the potion in one gulp.

Marla gaped at him for a few seconds, confused about what was happening. By the time she decided to act, the master's grunts and his writhing body slowed.

She cast several lower healing spells, back-to-back. Those, at least, came more easily since she had practiced them so many times. She honestly couldn't think of anything else to do.

A few agonizing minutes passed and the master gradually looked better. He sat back in his chair and breathed easily.

"Whew," he said. "I did not expect that. Usually, I'm not wrong when I choose to prod students into action by putting myself at risk. That was a close call."

"You...you weren't acting?" Marla asked. "You actually drank poison?"

"I did. I had the antidote, of course, but I delayed taking it, as you saw. Thank you for the lower-level healing. It took care of the cuts I obtained in biting into the vial. I hadn't accounted for the poison affecting my motor functions so thoroughly."

"Gods," Marla said. "You almost died. I almost killed you."

"Not so, my dear. At most, you would have been responsible only for failing to aid me, not the death itself. The blame for that would be on me."

Marla couldn't figure out if she was sad or angry or afflicted by any one of a dozen other emotions. Her hands shook as the situation caught up to her.

"Don't blame yourself, Marla. I have used the technique before to squeeze a bit more out of my more exceptional students. It was my lapse in judgment that made it an issue. Honestly, I'm surprised that you didn't cast the spell right off without a problem. Would you care to explain how it is that you did not? It's not like you at all."

"I've had a rough few weeks. I haven't been able to study or practice as much as I'd like. I'm so sorry, Master Videric."

"It's not your fault, and there will be no lasting harm. I can heal and cure myself of any residual issues, don't you worry. I do believe, however, that you should take some time for yourself. What you describe happens to students on occasion, especially the best of them. You're doing too much. We'll end our session here. Maybe you can take a nap or go somewhere to take your mind off things. Inform me when you have regained your focus. A good healer knows that their own bodies are as important to take care of as those of our patients."

After several more apologies, Marla left the master's office and headed toward her next appointment at the School of Air Magic. She was scheduled to teach a class for Master Esiyae. There wasn't enough time to do anything except take her time in walking to the lecture room she would be using, so she did so, thinking about what had just happened.

As she did, she grew madder and madder. Not at Master Videric, not at her schedule, but at herself. Because of her attitude and her lack of attention of late, she had failed to save Master Vederic. True, it irritated her that he would be so cavalier with his own life, but she knew the blame was primarily on her. If she couldn't even cast an intermediate spell, what was she even doing at the Academy?

She arrived at the lecture hall much earlier than desired, but utilized the extra time by practicing the cure spell Master Videric had tried so hard to get her to cast. By the time the students started to arrive, she'd cast it dozens of times and felt better about being able to do it in a stressful situation. Of course, *not* being able to cast it in a stressful situation did bother her. When had she started panicking like that? It was not something she did. Usually.

The School of Air Magic was one Marla had mastered and the students she was lecturing were in the beginning stages of the curriculum, so Marla could have done the lecture in her sleep.

Unfortunately, she ended up doing it in *others'* sleep. It struck her as she modulated her voice more, increased her volume, quickened her pace, and tried to inject more energy into her speech. None of those things helped, though, as most of the class seemed to barely pay attention.

She was already drained of her motivation because of what had happened earlier, so she let it go rather than to directly address the lack of interest with the students. They would be responsible for knowing what she'd told them, so the load was on their own backs, so to speak.

Still, it didn't do wonders for her mood. It wasn't quite noon and she was already getting irritated enough that if she could have, she would have skipped her next appointment.

Once she was in the middle of it, she wished she had.

After a quick lunch, she was responsible for teaching a double-length practical session in the School of Edged Weapons. She'd mastered that school, of course, and it held a special significance in her repertoire of abilities, and not just because it was presided over by her favorite master. She saw it as a privilege to teach classes for Master Yxna, even if they caused her mood to sour sometimes.

Like today.

Marla had been setting up the area in the training ground for the class when a group of the students filtered in. They averaged fifteen or sixteen years old, though there was one exceptional student who was younger and a few that were older.

There was also Erol Denagian. The young man was sixteen and he was a good student overall. He was also an arrogant bastard that Marla could hardly stand being in the same room with.

Erol bragged to his friends about all his many qualities, not the least of which was—according to him—that he was much too advanced with weapons to be in such a remedial class. He joked how he should be the one teaching the class and that if the guest instructor wasn't careful, he would show them a thing or two.

Marla closed her eyes and took a few breaths. She had hated students with personalities like Erol's when she was younger—still did, to be honest—and in her current mood, she definitely didn't want to deal with him. She repeated to herself that she would be calm, she would not get mad, and she would make Master Yxna proud in the way she handled the class.

Once all the students gathered in front of Marla, she greeted them.

"We're here for a practical in edged weapons. I will be demonstrating some sword techniques and then you will practice them. Once you're all comfortable with what we've learned, we'll do some light sparring. First, I would like a volunteer to aid me in demonstrating the techniques."

Erol Denagian raised his hand. Only Erol. Marla wasn't sure if it was something that was planned or if it was a coincidence. She waited a good minute for someone else to volunteer, all the while Erol stood with a cocky smile on his face.

Marla pointed to Erol to join her in the front. *Damn it all.*

EIGHT

Erol strutted to the front of the class. He was about an inch shorter than Marla, but he'd overtake her height in a few years. The way he stood, disdainful cast to his face, you'd think he was already a foot taller than her. He swept a wavy lock of dark hair to the side and smiled at her and everyone else in turn, like he had just won some great contest. She refrained from actually shaking her head at him, but just barely.

"Today, I'll be covering a very important concept," she said. "It may be one familiar to you, especially if Master Shanaera has given you instruction in unarmed combat. If you grasp and practice this concept, I guarantee your combat ability—either armed or unarmed—will increase dramatically.

"The concept is simultaneous defense and attack. By this I am not talking about maneuvering different parts of your body or different weapons to defend with one, and attack with another, though that skill folds in nicely with what we'll cover. What I'm talking about is using a defensive move as an actual attack, thereby fulfilling both offense and defense with a single move.

"Please raise your hands if you are familiar with what I'm speaking about."

Erol raised his hand high. No surprise there. Another girl, too, raised her hand. Marla was surprised that she was one of the younger students in the class. She must be one of those people who had decided from the beginning to be a combat specialist.

"Two," Marla said. "That's good. It means the rest of you will learn something new today. It also means the two who have been exposed to these techniques will have an opportunity to add to and refine what they've already learned."

Marla caught the eye roll from Erol as she said it, but gritted her teeth and clenched a fist to keep from responding.

The young man had a pretty face. Not handsome; more feminine than rugged. She was sure many of the female students would have found him attractive physically, as long as he kept his attitude suppressed and didn't open his mouth to speak. She knew his type and, unfortunately for both of them, people like him disgusted her. Attractive, accomplished individuals, both male and female, who knew their advantages and constantly brought attention to themselves naturally made her want to punch them in the face. Not the best thing for her current mood.

"Okay, let's start off with the basics, shall we. Erol, select a one-handed weapon from the rack. I will do likewise."

Erol sauntered over to the weapons and picked up a wooden short sword. Marla grabbed the wooden version of one of the thin straight swords from Shinyan. All the practice weapons were wood, but there was a great variety, from clubs and staffs to knives, all the way up to great swords and even polearms. A simple one-handed weapon would be best to demonstrate the basic techniques, though.

"Now," she said to Erol, "I want you to slowly slash at me. The rest of you, watch the action I take in defense."

Before Marla even finished her sentence, Erol charged in and cut at her with a fast downward diagonal slash, like he was trying to split her skull. She shifted her hips, flicked her sword out in a parry and, in the same motion, brought the blade to Erol's neck, stopping it with barely any contact. A couple of the students oohed at the exchange.

"Okay. Perhaps you can try a little slower. I'm not sure the others quite caught what I did."

Erol's smirk widened. The idiot seemed to think he had come out ahead, even with her sword edge resting against his neck.

Without a word, he knocked her sword away and lunged with a thrust toward her eyes. With her weapon already in motion from him knocking it away, she raised her elbow to angle her blade, deflecting his. She continued her forward motion to ram the point of her weapon into the soft spot just below the solar plexus. She didn't want to hurt him too badly, after all.

Erol grunted and backed up a couple of steps, then brought his sword up in preparation to attack again.

"Hold," she said, putting a finger up. She turned to the other students. "Did you catch the motions on those two attacks?"

No one had, so she explained them. "With the first defense, I used my energy efficiently in parrying the strike coming in." She repeated the motion, utilizing her hips and shoulders, with a flick of the wrist when the blades met.

"Then, I let the momentum of my parry carry my sword forward, guiding it slightly to the critical spot on his neck. If these had been sharp blades, and I had not stopped mine, I would have cut halfway through his throat and he would have been dead in a handful of seconds."

Erol snorted at that, but Marla ignored him. Again.

"With the second strike, a straight thrust following what amounts to a block to knock my sword away, I harnessed the momentum he imparted to my blade, twisted it to deflect his, and essentially leaned forward and let the sword continue to punch into his abdomen, though I purposely aimed it a little lower than I normally would so as not to take all his breath away and possibly caused him to lapse into unconsciousness from striking the nerve bundle there. Again, if this was sharp steel, even striking low, it would have been a fatal blow, though his death would have been longer and more painful in coming."

A chuckle beside her nearly caused her to flick her sword out to shut him up, but she gripped her hilt and wrangled her temper under control.

She took a deep breath. "Are there any questions about what I've said or demonstrated so far?" She prayed for all she was worth that Erol could keep his mouth shut. Surprisingly, he did. None of the other students had questions, and for a change, they all seemed to be paying attention.

"Okay," she said, turning back to Erol. "Let's give everyone a few more examples. It would be very helpful if you would move more slowly, Erol, so your classmates can see clearly what is happening."

"About that," he said. "This is really as slow as I can move. If it's too much for you, maybe we can get an instructor here who's better than you."

Marla couldn't help but to flick her gaze at the practice sword in her hand. An image of ramming it through the idiot's eye was so overpowering, she actually started to take a step toward him before she regained control of herself. She knew damn well that he was attacking at the highest speed he was capable of. It was nothing compared to what she could do, though. She wanted badly to demonstrate that to him. Maybe she would...in a controlled manner.

"Fine, if you are incapable of controlling your body, then I suppose we'll just have to deal with it," she said. "Go ahead and attack again. Let's do three and then we'll stop to explain."

He grinned, not even realizing she'd insulted him.

With what he probably thought was a battle cry, Erol cut downward at her again. Like the first time, she parried and struck him on the side of the neck. Exactly like the first time. He circled his sword around and swept his blade at her horizontally from her left to right. She flicked her sword in a tight circle and tapped his blade toward the ground, almost causing him to cut strike his own leg. Her sword bounced slightly from the impact and she continued its motion to slash upward in a cut that would have sliced open his sword arm for almost its entire length.

Undeterred, he looped his sword around again, performing a sloppy horizontal cut from the opposite direction. For this one, she stepped toward him, raised her hilt high so the sword was vertical, point down, and jammed his strike low on his sword. With a turn of her hips, his sword stopped, she dragged her blade along his arm, the she struck him hard in the face with her pommel.

Erol slammed onto the hard ground on his back, his sword bouncing out of his grip. He shook his head, his eyes unfocused, and started to work his mouth. When he opened it, his teeth were bloody and he spat. One of his teeth landed on the ground.

Marla felt bad for a solid second before she decided there was no real harm done and that Erol deserved every bruise he got. Still, she cast a simple healing spell on him, which regrew his tooth and stopped his bleeding.

After going through what had happened step-by-step, Marla had to decide if she would continue with the demonstrations or give up on trying to show them just how powerful the technique could be and start letting them practice. She figured she'd give it one more try.

"Right, one final demonstration," she said. "Are you up for this, Erol?"

He gave her his cockiest smile. There was still some blood on his teeth, but she didn't bother telling him. "Why, did I wear you out?" he sneered. "You can quit if you want. I can teach the class."

She blinked at him. "Uh, no. Let's make it a little more complex this time. Can you use two weapons at once?"

"Of course," he said. "Can you?"

She did her best to ignore the question, though she felt the heat rising within her. "Select your two."

He chose another short sword and she replaced her Shinyan straight sword with a battle rapier and a long dueling knife. All of wood, of course.

Erol hefted his two swords. "I'm an expert with two swords," he boasted. "I understand your brother tries to use two. Tell him that if he asks real nice, I might give him a free lesson."

For a moment, Marla considered sending someone to track Aeden down so he could kill the moron himself, but that would deprive her of inflicting some pain on the arrogant little prick in front of her.

"Worry about the opponent in front of you, not the next one who will kill you."

His smile slipped a little at her tone, but it slid back up when he glanced at the other students. He whipped the swords around him with a flourish, trying his best to show off. Marla picked out four separate holes in his guard as he did so and had to keep herself from exploiting them right then.

"As before," she said. "Attack me when you're ready. Though you insist on using your full speed, I will slow myself down to match yours so that maybe some of your fellow students can see what happens."

He gritted his teeth and swung his swords around in a figure eight configuration, pressing in on her.

Marla had to remember the point of the lesson. Though normally, she would rush in and attack, breaking through the defenses of someone like Erol and ending the fight quickly, she wanted to make it worthwhile for those she was trying to teach. With that in mind, she responded conservatively to the slashes he aimed at her.

From the simple parry-and-extend type of motions to more elaborate movements that utilized the force of bouncing her blades off his, she kept every strike from getting anywhere near her, while at the same time stopping strikes at his neck, eyes, heart, and even the femoral artery in both legs. As he tried harder and harder, she could see the effects of his frustration. He became wild, wanting only to kill her with a single blow.

While they moved, she explained briefly what she was doing, stating "hit" or "killing blow" as she methodically took him apart. Yet she didn't strike him hard. Her purpose was to show fight-ending blows, so any lack of control could seriously injure him. Once she'd "killed" him more than ten times, though, she decided it was time to pay back his arrogance. At least a little bit.

The next strike, a combination of both blades coming in horizontally from both sides, was a perfect opportunity. Using the handguards on both her blades, she pushed both of Erol's swords downward so they clashed into each other. At the same time, she snapped a lightning-fast front kick into the center of his chest, slamming him back and off his feet to land on his behind and slide in the dirt. Both swords flew from his hands on impact.

He got back up, face red and eyes blazing in anger. After scrambling to pick up his practice weapons, he charged again, throwing wild attacks at her.

"You'll note," she said, casually while batting aside his blows, "that Erol has lost control." Her leg shot out and jammed a horribly sloppy kick that would have probably cost him his leg if Marla had a real blade. "He isn't thinking clearly and his defense is suffering."

Erol began to whirl, gaining momentum for powerful strikes, though sacrificing accuracy and defense.

"This isn't part of the original lesson, but it's something to remember. If you find yourself losing your calm battle sense, you need to make a change." Marla parried a sword thrust with a crescent kick, easily fast enough to kick the flat of the blade to move it out of the way. "Sometimes, that change could and *should* be retreat. Pride has no place in a battle such as this. If you must choose to protect your ego or your life, it would be better to turn and run."

Erol growled and attempted a complex set of movements that he was no doubt hoping would confuse her. She simply evaded most of them and deflected the only two that were within range to strike her.

"One final lesson," she said. "You must be very careful

in striking with elbows, a shoulder, knees, or kicks when in combat with weapons. On the one hand, you put your vulnerable body parts at risk with such moves." She lifted her lead leg as Erol tried to cut at it, as if he was listening and it had given him an idea on how to cheat.

"On the other hand, if you have the skill—and the speed—you may surprise your opponent with such unorthodox attacks."

Erol lunged in with both swords in ridiculously telegraphed straight thrusts. Marla slammed her sword down on both his blades, driving them toward the ground. She pivoted and swept her leg to kick him hard on the back of his calves. The result was his feet flying out from under him as his body went completely horizontal. Her kicking leg didn't even touch the ground, converting the powerful motion into a circle and coming down in a high arcing axe kick.

Marla's heel slammed into Erol's chest with the downward force of a fully-loaded wagon. The cracking she heard was no doubt several ribs losing the battle against her leg strike. The blow slammed Erol onto the ground, flat on his back. Whatever air was left in his body rushed out with a grunt that mingled with the dull thud of his body landing.

Marla calmly returned her weapons to the rack. "Does anyone here know magical healing?" Two hands raised and she motioned toward Erol, who was still lying on the ground, gasping for breath. "Please see to him. If it's beyond your abilities, let me know. Also, Kinan, would you please collect Erol's weapons. He seems to have lost hold of them. Again. Please put them in the rack. Thank you."

While the three students performed their assigned tasks, Marla went through the combat with Erol step-by-step, highlighting the actions she took and how they demonstrated the topic of the day's class. Once Erol was sorted out—she'd had to cast a few healing spells on what she believed were three broken ribs—the class practiced what she'd been teaching them. At a very slow pace.

She dismissed the class on time. Her anger hadn't been sated by the impromptu beating of Erol. It had helped momentarily by expending some energy, but she was still in a foul mood. She gathered up some stray weapons and prepared to go back to her room.

"Yeah, I just don't get it," Erol's voice said from the edge of the training yard. He was talking to a couple of girls who were in the class. "All I can figure is that she's the masters' pet. Malatirsay. Pshaw. Right. She's got a few years on me, but by the time I get to be her age, I'll be so much better than her at everything. It just goes to show you that if you get the masters on your side, you can be a completely incompetent moron and still spread rumors about how good you are. I guess some of us just have to prove we're the best.

"You just wait. A few years from now, no one's gonna even know who she is. It'll all be about Erol Denagian. Mark my words, you'll be hearing a lot about me. Hells, you won't even have to wait a few years. Once it gets around how I mopped up the training yard with her today, you'll be hearing about me this week."

Marla clenched her fist so hard her knuckles cracked. She wanted nothing more than to go and see if he could *mop the training yard up with her* when she was actually trying. She wondered how much trouble she'd get in if she actually killed the bastard.

Without letting herself dwell on it anymore, she fled in the opposite way from her dormitory. Every step made her want to turn around and go after Erol, but she knew it was her anger trying to get the best of her. Iven Danson crossed her mind and it gave her the strength to leave before she heard any more.

Marla took a wide path around and back toward her room. She was definitely going to need some alone time before she interacted with anyone else.

CHAPTER
NINE

Marla made it to her room without encountering anyone else who tried to talk to her. Behind her closed door, she took a moment to stop and breathe. Thoughts of all the little irritations of the last several days, culminating in her nearly killing Master Videric and then wanting so badly to actually kill Erol, brought up the heat in her body again.

Maybe she should have stayed in the training yard and destroyed some of the practice dummies to relieve some of the pressure building up throughout her whole body. She clenched and unclenched her fists, gritted her teeth hard, closed her eyes and shook her head. If she didn't get her breathing regular instead of the building, panting huffs it was becoming, she was going to end up blasting a hole through her wall with some spell just to sate her anger.

It took longer than it really should have, but she managed to drop to a cross-legged position on the floor, focusing solely on her breaths and on blanking her mind. She used an old technique she'd been taught by Master

Jusha when she was younger. A bright flame in her mind, into which she fed her anger and other strong emotions.

She battled herself—and her mood —until she finally slumped where she sat. Her hair was damp from perspiration and her body felt like it had been strenuously exercising for hours. But she was calmer than she'd been. She would still probably kill someone that angered her at the moment, but she no longer felt like she had to go and hunt someone down.

It was some improvement, at least.

As Marla transferred herself to her chair, a sensation similar a cooling breeze passed over her. Her room was shut up tight, window and door closed, so it couldn't be a literal draft, but it was soothing nonetheless. She faced it and tilted her head back, enjoying the sensation.

It only lasted a moment, and it didn't rustle her hair or clothing at all, telling her there was no true wind. A longing stirred in her with its demise, though. That familiar tugging she'd been feeling. She hadn't even realized before, but she was facing due south, the direction the "breeze" had been coming from. What the hells was that feeling?

Like breaking out of a trance, it was suddenly clear what she needed to do. She'd been thinking about it, dancing around the idea, but now it all made such sense. She stuffed some things into her pack—it was always at least half ready for leaving on a moment's notice recently anyway—put on her cloak, and cinched the pack over it.

Sweeping her gaze over her room to see if she had forgotten anything, Marla readjusted her sword, dueling dagger, and the knives in her left boot and right thigh. Then she was out her door and heading for the stables.

Surefoot met her with a soft whinny and she patted the horse's nose.

"You want to go out for a ride, girl?" Marla asked. Surefoot tossed her head and snorted. Marla would take that as a yes.

It didn't take much time to get the mare saddled. She took some of the provisions in the larder near the stables and stuffed them into her saddlebags along with the supplies she already kept in her saddlebags when they were stored in the tack room. She eyed the log book sitting on a table, but didn't bother to fill it out. Better she just head out without dealing with any of the formalities. It was fortuitous enough that none of the stable hands were around to ask her questions. She'd take that as a sign that what she was doing was the right thing.

Marla swung up into the saddle and walked Surefoot toward the main gate. It was the calm late afternoon time when most students were in their last class of the day, or were holed up somewhere getting some studying done before the evening meal, so she only saw three people out and about.

Unfortunately, one of those was Lucas Stewart.

The blond-haired student spotted Marla as she was nearing the front gate. He was some distance away, so she made sure not to turn her head toward him, only catching him waving at her in her peripheral vision. Though she had an urge to speed up, she continued at a walk until she reached the gate itself. Lucas had sped up to get her attention, but she continued to ignore him.

As soon as she passed the threshold of the gate, Marla veered Surefoot to the left to block Lucas's view of her. She put her heels to the mare's flanks and headed for the road toward the mainland. By the time Lucas emerged from the gate, she was past a bend in the road and hidden from him in the trees.

"Okay," Saria Gilwenys said. "I'm going to play some soothing strains at first to relax you. Then, I'll sing a few songs, using some voice magic to try to help you to be more receptive to your talent."

Fahtin nodded as she adjusted her position on the bed in her room. She'd found that relaxing her entire body was the key. Most of her clearest visions, at least since she'd been trying to seek them rather than wait for them to strike her unaware, were when she was completely at peace.

The Gypta glanced over at Evon, sitting in a chair in the corner of the room with an anxious look on his face. She gave him a smile and he returned it with a tentative one of his own.

Saria, as exotic and beautiful as she'd been when Fahtin first met her, sat on a stool a little closer to the bed. No, that wasn't true. The astri woman actually looked even prettier than when she'd first seen her, with her new clothing—without the blood stains and tears—and with her hair, brushed until it was glossy, over her left ear, showing her pointed lobe clearly.

One of the astridae. Who was Fahtin that she kept such company? The Malatirsay, masters of the famed Hero Academy, Erent Caahs himself? She even regularly associated with arba and the servant of a goddess. All that, and the Great Prophet himself had written a book specifically for her. All she wanted was to be worthy of all the privileges she'd been given. And to help Aeden and Marla save the world, of course.

She blinked as Saria began to strum her lute. Okay, the first thing she needed to do was to stop thinking about everything under the sun. It was time to relax, to clear her mind, and to let the visions come. She wriggled to settle into the bed and closed her eyes, letting the music wash over her.

As she drifted, with the feeling of her body lifting off the bed and floating around the room, Fahtin panicked for a moment and jerked as her eyes snapped open. She looked over to see Saria and Evon both watching her, the latter on the edge of his seat as if to rescue her from something.

"Sorry," she said. "I think I started to fall asleep and was dreaming I was flying."

Relief washed over Evon's face. The young man really did worry too much about her. It was nice, comfortable, but he didn't need to worry. She wasn't so weak that a bad dream would hurt her. She gave him another soothing smile, readjusted her head, and closed her eyes again.

This time, when she felt the weightlessness, she embraced it. Half asleep or in some kind of trance, it felt wonderful. Like she didn't have a single care in the world. As Saria began to sing, the comfort actually turned to pleasure. She had never felt anything so relaxing.

It wasn't like when the astri had sung that first night. Her voice was amazing, beautiful, mesmerizing, but the songs she had sung were just songs. Fahtin could feel the magic within the notes of the song now, could almost picture it flowing through and around her.

Suddenly, she could no longer hear the meaning in the words. Even the music had retreated into the background. What sprang up instead was a fully formed vision. Not the half-images and washed-out pictures she sometimes saw. She saw, felt, and heard herself plunge into the experience.

Twelve shadowy figures sat around a table. All of it was

familiar, what Fahtin recognized as the group called the Dark Council. She still couldn't see detail, but from her experiences and stories from her friends, she could pick out individual silhouettes. The woman who had attacked them when they found Tsosin Ruus's secret cache, Ren Kenata the Academy graduate, the others who although nameless, were familiar nonetheless.

One of them—Fahtin got the sense that she was a tall, thin woman—seemed to be the leader. She gestured and the shadowy people flew off in every direction. Fahtin suddenly saw from up above Dizhelim as the Dark Council members scoured the land, looking for something she couldn't figure out.

One of the silhouettes came near the Academy, their dark shape meeting with one of the darker swirls of color she'd seen in her last vision. The two whirled around each other, tangled and interacted. By the time they broke apart, they were the same color and Fahtin knew they had traded information. Important information.

One of the Dark Council silhouettes drew her eye like iron filings to a lodestone. She tried to tear her gaze away, but could not. A sense of rushing, wind whipping past her face, made her think she was being physically pulled toward the other. She felt a kind of kinship with the dark shape and she intuited that it was a woman. Almond-shaped brown eyes stared into hers and a name was thrust into her head. Amatia.

Fahtin's vision went blank. Not black, but a total absence of any color. Just as suddenly, Marla, her hair still burning like her last vision, appeared in front of Fahtin. Both of them seemed to be floating hundreds of feet above the ground, on a shoreline Fahtin didn't recognize.

Marla dropped like a great stone and plunged into the water. Fahtin could still see her hair on fire under the water, the red-yellow of the flame not affected by being underneath the waves. The sight gave Fahtin a fright, but didn't seem to affect the dark monsters circling around her. Some were humanoid, but others were differently shaped, multi-limbed and exuding danger. They circled, coming ever closer, and Fahtin knew they would attack. Yet Marla was too caught up in her own flame to notice them.

The scene changed again, the shapes she had seen in her previous vision coming to be instantly as before. She could pick out the forms of different animals, and even people, though they all lacked color and detail. This time, as they were formed, they flew into the sky, pulled by some irresistible force.

Fahtin thought for a moment all the shapes, which she knew for a fact were living things, would fall to the ground and die, but they didn't. Instead, they floated softly to a large land mass of lush forest mixed with grasslands. From her vantage point above the area, Fahtin noticed coastline both to the east and to the north, but she didn't recognize their contours.

The entire area in her field of view glowed softly as the things that had fallen to the ground began to build detail and, finally, color. She spotted horses, cows, dog-like creatures, cats, as well as a number of other familiar animals. She also picked out humans and—she thought—other humanoid people, like the astridae.

Off to the edge of one of the forests, Aeden and Lily, along with other familiar figures she couldn't quite identify, stood discussing something. As she tried to reconcile her friends' presence, the world dissolved in a wash of color and she was suddenly looking at another person she recognized.

Saria Gilwenys floated in the air, much like Fahtin felt she herself was doing at the moment. The astri seemed calm and relaxed, though she was very high above the southern part of the coast of the Kanton Sea.

A light swept up toward Saria. Fahtin wasn't sure, but she thought it might have come from the west. As it reached Saria, the light reversed, turning to pure, inky darkness. It began to wrap around the blonde woman. Fahtin tried to shout, to warn the apparently slumbering astri, but having no mouth in this place, the Gypta couldn't make a sound.

She watched, helpless, as Saria startled awake and began to scream. Instead of a yell, though, song came out, but not just any song. It was music made solid, like a ray of sunshine so bright it had weight and substance. Fahtin relaxed marginally, knowing that such magic would protect Saria from whatever threatened her.

Instead, the darkness moved faster than Fahtin thought possible and it swirled around the song light and entered into Saria's mouth. The astri immediately slumped and began to fall. At the last moment, another Fahtin, this one as solid as the world, raced to catch the falling Saria, the dreamer Fahtin was looking at. Right beside her, Aila was also there and the two caught the astri just before she impacted the ground and somehow were strong enough to withstand the force of the falling woman.

Fahtin jerked up from the bed, screaming in surprise and then whimpering in relief as the Aila and Fahtin in the vision saved Saria's life.

Evon was there in a second, and Saria barely a breath behind.

"Are you okay?" Evon asked.

Fahtin panted, running her hands over her body to convince herself she was real and not still in some vision. After a few breaths, she was able to get out, "Yes. I'm fine. Get your little book out. I have some things to tell you."

CHAPTER

TEN

Aeden and Khrazhti finished up their morning exercises in a meadow area near Batido. The Croagh had a sheen of perspiration coating his bare torso but, as always, Khrazhti did not. She wasn't even breathing hard. Aeden hadn't figured out yet if it was some special way her half-human, half-animaru body worked or if the blue woman was just so fit, a normal workout couldn't come close to making her exert herself.

He found that he was running his eyes over her, searching for the slightest bit of perspiration. He did like how she looked. She was a prime specimen of a warrior's fitness and the way she moved could take his breath away. So graceful.

"Is something wrong?" she asked him.

His eyes snapped up to her softly glowing blue orbs. "Ah, uh, no. Nothing at all. I was...ah, just trying to figure out why you never sweat at all when I—" he waved his hand indicating himself "—am covered with it. It's amazing, really."

A corner of her mouth turned up into a smile. "I do perspire, but I believe my metabolism is different than yours and it takes a higher level of exertion for it to occur."

"Oh. That's what I was thinking."

He couldn't for the life of him think of anything else to say, so he stepped over to the branch he had hung his shirt on to retrieve the garment.

"Have you spoken with Marla," Khrazhti asked, and he could have kissed her for filling the silence. A high spot in the grass reached up and grabbed his foot as he was thinking it and he stumbled.

"No, not since a few days ago when she got angry when I was trying to teach her the Raibrech. I'm worried about her, Khrazhti. She's been really tense lately, and her temper seems to be getting the best of her. I don't know what to do. I want to talk to her about it, but I'm afraid it'll make things worse. I gave her a little time and space, but it's clear she's not going to come around and offer to talk about it."

"I have noticed, too, that she is having difficulties. I would ask her about it, but I am ignorant of such things and could not commiserate with her."

Aeden started walking back toward Batido and Khrazhti took up a position beside him. "Do the animaru have problems with difficult situations and anger like that?"

Khrazhti cocked her head. "It is a struggle to be one of the animaru leaders. As with any soldier, there is a certain difficulty when your job is to engage in combat. As for emotions, though animaru have them, they are...muted. Anger is one of the more powerful, perhaps because it is more in line with our dark nature, but going into a thoughtless rage rarely happens."

"It must be nice," Aeden said.

"It may be. One must also realize, however, that the lack of strong negative feelings is also balanced out by the lack of strong positive feelings. Most animaru cannot appreciate humor, or the joy of being with ones they care about. I would trade having to deal with anger to feel fellowship and love more keenly."

"Huh. I never really thought about that. You seem to do really well, though. You have a great sense of humor and you laugh more and more all the time. It's almost like we're rubbing off on you."

"Yes. I think my human side helps me in that respect. I am glad of it. I cannot imagine how I passed so many centuries without laughing and smiling."

Aeden reached over and grabbed her hand, squeezing it. "I'm glad you can do it now. I love hearing you laugh."

"Truly?"

"Of course. And your smiles, they're fantastic. They can make me feel better, even if I'm in a foul mood. You may actually be able to help Marla, after all."

She smiled at him and he realized he was still holding her hand. He released it and cleared his throat as they reached the door to the common room. He opened the door for her and followed her inside to find nearly all his friends sitting at the tables eating their breakfast. He also noticed Lucas Stewart, the young Academy student the masters often used for sending messages.

"Hey Lucas," Aeden said. "Stopped by to have breakfast with us?"

"Um, no, Aeden. Good morning. I was about to tell everyone that Master Qydus has been able to schedule the meeting you all requested. He has time two hours from now. Will that work for all of you?"

"Meeting?" Aeden said. "Oh, so Fahtin can finally tell us about her most recent visions." Evon had gone right away to talk to the headmaster to try to schedule a time when they could explain Fahtin's visions to him and the other masters. Both Evon and Fahtin had insisted that the others wait until everyone was together before they described what she'd seen. Apparently they were fairly involved and Fahtin didn't want to have to recount them more times than she had to.

"We'll be there," Evon said. "We'll pass the message along to the rest of us here, but if you could track Marla down and tell her, that would be great."

"I tried to find her before coming here," Lucas said. "I tried her door and a few of the out-of-the-way places she goes to study. Maybe she hasn't come back yet."

"Come back?" Aeden said.

"Yeah. I saw her leaving the Academy grounds yesterday afternoon. She had her pack and her saddlebags were stuffed. I thought maybe she was going on a mission. Do you know when she'll be back?"

"A mission?" Evon said. "I don't know anything about a mission. Anyone else?"

No one did. Aeden got a sour feeling in his stomach.

"Thanks, Lucas," he told the young man. "We'll try to find her. Please let the headmaster know we'll be there. If you have time for a bite to eat, stick around and have breakfast with us."

"Thank you, but I already ate. I'll go tell the headmaster you'll be there. See you all later."

When Aeden and the others arrived for the meeting, they found the headmaster sitting at his customary position at the head of the table. Master Yxna Hagenai was sitting next to him on the right and Master Nasir Kelqen was on his left. Master Isegrith was there, as usual, and Master Goren sat solidly in a chair a few spaces away.

Master Marn Tiscomb was also in attendance, slumping in a chair as close to the corner of the room as he could be, a scowl on his face. It may not have been odd to include the Master of the School of Prophecy in a meeting about Fahtin's visions, but it was plain he didn't want to be there. In general, he had always taken every opportunity to downplay and even demean Fahtin's abilities.

Surprisingly, there was another new addition to the regular group of masters in their meetings. Master Tufa Shao, the Master of the School of Movement and Body Mechanics, sat at the far end of the table from the headmaster, her posture perfect. She wasn't sitting stiffly, though, somehow giving the sense of both relaxing and being ready to flash into action in the blink of an eye.

Aeden had spoken with Master Tufa several times and came away with valuable knowledge each time. Physically, the master looked as one would expect for an expert in movement. Toned, perfectly proportioned, and with the ageless type of features so many of the masters possessed. Her black hair was in a topknot, bound by rings close to her skull. Her sleeveless white top was snug, showing off not only her impressive chest and toned arms and shoulders, but also the fine lines defining her abdominal muscles. Her black pants were snug as well, but of some type of material that allowed them to stretch and provide her free movement. Aeden hadn't had a chance to spar with the master yet, but he had heard she could fight Master Shanaera, the Master of the School of Unarmed Combat, to a standstill. He believed it.

The master lifted her chin toward Aeden and gave him a

fractional smile. Aeden waved. It struck him that the master, though obviously fit and capable, didn't radiate a sense of danger. Not until one looked into her dark eyes. Even with a smile on her face, the depths of those eyes promised nothing but bad things for anyone who was antagonistic toward the master.

Aeden blinked himself out of his thoughts and took a seat as his friends found their own.

"Marla?" the headmaster asked after everyone was settled.

"We believe she may have left the Academy grounds yesterday afternoon," Aeden said. "Lucas saw her packed for a trip and riding her horse out of the gate. He, and we, looked for her this morning, but we couldn't find her."

"The log book?"

"I checked all the log books, Headmaster," Evon said. "She didn't sign out in any of them."

"That is unfortunate. It seems she and I will be having a discussion when she returns."

"Master Qydus, I'm worried about her." This time it was Fahtin who spoke. "She's been out of sorts lately and I'm afraid she either tipped over the edge and is not making wise decisions, or there is some danger involved."

"We have noticed she has been having troubles lately," the headmaster said. "Perhaps we should have taken action sooner. For now, let us put aside the issue of Marla and her troubles. I believe you asked for this meeting to convey to us visions you had that may contain important information?"

"Yes, Headmaster. Some of them seem to be more detailed versions of what I told everyone in the last meeting."

"Very well. Take your time and explain your new visions."

Fahtin went through all her visions, providing all the detail she could describe. Evon read along in his record of what she'd seen, written immediately after she'd had the visions, to make sure nothing was left out. When she was done, it was time to discuss what she'd seen.

Master Marn made scoffing noises throughout, loud enough that Aeden's irritation grew to the extent he felt like smacking the man, master or not. When Fahtin had finished, the master spoke first.

"Are we to believe that any of what she dreams up is true? Is this a meeting to read a girl's dreams or to discuss important matters?"

Master Qydus's sharp eyebrows drew down, crinkling his forehead. "Marn, do you have the ability of prophecy?"

Master Marn blinked rapidly at the headmaster, as if he was trying to understand the question. "I...hardly think that is of issue at the mo—"

"It *is* the issue. Do you or do you not have the ability to receive prophecy or to naturally scry without the use of devices or cast spells?"

"No." The answer was barely loud enough to be heard, and wouldn't have been had not everyone in the room gone still and silent.

"Then perhaps you should take more care not to discourage Miss Achaya, who has proven on numerous occasions that she not only has this ability, but wields it with a power stronger than any the Academy has seen in centuries, possibly millennia—

to the extent that the Prophet himself wrote a book addressed to her personally to aid her in using her abilities."

"A book no one else has been able to read," Master Marn said.

If anything, the headmaster's face grew sterner. "Do you advocate confiscating letters received by Academy students solely on the grounds that you want to know what they say?"

"I...uh, of course not, but—"

"Then what right do you believe you have to take what amounts to a personal letter—a very long personal letter, no less—written by the founder of this school solely for the benefit of this young woman before us?"

The Master of Prophecy finally showed a bit of intelligence and restraint and remained silent.

The headmaster turned back to Fahtin and his face lightened. "Now, Miss Achaya, pardon us for the interruption. If you would, please explain the different visions and what you believe is their meaning. As with all prophecy, descriptions, and even illusions in the visions, are never as understandable to others as they are for the one who received them."

Fahtin flicked her gaze back and forth from the headmaster to the still fuming Master Marn, his mostly bald head flushed and damp. "Yes, Headmaster.

"The part about the Dark Council means that something has happened and they are searching for something. I'm not positive, but I believe they know about the wells and are actively looking for them. I'm able to recognize Ren Kenata and Cara Moore, the woman who attacked us when we found the Prophet's secret cache of books. I can recognize the silhouette of their leader, but I don't know her name yet.

"The new one, whose eyes met mine, has prophetic or at least seer abilities. I don't know exactly what she looks like because she appears as a dark shape, but I believe that if I met Amatia, I would know her. It almost felt like she was watching me as I watched her, though I don't know what danger there is in that, if any.

"The part about Marla is disturbing. My other vision showed her agitated, her hair on fire symbolizing the extreme anger she was feeling. So strong that even plunging into the ocean didn't make it go out. When we found out this morning that she had left, I got a bad feeling that those dark shapes swirling around her mean her harm. I think we need to do something. She might be in danger.

"I'm not sure what the visions of the creation of animals and people have to do with anything. I understand now that the shapes springing to life represent the creative acts of Surus at the beginning of Dizhelim, though I don't know what it means that they were flying through the air and landing in another place, nor what Aeden and Lily and the other unidentified people have to do with it.

"The last vision, the one with Saria, is the most confusing of all. I don't know why she would be floating above the ground south of the Kanton Sea, nor what the light and darkness represent. My presence, and Aila's, doesn't make any sense. Why are we all there and what does the attack on Saria mean?

"I'm sorry, but that is all the information I have. I seem to have more questions than answers."

"You have nothing to be sorry about, child," Master Isegrith said. "Coming to terms with your burgeoning power is a difficult thing. You are doing admirably."

"Thank you, master."

Master Nasir leaned forward, the light glinting on the runes and scars on his face. "There are some things I would like clarified, if I may. First, I would like to determine how we are to view these visions. Are they prophetic or are they seeings?"

Fahtin moved her mouth, but wasn't able to formulate any words.

"Perhaps I can add a little to the discussion," Evon said. "I have been working with Fahtin and documenting her visions from the beginning, or nearly so. I think what you're asking, Master Nasir, is if we are to view the visions as things that *must* come true or things that *may* come true."

"That is accurate."

"Thank you. We—Aeden, Marla, and the rest of us who have been subjects in her visions lately—have discussed the matter and while I don't believe there is overwhelming evidence for calling them prophecies, our experience has been that it is advantageous for us to act in accordance with Fahtin's visions."

Master Nasir stroked his beard. "I see."

"To cut to the heart of the matter, I think the others will agree with me that when her visions specifically mention people doing things or being in a location, we will endeavor to act in a way to make those situations occur."

"Ah. Exactly what I was asking about. I am glad to see that your time in my school was not wasted, Evon. Well done."

"Thank you, Master Nasir."

"To clarify, then," Master Yxna said, "Aeden and Lily should go to wherever the creations landed and Fahtin and Aila need to be with Saria somewhere near the south coast of the Kanton Sea."

Evon nodded. "That is my opinion."

"I agree," Tere said. "Fahtin's visions have benefitted us before, when we acted in accordance with them. In fact, I believe that had we not done so, things would have turned out much differently and we most likely would have failed. I, for one, trust her abilities implicitly. They have not steered us wrong yet."

"Then Aeden, Lily, Fahtin, Aila, and Saria are not able to go after Marla," Master Yxna said. Heads snapped to the master as she said it. "What? It's clear to me that Marla is in some kind of trouble. We've established that the ones named are needed for other work, assuming the visions involve situations in the near future. I don't think we can safely assume that they are not. That leaves the rest to decide if they will join Aeden and Lily or Saria, Aila, and Fahtin."

"I will accompany Aila wherever she goes," Conren said. "I was charged with her safety by her father, my king."

"I'll go with Lily," Tere said. "She would be lost without me anyway." He grinned at her and she slapped his shoulder.

"Masters, I would like to go after Marla," Evon said. "With the use of one of Tsosin Ruus's finders, it should be an easy matter to locate her. I wish we had use of one when Skril disappeared. It could have made a difference. I don't want to delay with Marla. She can take care of herself, but, well, I need to go."

"Of course," Master Qydus said.

"I will aid Evon Desconse in finding Marla Shrike," Khrazhti said. "She is my friend and I would not leave her without allies."

"Me, too," Raki said, shooting a nervous look at Jia, as if afraid she would disagree with him. The former Falxen gave him a smile. "Aeden is like my brother and so Marla is like my sister. If Aeden and Fahtin can't go, I'll go in their place."

"And I will join you," Master Yxna said. Again, heads

swiveled toward her and eyes widened. "I'm not about to let that headstrong girl be hurt. Besides, she needs a talking to, and the sooner the better."

"Are you sure, Yxna," the headmaster asked. "Masters rarely leave the Academy for missions."

"We are in a time unlike any other in the history of this Academy, of the world itself. I believe it's time for unusual action."

"Very well. Evon, please provide a copy of your record of the visions we discussed and—"

Evon handed a small bound book to the headmaster. "I thought you might want that."

Master Qydus actually gave Evon a smile, a rare occurrence. Aeden couldn't help but notice the headmaster's eyes shifting to the pouting Master Marn before latching onto the book Evon proffered. "Thank you. I will discuss the matter further with the masters and think upon it. For now, those who are to chase after our wayward half of the Malatirsay, you may avail yourself of the Academy's resources, of course. For all others, continue with what you've been doing. Perhaps we will get news or Fahtin will have more visions that will indicate what we are to do with the other situations she described. Master Yxna, Evon, Raki, and Khrazhti, please remain for a few minutes before starting your preparations. We have a few things to discuss."

Aeden locked eyes with Khrazhti as he got up to leave. He was a little anxious about her going on a mission without him after going so long without being separated from her, but he immediately pushed the thought down. There was no one more capable of keeping herself safe than his animaru friend.

"I will speak with you after Master Qydus Okvius is finished," she said, patting him on the shoulder.

"Thank you," he said. He didn't like her going off without him and liked even less that he couldn't help with going after Marla, but duty rarely stopped to ask what its agents wanted. He headed back to Batido with the others, wondering if all of them were in for another series of journeys away from their home.

ELEVEN

Khrazhti finished packing items into the saddlebags on her horse, Twilight, outside of the stables. She eyed the beast warily, her glowing blue orbs locking onto the black eyes of the animal she would be riding for however long it took them to find Marla and bring her back.

The two had come to an unspoken agreement. Unspoken because the dumb animal could not speak, but it seemed to have the ability to reason out simple things. Things like if it did not behave, Khrazhti would thrash it soundly. *Her*. Marla had told Khrazhti several times that a mount was not a thing, an it. It was either a him or a her. Since the grey mare was a female, she would need to call the beast *her*. Fine.

"We are still in agreement, yes?" she asked the horse. She scrutinized Khrazhti as much as the animaru did the horse. "A token, then, of our agreement." Khrazhti produced a small apple from her pack and held it out for Twilight. The horse tilted her head for a moment before leaning forward and taking it carefully into her mouth and crunching down on it. The equine had learned not to snatch it up quickly when Khrazhti's reflexes had guided her hand to punch the horse on the side of the head once for her transgression.

"Good," Khrazhti said. "We have an accord." She patted Twilight's cheek as she had seen the others do. The beasts seemed to enjoy it.

Raki hid a smile, as did Evon while he passed her to go into the stables. Khrazhti looked behind her to see what they found so funny, but could not determine what had caused the reaction. Aeden said her sense of humor was getting better, but there were still times she felt as if she missed something that could make those around her laugh.

The group had opted to leave right away. The discussion with Master Qydus only lasted a few minutes, then speaking with Aeden and the others less than half an hour. As soon as they finished, they were gathering their supplies to meet at the stables. Raki and Evon looked the same as always, the Academy student in his runic and the boy in his black garb. She had been on such missions with them before.

Master Yxna, though, came prepared for the journey with weapons visible on her person. Though she was the Master of the School of Edged Weapons, Khrazhti had never seen her walk about with a sword strapped to her body. She did now. Not only that, but she also had two additional curved blades sheathed on her waist. Other than that, she had on the same drab clothing she normally wore.

If she were to admit it, Khrazhti was anxious to see the master in action. She'd seen Aeden sparring with her, but had not had a chance to spar with the master herself. Perhaps during this trip? The praise Aeden had for the master was high indeed. When Master Yxna had taken part in their exercise, disguised by illusion as one of the animaru, Khrazhti had been busy with fighting other foes and hadn't seen her technique. It had been said that she had turned the tide and ensured the humans' defeat single-handedly.

Evon emerged from the stables, leading his horse Lex. "I wish we had time to do a proper scrying so we'd know exactly where Marla was. The finders are nice, but they only point toward her, not give a specific location."

He had gone into Marla's room to use some of her personal items to train the finder to indicate where Marla was. Khrazhti thought it was a useful magic and could see its benefit in a wartime situation.

"Do the animaru have things like finders?" Raki asked.

"No. Some of the animaru are very good with magic, but as a whole, I do not think we are as clever as humans in the making of items. If something cannot be done with a spell, it would never occur to us to create a physical device to channel magic."

"Don't include yourself along with the others," Evon said. "Now that you've seen some of the things people have made, I'm sure you could invent a thing or two."

The statement seemed strange to Khrazhti, and she wasn't sure if she agreed with it, but the thought made her want to smile, that they had faith in her abilities.

"So," Evon said, holding the finder up. "It's no surprise, but she's to the south. Considering that most of Dizhelim is to the south, it's the way we'd go anyway. We're a full day behind, if Lucas's report of when he saw Marla leave is accurate. We'll need to make up some time. Is everyone ready?"

They were and as they mounted Khrazhti wondered where Marla was, and where she was going. There was so much of this world she had not seen yet. Perhaps on this journey, she would experience new places and see strange and wonderful things. She hoped above all that they would find Marla unharmed and convince her to come back to the Academy, but she couldn't help but feeling at least a little excited about exploring the world she had chosen to defend.

Out of the Academy, east over the bridge to the mainland, past Dartford, and finally onto the River Road, the group swung south. Evon checked the finder once they got to the major north-to-south road and found that it still pointed them almost directly in a southern direction.

"Evon," Master Yxna said as they rode along. "When the different groups of your friends split up, are you accustomed to bringing the message tablets along with you, the ones all synchronized to each other and to the one the headmaster keeps?"

"Yes."

"Did you happen to see if Marla had left the one that had been in her possession? Did you find it in her room?"

"Oh. No, I didn't see it, but I didn't look for it, either. Now that you mention it, I wish I had."

"One more question..."

"Yes, Master Yxna," Evon said with a grin. "I did bring one with me. Thank you. I hadn't even considered using it to try to contact her."

"Perhaps we can stop for a break soon and you can attempt to contact her using the tablet."

"That is a wonderful idea."

～

MARLA TOOK her time eating up the miles on the River Road. It had been so long since she had let Surefoot go at her own pace, she'd almost forgotten how nice and relaxing it was to move through terrain different than what she saw every day, and especially without worrying about being attacked at any moment.

Without the effect of others on her mood, she had calmed down considerably. Already, she was approaching a neutral mood as she passed between the high grasses on either side of the road. It had been a while since she had been so on edge that any little thing could set off her anger.

It had been a good choice to take this little trip. The tugging sensation was still there, drawing her further south, but other than that, she felt more normal than she had in a while. She was tempted to consider her mood approaching good, though maybe that was a bit of an exaggeration. She patted Surefoot's neck and settled in for another few hours of riding before stopping to eat something.

With her calmer disposition, Marla started thinking about her friends and how she'd left without telling anyone. Lucas had seen her go, so no doubt by now, everyone knew she was no longer at the Academy. But it was an irresponsible thing to do, something she never would have thought of doing had she been in her right mind. She had been so angry...

It occurred to her that she had the tools to let her friends know she was safe. One of the message tablets was stuffed into her saddlebags. The least she could do was to send them a message to tell them not to worry.

At the end of the River Road, the way split into two roads almost as large. To the west was the Genta Highway, which went through Sutania, the Great Enclave, and

Arania. To the southeast the Trail of Sarak led to Satta Sarak. She stopped at a small clearing alongside the road.

The terrain included more trees than even a few hours to the north, the forests near the mountain range known as Ianthra's Breasts beginning in earnest in all directions but west, in which direction the vegetation actually thinned going toward Arcusheim.

While she ate a simple cold meal of dried meat and bread, washed down with tepid water from her skin, Marla took out the message tablet to pen a short note. She found a message already waiting for her on the magical device. Of course her friends would have expected her to take the tablet, so they had sent her a message. She wondered how long it had been there, unread.

MARLA, IT'S EVON. WHERE ARE YOU? WHAT'S GOING ON? YOU LEFT WITHOUT TELLING ANYONE, NOT EVEN NOTIFYING THE MASTERS WHOSE CLASSES YOU WERE SUPPOSED TO TEACH. WE'RE ALL WORRIED ABOUT YOU. PLEASE RESPOND TO LET US KNOW YOU'RE SAFE.

Marla's face heated. She really had done something irresponsible. It was unbecoming an adult, let alone an Academy student. There would be consequences for her actions, she knew, and she regretted the situation. All she could do was to try to mitigate the results. The way to start that was to let everyone know she was not in danger, but that she needed a little more time away from things.

HI EVON. SORRY TO WORRY YOU, BUT I'M FINE. THINGS WERE GETTING TO ME AND MY ANGER WAS OUT OF CONTROL. I NEED A LITTLE BREAK, SO I DECIDED TO GET AWAY FROM ALL THE PRESSURE FOR A LITTLE WHILE. I KNOW IT'S IRRESPONSIBLE, BUT I NEED SOME

MORE TIME. I HOPE YOU UNDERSTAND. PLEASE TELL EVERYONE I'M SORRY AND THAT I MISS THEM. THINGS JUST GOT TO BE TOO MUCH FOR ME TO DEAL WITH.

That last part hurt to admit, but it was the truth. She didn't feel it necessary to tell them about following whatever it was that was drawing her south. She wasn't even sure what it was herself.

With that chore done and a bit of food in her belly, Marla got back in the saddle and took the Genta Highway toward the west. The tugging was coming from almost due south, but she had a feeling that going all the way around the mountains to swing toward Satta Sarak wouldn't get her to where she needed to go. With a long look northward up the River Road—toward her home—she set off to find out what wanted her attention so badly.

CHAPTER

TWELVE

E von read Marla's message to the others. Yxna Hagenai watched Marla's friends as they received the information that she was safe, but the master also recognized that it was something of a dismissal. She hadn't said where she was, had plainly stated that she would not be going back to the Academy soon. As Yxna expected, Evon picked up on those exact points immediately.

"I'm going to respond to her message. I don't like this game we're playing. We hide that we're following her because of fear of her running. She hides where she is in case someone tries to find her. It's enough for *my* anger to get the better of me."

Yxna could understand the frustration, but she had known Evon for some time, and she didn't believe for a moment he would lose his temper.

The young man scratched out a message on the tablet and then read it out loud.

MARLA, WE'RE SO GLAD YOU'RE SAFE. WITH EVERYTHING THAT'S

GOING ON LATELY, THERE ARE GROUPS OUT THERE WHO WOULD LIKE
NOTHING BETTER THAN TO GET HOLD OF YOU. WILL YOU TELL US
WHERE YOU ARE, WHAT YOU'RE DOING? WE'RE WORRIED
ABOUT YOU.

While the group waited for a reply, Evon used the finder
again.

"Oh. She headed to the west, probably at the Genta
Highway." He ran his fingers through his hair. "Do you
think she's heading to Arcusheim? What if we misinter-
preted things? Maybe Fahtin's vision about her and Aila
and Saria being south of the Kanton Sea meant they were
supposed to go after Marla. Did we make a mistake?"

Of all people, Khrazhti spoke up first to soothe Evon.
"Evon, please calm yourself. We have few facts and it will
do you no good to get agitated. Perhaps she is going to
where Fahtin's vision occurred, perhaps not. Even if the
location is the same, it might be that they are unrelated.
There is no temporal component to Fahtin's visions. For all
we know, the vision on the south coast of the sea may be
after we—and Marla—have already returned to the
Academy."

"I...yes. Of course. You're right, Khrazhti. Thank you. I
guess I'm just worried about Marla. She can take care of
herself. Usually. The way she's been acting, though..."

"Evon," Yxna said, "wait for her response. Until then,
we can continue to get closer to her. If she took the Genta
Highway, she's less than a day ahead of us. We're catching
up. Even stopping to sleep this evening, we'll get to the
crossroads before noon tomorrow."

When they did stop for the night, Evon checked the
message tablet, as he'd been doing at least every hour
since he had sent his message. No new messages had

been received. He immediately pulled out the finder to check it.

"I wish this device would better indicate how far something is. All it does it point and..." He blinked at the magical device in his hand and gave it a shake. "I think she left the Genta Highway. She's moving south, now."

"South?" Yxna asked. "What's south?"

Evon ticked off on his fingers. "It seems like she just traveled west far enough to get to the far side of the mountains before going south. There's Telna, the Dark Pinnacles, and...oh, no."

"Campastra," Yxna finished for him. "Why would she go there?"

"No, she wouldn't," Evon said. "That would be ridiculous."

Raki raised his hand and both Evon and Yxna turned to him. Khrazhti was watching all three at once as she sat some distance away.

The young Gypta took the looks to mean he could talk. "I know I've heard that word before, but I don't know anything about it. What is Campastra?"

Yxna gestured to Evon and the young man answered the question. "It's a large area stretching from the small mountains on the east of the Sittingham Desert nearly to Telna, and down to the Aesculun Ocean in the south. Have you ever heard of the Arunai?"

Raki shook his head. "It sounds familiar but I'm not sure where I heard it."

Well, two centuries ago, there was something that happened with someone calling himself the Malatirsay. He was a charismatic man who gathered many followers. The world was having trouble at that time and many believed when he said that they were in the last days, as told by the prophecy.

"Not only did he gather thousands of followers, but once he made his way to the Academy, he convinced many more there that he was the one the world had been waiting for, the one to fix all Dizhelim's problems. Even a few of the masters were convinced." Evon looked over at Yxna with a sympathetic look, but she waved the matter away. It was true that some of the masters had backed the man, but she had no embarrassment over it. It was before her time.

Raki's eyebrows went up. The boy must have remembered where he'd heard the name. Yxna smiled. She'd heard how much he enjoyed stories.

"Anyway, he left the Academy and came south, promising his followers that he knew what he was doing and that he had a plan. A fair number of Academy students joined him, though even the masters who believed him didn't go.

"They ended up in Campastra. It was more populated then, with large tribes who had been there for long periods of time. Some were nomadic, while others had villages and even what might be called cities. There was constant war between the different tribes, but few of them had any desire to increase their territory outside of Campastra's current borders, so the rest of the world left them to themselves, not interfering.

"The thing about the tribes of the Campastra was that they are very dark-skinned. Once the so-called Malatirsay arrived in the area with his followers, that fact became very important. The people had been called Arunai, a term that originally had been derogatory, but the tribes had embraced the name, using it proudly, taking the power from their detractors. *Arunai*, of course, came from Alaqotim and meant *dark* or *black*.

"The leader said that these were the creatures of the prophecy, these were the animaru. He commanded his followers to attack. The battles were fierce and for a time, it looked as if the entirety of the Arunai might be destroyed, but then the tribe chief and great hero Jintu Devexo rallied the remaining Arunai, gathered them as one fighting force, and attacked so savagely that the False Malatirsay's forces broke.

"Nearly all of them were hunted down, including those from the Academy who had taken part. Some had realized they'd been duped and returned to the Academy before the battles started in earnest, though they were not welcomed back with open arms. The False Malatirsay himself was killed in single combat with Jintu himself.

"All of that is to say that since that time, the Arunai have loathed anything to do with the Academy. The hatred for those who almost slaughtered their entire race is strong. If Marla is going there, that's not good news at all. It's not difficult to identify someone who has been trained so highly at the Academy, not for those who look for such things. The Arunai constantly search for such traits that would identify an Academy graduate."

Yxna shook her head. Evon had done a good job in telling the story briefly, but there was so much more detail involved. Detail she knew well. She respected the Arunai—they were fine warriors and maintained a strong sense of honor—and she didn't blame them for their hatred. She also didn't look forward to fighting an entire tribe if Marla got in trouble in Campastra. Win a battle like that or lose it, the consequences could be dire. Especially with the world's current difficulties.

"You don't think she's going there to try to recruit them to our cause?" Evon asked.

Yxna felt a laugh coming on, both for someone having the guts to do such a thing and also that Marla would somehow be acting like an unofficial emissary to an entire territory of people who hated all things Academy. "Why don't we follow Khrazhti's advice from earlier and wait until we have more information. Marla is a smart and talented woman. We have to trust she knows what she's doing."

She had better, the master told herself. *If she gets hurt, I'm going to kill that girl.*

Sirak Isayu reclined in his favorite chair. He had been working so hard on his projects for the Dark Council lately, he had not had time to relax in his home. It was an honor to be part of the Council, he knew, but at times he wondered if he had made the wrong choice.

His family was powerful in his tribe and he had been trained to contend for the position of chief as he was growing up. Unlike some of the tribes of the Campastra, the Anen-Shuken tribe did not simply hand over the chieftainship to the firstborn son of the chief. To ensure that the leader was always the most capable, there was a selection process.

It wasn't like the stories he'd heard of other peoples, where a chaotic kill-or-be-killed mentality was adopted. No, warriors did not simply challenge the current chief. That would be disrespectful. Dishonorable. Instead, when the chief believed he was at the end of his power and the tribe would be better served with a younger man, the chief would open the selection for a new chief.

It was for this that Sirak Isayu had been raised, trained for, molded. That was, until his father became ill and it was clear that he would not live long. Sirak still remembered the day his father had told him his secret, that he was part of a Dark Council, a committee nearly three thousand years old, instituted by a great mage to protect all peoples from the end of the world.

It was a shock and Sirak, who had always respected and honored his father as a man and a warrior, dropped to his knees and made obeisance to the man. Just when he had thought his father was as great as he could be—nothing short of being clan chief would have magnified him in Sirak's eyes—he found the answer to the riddle that had always puzzled him.

The current chief was a great man, true, and also a great warrior, but it always seemed that if Sirak's father would have asserted himself a bit more, he could have become the chief himself. On that fateful day of his explanation, his father elucidated that he would have had to spend too much time dealing with tribe issues and he would not have been able to serve the Dark Council with his whole heart. So, he gave up his chance to be chief for a greater responsibility.

And now, Sirak Isayu would have to take his father's place on the Council. A mirror of his father's decision, he chose the honor of the Council. He would not put his name forth when the selection for chief came to pass. He would do as his father had done, silently and humbly working to protect the world while another man would become chief.

Sirak had thought much about that decision over the years, starting with the year and a half his father trained him before finally succumbing to his illness. Now he was busier than any chief. It was the time of the end, the days prophesied. Not in that drivel the rest of the world sang of, but in the true prophecy. Given directly to the Dark Council by the mage who had created it: Aquilius Gavros. The Dark Prophet himself.

He supposed he had made a good choice, but still, it was nice to be able to relax occasionally. A man could not be all work.

The stone Sirak kept on a leather string around his neck vibrated and grew warm against his chest as he pondered. He pulled it out and saw it flashing. A summons. He would have to relax another time. For now, he was required to be in a meeting.

Sirak stepped inside the small room he used for his meetings and closed the door behind him, locking it. His tribe was more stationary than some of the other Arunai and had a village—a city, really—with permanent buildings. His family was an old and honored one, so they could afford more than basic necessities. Not that he needed more than that.

Once seated at the narrow table, he placed his meeting stone on the stand he'd had made for it and he activated it with the words of power. A brief sensation of falling afflicted him, but he recovered quickly and opened his eyes to find the familiar sight of the meeting room at the Vituma's estate. Alloria Yurgen was seated in her customary position at the head of the table.

"Vituma," Sirak said, bowing his head in greeting.

"Sirak, good. We will start momentarily, but you are the guest of honor for this meeting."

He didn't like the sound of that. Had he failed in some way and this was one of the shockingly common meetings to scold him and mete out punishment they'd had lately? The Aruna kept his face as neutral as he could—though his belly roiled—as he reviewed his activities for the last few weeks, trying to pinpoint what he might have done wrong. He was so caught up in his thinking, he didn't even notice which members were already present and which appeared, until the Vituma spoke again.

"Very well. We are all here. My apologies for yet another meeting, but this will be short. You may, of course, speak about what you are currently working on if you would like, but I'll not ask for updates.

"We received information from Thalia's agents, who have been tasked with watching the bridge from Munsahtiz to the mainland so that we can detect when groups of the Academy operatives leave. They observed Marla Shrike leaving the Academy and taking the River Road south. Alone. We are not sure what her purpose is, but we cannot let the opportunity pass to capture the girl. She has been declared to be half of the Malatirsay, along with her twin brother Aeden, and we could cripple the Academy's efforts if we can get her or, if necessary, kill her. Thalia?"

The black-haired, black garbed Council member cleared her throat. "I trailed her for two days. I believe now is the time to act. Marla is going toward Campastra."

Sirak's head snapped up. *Campastra?*

"I'm having trouble keeping up with her," Thalia continued. "I can't stay too close and she left the road, so if she spots me, it will be obvious. I have to stay back. She's heading toward Telna, but even if she doesn't continue south, Campastra is the closest place where we have a Council member." She glanced over at Sirak.

He could only nod dumbly. Not a scolding or punishment, then, but an assignment. An opportunity.

The Vituma cleared her throat. "I assume you are still in Ikali, at your home?"

"Yes, that is correct," he said.

"Good. This is an ideal opportunity for you, as well as the rest of the Council. Capture or kill Marla Shrike and it will be a heavy blow to the Academy and an important victory for us. Gather what resources you have and find where the woman is. Do whatever you must, but do not let her escape. Watching the others to see what they are working on is practical, but we will likely never have this chance at Marla again. Do not waste it."

"Yes, Vituma. I have warriors that are loyal to me and who have performed work such as this for me many times. I will gather them and find her. It could be tricky, however, if she is in the lands of other tribes. Tension is high and it could cause war to break out among the Arunai."

'I understand. Handle it delicately. But if war results from us capturing or killing Marla Shrike, then so be it."

"Understood," Sirak said slowly. "Shall I begin immediately or is there something else I am needed for in this meeting?"

"You are excused. If we discuss anything important to you or your mission, I will inform you of it."

"Thank you. I will report on my progress as I am able. Good evening." With that, Sirak shut down his meeting stone and was instantly in his small room again. Actually, he'd always been there, but now he could see it and feel like he was actually present in it. Strange things, the meeting stones. After all this time, he still was unaccustomed to the feeling of his consciousness being transferred to another location for speaking with the rest of the Council.

Sirak opened the door and went to the room where he

knew his lieutenant would be. As expected, the man was relaxing in a chair, drinking from a goblet of wine.

"Cholu," Sirak said. "We have work to do."

The man sprang to his feet, all nearly six and a half feet of him. He wore the typical garb of the tribe. That was to say, loose cloth covering his waist and groin, with little else other than the soft leather boots and the rings and bands on his arms. Campastra was a warm place and its inhabitants dressed for the weather.

"Gather the men," Sirak said. "The full complement. It is important work we will be about."

"The, uh, men?" Cholu asked hesitantly.

Sirak shook his head. "You know what I mean. All the men...and Ellia, too. Unless you want to try to explain to her why all the others will go and she was not told."

"No. No. I only wanted to make sure. I will inform her first." He gave Sirak a goofy grin and was out the door to do as he was asked.

Marla Shrike. The rumor was that she was the best of the Academy students, including all the graduates who had already left. He would see if there was truth in that. Not that he had a high opinion of those from Sitor-Kanda. The Arunai had not forgotten about how that Academy lackey had nearly destroyed them for good all those decades ago.

He would test the woman and he might engage in a little vengeance for his people while he was at it. Sirak headed toward his bedroom to fetch his weapons. They would be on the hunt soon. His white teeth flashed as he prepared to do his duty.

CHAPTER
THIRTEEN

Yxna Hagenai has been something of a prodigy. From the first time she picked up a blade at not yet six years of age, weapons had made sense to her. The way they moved, how they could be utilized for both attack and defense, it was all glorious, almost mystical to her. She had been accepted to the Academy solely on the way she demonstrated her abilities to the Academy recruiters visiting different towns and villages, something they did infrequently, even then. They rarely did such things at all anymore.

The recruiters had tested her for magical affinity of well, of course. After all, the purpose of Sitor-Kanda was to find and train the Malatirsay. Though it had become more of a genuine institution of group education, that purpose was still at the Academy's core. So, yes, they accepted students who were quite clearly not of the caliber to be the Malatirsay, but even those had to have at least a shred of magical ability. Not natural talent as some had, but the capacity to learn to cast spells with education and practice.

She had learned magic, but it was always the physical

123

combat that excited her. She mastered all the schools of combat and several other schools, at a pace that had both the students and the masters excited that she might actually be the one. The Malatirsay. She knew she wasn't, and the attention wasn't something she enjoyed.

The previous Master of the School of Edged Weapons was killed in an unlikely accident, torn by wild beasts as he slept when off visiting his family. He fought them, killing a handful and scaring the rest away, but he had been too injured to survive, even knowing healing magic. Word of his death came back to the Academy and the masters were distraught, as they always were when a master's service ended.

It was Master Qydus Okvius who called Yxna to his office a day after the news about the Edged Weapons Master had died.

"Yxna, I would like to ask you something and I would like your honest answer."

"Of course, Master Qydus."

"What are your plans? You have mastered seven schools and you are still young. Will you stay and master more or will you go out in the world and try your hand at being a hero. I know that despite what others say, you do not believe that you are the Malatirsay. I agree with you. Not because I find you unworthy—we would be fortunate to have one such as you as the prophesied hero—yet sadly, you do not meet the criteria set forth in the Prophecy."

Yxna had sighed in relief at that. Finally, someone who agreed with her. "I know I'm not the one, for the reasons you state, as well as some sense I have. I can't explain it, but I don't feel the pull of the Prophecy."

"As I have guessed. My question stands, then. What will you do?"

"I'm not sure. I have learned so much. Traveling the world sounds exciting, but I don't know if that life is for me. Maybe I'll become an Academy operative? That way, I'll still be connected to Sitor-Kanda and could even continue to learn, but still go out into the world, too. I just don't know, Master."

Master Qydus tapped his steepled fingers on his chin. "I see. Would you perhaps consider being a master?"

"A master? I have mastered several schools, so I am—"

"Do not be coy with me, Yxna. I will be more clear. Would you consider being the new Master of the School of Edged Weapons?"

She had thought that was what Master Qydus was getting to, but to hear it put so plainly...it made her head spin. "I'm so young."

"You are. There is precedent, however. Other masters have taken up their positions as young as you. Not many, true, but I—and many of the other masters—can see no one else who would do as well. You are more accomplished, more efficient, more 'master-like' than any other we could name. To be honest with you, Yxna, if anyone else were to take the position, I would be very disappointed. I would not say that to the incumbent, of course. Let that be between you and me.

"I am asking if you would want to take the position. Think for a moment not on whether or not you deserve it or if the students would respect you or any of that other nonsense. How would you feel about becoming a master of the Academy?"

"I would...be honored, of course. I hadn't really thought about it before, but I believe I could enjoy it and perform the duties adequately. Admirably. Yes, I could do it."

"But would you?" Master Qydus asked.

"Yes, Master Qydus. I believe I would."

She had been the Master of Edged Weapons at Sitor-Kanda for nearly thirty years now, and she had always been glad of her decision to take the position. Helping students, especially those she felt a special connection with, like Saria and Marla, was her life's joy. Still, she did sometimes think of the opportunities she hadn't had...

Evon and Raki were bantering at the fireside in their camp for the evening. Khrazhti kept herself apart, as normal, though not in such a way that she seemed ostracized or anti-social. She would speak occasionally, and watched the two boys, even as Yxna was doing, but it was the camaraderie that Evon and Raki showed that amused the master.

"I'm telling you," Raki said, "there was never a hero like Erent Caahs. I know all the stories and he's just the best."

"And the fact that he's your friend and the one who first taught you to move more quietly, or that he saved your life, doesn't have anything to do with it."

"Psht. Of course not. Using that logic, Jia should be the best hero ever because she has taught me way more and she's saved my life lots of times. Now that I think about it, she is a great hero. But so is Aeden, and Marla, and Khrazhti. You, too. But I'm sorry, even surrounded by heroes, I still think Erent Caahs is the best." He tilted his head. "Oh."

"Oh, what?" Evon asked.

"I just thought about whether I would call Erent Caahs or Tere a better hero. That's a tough one. I guess it's good they're the same guy."

Evon burst out laughing. Raki glared at him at first, but then lightened up and smiled.

That, the friendship, the closeness that could only be

had by those who had faced danger and death together, that's what Yxna had never had the chance to experience. She'd had friends over the years, but they had never quite seemed like family to her. Not really.

"So," she said, taking advantage of the lull in real conversation, "I've heard that you insist on people telling you stories, as often as every night. Is that true, Raki?"

The boy seemed to shrink upon himself, almost threatening to go invisible. The smile disappeared instantly and was replaced by a nervous slant to his closed lips. He took a few seconds to answer. "I like stories."

"Don't we all?" she asked, trying to force a smile. She knew what she looked like, had been told that her normal expression was as blank as a statue. She couldn't help it; her face wasn't really made for expression.

"No, Master," Evon said. "He really, *really* likes stories. He pesters us constantly to tell him more."

"That's not fair," Raki grumped. "I tell stories, too. It's just that there are a lot more of people who are not me, so it seems like others tell more of them."

Evon laughed. "Fair enough."

"My point," Yxna continued, "is that we have been together for several days now and I have yet to hear a story, other than Evon's respectable summary of the tale of the false Malatirsay. I haven't even heard anyone claim that as the newest member of the party, it's my obligation to tell one."

If Raki's face looked nervous before, now he looked absolutely mortified. His mouth started moving, stammering over something, but she stopped him before he worked himself up too far.

"Calm down, Raki. None of you have ever indicated that you'd make such a statement." She looked over at Khrazhti, who had a mischievous smile on her face. The animaru not only failed to be dazzled by titles or rank, she also had a keen mind and no doubt knew what Yxna was going to say next. "I believe it's past time for us to engage in your story-telling habit."

Raki looked at her in confusion, shifting his gaze from her to Evon to Khrazhti, trying to look for an explanation.

"I'm offering to tell a story, Raki," she said. "If you would like to hear one."

"Yes, Master Yxna. Yes, of course. I would never ask, but you must know a lot of great stories and you can tell one if you want but I don't want you think that you have to because the storytelling time doesn't really apply to you only to us because you're a master and—"

She couldn't help laughing out loud. It seemed that she had found the secret to making him talkative. "Breathe, Raki. Breathe. I was thinking of a story earlier. A myth, really, but aren't all myths just old and important stories? Since we're heading south toward the ocean, I thought maybe I'd tell the tale of how the Aesculun Ocean came to be."

"The...Aesculun Ocean?" Raki said. "Wasn't it created with all the rest of Dizhelim in the beginning of things?"

Evon's mouth dropped open. "Wait, do you mean that you don't know the story of the Aesculun Ocean? I thought you knew just about every story out there. You're Gypta and even for them, you're obsessed with stories."

"I never said I knew all the stories. That would be stupid. No one can know them all. Except maybe Master Aubron, because that's kind of his job."

"I have the privilege of telling you a story you haven't heard?" Yxna asked. "That makes me happy. "Khrazhti, have you heard the story?"

"I have not, Master Yxna."

"Then I believe we have settled upon our story for the night. You'll pardon me if I can't tell a tale as Master Aubron can. Few can match the Master of History and Literature in that task. I'll do my best, however."

"In the first age, the Age of Creation, Surus and the other gods created all things. At that time, there was but one continent on the face of Dizhelim and though the creation of people and beasts were done in the same location far to the south, the new life spread outward, searching for a place of their own. They were not many—yet—but within all living things was a desire to go and explore, only to settle into place once they had found where they belonged.

"Aesculun, God of Waters, took delight in making the creatures of the seas, lakes, and rivers. Things that swam, crawled, or propelled themselves through his liquidy world were all of his design. None were the match of the people, however. Observing the thinking creatures was the joy of all of the gods.

"With the vast deeps surrounding the one continent, Aesculun allowed Mellaine to control the rivers and streams, since they were so integral to her natural world. For himself, he retained lakes, seas, oceans, and other large bodies of water.

"As the people explored and spread, some gathering to make communities and others opting to live alone or in very small families, they admired the rivers and expressed their thanks to Mellaine for them. They venerated the Goddess of Nature and built shrines of wood and other natural materials. Some even mistakenly thanked her for the lakes as well.

"This didn't sit well with Aesculun. Year upon year and

generation upon generation continued to bow to Mellaine, with hardly a word for the God of Waters. Finally, he had enough and in a fit of rage, took action. He struck Dizhelim itself. So powerful was his blow that he fractured the continent, splitting off huge chunks of it and causing them to spread apart.

"He wasn't done, though. When he saw what his blow had accomplished, he allowed water to rush in from the deeps and fill the voids between the parts of the continent. In this way, the islands and other continents were created.

"The intelligent races on Dizhelim raised their voices to complain and express their woe at what had happened. Again, however, they called upon Surus or Mellaine, few upon Aesculun himself. Rather than have his anger sated, Aesculun felt slighted, abandoned by the people.

"'You have thirty days,' the god said to all living on the surface of the world. 'You have that time to cross the waters I have caused to be between the pieces of what used to be the one continent. After thirty days have elapsed, I will cause the monsters from the deeps, the vicious hungry creatures, to inhabit the ocean between the land, and will cause whirlpools, dangerous tides, and other hazards to appear. Any who desire to brave the water after that will surely be hunted and eaten by my monsters or be dashed onto rocks by the raging waters. Thirty days to join your brethren on the main remaining continent, which shall be called Promistala.'

"The people of Dizhelim had learned to build boats to travel the rivers and lakes, but none had desired to explore the deeps that surrounded the one continent. Those who had been on the parts of the one continent that split off could use their boats to flee to Promistala. Most did, though with difficulty.

"People lost their lives in their travels, their river boats no match for the rough ocean waves. Most survived, however, and came to settle on the main continent, where there was plenty of space for all.

"As Aesculun promised, thirty days after his proclamation, great sea monsters rushed in to inhabit the new waters. Huge beasts they were, able to capsize and crush even the greatest of boats made since then. Also as promised, the seas grew haphazard and dangerous.

"Some few people decided to remain on the splintered land, and of them there is no record. Whether they survived or not, no one can say. To this day, the waters are not braved except the Catillan Ocean to the north of Promistala because Aesculun takes such pleasure in Ascesh, the land of frozen waters, and he prohibits the monsters from being hazards there.

"To remind everyone of what he had done, Aesculun called the waters south of Promistala the Aesculun Ocean, and even now, boats only travel in the shallower areas along the coastline, hugging the land and never straying into deeper waters, which would mean their deaths. Though brave explorers have attempted to find the lost races on the other land masses within the ocean, none have ever returned.

"And that is the story of the Aesculun Ocean and the reason even the masters at the Academy don't know what lies on the lands south of Promistala."

CHAPTER
FOURTEEN

Marla stopped Surefoot and patted the mare's neck. They had passed by the kingdom of Telna and emerged from the forested areas surrounding the southern tip of the Dark Pinnacles mountain range. As she traveled farther south, the trees thinned and the terrain grew more rugged.

She hadn't been in the area before. The truth was, she hadn't ever been that close to Telna, so she'd been traveling unknown territory for some time now. It always fascinated her how the world seemed to be separated into zones. Forest, desert, grasslands, and all the others. If she had to label where she was at the moment, it would probably be scrubland, though the trees were still thick yet for that. It did seem that's what type of place the land was transitioning to, though.

That meant she was entering Campastra. The vast land had different types of climates, but large swaths of it were full of hardy vegetation that seemed to need to scratch out its survival as if it were an animal digging in the hard dirt to make its home. This was no rich, verdant place, but a region of scarcity and toil.

It also probably wasn't the best place for someone from the Academy. The bad feelings were still strong in the place after the False Malatirsay debacle. Still, the power tugging at her led her this way. She hoped it didn't stop inside Campastra, but knowing her luck, the source of the feeling would be smack in the middle of an Arunai city.

She was feeling a little guilty for not answering that last message Evon had sent. How could she, though? She wasn't about to tell them where she was, and she wasn't comfortable explaining what was going on with the pulling sensation. It was better they stayed at the Academy and worried about her. She would face the consequences when she went back, both with the masters' disapproval and her friends' disappointment. It was something she had to do.

Being alone was helping her with the angry, irritated feelings she'd been having, though. That was good, at least. She hadn't wanted to kill someone for more than a day now. One had to recognize progress when it occurred.

Movement off to her side drew her eyes to the left. Before she could react, a group of six men materialized from the low scraggly bushes that were so abundant in this place. Her sword was in easy reach, and several nasty spells came to mind, but she didn't attack. The men strode toward her, their spears and bows at the ready, but not held as if they would attack right away.

All six were wearing little more than loin cloths with soft, low boots. They were muscled, but not so heavily as some warriors she'd seen from other southern tribes. They were leaner, like people who could chase game for an entire day without tiring, their strength and stamina of the type more useful for intelligent combat rather than the brute force swinging of a weapon.

Oh, and they all had skin that was as dark as any she'd ever seen. Arunai.

"This land belongs to the Den-Uto," one of the men said in a rich, deep voice.

"I mean no harm," she said, making sure to keep her hands where they could see them. "I am traveling south."

"To what destination?"

Ah. Well, that was the tricky part. "To the shore."

"There is nothing for any but the Arunai on the shores in this place. You should be farther east if you want to get to Hirsen."

"Thank you for the information. I'll head that way now." She turned Surefoot's head to the east and started her walking.

"No." The weapons went up now, spears pointing at her, along with the arrows in two bows. "You have trespassed on Den-Uto lands. We will bring you to the chief so you can explain yourself and he can decide what is to be done with you."

A sharp spike of irritation pricked at Marla, but she pushed it away. She had no doubt she could take these six men. They might be tribe warriors, but more likely they were a hunting party. They didn't stand a chance against her skills, let alone her magic. But was that the right thing to do? She was in their land, after all. If she killed, or even incapacitated them, she would have not only made personal enemies of the Arunai, but she might well start a war between them and the Academy. Somehow, she didn't think the masters would be forgiving about that, given their current need for all able fighters to defend against the animaru.

The Arunai stood tensely, ready to spring—or launch weapons—given any provocation at all. Marla kept her eyes locked on the one who had spoken, assuming he was the leader. She still wasn't sure if she should make a run for it or give in. With a magical shield in place, she could probably escape without injury, but then she'd be on the run. On the other hand, if she was trapped in one of their cities or villages, it would be a lot tougher to get out alive if things turned sour.

She sighed and slowly dismounted, holding Surefoot's reins in her hand. "Fine. Lead me to this chief of yours."

THE ANIMARU GUARD led Toross Iardisith to a small room to wait. His escort wasone of the seren types, a common worker and all around fodder type for the animaru army. How was it that he didn't even rate being escorted by a semhominus or one of the other upper-class animaru? It was just insulting, is what it was.

Toross provided a valuable service, after all. He opened portals to bring more of the animaru from their world of Aruzhelim to Dizhelim. Really, the entire war effort was based on his work. As always, though, he never received the credit he was due.

Footsteps in the hall brought him to his feet. Would it be Kirraloth, the leader of all the animaru in this world? It was about time he was being treated with the respect that was due. It took the filthy beasts long enough to figure it out.

The door opened and a familiar tunic appeared, wrapped tightly around the pudgy figure of Jandar Zumlee.

"Oh, it's just you," Toross said.

"Ah, yes, evidently it is just me."

"They called you in for a report the same time as they summoned me. No doubt they'll press us, trying to get us to open portals faster again. I've told them before, we can't speed up the process. The timing must be correct. One can't change the way the magic flows."

Jandar tilted his curly hair-covered head at Toross. "No need to explain it to me. I know as well as you how it all works."

Toross very much doubted that, but he let the comment slide. "Quite a difference from when we were students, eh? We're important men now, even if they don't treat us accordingly."

"Toross, what do you expect from them? The longer we toil for the animaru, the more I think it was a mistake to start doing it to begin with. It's not like we can stop and I have lingering doubts they will hold up their end of the bargain and let us live in our own nations, ruling over those they capture and allow to live after the war is over."

"They will follow through if they know what's good for them. Two graduates of the Hero Academy—they better respect our abilities."

Jandar didn't answer and Toross looked over at the man. They hadn't been friends at the Academy, though they'd known each other then. He doubted they could be called friends now, though they did interact quite a bit. Toross hadn't met any other people creating portals for the animaru, so the two of them had that in common. Not the basis of a great friendship, but it was something.

Jandar was staring at the wall. Toross pushed his shoulder, nearly knocking him off the seat on which he was perched.

"You did it again," Toross said. "That thing. The staring at nothing."

"Ah. Oh. Sorry. I don't know what it is. When something occurs to me, it's like my brain takes over everything and wants to think about it right then."

"What is it this time? Some new experiment you want to conduct? A way to make the portals more efficient?"

"No, no. It's—"

A seren animaru opened the door opposite the one the two humans had come through and motioned them to follow it. The creature led them into a larger room, one Toross was well familiar with.

The two semhominus animaru Sastiroz and Jarnorum were already there. *Finally*, Toross thought. *Finally we are to speak to someone of a higher class than the army grunts*. Not only were the two users of magic, they were on the second level of command, underneath only Kirraloth.

"You must open more portals, and more often," Sastiroz said without preamble. Toross distinguished him from the other general by his greater height. "The rate is too slow, especially as you are bringing over more powerful animaru. We must have more to start the main assault."

"Ah, as to that," Jandar said. Toross was glad of it. Let the man get himself in trouble. There was no good answer to what the animaru leader said. "We have explained before that it is impossible. In order for the magical technology to work, the magic of the ley lines must be aligned. This occurs on a regular cycle which cannot be sped up or fabricated at need. Without the alignment of the magics, a portal cannot be opened."

"Kirraloth demands more portals," Jarnorum said. "Failing that, he may be satisfied with increasing the potency so that more animaru can be brought through at once."

Jandar frowned at the two animaru, lucky that they didn't understand human expressions well. It was plain he wasn't going to speak again, so Toross would have to. "Please, honored leaders, you must understand. There is a finite amount of magical energy that can be accessed with a portal. For that allotted energy, we can bring forth many of the lower types of animaru, seren and the like. If more powerful animaru are brought, ones who have the use of magic such as you, the numbers are drastically reduced. It's like paying for passage on a ship. A noble deserves a private room and exquisite accommodations. The price the noble pays could pay for two dozen commoners who would sleep atop one another in a damp corner of the boat."

Both animaru glared at Toross, or at least the looks they had on their faces seemed like glares. They were apparently too ignorant to understand his very fitting analogy.

"I have some information that might satisfy Kirraloth despite us not being able to bring over more animaru," Jandar said. Toross's head snapped to his companion. *Information? Why hadn't he shared it?* How was Toross to steal information from him to give it to Kirraloth so he could gain favors if Jandar didn't tell him first?

"Information?" Sastiroz repeated. "What information?"

"Something I got from a friend still at the Academy. It's very important. Maybe the most important. It's about what the masters and all their minions are working on."

"We have information on what the humans do."

"It's about what the Malatirsay is doing. Uh, I mean, the Gneisprumay."

That seemed to get their attention. The two leaders traded looks and Sastiroz went through another door.

When he returned a few moments later, he waved toward the door. "Come, Kirraloth will hear your information."

The two humans had not seen the highest animaru on Dizhelim before. It was significant that they were doing so now. Obviously, even these mindless beasts finally had come to recognize Toross's importance. He wasn't sure of the protocol for meeting Kirraloth, but he stepped forward to speak first and make a good impression, one of strength.

Darkness boiled out of Kirraloth and pressed Toross to the ground. His knees hit the stone floor painfully and he let out a grunt, but did not speak. A glance to the side revealed that Jandar had not been manhandled by the dark magic as he had.

"You will speak when spoken to," Jarnorum said. "Aside from that, be silent."

The pressure kept Toross on his knees, but did not prevent him from lifting his head up to study the leader of all the animaru in this world. Kirraloth was tall. Very tall. More than six and a half feet, probably closer to seven, the animaru didn't look like the typical semhominus. He was startlingly thin, almost like one of the scaled colechna, but without the fine scales. His skin was a rough dark hide, hairless and almost like bark, but the animaru moved easily and gracefully. The most distinguishing feature was his eyes.

They glowed with a sickly red, something he'd not seen in any other animaru he'd encountered. Those eyes were enough to make Toross gulp and do his best to keep from meeting them.

"You have important news for me from the place called Sitor-Kanda?" Kirraloth asked. His voice was smooth and somewhat soothing, which maybe frightened Toross more than if it had been rough and grumbling.

"I...I do, Lord Kirraloth," Jandar said.

"Speak it and we shall see if any deaths result from interrupting me."

"It's information one of my acquaintances at Sitor-Kanda overheard. It is not widely known yet. On several occasions, operatives of Sitor-Kanda have encountered sources of magic, vast quantities that were somehow locked away for countless years."

"We know this. Some of my mages have detected such things and have begun to investigate them."

Toross didn't like where the conversation was going. If Jandar had bothered the animaru lord to reveal something Kirraloth already knew, he or Jandar—probably both—would be punished, maybe even killed. That last was not likely because of their importance in opening gateways to allow more animaru to come to Dizhelim, but still, gaining Kirraloth's displeasure would not be good.

"Yes, Lord Kirraloth," Jandar continued. It was as if the stupid man didn't understand how much trouble they were in. "They have started calling them Wells of Power. These stores of magic, though, each of the wells is of one type. Two wells will be two different varieties of the same pure magical power. Apparently, when the groups have found these wells and gotten through the traps set to protect them, they have found how to release the magic."

Kirraloth trained his red eyes on Jandar. "That I have not heard. You say each of these wells is of a particular type of magic?"

"Yes. One they have found was full of dark magic. They released it into the world. I have a small affinity for that type of magic and when the magic was set free, I felt it, though I didn't know what it was then."

"Dark magic. When was this dark magic released from its well?"

"Three weeks past."

Kirraloth considered Jandar silently. Toross didn't have any talent with dark magic, though he had felt magical shifts before. Were those all these wells Jandar was talking about?

"How many of these wells are there?" the leader of the animaru asked.

"They don't know, or at least, my contact hasn't heard if they do. It seems like they are still looking for them."

"To use them as a weapon?"

"I...I don't know, Lord Kirraloth. If there is a way to harness the magic instead of releasing it into the world, I don't know about it. I'm sorry, but that's all I know."

"I see." Kirraloth shifted his gaze to Toross, who looked at the animaru's feet. "That is very useful information. Thank you, human. Your name is Jandar?"

"Yes, Lord. Jandar Zumlee."

"Good work, Jandar Zumlee. Be sure to inform me, Jarnorum, or Sastiroz if you should happen upon more useful information."

"Yes, I will."

The pressure that had been pressing upon Toross released. He sighed, able to breathe easier without the weight.

"You may go. Sastiroz, Jarnorum, stay with me. We must discuss what to do with the information we have just received. I also have a special mission for you to handle, Sastiroz."

CHAPTER
FIFTEEN

Marla allowed herself to be led by the Arunai tribesmen. The men didn't speak as they traveled, which suited her just fine. She wasn't there to be social and still wasn't completely certain she should be going with them. As they strode toward wherever their village was, she vacillated. Not fighting, or at least escaping, might be exactly the right thing to do or might be the worst mistake she'd ever made. If she went to the chief and was met with hostility, she would be out of choices. She didn't want to have to fight off an entire tribe.

She knew of the Arunai, of course, though there was not a great amount of information on the way the communities worked in Campastra. That was a result of the terrible situation with the False Malatirsay and how he nearly destroyed the Arunai as a people. Even simple requests for knowledge had been met with hostility when the Academy tried to learn about the area. She was going into the situation essentially blind and ignorant. Hurrah for her.

On the other hand, if she managed to not be killed, she might be able to glean a little information to bring back to the masters. New information was always welcome and it might help to mitigate the trouble she was in for leaving so abruptly.

All her introspection stopped as the group finally came within sight of what she assumed was Den-Uto. From how the group had referred to the place, she was pretty sure the name applied to the tribe *and* to the village itself. Scanning the community in front of her, she revised that thought. It was too big to be a village, even if that's what the Arunai called it. This was at least a town, maybe a city.

There were no real walls to speak of, but there were plenty of buildings. Marla would have thought the Arunai lived in tents, but that was probably because they were nomadic historically. Before the time when the Academy was no longer able to get information from the area. She understood that some tribes stayed in one place, but for some reason, she had never thought the people would have solid structures.

But there they were. The edifices were not too unlike what was in towns and cities throughout Dizhelim. Some were made of stone, a very few of wood, and many out of what looked like bricks smeared with sun-cured clay. Mostly, they were squat, much wider than they were tall. The surrounding trees attested to the strong winds that must blow in the area, with their trunks and branches leaning toward the southeast.

Marla didn't spot any chimneys, but smoke escaped the tops of many of the houses, so they must have had fires or ovens within. She wondered what they did for water in the rough, arid land. As the group got closer, she saw the answer to her question. In the center of the city was a body of water. An oasis. It appeared that the structures had been built around the source of water and in so doing, it was protected by the closely spaced dwellings that acted like a defensive wall.

Arunai bustled everywhere, some stopping to look at her. She saw few horses, but Marla had a feeling it wasn't Surefoot they were gawking at. The same thing that made it so hard for the Arunai to hide in most of Dizhelim made Marla stand out, too. Everyone's skin was very dark brown or even black; her's was ruddy at best. Probably a more apt description was pale. Yes, she definitely stood out.

Thankfully, being within the ring of the warriors who found her, none of the other residents seemed to be alarmed about her presence, so even if they looked, no one threatened her in any way. In fact, the most notable thing about the reactions was the shock and surprise in the faces of the young. With the isolationist tendencies, it was clear that those with skin of her coloring were rare, even more so because of her hair. As far as could be seen, there was nothing but dark hair in all but the older Arunai, who had their share of grey or white. Marla stood out like a torch in the middle of a field on a cloudy night.

"We will take your horse," the speaker of the group said to her. "No harm will come to her unless the chief declares you an enemy. Even then, she will not be injured. Horses are too valuable for us to mistreat her."

Marla nodded. It was a strange way to explain it, but she understood. Surefoot wouldn't be injured, though Marla might be. Wonderful.

The mare snorted at her and Marla patted her on her cheek. "Go with them. I'll see you in a little while. Behave."

Surefoot moved her head to stare into Marla's eyes for a moment, then huffed. Maybe she didn't agree that this was the best option. It was too late to change direction now, though.

Once Surefoot was led away, Marla was guided toward a large building closer to the edge of the lake in the center of the city. No doubt it was the city meeting place or the chief's residence. It was time to see what kind of official reception she was going to get.

Strangely, the Arunai hadn't taken her weapons. Marla tried to dredge up from her mind what kind of tradition would keep them from disarming her, but was not able to recall anything. She was glad, no doubt, but it was a bit concerning that they felt so confident in their ability to match her even if she still had her weapons that they didn't take them.

"Wait here," the Aruna told her when they reached the front of the building. He went inside for several minutes. The voices from within were unintelligible and while it was easy to hear that there were at least three people speaking, the tones didn't reveal any hint of how the knowledge she was there had been received.

After several minutes, the Aruna came back out and motioned for Marla to enter. "The chief will see you. Be respectful or I may slay you where you stand."

Marla looked the man over and scoffed. Not on the best day of his life could the man *slay* her, as he said. She motioned for him to go in first, an action that caused his eyes to widen and his hand to rest on the long knife at his waist. It looked like he might balk, but then he turned and entered, letting the door close in Marla's face.

"Rude," she said as she opened it again and stepped into the building.

She blinked and opened her eyes more widely to help her adjust to the dimmer light. Several stand lamps lit the space, as well as a fire at one end of the large room, but after the sunlight she had just been in, the place almost looked dark.

Once she could see well, she spotted the man who had led her to the city and into the building. Four older men sat in sturdy wooden chairs spread around a central chair, one larger than the others, with elaborate carvings across its surface. The man in it sat up straighter, but didn't move to get up. To his side stood a tall woman in the typical minimalist Arunai garb.

"You stand before Naxun Den-Uto, chief of the Den-Uto tribe and ruler of this and all other villages of the tribe," her guide said. The man in the big chair, obviously the chief, said nothing. He stared at her for several long minutes. He didn't look surprised to see her pale skin, nor did he look particularly hostile toward her. In fact, he almost looked bored. Marla mirrored his look of boredom and stared back at him.

"Who are you and what are you doing in my lands?"

"Is this how the Den-Uto treat those simply passing through a corner of Campastra where they bother no one?" Marla asked.

The man who brought her gritted his teeth, anger in his eyes. He went to draw his knife, but the chief raised his hand to forestall any violence.

"You have trespassed on our land. Simply walking upon it bothers my tribe and our ancestors. Answer my question or I will declare you an enemy and you will be executed."

"Just like that? What ever happened to common courtesy in Dizhelim? My name is Marla Shrike and, as I said, I was merely passing through. I knew not who claimed the territory through which I rode. There were no problems in Telna when I passed through their kingdom."

"This is not Telna. This is Campastra. What is your purpose?"

"Passing through. I am trying to reach the shore of the Aesculun Ocean. I mean no harm to anyone, nor do I plan on any mischief."

"From where do you come?" the chief asked.

"From the north."

"Everywhere is north from here. What is the name of the place from which you come?"

Marla was tired of the silly game they were playing. It was time to answer the man straight, come what will. "I come from Munsahtiz."

This time, the Arunai warrior actually drew his knife and took a step closer as if he was about to attack her. Marla hoped he didn't. Killing the man in front of his chief wouldn't endear her to them.

The chief hissed and the knife went back into the sheath immediately. "You come from Sitor-Kanda?"

"I do."

"Yet you say you are here to do no mischief and cause no harm."

"It's true."

The chief slammed his forearm onto the rest on the chair. "There is nothing but harm and mischief from the devils from the Academy. The last time they visited, it was to wipe the Arunai off the face of Dizhelim."

Marla's anger was building. It was not the time for it, she knew, but she couldn't help it. If this went much further, there was going to be bloodshed. A *lot* of bloodshed.

"We are not of that time. Hundreds of years have passed. There is no need for hostilities."

"So you say. If your fathers and mothers had been

147

slaughtered for no other reason than they were different, you would not treat history so lightly."

Marla stared into the chief's eyes. "I did not perpetrate those actions, nor did you personally receive injuries by my hand. We would do well to continue with that condition."

"You dare—?"

"If I may?" the woman standing next to the chief said in a calm voice.

The chief, despite being interrupted, didn't lose his temper and get angrier. If anything, he seemed to calm a little. "Of course, Honored One."

Something about the woman made Marla decide that she was not only respected because of her obvious physical attributes, but there was something else at play here. She was statuesque and fit, with weapons strapped about her person and the posture of strength and confidence, but that wasn't all. She looked...regal.

"Perhaps this conversation has taken a turn which is unfortunate," the woman said. She spoke Ruthrin, but had a slight accent that, for some reason, reminded Marla of the elite classes in several different nations. Maybe it was the confidence, the ring of command. It didn't beg respect; it demanded it. "I am Masseni Devexo. It is my honor to meet you, Marla Shrike."

Devexo, Devexo. Marla's mind scrambled to recall the name. It was important. It was..."Devexo. You are a descendent of the great warrior and leader Jintu Devexo."

Masseni gave Marla a predatory smile. "You know of my ancestor. Good. Do you also know that a Devexo still holds the position of high chief over all the tribes of Campastra?"

"Your father, I take it?" Marla asked.

"Truly. Now that we have become acquainted, I would

ask you what Chief Naxun asked before: what is your purpose in traveling through Campastra."

"I gave an honest answer. I am trying to reach the shore."

"You are doing so for some machination of the Academy masters?"

"No, this is a personal quest, one I will not discuss with those I don't know."

"That is unfortunate," Masseni said. "We have heard of strange things happening in the world." She quirked an eyebrow, noticing something in Marla's reaction to her statement. "We do get news. We are not completely isolated, though it might seem so to those in Sitor-Kanda. You must know that even after all this time, there are no people the Arunai hate more than those from the Academy. But as I was saying, there are things occurring in the world. What can you tell me of them?"

"A lot, actually. I can tell you from personal experience that the dark monsters of prophecy have arrived. They have come from another world and are even now trying to destroy all life in Dizhelim. You may not want to hear it, but the Malatirsay has come and has been recognized by the entire body of the masters of the Academy. The true Malatirsay, not the cheap fake who deceived so many of old."

The Arunai warrior looked ready to draw his knife again, while the chief and what Marla figured were the tribe elders shifted in their seats. If anything would make these people uncomfortable, it was talk of the Malatirsay.

"So, your Academy companions are off hunting more innocents to further their agenda?" Masseni asked wryly.

"No. Listen, you and I both know what happened all those hundreds of years ago. That was one man who was charismatic enough to gather followers and do unspeakable things to your people. Yes, there were some Academy students involved, and even a very few masters who were also duped into believing he was the one the Prophecy predicted. All the rest of the masters and students did not agree, however, because the man didn't fit the criteria the Prophecy set out to identify the Malatirsay.

"It was a horrific thing and if your ancestor hadn't bravely stood up and gathered all the Arunai, they might have all been wiped out. If that had happened, or if the False Malatirsay had escaped, I guarantee you that the man would have been hunted down by the Academy and executed. The masters were as shocked as any over what the man tried to do. In fact, some of those who had originally joined him abandoned him when he made it clear what he intended.

"All I ask is that you think on it logically. Your people interacted with Tsosin Ruus himself and, from what I understand, you know that his Prophecy is the truth. He—and we of the institution he created—cannot be held accountable for someone using that Prophecy to fool a large number of people to commit unthinkable violence. So, too, I ask that you hear your news, look at the signs, and realize that the end times are now. All nations of the world will need to gather together to fight the animaru threat. I have fought these monsters and even with all of us fighting together, it will be a close war. They cannot be killed except with life magic. If you have those who can use such things, you should probably get them to train as many more as you can find.

"Join us. We already have Teroshi and the Great Enclave committed to standing together with us. With your warriors, we will be more formidable an adversary against the monsters trying to destroy our world."

Masseni considered Marla for a time and Marla stayed quiet to let what she said sink in. Then, surprisingly, Masseni Devexo barked a laugh.

"I think I could like you, Marla Shrike. Your fire, your passion, it reminds me of stories of Jintu himself. That is a good thing. What you say is interesting, though I am not sure how much to trust it. I think we will listen for more information. As for joining with you—with the Academy— I very much doubt that will ever happen. The hurt of what happened is too near, both in time and in emotion. I find no fault with you, but I am merely here to coordinate with the Den-Uto tribe. It is their land, their city, and their rules apply."

"I've said what I need to say," Marla said. "I hope it will start a discussion. Artuyeska and Kruzekstan have already fallen. It will be some time until the animaru get this far west, but when they do, they will roll over this land and crush every last one of you, life magic or not. Only all of us banding together can stem the tide."

"We shall see."

Masseni nodded toward the chief, but as he opened his mouth to speak, another warrior opened the door and stepped in.

"Chief Naxun, a large group of warriors from the Anen-Shuken tribe are here. They demand we hand over the stranger to them, the pale woman. They state that she is a criminal and that they have the right to pass judgment on her."

Marla's mouth dropped open. As if things weren't bad enough already, now she had two Arunai tribes fighting over who was going to kill her. She wondered if it was too late to fight her way clear and escape.

SIXTEEN

"Have the Anen-Shuken wait," the chief told the warrior with the message. "I will be with them shortly."

The man left and Naxun Den-Uto called the elders to him at the far corner of the room. The knife-happy warrior stayed near Marla, ostensibly to keep her from causing mischief. Marla frowned at the man, but remained where she was.

The chief was an older man, but not the oldest among the group. Another was far older, his ancient body looking like weathered leather wrapped over gnarled wood. He moved well still, though she was sure it was his experience that was most valuable to the tribe. The other two elders looked to be slightly younger than the chief, one of them a big man with barely any grey in his hair. He looked formidable, even if it was probably strength he focused on rather than speed.

The chief and the elders whispered softly enough that Marla couldn't hear what they were saying, but she had a remedy for that. For every powerful magical attack or defense an Academy student learned, they learned at least one simple and seemingly unimportant spell. At least, she had. The existence of such minor magics were to train students to manipulate the qozhel and learn to more capably wield magic, but they had their uses, she'd found.

Case in point, the magic she called up with a small gesture of one hand while whispering a word of power almost soundlessly. Instantly, the voices of the men came to her like they were speaking in a normal speaking voice right next to her.

"Relations with the Anen-Shuken are still strained," one of the older men said. "Any mishandling of this may result in them trying to attack us. The small party present will not do so, of course, but they will go back to their village and rouse their warriors if they feel slighted. It could mean open warfare again."

"They are unreasonable and would find fault with whatever choice we make," the oldest said. "Anything short of bowing to them and handing over the pale woman might result in violence."

The youngest of them, the massive wall of muscle, held up a fist. "Their tribe probably does not know they are here, if they have been following the woman. We can kill them and the Anen-Shuken will not know anything but that their warriors disappeared."

The chief put his hand up. "We will not bow to them. Neither will we kill an entire party of another tribe's warriors unless provoked. I must speak with them and find out why they believe the woman should be given to them."

"But if we admit to having her, then we will have to give her unto them," the eldest said.

"I will not admit to having her here. They say they know

she is with us, but are they truthful? Did they see her enter our lands, see her escorted by our warriors to Den-Uto?"

Marla stared at her hands as the elders and the chief spoke. She'd almost forgotten that Masseni Devexo was still nearby. She stood stone still, watching Marla. Marla hoped she hadn't betrayed that she could hear the men speaking with any expressions.

"Relations between the Den-Uto and the Anen-Shuken tribes are strained to the breaking point at present," the tall Devexo woman said. "They no doubt are trying to decide if they can hand you over without seeming weak or if they can keep you without sparking a war between the two tribes. Hostilities are common and tempers are hot."

"It's easy enough," Marla said. "Tell them to let me go. Then they can tell the Anen-Shuken I'm not here. They won't be giving the other tribe what they want, but it can't be proven that I was here. They can let the warriors look around to be sure I'm not here."

"How would that benefit the Den-Uto?"

"I think we're past what can benefit them. Now, it's a matter of seeming weak to their enemies or getting entangled in a war. Unless the chief decides to kill me and does it quickly, the most advantageous way out is if I leave. They can even make it look like an escape."

Masseni considered Marla, nodding slightly. "I will speak to the chief."

When the high chief's daughter stepped over to the men, apologizing for interrupting before doing so, the warrior watching Marla took a half step closer to her. She hoped he wasn't stupid enough to try to take advantage of the distraction to attack her. She had no qualms about ending his life instantly if he came at her with a weapon, though that would mean she would probably be up to her eyebrows in other warriors attacking her if it happened. Maybe she'd just make the warrior lose consciousness.

Her spell picked up the conversation with Masseni.

"Maybe it would be better to let the woman go. Perhaps make it look like she escaped. That way, you would not have to bow to the Anen-Shuken's wishes to give her over and you also wouldn't foment a war by refusing to do so."

"What is the benefit to us?" the chief asked.

"You will not have to go to war and you will not look weak to your enemies."

"What of the woman? Should we set loose one of the hated Academy people?"

"Will you kill her?" Masseni asked. "If so, you will have to do it right now, before you speak with the Anen-Shuken. That way you will be able to tell them truthfully that you disposed of her. Still, they may want her body, which is only slightly less than handing her over alive. Be aware that if the Academy finds out you have killed one of their own, they may declare war themselves. Would you pit yourself against an entire institution full of users of magic?"

"There are no good choices," the chief said. "We will speak with her and I will make my decision."

The small group broke apart and came back to where Marla was waiting. The warrior took two steps back, having missed his opportunity to harass her.

"What will you trade for being allowed to leave this place without us executing you or turning you over to the Anen-Shuken?" the chief asked her.

"What would you have of me? I have only what is in my pack and my horse's saddlebags. I could speak to the masters for you, maybe broker a deal or some kind of peace accord. The Academy is a good friend to have. We make useful items—even weapons—many of them magical. We could trade a little, try to build trust between us again."

"No one desires trade or good relations with murderers."

"I don't know, then. If we make it look like I escaped, I'll let the visitors see me fleeing. That way, they will take up the chase and know at the same time that it's no use in trying to talk to you further about me. You won't look weak, you won't be giving into them, and you won't be forced into a war. It's about the best I can do."

The chief closed his eyes, thinking. "I do not like any of these options. I believe it would be better to kill you, as is the tradition since the attack on my people."

"That would be a big mistake," Marla said. "It would pit you against the Academy and the forces we've already gathered to fight the animaru. You will be declaring yourselves our enemies, which means they would have to wipe every Arunai from the face of Dizhelim to prevent having to fight a war on two fronts. Are you ready to go to battle not with armies carrying weapons, but several hundred of the strongest mages in the world?"

"You boast," the chief said.

"Do I?" With a quick motion, Marla cast Gale, a moderately powerful wind spell. The effect was immediate. Every person in the room except her was thrown off their feet to slam into the walls. By the time they scrambled up, Marla had disarmed the warrior that had been antagonizing her and had his own knife in her hand, edge to the man's throat. "That was a weak spell. I am trained well with my weapons, or even with empty hands, I can cast dozens of spells—some of which can burn the flesh off your bones in an instant—and I am not in a particularly good mood. I ask you again, Naxun, chief of the Den-Uto tribe, are you willing to go to war with three hundred just like me? I can give you a more potent demonstration if you insist, but if I do, there will be injury and death. Make your decision. I am ready to die today, as I am ready to kill today. How about you? How would your tribe fare without both chief and elders, not to mention the loss of the high chief's daughter."

The chief gritted his teeth and Marla figured she had gone too far. So be it. If she had to fight her way out of an entire city, then she was willing to do so. She might die, but so many more of them would see death first.

"Stop." It was Masseni Devexo. "I cannot speak to any interactions between the Arunai and the Academy in the future, but I do know that I will not be party to the decimation of an entire tribe of my people. Chief Naxun, what do you think will happen if Marla Shrike unleashes her magic upon your tribe? You may kill her, true, but she will kill many of your warriors. Once weakened, the Anen-Shuken tribe will attack you and finish the slaughter, taking your sons and daughters as slaves. Then, should the Academy find out, they may bring all their strength to bear. We do not know if Marla is important to them, but even the lowliest student's death would be an insult. Do you really want to insult Sitor-Kanda?

"As I have the authority to speak for my father, I declare that you will allow Marla Shrike to leave. You will stage it as an escape and she will promise to draw away the Anen-Shuken warriors searching for her. Are there any arguments against this?"

The chief looked like he would disagree, but he couldn't very well go against his high chief.

"So be it. Marla Shrike, you will get your horse and you will *escape*. You will lead the Anen-Shuken from us. Furthermore, I would ask that you remember that this situation could have been resolved in other ways, ones that would see you dead, injured, or captured by the Anen-Shuken."

"I thank you, Masseni Devexo," Marla said. "You are truly your ancestor's descendent. Think on what I've told you. The true animaru are here and none in the world are safe. You can send a messenger and I will meet with you or your father if you would like to discuss it further. It's time for all Dizhelim to stand together."

"I will report this to my father," Masseni said.

While Marla waited for the Arunai to bring Surefoot back to her, she analyzed the situation. There was a chance that they were playing her for a fool and that as soon as she mounted her horse, they would attack her. She immediately threw the notion out, though. There would be no reason for it. They already surrounded her and besides, if history had told her one thing, the tribal societies on Dizhelim acted with honor. More so than the so-called civilized lands. She would have to trust them, just as they were trusting her to hold up her end of the agreement.

The warrior Marla had disarmed and threatened with his own knife sulked as she mounted Surefoot. She felt like smirking at him, just to irritate him, but it would serve no purpose but to be petty. She laughed inwardly that that was a good enough reason for her. Other things were more important at the moment, though. Like putting on a good performance at escaping and the little matter of surviving allowing the visiting warriors to get close enough to see and chase her.

"Where are the other tribe's warriors?" she asked from her saddle. One of the Den-Uto warriors pointed to the southeast. "Okay. Do you want me to knock down some of your warriors to make it convincing?"

"We will shout that something is happening. Break free of the city. My warriors will not know it is a ruse, so they may attack or try to stop you. I ask that you do not kill any. If they are injured, we will understand, but do not cause unnecessary injury."

"I'll do my best. I'll go now."

With that, she kicked Surefoot into motion, angling near enough to where the Anen-Shuken warriors were to get their attention, but not so close that she would run into the center of them. It didn't sound like they had dozens of warriors, but it seemed they were a fairly large group.

A few seconds later, after dodging swung and hurled weapons, she emerged from between two buildings and saw the edge of the city, and a tight group of nearly twenty warriors with a different style of minimal clothing than the Den-Uto. She met eyes with the one who she thought was the leader, a big man with an air of authority. His eyes grew bigger, as hers did, and she cut to the left and had her horse sprint for all it was worth.

The warriors sprung toward her to stop her from escaping.

CHAPTER
SEVENTEEN

A smaller group of the Den-Uto warriors came upon Marla on her left side. Some of them hefted spears, ready to throw, and one had a bow with an arrow already nocked. They were closer than the pursuing Arunai of the other tribe, and the distance between them was shrinking as she moved forward. There was no way they would all miss her.

Reins in one hand, she cast with the other hand, the same spell as earlier. A wall of air rushed out and struck the Den-Uto. They weren't as close as the elders and chief had been earlier, so they weren't picked up and thrown, but they were knocked down and unable to reach her with their weapons.

As soon as Marla passed them, she cast again, this time bringing up a shield around her. No sooner did it drop into place than she felt the impact of several missiles from the Anen-Shuken group. One more weak impact vibrated her shield and then she was too far for them to reach.

That had been entirely too easy and she expected another group of warriors to jump out from behind a rock formation ahead of her. She swung wide around it, just in case, but she needn't have bothered. She'd made a clean getaway. Marla allowed Surefoot to slow, though still keep a faster pace than the pursuers could run, as she looked ahead and planned what she would do. The tugging sensation was still there, off to her right, so she'd need to go that way, but for now, she wanted to keep as many things between her and the Arunai chasing her as possible. If they didn't see her, they might slow down a little and allow Surefoot to travel at a pace she could maintain indefinitely.

Marla wasn't sure, but she thought maybe she was heading into the territory of the Anen-Shuken tribe. If so, she could find herself being captured again. This time, though, she wasn't going to give up meekly, not with some of them chasing her already. It was going to be tense for a while, until she put enough distance between her and her pursuers, probably until she got out of Campastra completely. There wouldn't be much sleep for her in the next few days. It was one disadvantage to traveling alone: no one to watch while she tried to grab a little rest.

It occurred to her that she felt better than she had in days. There was a low level of irritation—at herself for getting into the situation, at the Arunai for chasing her, at her quest that caused all this trouble to begin with—but the excitement of possible combat and the rush of the escape gave her a thrill that counteracted some of the anger that had been sitting just below the surface for so long.

She decided she had two objectives to complete before she went back to the Academy. She would figure out what the sensation pulling her south was and she would get rid of whatever foul mood or mindset was making her angry all the time. If she didn't do both things, she wouldn't feel comfortable going home. Things would still be tense and she would inevitably drop back into an angry state. She didn't want that. So, with her mind made up, she threaded her way through the scattered trees and rocky hills until it felt right to turn due south. If she could keep from being spotted for a few more hours, she'd have the cover of night to travel through. She had no doubt that mounted, she could get clear of Campastra without any more mishaps.

After traveling all night and half of the next morning, Marla thought she might be at the edge of Campastra, near the no-man's land that technically was part of the Saraki Principality, though it could be the very southern tip of the kingdom of Telna.

Somehow, in her nighttime travels, the terrain had become softer, from rocky hills and rugged landscape to gentle hills and even some stands of trees visible. There weren't any real forests, but seeing trees clumped together and standing relatively straight instead of being curved and twisty helped her to relax her vigilance, if only a little.

Scanning behind her often, she wondered how serious the Anen-Shuken Arunai were about finding her. They'd told the Den-Uto tribe that she was a criminal and they were going to deal with her. What was that about? She hadn't done anything other than trespassing in their territory. Would the group chasing her give up and go back to their own tribe, or was whatever crime she supposedly committed worth leaving their territory to come after her?

She shrugged and angled more to the south than the east. Whatever happened would happen. At the moment, all she cared about was how tired she was from traveling all night and how irritating the sun was as she headed roughly toward the great, bright ball low in the sky.

Marla had been walking for an hour when she noticed shapes dancing in her vision to the north. She was giving

Surefoot a little rest from having to carry her and trying her best to keep awake and alert. Endless time in the saddle tended to tire her out, especially with no sleep for more than a day and a half, and that after all the excitement of her escape. She shaded her eyes as best she could with her hand and picked out what looked like individuals moving toward her. Great.

Marla checked her weapons to make sure they slid easily out of their scabbard and sheaths, stretched her neck and back as she walked, and prepared her mind for magical combat. She thought for a moment about getting back in the saddle, but as the figures grew closer, she recognized that they were mounted as well. Not the warriors who were after her, at least, but with horses of their own, she wasn't going to outrun them. She fought better on her feet, anyway.

She continued in her southern direction, glancing at the group to gauge when they would reach her. When they were within half a mile, she stopped, patted Surefoot as she shook her head, and waited. Soon enough, the mysterious figures arrived, not nearly as mysterious as they had seemed at first.

"What the hells are you doing here?" she asked when they pulled up and dismounted in front of her.

"Trying to find a wayward girl with no sense of responsibility." Until she had spoken, the fourth member of the group had managed to keep the others between herself and Marla. That voice, though. There was no way Marla wouldn't recognize it.

"Master Yxna?" She regretted her words from a moment before.

The lithe master, wrapped in a cloak that made Marla feel a little bit better about not recognizing her, approached and held her arms out. Marla accepted the offer and wrapped her arms around the master.

"I'm glad you're all right. You've led us a merry chase."

Marla released the master and found Khrazhti in front of her, the one figure she had recognized first. She hugged the animaru, too, then Evon, even Raki. She wasn't a big hugger, but it seemed right and felt comfortable.

"I'm sorry about that," she said. "I hadn't planned on you coming all this way looking for me."

"Well, now that we have found you, we can go back home," Evon said, eyeing her warily.

"Uh, no. I can't do that. I have things I need to do."

"How did I know you were going to say that?" he said.

"Sorry. First thing, I have something like twenty Arunai warriors chasing me. They're not mounted, so they're not too near, but I'm not sure how serious they are. I was prisoner with another tribe and these came to try to take me, saying I was a criminal and they had the right to prosecute me."

Master Yxna shook her head. "How could you get into so much trouble in so short a time? You can't have been in Campastra for very long."

Marla looked at the ground. "You know how the Arunai feel about the Academy. It's not too hard to figure out that I have been trained there."

"Which makes me wonder why you would enter the area to begin with."

"Oh, uh, it's kind of involved."

"We just followed you hundreds of miles," Evon said. "I think we can spare the time to hear your convoluted reasoning before we tie you up and take you back home."

A hot spike of anger lanced through Marla and her first urge was to snap at her friend. She swallowed it, though, mostly because she didn't want to seem like a spoiled child in front of Master Yxna. "I'm not going back. I know Master Yxna could beat me into unconsciousness, but if you try to drag me back to the Academy, there will be fighting involved."

"Whoa. I was just joking, Marla. I know you've been having a rough time. How about we sit down and you tell us what's going on?"

"We're only here because we care about you," Master Yxna added. "Let us help you."

Marla huffed out a breath. "Fine. Yes, I'm a little irritated. I haven't slept because I was fleeing from those Arunai. I didn't think it was a good choice to fight them all, what with me being in their land and surrounded by thousands more of them and all. I thought about it, though."

They settled into an open area with several convenient rocks they could sit on. Her friends shared some of their food with her, which she appreciated, and she tried to explain things to them.

"I don't know what's going on. My temper gets worse every day and with the time I had just before I left, it was clear I needed to get away. You don't understand how close I came to killing a few students. One in particular. Visions of going over the edge like Ivel Danson keep popping into my head."

"Ivel Danson?" Evon asked. "Was that the guy several years ago who flipped out and killed another student because he was having a bad day and the student kept pressing him?"

"Yeah, that one. I never understood before how he could have done something like that, but lately, I can."

Master Yxna patted Marla's hand. "I know you've had issues with your anger, Marla, even more so lately with all the pressure put on you. I can understand wanting to get away from things. The way you went about it, though, leaves something to be desired."

"I know. Honestly, though, if I hadn't gone when I did, something bad would have happened. Even dealing with stupid protocol, informing people I was leaving, filling out the log book, all that, could have sent me into a rage. Then there's the tugging."

"Tugging?"

"Yes. For something like two weeks, I've been feeling a sensation, like someone had tied a rope around me and was gently pulling on it. I don't know what it is. Something magical, obviously. It wanted me to come south."

"Toward where?" Evon asked.

"I don't know. I followed it and ended up in Campastra. Turns out, though, that wasn't exactly where it was coming from. I still feel it right now. It's that way." She pointed almost due south, maybe a little toward the southeast.

"Fahtin had visions of you with your hair on fire," he said. "We all figured it was symbolic of your anger. The most recent one showed you plunging into the ocean and dark shapes all around you."

"It does seem like I'm heading toward the ocean," Marla admitted. "I don't know about the dark shapes, unless it's the Arunai chasing me." She paused for a moment, reflecting. "Listen, I'll make this simple. I've decided I won't go back to the Academy until I resolve two things. I need to find out what is pulling on me and I need to somehow get a handle on the unreasonable anger I've been feeling lately. If that pits me against you and your plans, then I'll tell you right now, you will need to render me unconscious and drag me back.

"The way I look at it, you have two choices. You can try

to overpower me—though as I said, I will fight and any time I'm not unconscious on the way back, I'll do my best to escape—or you can go with me and help me resolve these two things. I'm desperate here. I don't want to lose my mind and hurt people around me. I have to take some time and get things under control."

The way Evon and Master Yxna traded looks, she almost thought they were going to attack her right then. She itched to bring up a shield, and her body tingled in readiness for combat. She wasn't sure if she could take all four. Hells, she didn't know if she could take Master Yxna by herself. Obviously she couldn't fighting physically, but Marla's magic was stronger and more refined than the master's. She hoped so, anyway. But still, four against one? Evon was no slouch and Khrazhti was a powerhouse. Who even knew what Raki was capable of?

Evon's laugh caused Marla to jump. "Gods, Marla. I can feel your body vibrating, getting ready to fight. If I had any doubt you were serious about fighting us, I know for sure now. It's really up to Master Yxna, but for me, the most important thing is to help you. If that means bringing you back to the Academy, I'll sacrifice to do that. If it means following you to find whatever magic is affecting you, then you know I'm with you. You're my best friend. I'm not going to abandon you."

Marla nodded, then looked at the master.

"You're like a daughter to me, Marla. We didn't come to force you to do anything. This is the first time I've left the Academy in some time. If there's more I can do to help you, I'll do it. I don't like the things that have been happening to you lately. I cannot speak for the rest, but I'll go with you as well."

"I'm in," Raki said. "You'd never leave us to deal with something like this without helping."

"You are as close to me as a sister," Krazhti said, "though animaru really do not have such things. You may count on my help as well."

All the tension from the moment before bled out of Marla and she slumped. "Thank you. I might not be able to do this without you. Can I ask one thing before we get started?"

"Sure," Evon said.

"I'm not sure if the Arunai are still following me. Can you stand watch for a few hours so I can get some sleep? I'm tired."

CHAPTER
EIGHTEEN

T hree hours later, Marla roused herself from her nap. She rubbed her face and looked around to find her friends sitting and chatting softly.

"Did I miss anything?" she asked.

Evon stood and stretched. "Nope. Just sitting around listening to you snore."

"I do not snore."

Even Khrazhti laughed at that. A little.

"Oh, shut up. Are you ready to get going?"

They all mounted and followed Marla as she headed toward where the tugging sensation was coming from.

"How did you find me, anyway?"

"One of Tsosin Ruus's finders," Evon said. "They're more flexible—and faster—than the scrying locators."

A sudden sadness struck Marla. "I wish we would have had one to use when we were looking for Skril. We might have found him in time."

"I know. I said the same thing. The only finder back then was the one in the museum and we would have never been able to get it to use."

Half a day's travel later, the group stood on a cliff overlooking the vast blue-grey expanse of the Aesculun Ocean.

"Well, damn," Marla said. "I knew there was a possibility of this, but I'd hoped it would be somewhere more... accessible."

"Do you still feel the magic pulling you?" Master Yxna asked.

"Yes, from that way." Marla pointed to the southeast. "It does feel stronger, though, like it's closer. It actually seems that it's closer to east than southeast at this point."

"What's that out there?" Raki asked, pointing out into the ocean.

"It's the ocean," Evon said. "You know, the Aesculun Ocean. The one from the story Master Yxna told us."

Raki gave Evon such a look of incredulity as they boy rolled his eyes, Marla snorted.

"I know that. I mean, what is that, way out there?"

"I don't see anything."

Marla didn't either, though she squinted her eyes. As she moved her head slightly, there was something that broke up the endless water, but it could have been a wave or even an optical illusion along the horizon.

"It is land," Khrazhti said. "Rock."

"Oh," Evon said. "It must be the island. Iracundia."

"Island?" Khrazhti said.

"Yeah, it's land in the middle of the water. There are several out there, apparently, though like Master Yxna's story told us, people can't get to them because of the rough seas and the monsters. Actually, some people have made it to Iracundia because it's so close and the seas are shallow between it and the mainland, but not from this end. It's over twenty miles away from here, but only eight miles or so near Bandit's roost and the city of Hirsen. No one has explored the island yet, though, because any who set foot on it are never heard from again."

"The name of the island is…Iracundia?" Khrazhti asked.

"Yes."

"That is very strange."

"What do you…?" Marla asked, then groaned. "Oh, gods, how stupid am I? Iracundia. It's Alaqotim. It means—"

"Wrath," Evon finished for her. "Do you think the pulling is coming from there?"

"Seems likely. I wonder if we could get someone to bring us there from Hirsen. Several explorers have made it to the island but not actually set foot on it. They returned to tell about it. That's how we know its rough shape."

Evon stared out toward where Raki said he'd seen the island. "It might be possible. It will at least tell us if what you're looking for is coming from the island. We probably shouldn't take a chance on getting off a ship there, though."

Marla hardly heard him. She tapped her fingers on her saddle, thinking it through. With a name like Iracundia—wrath—it had to be the place she was looking for. She had been to the most dangerous parts of Promistala and survived. What could an island to do her that she hadn't faced before?

"Let's follow the coast and head for Hirsen," she said. "We can figure out what we'll do when we get there. Remember, you can choose whether or not to follow me. You're under no obligation. Just don't try talking me into going back to the Academy without solving this mystery."

As they moved to the east, staying mostly within sight of the ocean, the distance between the mainland and Iracundia grew so that even Raki and Khrazhti couldn't see it. Four days they traveled toward the northeast before the edge of the continent kicked back toward the southeast. Another two days and they reached Bandit's Roost, an old fortress high on cliffs looking over the Aesculun Ocean.

"This is where Erent Caahs and Raisor Tannoch killed the Bandit King, the man who murdered Erent's whole family," Raki said, looking up at the deteriorated walls in wonder. "The two of them scaled the walls, found the bandit lord Dartran Finis, and killed him and most of his bandits. Then they brought Dartran's young son to Hirsen to be raised."

"I always liked that story," Marla said. "We'll have to ask Tere about it sometime. It was his first really big heroic adventure."

The group passed the fortress, which had only grown more dilapidated since the time Raki was talking about, in awed silence. Marla could hardly imagine two people assaulting such a monstrous place, but then, things like that were why Erent Caahs was such a famous hero. She wondered if the actions of Tere—and the rest of her friends—would make as much of an impression on people hearing their stories in the future.

Finally, as the coastline twisted to head even more south, the island came into view out in the ocean, a green and grey blob in the middle of the blue waters. All of them could see it by the time they reached the outskirts of Hirsen, one of the largest cities on the coast.

Marla had never been to the city, but she'd seen some drawings and a few paintings of it and its surrounding area, so she was prepared for the sight before her. Others were not quite as prepared.

"Whoa," Raki said. "It's so...high."

"Wait," Evon said. "Your caravan never came to Hirsen? I thought you traveled the world."

"We did. We do." Raki's voice was so soft, Marla had to strain to hear it. "We've been here before, but always on the outskirts, more inland. A lot of cities don't let us come too close. My nani never let me go exploring, not after what happened with my family."

"Oh."

"It's amazing, though." The excitement was back in the boy's voice.

The city did provide quite a sight. Along the shore, where the docks were, it looked like a typical port town. As the city went inland, however, it also went upward, like a huge bowl. Or an amphitheater. From where they sat on their horses, they could see the streets criss-crossing up the cliffs, where it looked like the city was literally carved into the rock.

The bottom of the city, nearer the water, was jumbled and crowded, the streets and alleys and the sheer variety of buildings giving a look of barely contained chaos. As Marla's gaze swept up farther, she could pick out evidence of more intelligent planning for the structures, some larger areas she figured were marketplaces, and even some parks higher up. At the pinnacle of the city were the estates, sprawling homes surrounded by greenery and gathered around a cental feature of Hirsen: the Prime's palace.

Jutting proudly into the blue sky, the Prime's palace was a magnificent structure of stone. It resembled what she used to picture when she heard tales of fairy palaces in some of the children's stories.

"That's where the Prime lives," she said, pointing up. "Though the city is part of the Saraki Principality, it is also the capital of Skegge Naes."

Khrazhti looked to be taking in the information about the city, while Raki's gaze darted to and fro, trying to see everything. Marla wondered if she'd ever had such excited wonder. It seemed to her she'd been jaded for as long as she could remember. Such was what happened when a child saw magic every day at the Academy. She was hit with a pang for a lost childhood, but pushed it away. She'd had a good life and she could always enjoy seeing new things vicariously through Raki. He had enough energy for several people.

"What do you feel?" Master Yxna asked, pulling her cloak around her as if she needed to hide for some reason.

"Feel?" Marla was confused for a moment before she realized what the master was asking. "Oh. Yes. The tugging is coming from that way." She pointed directly south. Toward the island of Iracundia.

"On the island or past it?" Evon asked.

"I don't know for sure, but I think it's probably the island."

"Then our next step is to find a boat to take us there," Master Yxna said.

Raki held up his hand. "Umm, Master Yxna?"

"Yes, Raki?"

"Didn't you tell us that we can't go into the ocean? That story you told, the way you explained it. The monsters and the rough seas."

"Generally, yes, you are correct. Like I mentioned, though, that doesn't apply in the Kanton Sea—since it's an inland sea and doesn't have those problems—the area between Promistala to Ascesh and Teroshi in the north, and the island in front of us, by virtue that it's close enough that the water is shallow enough to be safer. Not safe, really, but safer."

"Look at it this way," Marla said. "You know how there are boats all along the coast that bring things to trade to all the different cities? They don't go out far into the ocean, but stay within a few miles of the land. In that shallow water, there are fewer problems with the strange currents, huge waves, and monsters. There are some—no travel in the oceans is really that safe—but the traders see it as an acceptable risk. We should be able to find someone to bring us eight miles to the island, but they won't want to harbor there, or to go ashore."

"Then what will they do?" Raki asked.

"If we can get them to take us," Evon said. "they'll drop us off. And hopefully pick us up."

The boy nodded, his eyes darting out toward the open water.

"Come," the master said. "We can see about a boat and maybe find rooms for the night. I would not argue with eating food at a table or sleeping in a bed. I've brought plenty of money, nearly enough to buy our own boat."

With a last look at the Prime's palace, Marla directed Surefoot to follow Master Yxna. Khrazhti came next, wrapped from head to toe in her own cloak and hood, then Raki, and finally Evon. She wasn't sure what would happen in the next day or two, but despite the anxiety, she felt better than she had for some time. She was well on her way to discovering what magic was pulling on her. Maybe she could figure out how to fix her anger problem as well.

NINETEEN

I t was late afternoon by the time the group got down to the waterfront.

"The place looks even more crowded at street level than it did looking at it from above," Evon said. "Should we dismount?"

Marla's irritation was spiking at the crowd around her. What she felt like doing was kicking everyone close to her in the face to make them move away. Or maybe she's have Surefoot *accidentally* kick some people out of the way. She stood in her stirrups and looked over the crowd.

"It opens up a bit over there. I'm hoping it's not normally like this. Follow me."

She let her horse's bulk nudge people out of the way. A few grumbled about it, but no one challenged her. Soon, she and her friends were in a less-crowded place. It was still a cramped street, but at least it wasn't shoulder-to-shoulder people. Evon was right. Not only did it look more congested than it had seemed from up higher, but being in the middle of it, Marla was definitely not impressed with the condition of the place.

The buildings, in addition to being placed haphazardly, were run down and most were filthy. The dirt caking them looked like soot, but she couldn't hear any anvils ringing, so she doubted it was from coal smoke. The scent, too, was something she could have done without ever experiencing. Something in between salty rotting fish and forty-day-old garbage.

Master Yxna, as unflappable as ever, turned from her own observation of the place. "I think it would be best to go back up and find a suitable inn. Then, we can walk back down to the docks to search for a boat. I would also suggest we eat at the inn, in the...cleaner part of the city."

The others all readily agreed, all except Khrazhti who was busy looking at everything. She didn't have to eat anyway, so the animaru probably didn't care where they stopped to eat.

After backtracking—the crowded area they had come from had loosened up and only maybe half as many people remained—they found an inn, though they had to travel nine blocks up until they were satisfied with the area.

Tide's Blessing wasn't a fancy establishment, but it was clean. The innkeeper, named Penna Holsen, a hefty woman with a friendly face and even friendlier demeanor, welcomed them. While Master Yxna discussed getting rooms, Marla noticed three toughs leaning on the walls in different areas of the common room, all with similar features to Penna. They must be her sons. There was no way four people with faces that lumpy in the same places could be in one place and not be related.

Marla turned her attention to the negotiation as it concluded. "Yes, yes of course, Madame Yxna," the innkeeper said. "It'll be no problem. Just let me know how long you think it will take to conclude your business and we'll settle accounts at the end of your stay."

"Actually," the master said, "I'd like to pay you in advance for tonight, as well as for stabling the horses. I should be able to tell you tomorrow how long we might stay."

"Oh," Penna said. "If you insist. That will be fine. Will you be taking supper here as well?"

"We will, but we have some business to engage in first. We'll return later."

"Very well. I'll be here. Simply let me know—or any of the girls—and we'll work on getting all your bellies full." She barked a laugh and Master Yxna smiled at her and thanked her.

"Why don't we put our saddle bags and packs in our rooms and then go ot the dock," the master said. "We can look around and make some inquiries before coming back for dinner."

They did as the master suggested and were soon walking along the shoreline. There were all kinds of ships lined up along the docks. Marla and the others followed Master Yxna, who seemed to know what she was doing. The master would stop occasionally at one of the larger boats to ask if anyone would make the trip to Iracundia, but she wasn't having any luck.

Meanwhile, Marla watched Khrazhti. The animaru seemed fascinated by the ocean.

"You don't have large bodies of water in your world?"

Khrazhti shook her head. "No. We do not have water at all. Until we came here, I had never seen such a thing. This... ocean, it is beyond belief So much water, all in one place. And it seems to think and move."

"It's something alright. Once we find someone to take

us out, you'll get a lot better look at it. I think you'll find it interesting, how it feels to be on a boat.

"I'm telling you, Asgeir, you don't have a choice in this," a voice said from a section of a dock crowded with crates. "You wouldn't want anything to happen to your boat."

"Please. Business hasn't been good. I don't have money to pay you."

"If you can't pay to protect your business, maybe you should sell your boat to old Kresk. He'll take it off your hands for a fair price."

Marla traded looks with Evon and headed toward the sound of the arguing. First he, then the others, followed her. When she came around a pile of crates, she got a good look at who had been speaking.

A thin man with bare feet and the kind of loose pants that seemed common among the seafarers stood in front of six other men who were definitely not sailors. They had the rough clothing of city-dwelling commoners, more specifically, the type of dress that fairly screamed street thug: mismatched tunics, ill-fitting pants, and heavy boots. They also all had weapons of one kind or another, even if it was a length of crooked metal rod that looked like it had come from a smith's scrap heap.

Marla cleared her throat and seven heads turned to her. "Good evening."

"You're in the wrong place, bitch," a man said. It was the same voice as before, probably the leader. "Shove off."

The anger building in Marla expressed itself as a wicked smile. "Do you know me?"

"What? No, I don't know you. Everyone will know you for the corpse that was found on the dock unless you clear out of here. This doesn't concern you."

"If you don't know me, then how do you know I'm a

bitch? You're correct, of course, but how could you know that? You strike me as a man who doesn't know much."

"I'll strike you, alright. Jenden, Kaleb, take care of her."

Two of the biggest of the other men rushed at her, one with a knife and the other with that crooked piece of metal. Their eyes grew in size when they came nearer to her and saw Evon and Master Yxna behind her, but they continued toward her.

Marla didn't bother drawing her weapons. It wasn't worth the effort. The metal rod came down at her head while the knife shot straight toward her belly. She waited until the last second, then sidestepped the knife to the left, darting her head down and around the rod, and slammed a hard kick into the rod-wielders torso. She could feel the crack of at least two ribs.

At the same time, she had pushed the knife outside of her center line and flexed her wrist, twisting it in a circular motion to snatch the wrist of the hand holding the knife. As her kicking foot dropped to the ground, she used the motion of her body settling into a stable stance and pulled on the wrist, rotating her hips to slam her palm into the knife-wielder's elbow. A savage crack, followed by a loud scream, announced to everyone within fifty feet that his arm had been shattered and was now unusable.

Somehow, the rod-wielder still held onto his weapon, though he was bent double, trying to breathe in shallow gasps through the pain his ribs were in. Marla helped him out by stepping past the man with the broken arm and delivering a powerful front kick to the bent-over man's jaw. The strike landed with so much force, it flipped him backward and caused his feet to leave the ground. As he crashed down on his back, the rod clanged on the dock and bounced away.

"Now," she said calmly, as if she hadn't just broken several bones while defending herself empty handed from two weapon-wielding thugs. "I suggest that whatever scam you are running on this man, you pack up your little friends and leave. I'm not in the best of moods and I really, *really* don't like it when people come at me waving weapons around. I will give you this one chance to show some intelligence and leave."

"You talk big when you have a gang behind you," the man said.

"Oh?" Marla looked at her friends. "Don't worry about them." She addressed her group. "Guys, don't interfere, okay? This is between me and these four."

"No problem," Evon said. He looked around, found a suitable crate, and sat down to watch. She could have kissed him. She caught Master Yxna rolling her eyes, Khrazhti looking back and forth between her and Evon, and a slightly denser than normal shadow that she was sure was Raki.

"Okay, good. Now, where were we?" She tapped her lower lip and looked up at the rapidly darkening sky. "Oh, right. *You* were going to apologize for bugging this man and then you and your buddies were going to scurry along. Meanwhile, *I* was going to stand here being a bitch, but not killing all of you." She gave him the biggest, fakest smile she could manage. "Unless you are too stupid to understand what's going on and attack me, which might end in death for some of you and definitely will end in pain and probably disfigurement for most of you. Your choice. Make it quick, I have things to be about."

The man looked at the two he'd sent to attack me. One was unconscious on the dock and the other was cradling his ruined arm and whimpering. Neither were going to try to come at me again. Then he looked over at the sailor he'd been harassing and Marla's eyes narrowed in on him so intensely, he actually jumped.

"If you try to harm that man, you will be dead before you take one step. Don't you test me in this, little man. Attacking me is irritating, but make one move toward him and it will be the last thing you ever do. You've been warned."

The man traded looks with his minions and jerked a nod, at which point everyone exploded into motion. The three remaining thugs came at Marla, one of them stooping to pick up a gaff lying on the dock as he came. The man she'd been talking to raised the knife he was holding and lunged at the sailor.

"Wrong choice," she said.

Before the three got anywhere near her, Marla cast one of her favorite spells, Fire Missile. All it took was a simple gesture and a word of power and half a dozen projectiles made of condensed flame rocketed toward the leader. They struck so closely together on his head, they blew a hole all the way through half the size of her hand. He dropped dead at the sailor's feet.

She shifted her attention to the men coming at her. They hadn't seen what she did to their boss, too intent on getting to her. Well, they'd see, if she only incapacitated them and didn't kill them.

One of the men swung a length of heavy chain at her, while another had drawn two knives. It was obvious he was right-handed and had not trained enough to be as proficient with his off-hand, because he moved the left knife clumsily as he prepared to slash at her. The third man, the one with the gaff, held the pole toward the end, giving him a better reach than the others, but his delay in picking up the weapon meant he'd probably get to her last. She didn't worry about any of it. She was used to sparring with several highly-trained Academy students at a time. These clumsy thugs wouldn't even touch her.

Marla was well familiar with the flexible weapons like the Shinyin rope dart or chain whip, having sparred with practitioners of those weapons. She'd tried them out herself and found them to be frustratingly difficult to control. When trying to aim something as long and unpredictable as a rope with a weighted dart at the end, any unnecessary movements could cause the weapon to spin off into an unexpected direction.

So it was with the chain the man was swinging at her. True, he wasn't trying to do anything too fancy, but the simple fact the object was long and flexible, not to mention heavy, made its use difficult. The man attacked her with a simple swing, coming down diagonally, his goal to pummel Marla and wrap her up in the weapon. She danced to the side, letting the weapon pass without touching her as she took a step forward to meet the knife-wielder.

The chain bounced off the dock and the man using it over-rotated to get it under control. Marla slipped her dueling dagger from her belt to block the knife in her attacker's right hand while slamming her open palm into the man's left wrist. The strike deadened his hand, allowing the knife to clatter to the ground.

The attacker with the gaff swung the sharpened hook at Marla's face, and she leaned back to let it pass by without touching her. It kept her from doing more to the knife-man than pushing him away, using her blade to push his knife.

Meanwhile, the chain-wielder came around for another swing. He'd already lost a bit of control of the chain and was fighting to make it go where he wanted it to strike. Marla pivoted, planted a roundhouse kick on the gaff-man's side, then backed up a step. As intended, the gaff-wielder stumbled into the path of the chain. It struck him solidly on the shoulder and wrapped around to slam into his back. He cried out and nearly lost his grip on the long weapon.

With the chain's momentum arrested, it was time to finish the engagement. Marla lunged in, dodging another knife swipe to cut the attacker's forearm with her dagger. The incision went deep enough to cut some tendons and his hand sprang open, dropping the knife. She snapped a front kick to the bottom of his jaw and his eyes rolled up in his head and he fell hard to the dock.

The gaff came back toward her and Marla deflected it with her empty hand, manipulating its trajectory and guiding it around in a circle. The man using the weapon opened his mouth in surprise as Marla moved the gaff around to slam into the chain-wielder's shoulder, puncturing the muscle with the sharp hook. He screamed and dropped his chain, jerking back so violently, it not only tore his injury wider, but pulled the pole from his companion's hand.

Using the momentum from her defense, Marla spun and delivered a heel kick to the chain-man's face with such force that he flew off to the side, bounced on the dock, then lay motionless, groaning.

The final man, now weaponless since his gaff had been torn from his grasp, turned to run, but there would be none of that this day. He'd made his choice earlier and he would deal with the consequences. Marla softened him up with several hard punches to the face with her empty hand, three lightning-fast kicks to his abdomen, then followed up with a powerful strike to his jaw with the hilt of her dueling dagger.

The bone crackled as the heavy metal slammed into his jaw and he bounced backward to land on his back, his ruined jaw and mouth a bloody pulp.

Marla stepped calmly to the closest man—the knife-wielder—and wiped her dagger on his clothes as he cradled his cut arm and whimpered. She scanned the carnage she had wrought, nodded, and stepped up to the sailor who had frozen while she dispatched his harrassers.

"Captain," she said. "Are you hurt?"

TWENTY

The sailor's eyes wandered over the men lying around him on the dock. When they reached the leader who had been in the process of charging him, he blinked and jumped back half a step. Marla had to admit the fire pellets had really done a lot of damage to the man's head, turning it into so much pulped flesh and bone, though the rest of his body didn't show any signs of injury at all.

The boat captain pointed to the corpse. "He...I...that...dead."

Marla stepped slowly over to the man and took his arm. "Come here. Sit down and take a few breaths." She guided him to a nearby crate and sat him down, letting him close his eyes and breathe as she had directed him.

"Are you hurt?"

"N-no. They hadn't reached the point where they would physically attack me. Yet." He looked back at the leader's ruined head. "I mean, before you got here. They were still trying to scare me into giving them money. But I didn't have any."

"They did this often?" Evon asked. He'd given up his seat and wandered over toward where Marla and the captain were.

"Yes. It's a regular thing. They go after the smaller boats, take money from us. If we don't pay, they hurt us or even destroy our boats."

"You didn't report it to the constable?" Master Yxna asked.

"They said they have enough to deal with. They don't want to get involved with protection schemes."

"Well," Marla said. "This guy won't bother you anymore, nor will what's left of those thugs. Not anytime soon. Does he work for someone bigger, a crime boss or something?"

"No, it's just them."

"Then it seems like your problem is solved."

"I...yes. Thank you. I was afraid he'd really hurt me this time."

"I have a special dislike for bullies," Marla told him. "And I've been looking for a chance to blow off some steam. I think it all worked out."

The captain looked back to the dead leader again. "Thank you. How can I repay you?"

"Don't worry about it. Glad to help." Marla turned toward the main docks, but then stopped. "Unless you can help us with some information. We're trying to find a boat that'll take us to the island. If you know someone who might be willing, we'd appreciate it."

"To the island? To Iracundia? It's not safe there. No one who has ever stepped onto it has returned."

"We mean to be the first. I know boats have gone there, even if they didn't disembark. We're just looking to be dropped off, then picked up after we're done."

The captain wrung his hands nervously. "I've made the trip several times. The crossing is dangerous, but not like going out into the open sea. It's shallow enough that there aren't a lot of monsters. They seem to like the deeper waters."

"Will you take us there?" Marla asked.

"I could, yes."

"Don't worry, we'll pay you well."

"No, you just saved me from at least a beating, if not being killed or having my boat burned to the waterline. I'll take you there. I wouldn't think of charging you."

"Nonsense," Master Yxna said. "We will pay you. We heard you tell these goons that business hasn't been good. We would not expect you to spend your valuable time taking us for free when you could be earning money. We'll pay you twenty gold up front and another twenty when you pick us up."

The man's mouth went wide. "That's way too much for—"

"Captain, a little word of advice. When someone offers you money for a job you would do for free, take the money."

"Uh, yes ma'am."

Marla put her hand out to the man. "Good, I'm glad that's settled. My name is Marla, and my friends are Master Yxna, Raki, Evon, and Khrazhti." She pointed each one out as she said their names.

"Master?"

"Yes, she is a master at the Academy at Sitor-Kanda."

"The Hero Academy?"

"The very same."

"Oh. I'm Asgeir Balstad. My boat here is called the Breath of Gelendia."

"An apt name," Master Yxna said.

189

Marla shook the captain's hand. "It's a pleasure to meet you, Captain Asgeir. Would it be acceptable to sail tomorrow morning? We have rooms at an inn in the city and would like a good night's sleep before departing."

"That suits me fine. Meet me right here and we'll shove off in the morning."

The group went back to the inn, enjoyed a fine dinner, and got the sleep they'd been missing for the past several days. Master Yxna worked it out with the inn keeper to board the horses until they returned. She paid for three days in advance with the promise that they'd pay the rest when they returned.

In the morning, the party was up early. They ate breakfast, stopped at a trader's shop to buy provisions, and met Captain Asgeir at his boat. The men Marla had decimated the day before were gone, though a few blood stains remained. The captain, though, seemed in good spirits, especially when Master Yxna dropped the gold coins in his hand.

In no time, they were underway. The crew of the Breath of Galendia consisted of four rugged sailor types, along with the captain, and they seemed to know their business. It made Marla wonder that with five tough men, why they hadn't stood up to the thugs bilking money from them. She figured it probably came down to not knowing how to fight. Someone could be tough and strong, but that wouldn't matter if they were pitted against someone who knew their way around a weapon. Just as the men the previous day had found out.

From the start, Khrazhti spent much of her time sitting at the bow of the boat, watching the water as they cut through it. Raki hung around her, a wild grin on his face, his hair blowing back and streaming in the wind. Evon and

Master Yxna bided their time on a bench attached to the deck near the wheel. Marla joined them.

"We appreciate your doing this, Captain," she told Asgeir. "We tried to find other captains who would take us, but none would.

"The trip isn't that bad," he said. "I've made it several times. The water can get rough and sometimes smaller monsters will show themselves, but it is a beautiful path. The island, untouched like it is, is wild and rugged. Too bad it's so dangerous." He laughed. "It's funny to me that the other captains don't want to make the trip. You should meet my brother Tesnair. He sails out of Squalls Landing. He's always telling me he's going to go to one of the other islands. The man's a damn fool to want to cross the deep waters, but he swears he'll do it. One day. It'll probably be the last day anyone will ever see him, but he's set on it. He'd bring his boat down here to make this crossing in an instant. I guess crazy runs in our family."

"We're glad of it," Marla said, smiling at the man.

"But this going onto the island, actually putting your feet on the ground of the place, that takes all. Please don't do it. You all seem to be decent folk, and you're more competent than most, from what I saw you do yesterday, but this isn't some two-bit thug on a dock in Hirsen. Strange sounds come from the island. Calls and screams. There are wild beasts there, at least, and most probably monsters. Monsters! How can you fight them? Why would you want to go there?"

"We appreciate your concern, Captain Asgeir," Master Yxna said, "but sometimes one must do things that others never have before. This group knows that better than most. We will return. You can count on it."

"Yes, Lady...uh, Master Yxna. If you say so. But how will

I know to come get you? I can't very well anchor off the shore. The currents can be tricky and can change in a moment. I'll end up on the rocks."

"I've thought about that," Marla said. "Here's what we'll do. I will give you a signal. Look for it at just before sunrise and at dusk. It will look like this." Marla swirled her hands and muttered words of power. A fist-sized ball of red fire shot up from her open hand into the sky.

Captain Asgeir flinched away at the display of power. "What was that?"

"Just a simple fireball flare. In the dim light, you should be able to see it from Hirsen. I'll shoot several of them up and toward the city. When you see the flash, come and get us. Keep in mind it may be several days until we have finished what we need to do."

"How did you do that?" he asked.

Marla gave a little shrug. "I was trained at the Hero Academy. Why would you ask that?"

"It's true, then? They teach heroes how to throw magic at that place?"

"Oh, yes," Master Yxna said. "That, and so much more."

The three relocated to where Khrazhti and Raki were peering out at the ocean, not wanting to make the captain any more nervous with their conversations. All of them sat silently, listening to the water lap against the boat as they cut through it. The island filled their view now, getting larger as they approached.

They headed for a promontory with a suitable beach beneath the cliffs. Parts of the island were choked with trees, but closer to the shore, the land was clearer. Marla couldn't see anything moving, but that didn't mean much. They weren't close enough to pick out that kind of detail.

"I found a small work by the Prophet in the cache we

found," Evon said out of the blue. "I believe it was one of the last things he'd ever written. It was about the gods, their departure from Dizhelim, and the changes in the magic of the world."

Marla didn't usually get as excited as Evon did about scholarly pursuits, but what he said seized her attention. "I didn't know he wrote anything about that."

"No one did. He saw a few of the gods leave at the end of his life. Their exodus wasn't complete until after he was dead, but he saw the beginning. It's fascinating. He proposes that the gods are so closely tied to the magic of Dizhelim, it's nearly a symbiotic relationship. With the extreme imbalances in the world's magic, he says it probably affected them like a sickness or a physical wound.

"It wasn't so severe that they were in any danger, he wrote, but it definitely must have been uncomfortable. When they left, it accelerated the degradation of the magic, taking most of the stable sources of qozhel from Dizhelim."

"All except for the magic locked away in the Wells of Power," Marla said.

"I've seen no indication that the Prophet knew of any of the wells. He was aware of concentration of magic in the world, such as in the area where we found his cache of books, but I don't think he suspected such things existed, or that they could think and act they way they do, let alone that the magic could be released. If he had known, he would have started to release them himself and would have put in place a group to find all of them. Can you imagine him not doing that when he knew the Malatirsay wouldn't have as much magic available as previous generations to fight the animaru?"

"So the gods were weakened by the magic deteriorating, but when they left, the world's magic got even weaker,"

Master Yxna said. "There is the perennial question, however. What caused the weakening to begin with?"

"General understanding was that it was the abuse and overuse of magic during the War. Not only was more qozhel manipulated than at any other time since the creation of all things, but much of it was used in violation of the natural way of things. Stealing it from living beings, stockpiling it for use in massive amounts at once, all those things are thought to have weakened the magical matrix of the world."

"I don't buy it," Marla said. "Not completely. I can see how some things would be affected, but to drain the magic from the entire world? I don't think that's possible. If so, why didn't the gods—Migae, for example—simply restrict how much could be utilized?"

"Maybe he did. That could have started the world on the road to where we ended up. The gods are old and are super-powerful, but they're not perfect. What if they did try to keep things from getting worse, but they couldn't foresee what their actions would do?"

Marla stared at Evon. "Are you saying that the gods made mistakes and made things worse, then when they realized it, they ran away?"

Evon shrugged. "Not in so many words, but it's something we have to think about. Everything involving magic is so incredibly complex. We forget that sometimes and get complacent because we use it all the time. The gods could fall prey to the same thinking. It's just an idea."

Master Yxna considered Evon for a moment. "Evon, I ask that you please never mention what I am about to say to anyone ever again, but how I wish we would have pushed you to take the position of Master of Prophecy."

Evon's face went blank and he sputtered unintelligibly,

his eyes going liquid. He finally dropped his head and muttered, "Thank you."

Marla had to agree with the master. She'd said it often enough, many time in jest, but Evon, though young, was one of the greatest assets the Academy had. She smiled at her friend, then shifted her gaze to the island they were fast approaching.

"We'll be able to launch a dinghy in a few minutes," Captain Asgeir shouted. "I suggest you gather your supplies and get ready. I can't keep the ship steady for long in this chop."

TWENTY-ONE

"Watch for my flare," Marla shouted to Captain Asgeir as she joined her friends in the dinghy bouncing along the side of the ship. Two of Asgeir's men and all of Marla's friends were already in. "I will watch, hoping to see it. Safe travels to you."

Marla sat on the bench next to Master Yxna and nodded to the men holding oars. They cast off the rope tethering them to the ship and pushed away from it before dipping the oars into the water to start toward the shore.

The water was rough, and the little boat rose and dipped, sometimes quickly enough for her to feel a strange feeling in her stomach. It was uncomfortably like the feeling when something suddenly went wrong, a dropping sensation that nearly took her breath away. She hoped it wasn't prophetic.

Raki sat near the edge of the boat, not concerned in the least with the spray the wind blew into his face with each stroke of the oar near him. The grin he wore displayed pure joy as he trailed his hand in the water.

Khrazhti, on the same bench on the other side of the

boat sat straight, as always, with her eyes searching the expanse of grey-green water between them and the strip of beach they were heading for. Marla wasn't sure she would be so calm sitting in a tiny boat moving so much in the waves if she didn't know how to swim. Maybe it was a matter of Khrazhti not knowing what drowning was, since she was so unfamiliar with water. Then again, Marla wasn't sure an animaru *could* drown. Did they even need to breathe? She didn't need to eat and drink, after all.

Evon sensibly sat hunched up, cloak wrapped tight around him with the hood covering as much of his face as possible. He'd traveled by water before, within the Kanton Sea, so the picture in front of him probably wasn't too interesting. Unlike him, Marla and Master Yxna sat as if simply tolerating the trip, not excited but not too put out by it, either.

Marla wasn't sure what the master was thinking, but she was wondering what they'd find on the island. Was it really so dangerous that they might not make it back alive? With their magic and skills, she was confident they'd survive it, but she'd been overconfident before. Was she putting her friends in danger on a whim?

"It's something you need to do," Master Yxna said, patting Marla's hand. "This feeling, the tugging, it has a hold on you. You need to find out what it is. We will all watch out for each other."

Marla smiled at the master. "Thank you." They had such a connection that Master Yxna seemed to be able to read her mind. It had been irritating before—especially when Marla had tried to misdirect the master—but she was glad of it now.

She watched the shoreline, looking for anything that moved, but saw only the waves and the trees some distance away swaying in the wind. The feeling she'd been having, the pulling, left no doubt that it wanted her on this island. She wasn't sure how she knew, but she was positive it wasn't coming from anything past Iracundia. Whatever it was, she'd find it here.

As far as Marla could see in either direction was a narrow sandy beach, butted up against a series of cliffs and hills. The first half mile or so was clear before the trees started and became thick enough that she thought they might have trouble passing through them. If she were a predator, those trees were where she would hide.

The boat scraped the sand and slowed to a stop. One of the rowers leaped out and pulled it a few feet more to stabilize it. The man winced as his feet touched the ground, several inches under the water. "Time to get off," he said. His expression showed that he would prefer they did so quickly, his darting eyes looking for danger in every direction.

Marla was off first, jumping to land in barely an inch of water. She would prefer not to start the day with her boots full of sea water. When she landed, a jolt ran up her legs, tingling with magic. The feeling irritated her and, along with splashing herself and needing to move out of the way so the others could disembark, her anger spiked. She grumbled as the slogged up the beach, wondering again if her choice to come to the island was the right one.

In short order, the others made their way to her and they all watched as the rower pushed the boat back into the surf and hopped in to take up his oar. Both men waved at them and put their backs into rowing away from the island as fast as they could.

"Well, we're here," Evon said, a bite in his voice that Marla had rarely heard. She blinked at him, but didn't want to say anything. With her mood, suddenly foul, she would probably say the wrong thing anyway and start an argument. Better to keep silent.

"Which way?" Master Yxna asked. Marla glanced at the Master of the School of Edged Weapons. Was she trying to annoy Marla, poking at her to see if she would rise to being baited? The woman's smooth and too-young face showed no more emotion than it normally did, but she often looked like that, even as she joked around.

Marla shook her head. What was she thinking? Master Yxna was like a mother to her. She would never do anything to purposely prod her anger. She took a breath, looked around them, and answered. "It feels like whatever it is is over in that direction." She pointed to the south. It really didn't matter as far as the terrain was concerned. That damn forest stretched across the island for as far as they could see in any direction. "Let me look around here first, before we head to the trees. I want to see if I can find any tracks or evidence of other...things here."

Master Yxna nodded. "Good idea. Do you want help or should we just stay out of the way?"

Marla wondered why the master had put it that way, but after thinking about it, she realized that's exactly what Marla would have told them, had she not been as tactful as she was. "Staying out of the way would be good."

The master walked over to a fair-sized piece of tree trunk that had been washed up onto the beach. She sat down, swiveling her head to scan the surroundings. Thankfully, the others took her lead and did the same, though Evon kept glancing at Marla for some reason.

She dropped her pack and didn't pay attention to him, instead focusing on the beach itself. The sand and pebble mix crunched with every step, sending little vibrations up through Marla's boots. She glanced back and though her footprints weren't as sharp as they would be in pure sand, the marks that someone had passed were unmistakable. Good. That would help her to see if there was evidence of anyone or anything else traversing the strip of beach.

For half an hour, she walked along the beach to the northeast, then back down to the southwest, following the water's edge, but she found nothing in between the driftwood and shells littering the coast except strings of seaweed and kelp. At least there would be that to eat if it turned out that nothing else on the island was edible. With the look of the forest, though, she doubted it would be a problem. There had to be animals in there and if not, edible plants, mushrooms, and roots. Besides, they had enough food in their packs for at least five days. Surely it couldn't take them that long to explore, especially since they knew exactly where to go. That tugging sensation would bring them right to where they needed to be.

When she returned to the group, the tension was almost palpable. Raki looked to be sulking off away from the others a little bit and Evon darted glances at the boy, one edge of his lips turned upward.

"What's going on?" she asked.

"Are you finished walking around now?" Evon asked her. "Can we head toward whatever it is we're here to find? I'd like to get off this island as soon as possible. I hate it here."

Marla had an urge to back up a step at the venom in Evon's voice. What was his problem? Before she could make an appropriate reply, he blew out a breath.

"Sorry. I don't know if it's the anticipation or if I'm tired from the trip. I'm in a bad mood for some reason. Did you find any tracks or anything?"

He acted like a simple apology would eliminate his rude speech. Marla had a mind to call him to task for it, but then realized that her mood wasn't the best, either. No use in her aggravating him more. "No. Nothing bigger than a mouse has walked across the beach that I can see. I'm not sure how high the water gets with the tide, but for at least several hours, we're the only things that have been here. Yeah, let's get started. We've got most of the day still before we need to make camp."

She picked up her pack and crunched toward the forest.

Once she reached the edge of the gritty sand, the ground became firmer, grasses and weeds holding it together and providing a springy plaform for walking. Shortly after it solidified, the land kicked up into a hill. On either side of them sat cliffs of crumbling stone and dirt. A few areas that could be paths upward snaked around the scree and weeds, but the hill was a better option. It didn't look like any animals had used the paths up the cliffs—not that it looked like they'd used the hill the humans were using either—but Marla was all for taking the easiest path.

The hill wasn't too steep and they were soon standing on top of it. The rise provided a good vantage of not only the entire beach, but also more of the forest that she couldn't see from the waterline. The one thing that didn't change was that, other than the narrow belt of the beach and the cliffs, it appeared the whole of the island had been taken over by the dense forest.

Marla sighed, adjusted her pack, and led her friends directly toward the wall of vegetation.

From the first step, she knew they were in for a fight. The trees, of varieties she had never seen, were split about evenly between those with straight trunks shooting up into the sky, and those that seemed more bush than tree, except for the obvious quality that their trunks were bigger around than she was. The latter were the most irritating, curved and twisty, sending their branches out to the sides as much as upward. Added to that a broad-leafed type of bush that shot its branches out horizontally, and every single step was a battle as the vegetation conspired to interlock and—seemingly—not only prevent them from going forward, but also to push them backward.

"Gods damned plants," she spat, and contemplated using fire spells to burn a path through. Fortunately for all involved, she decided it probably wasn't a good idea to do something that most likely would catch the entire place on fire. Still, she was tempted.

The soft ground was treacherous as well. Though the soil was well-suited for growth, soft and springy, it was also shot through with roots that were either half submerged or were growing along the surface entirely. After the fifth time one of the surprisingly strong but string thin roots reached up and snatched the toes of her boots, she revisited her idea of using the fire spells.

Not that she was alone in her misery. Even Master Yxna muttered what sounded like choice curses under her breath. Raki had disintegrated into prolonged sub-aural rants, and Evon had taken his sword to a few bushes before he realized it did nothing but tire him out and dull his blade.

Only Khrazhti seemed unaffected by the very land gathering together to repel them. The animaru calmly pushed through the vegetation to Marla's left, applying only the pressure needed and not attacking the bushes. Marla was impressed—and irritated—at that.

"Has anyone else seen anything that might look like an animal trail?" Marla asked at one point. "I'd actually welcome a path trod often by a large predator over pushing our way through this mess."

"I haven't seen any," Evon said. "I also haven't seen any small animals. Not even birds. Is this whole place devoid of anything but plants?"

"Maybe the island kills all animals that come here," Raki said. It was soft enough that Marla thought maybe he was saying it to himself, barely audible through the crashing they were making through the foliage. He did have a point there, though.

Raki's statement had effectively ended conversation for some time. For a few more hours, the group battled their way through what had to be the thickest and most tangled vegetation in the world. All the while, Marla continued to lead them toward where she could feel the magic was.

At what she thought was probably a couple of hours from sunset—something that would come quickly in the wall of trees they were in—they lucked upon an area where three large trees had fallen, smashing down the smaller surrounding trees and making what was probably the closest thing they'd find to a clearing.

"What do you say we stop here for the day," Marla said, fully intending to do so even if the rest didn't agree. "I want a fire and to enjoy a little time where I can actually swing my arms around without hitting ten damn trees or bushes at the same time."

No one had any objections. In fact, none of the others bothered to say anything, instead staking out a spot to drop their packs and sit down. Marla did the same before deciding to separate out an area to be a fire pit.

Despite the verdant growth, the forest wasn't too damp. She'd gone through vegetation like this before, with little water drops hanging everywhere. After only a few feet, anyone passing through was soaked to the skin. She was surprisingly dry now, aside from where she had perspired through her clothes in the center of her back, under her arms, and between her breasts. With a fire and some time, she'd be dry and comfortable.

Evon and Raki helped to clear out some of the plants and dig a shallow hole, then locate some rocks she used to line the pit. Deadwood was no problem to find. Between what was on the ground, what they could take down from dead branches still on upright trees, and some of the larger branches attached to the three large fallen trees, they had enough wood to easily last the night. She soon had a blaze burning, its soothing light helping her to feel not-so-horrible as she had earlier.

At least, that was the case before the creatures showed up.

CHAPTER

TWENTY-TWO

I t started with a small sound. Marla sat on the ground, leaning against one of the fallen logs, her boots off and her feet warming in the fire's glow. She breathed in and out with regular, measured breaths, forcing herself to relax even though she felt like they'd wasted so much time bashing through the forest and traveling maybe a mile or two in more than half a dozen hours of work. Irritation pressed at her, trying to take over her thoughts, but she set her mind in a loose, peaceful state and closed her eyes.

Scritch-scritch.

She opened one eye, expecting to find Raki drawing in the dirt or some such nonsense. She spotted the boy, on the other side of the fire sitting cross-legged with his eyes closed. He looked to be meditating, something she'd seen him do before. Jia had been working with him on using some form of mental magic. He wasn't moving a muscle, so the sound hadn't been him.

Scritch-scritch.

What the hells was that? If she were anywhere else, she would say it was a squirrel or a bird flitting around on the forest floor looking for hidden treats. They hadn't seen any evidence of animals at all, though. No sightings, no tracks, no droppings, no nests, nothing.

She had both eyes open now, scanning their little camp-ground. "Hey," she said. "Did anyone else hear—"

A flash of pale grey darted across her legs, making her jump.

"What the—?"

She might have thought she'd imagined it, but after whatever it was had crossed over her, she heard it dive into the vegetation. She pulled her boots on, drew her sword, and used it to poke around in the plants where the thing had gone.

"Did something just move over there?" Evon said from another spot across the fire from her.

"Yeah. I couldn't catch what it was, but it actually ran across my legs." She shivered. She wasn't generally squea-mish or nervous about small animals, but the damn thing had run across her legs!

For a good fifteen minutes each member of the group tried to follow the little sounds and movements that betrayed whatever it was that had trespassed in their camp. It seemed unlikely that any kind of animal could be so elusive and Marla started to think it was a spell, with some caster sitting well away from them, laughing at their antics.

They spread out, each with their weapons out, eyes darting at the wall of plants surrounding their little island of space. The more minutes ticked by, the more aggravated Marla got. When she finally got hold of whatever it was, she would...

A screech rang out and all eyes turned to where Raki stood, looking down at the ground. Something down there twitched a few times, rustling the detritus on the forest floor, then went still.

Raki had a look of horror on his face. "I'm sorry. I didn't mean to do that. It was reflex, from all the training. I—"

Marla stepped over to the boy and saw what he was staring at. It was probably the ugliest creature she had ever seen, and that was saying something since she'd seen all kinds of animaru. The animal—she thought it was an animal—was the size of a small dog, or a large cat, half bald, with long, wiry hair spouting mostly from its back. It had the appearance of a very large rat, though its forelimbs and back limbs were about the same size. The toes, or fingers, on all its appendages, seemed articulate, long and segmented with sharp claws on the ends. Ears much larger than they should be for the size of its head stuck out from the upper sides of its skull, the top half black and the bottom a light grey color, the same as the skin on its body. A long tail, scaly like a rat's, was more than half the length of the thing's body. Big yellow eyes sat on either side of its pointed head, just above a sharp snout that Marla had no doubt was full of razor needle teeth. Stuck through the center of its body was one of Raki's throwing spikes.

"What is it?" Evon asked. "I don't recognize it as any animal or monster I've ever seen, not even ancient ones that are extinct."

"I know of nothing like that, either," Master Yxna said.

"I didn't mean to kill it," Raki said again. "It didn't do anything to us. It was just running around."

"You did good, Raki," Marla told him. "If it's not too afraid to run across me, it wouldn't have been too afraid to bite one of us. Who knows what kinds of diseases it could have given us."

The boy still wasn't having any of it. Instead of going to

retrieve his spike, he backed up a step, genuinely horrified at his actions. Marla pulled the spike out and wiped it on a large leaf nearby, then handed it back to Raki. He took it hesitantly, making it disappear into the sheath he'd taken it from.

"I guess that answers the question about whether there are any living things here besides plants," Marla said. "Nasty, ugly little thing. We can only hope that's the most dangerous thing we'll come up against."

"Don't count on it," Evon said. "If these were the only things on this island, the place would be overrun by them. We'd have seen them all over the place."

"Maybe there are plants that eat them," Raki said. "Like the plant that shot me with poison darts and tried to eat me in the Grundenwald." The others all stared at him, mouth open. "What? That's how we met Urun. Tere, Aeden, and Fahtin had to carry me to Urun so he could heal the poison. I almost died. Maybe they have mean plants here, too."

Marla cursed under her breath. As if she had needed that image in her mind. She took a hard look at the foliage surrounding her and suppressed a shiver. "Not that we weren't going to do it anyway, but we're definitely keeping watch every night while we're here."

Khrazhti, who had been silent for most of the day, Master Yxna, and Raki went back toward the fire, the crisis now averted. Evon examined the creature from a few feet away.

"Do you think it's safe to eat if we cook it?"

"I'm not eating that thing. If anything ever looked like a scavenger, it's that disgusting animal. I'll eat a rat if I'm starving, but only as a last resort. We should either bury it or burn it in the fire or one of the things you say are probably here might come looking for what smells like food."

"I'm not digging with all the roots here. Burning it sounds like the right thing to do."

He turned and joined the others, leaving Marla near the carcass. She sighed, picked the monstrosity up by the tail, and brought it to the fire to burn.

After the stench of the burning creature finally faded, the group sat around the fire eating a cold meal. The rations they'd brought didn't need cooking, so they chewed their food, mostly silently, and enjoyed the warmth of the flame in the rapidly cooling evening.

"Are you well, Raki?" Khrazhti said, surprising Marla, since the animaru had been so quiet all day.

"I'm fine," he said a little too quickly. "I don't like the idea of killing something that was only moving around in its home. I'm trespassing into its forest; I had no right to throw a spike at it."

"You have killed before. Many times."

He shrugged. "I know. I don't like killing at all, but it's different if someone is trying to kill me, or if they're hurting someone else. Or if something is going to try to eat me. In those cases, where it's me or them, or someone else may be hurt or killed, I can do it. I don't know what that animal was doing, but it didn't hurt anyone and didn't attack us."

"You have a good attitude, Raki," Master Yxna said. "Keep thinking that way. I've seen too many learn to use weapons and get to like hurting their enemies too much. I'm glad you feel like you do, but is it bothering you a lot, making you depressed?"

"No. I try to remember how I should think. My nani told me a story that I think about a lot. It helps me to put things in perspective."

"A story?" Khrazhti asked. "Your...nani told you stories?"

"Of course. All Gypta tell stories. It's how we learn. There are stories for everything. How we should act, or think, or be; what we should do when we're in trouble; to teach us how the world works. It's why I love stories so much. It's not just about hearing how heroes battled enemies and destroyed monsters. It's how they faced problems, even ones that seemed to be too much for them, and how they won. Not because of their special magic, or at least not only because of that, but because of who they were."

Evon barked a laugh, and Marla seriously thought of smacking her friend. Apparently she wasn't the only one because Master Yxna glared at him as well, and Raki blinked at him, as if he didn't believe what Evon had just done.

"No, no," Evon said. "I'm not laughing at what he said. I laughed because all this time, I thought Raki loved stories because he's young and we all loved stories when we were younger. I just figured it was him being boyish and liking the excitement and entertainment. Now he turns that all on its head with a few sentences, making me realize how much wiser than me he is."

Raki dropped his head, his cheeks darkening. "I do love the excitement of hero stories, but I like the lessons, too."

"The story," Khrazhti said, her head swinging as she tried to keep up with the changing moods in the group. "Your nani told you a story that helps you not to be too sad?"

"Yes. It was when my whole family was killed and I was left alone in the caravan, with her being my only relative. I spent a full week barely eating any food, not sleeping, not really doing anything. I didn't see a purpose in things and I only wished I could never feel again. It hurt so bad, thinking about them being gone forever. At the end of that week, I decided I was going to push it all away, not let myself feel sad. If I could be unfeeling, like a rock, then I wouldn't hurt anymore. Ever again. She told me the story to help explain why that wasn't the best thing to do, that it was probably the worst."

"Will you tell us?" the animaru asked. Marla hadn't witnessed Khrazhti asking for stories before, though she paid close attention to them, as she did with any new information she was exposed to. She wondered if her request was more out of her own curiosity or to help Raki work through his sadness as killing the little creature.

"I...I can. It's probably my turn anyway. Some people say I never tell stories, but that's not true." He looked pointedly at Evon, who had the grace to look at the ground.

"Yes," Master Yxna. "A story. Just the thing we need to get us ready for a night's rest in a strange place."

"Okay. I'll try to do a good job."

CHAPTER

TWENTY-THREE

Marla watched Raki as he straightened his posture for a few seconds, before slumping back into his normal sitting position. The boy cleared his throat and prepared to tell the story he had promised. The story his nani Jehira had told a young boy to deal with the slaughter of his entire family in one night.

After her initial flash of anger at Evon's laugh, she found that she thought the same way her school friend did. She'd always thought Raki a simple child, excited about stories of danger and fighting and no more. The way he explained it was so...grown up. It shocked and surprised her. She already had respect for the kind, gentle person Raki was, not to mention his extreme skills in not only disappearing and using dark magic, but the unerring aim he had with any type of thrown weapon. Now she saw that she hadn't given him even half the credit he deserved. At sixteen years of age, he had sounded like a wise adult when he explained the value of stories. It was the way she had heard Master Aubron explain why tales of the past were so important in the lives of everyone. She had been so wrong about Raki's simplicity. What else that she thought she knew was she wrong about?

She quieted the conversation in her head as Raki began to speak.

"This story was in a time long ago, maybe at the end of the Age of Creation or near the beginning of the Age of Magic. So, over twenty-eight thousand years ago. It was a time when there were fewer people and their connection with the gods was stronger.

"In that time, there lived a man named Apatholonus. He was a devout follower of Eruditen, the God of Knowledge and Learning. He spent nearly all of his time learning all he could. As the things he knew increased, he branched off into other areas of thought. It was no longer enough for him to learn about the land and the sky, the water and the plants, all the animals and other creatures on Dizhelim. He wanted to become more efficient at learning. It was the only way he had a chance of learning all there was to know.

"He prayed to Eruditen, asking for the god's guidance in making his mind more efficient. Eruditen answered him by appearing in person to the man, teaching him to go within himself to improve. The god taught him the basics of meditation, allowing Apatholonus to separate himself from his normal reality and dwell within his mind for hours at a time, working hard on the pathways of his thoughts to become more proficient at thinking and learning.

"Every day, he began to spend at least half his time experiencing the wonders of his meditations, reducing the time he used for studying all the other subjects in which he was interested. His new practices bore fruit and he was able to learn more, and faster, than he had before. His gratitude toward his god was immense, but he knew that Eruditen was not one for rituals and offerings. Instead, the god appreciated more than anything else the education of his folowers. So Apatholonus worked hard to become better and better.

"For decades, he worked his keen mind, molding it into a wonder to all the people who knew him. He became famous for his wisdom and knowledge, all of which made Eruditen happy.

"Then, one day, Apatholonus stumbled upon a thought during his meditation. Earlier in the day, a commotion had interrupted his study, several men arguing outside his home. Their inconsideration irritated the scholar and, try as he might, he couldn't shut out completely the escalating shouts of the people. When he finally rose from the mat on which he was sitting, he stepped outside to scold the noisemakers.

"As he left his door, the argument had gotten out of control and one of the men attacked another, striking him in the head with a large rock in his hand. The struck man dropped to the ground, but the attacker followed him, striking him several more times before two other young men standing nearby wrestled him to the ground and took the bloodied rock from his hand.

"The man who was attacked was dead and the attacker was taken off to be judged by the elders of the community. Apatholonus was shocked, watching the whole thing unfold in front of him.

"After the crowd dispersed, taking the body of the victim, the small puddle of blood was the only thing to show what had happened. Apatholonus stared at it for a time, trying to come to grips with the violence that had occurred. At that time in history, there was little conflict, with the relatively few people living peacefully in accord with their gods' strictures.

"When he tried to settle back into his meditation, he found he could not. The irritation he felt previously lingered still, but more strongly, he felt a great sadness. A man had lost his life in front of the scholar. Not only that, but if Apatholonus had reacted sooner, he might have been able to help prevent what occurred. His emotional state would not allow him to use his mind as effectively as he was accustomed.

"He thought upon the problem for several days, finally slipping back into easy meditation four days after the incident. The analysis continued, though, until he reached a conclusion. His emotions, both the irritation and the sadness, had hindered the efficient use of this thinking. It wasn't a great leap to see that all emotions would do similarly.

"Apatholonus realized what he needed to do to become even more efficient. He would have to push out all emotions, no matter the type, and only by doing that would he truly be efficient in thinking and learning.

"For years more, he worked on the problem with single-minded determination. Little by little, he trained his mind to reject anything that would make him feel emotion. As he did, he found that what he had thought was the pinnacle of mental efficiency and learning was not nearly as good as he could be.

"It came to pass that Apatholonus became so good at thinking logically, without emotion affecting anything in his life, he became like a stone. He learned, he meditated, and he solved great problems, but he found no joy in it. In fact, he found no joy in anything. Nor happiness, sadness, anger, or any other feeling.

"One fateful day, during his meditation, he realized something profound: there was no purpose to his life. Yes, he could think and learn and do many things, but so what? Inpecting his life and his everyday actions coldly and logically, he saw no real value in himself as a person.

"Apatholonus calmly ended his meditation and rose from his mat. He walked with his measured, efficient stride to the land beyond the edge of the village in which he lived and peered out over the vast landscape beneath him. With a single step, he left the ground, plunging off the cliff he had been standing on, and crashed to the ground far below, dying instantly."

Raki's eyes grew liquid and he blinked several times, letting a few tears fall so his vision cleared. "So my nani told me that to try to push out all emotion wasn't good. Instead, I needed to accept it...accept the pain of losing my family, and from that pain I would learn to be stronger, but not only that. The pain would teach me what was precious, because all precious things spring from pain of some kind.

"She reminded me of that story whenever I had problems with any emotion. When I was afraid of the dark when I was younger, when I was too eager for something, when I got mad, and especially when something made me sad. She reminded me that if I tried to get rid of those feelings completely, my life wouldn't mean much and I might feel like there was no reason to live. So, whenever I feel emotions too strongly, instead of trying to reject them, I try to take them in and let them be a part of me.

"I'm sad I killed that little creature, and being sad is good because the alternative is to either not care or to be happy about it, and that would turn me into something bad."

Of all people, Master Yxna went to the boy and pulled him into a hug. The other three members of the group sat silently, watching. Marla still wasn't much of a hugger, but she was glad the master had taken the action she did. As for herself, she revised her opinion of the young Gypta yet again. Not only had he been subjected to a rough life, but he was amazingly wise and resilient because of it. It made her want to be better herself.

The story—and Raki's emotions in relation to it—seemed to calm everyone down. Marla knew it did with her. She was ready to sleep, even though it had only just become full night a short time before.

"We need to set up a watch rotation," she told the others.

"I will keep watch," Khrazhti volunteered.

"Great, you can take the first watch."

"No, what I meant was that I would watch all night and allow you to sleep. I do not need to sleep, if you remember."

It was hard to argue with the animaru's logic, but for some reason, it still didn't feel right to Marla. "Khrazhti, that's very kind of you, and we appreciate it, but we can take turns watching. I've seen you sleep a few hours at a time."

Khrahzti tilted her blue head at Marla. "I partake in rest and in food or drink, mostly because it makes others more comfortable if I do so. Though I do derive a small benefit from those things, it is in no way necessary."

"I don't like it," Marla said. "It seems unfair to you." The animaru's insistence was beginning to annoy her.

"How about this," Master Yxna said. "Khrazhti, we appreciate your offer and we will accept it, with one slight change. If you would be so kind as to take most of the watch, allowing someone to take the task for maybe two or three hours, then you can rest and derive that small benefit you referred to and at the same time we can feel as if we're doing our part. I think Marla feels as if we would be taking advantage of your kindness, and in turn, her kindness makes her feel bad about it."

"Of course," Khrazhti said. "I do not attempt to make any of you feel uncomfortable. I offered because it is the most efficient manner in which to provide a watch over those sleeping. I will wake whoever you direct me to at two hours before dawn."

Marla grumbled inwardly, but had no real basis for argument. She must really need sleep if she was getting miffed at someone trying to make things easier for her and the others.

"That sounds like a good plan," she said. "Khrazhti, I'll take the other watch, so you can wake me up." Without waiting for anyone to disagree, she rolled up in her cloak near the fire and closed her eyes.

CHAPTER

TWENTY-FOUR

There were no disturbances during the night, either on Khrazhti's watch or on the short stint Marla did. Most of the others woke as the first rays of the new day's sun filtered through the trees. All but Raki. She had to nudge the boy—several times—before he would actually sit up.

By that time, Marla was well familiar with their little open area. She watched the bushes as the light grew brighter, wondering if any more of those little animals would start moving around them, foraging or whatever they did to greet the new day. The only movements and sounds were from her companions, though.

Master Yxna dropped her pack next to the log Marla was sitting on and sat down next to her, chewing some bread with pieces of dried meat and cheese in between.

"Apatholonus," she said.

Master Yxna looked at her. "What?"

"Apatholonus. From Raki's story last night. His name. Do you think the root of the Aloqotim word for *apathy* came from that story?"

The master smirked at Marla. "I would expect that to be a correct assumption. Interesting."

They sat silently for a moment before Marla spoke again.

"I was thinking about it while I was on watch," Marla told the master. "This place is called Iracundia."

"Yes."

"And that means, roughly, wrath."

"It does."

"Who named it? I mean, I totally agree that the name is appropriate. Not only does the place piss me off on general principle, but it seems a lot easier for me to get angry here. I felt it from the first footstep on the beach."

The master finished chewing her food and swallowed, nodding her head gently. "I felt it, too. Still do."

"The thing is," Marla continued, "according to what everyone has said, no one who ever set foot on the island ever left. If everyone was killed—or disappeared, or whatever—how would anyone know about the angry environment of the place to name it?"

"I don't know for sure, but I have my suspicions," Master Yxna said. "Remember that the land was split and the waters poured in many thousands of years ago. From then until now, there were people on Dizhelim. During the height of the Age of Magic, there were powerful mages walking the world. The magic of this place, and the monsters and magic of the waters, were also exponentially stronger than now. That means that though a skilled mage could survive the dangers the way they are now, she wouldn't have been able to withstand them then. What they probably could do, though, was to sense the magic and *personality* of the island from offshore, without setting foot onto the dangerous place. It would only take one such attentive explorer to give this island the appropriate name."

"Huh. That makes sense. I'm still not certain about how dangerous this place is, though. Sure, it's irritating, but we've been here almost a day and gotten at least a few miles in from the water, but we're fine. If we turned back now and signaled Captain Asgeir to pick us up, we'd have already done what no other person before ever has. At least as far as we know. It seems so easy. A group of completely mundane explorers could have accomplished what we did so far, killing one crazy rat thing."

"You're assuming that going back will be the same as getting to this point. Maybe the island—or whatever magic or monster is here—knows we plan on going futher, so it's not in a hurry to attack. If someone tried to step onto the beach and planned only to do that and leave, they might get attacked right away."

"That's imbuing a lot of intelligence in this place," Marla said.

"True, but better to prepare for intelligence and be met with the lack of it than to expect thoughtlessness and be confronted with clever thinking."

"Touché."

After her long sleep, even though she had to get up earlier than the others to take the final watch, Marla had high hopes for the day. She wasn't sure how wide the island was, but Captain Asgeir had told her it was much longer from northeast to southwest than it was wide. They were currently heading southeast, so it was clear to her they were cutting across the narrow part of the land mass. Maybe the day would bring them to the source of the magic she felt and she could solve that mystery.

They pushed through the tangled vegetation as they

had the day before. Not needing to worry about strangers seeing her blue skin, Khrazhti had removed her cloak and strode through the plants with the small articles of clothing she normally wore. The temperature was mild, and the plants didn't seem to snag on her smooth skin as they did on Marla's clothes. Maybe the animaru had a good idea there.

The amount of light they saw through the trees dimmed a couple hours into their trip and the air gave the feeling of a coming storm. Sure enough, the soft patter of rain on the upper boughs of the trees confirmed that it had indeed started raining. If there was one good thing about the infernal forest they traveled through, it was that the leaves above them were so thick, little of the rain actually made it through to them. They could hear it, but she only felt a few small drops.

Until the sound grew as the rain came harder.

Within an hour, it seemed that they were in a proper storm, with more of the water getting through, sometimes in big splashes as it collected on upper branches and leaves and suddenly gave way. One such miniature deluge struck her shoulder, splashing water down her left side. She growled at the thought of traveling wet.

A few more close calls and she decided it was time to put on her cloak. Getting through the forest was bad enough without doing so wet. The temperature had dropped with the rain and, although it wasn't chilly, it was cool. That combined with damp clothes would at least make things uncomfortable, if not dangerous. Evon put his cloak on at the same time, either seeing her and thinking it was a good idea or having the thought at the same time as she did. Master Yxna didn't bother, she couldn't see Raki to know if he took out his cloak, and Khrazhti continued on, the only indication that she was getting wet the look of wonder on her face at water falling from the sky. She'd been in rain before, but it was still a novelty to the animaru.

Within ten minutes, the whole situation had Marla cursing out loud. If plowing through the trees and plants was bad with a full set of clothes on, doing it with a cloak was ten times worse. She tried to wrap it tightly around her —even using a short length of rope to tie it in place—but every plant within a quarter mile successfully snagged the cloak and slowed her pace. It got caught so thoroughly a few times, she thought she might lose the article of clothing completely. The worst part was that while she wrestled with it, trying to keep it on her body and prevent it from getting torn, she scraped the branches of other plants with her clothes underneath. Every drop of water on all those leaves transferred to her and soaked into her pants and her leather armor.

The end result was that she took her cloak off, rolled it up, and tied it to the outside of her pack. She was already soaked all the way through, so there was no need to cover up anymore. For the briefest of moments, she took consolation—almost a little bit of pleasure—that Evon had suffered a similar fate. It was then that the forest decided to reward her smugness by allowing one of the large splashes to land in the exact center of the top of her head.

It was like someone had dumped a large bucket of water on her from several feet above. It soaked her hair to the scalp, drenched her shoulders, and ran down between her breasts and past her belly. It finally stopped just below her navel, which she appreciated. Cold water up top was bad enough, but to have it drench her nether regions would be plain horrible.

One step was all it took until the world figuratively

kicked her right in the crotch. The wind whipped up in a gust, knocked another thousand gallons of water—or something similar to that—from the trees above, and slammed it full on her front to gush down her pants. She thought she'd been cold already, but that little maneuver sucked the breath right out of her lungs.

"Gods damned forest," she growled, face down as she did the only thing she could: push on. If she looked up and saw someone—like Evon—smirking at her, not all the gods who left Dizhelim could stop her from murdering him.

Thankfully, that was the worst of the experience in the storm for her. Of course, there wasn't much worse it could get, so that went without saying. She was cold, uncomfortable, and soaked through and through as she led the others toward the magic only she could feel. She threw all of her mind toward getting to it so she could solve its mystery and leave the thrice-damned island.

It was because of that focus that she didn't notice when the rain actually stopped. In fact, she not only missed the ceasing of the showers, it was some time before the aftereffects of the storm, the incessant dripping and draining, tapered off.

When she finally recognized it, something deep within her pushed the idea into her head that maybe, just maybe, things would improve. The heat of her anger was keeping her warm, and she wasn't sure exactly where the hope came from, but she let it pass. It *could* happen. Sometimes things worked out.

As she should have known, that was when the first of the rat creatures showed its ugly, half-bald, scraggly head.

CHAPTER

TWENTY-FIVE

Khrazhti missed Aeden.

The former leader of the animaru enjoyed her other friends, had grown close to them, but not as much as she had with Aeden. The training each morning, the things he taught her about the still-strange world of Dizhelim, even the way he reacted to things and interacted with others, all of these made her feel more comfortable. Less an outsider.

Not that her friends did anything to make her feel isolated. It was not something she could explain, even to herself. She found part of her mind wondering what he was doing as she was walking through the plants on the strange island they had come to.

A flicker of movement caught her senses. It wasn't something that she could see with her eyes, only a feeling. When she turned to see what it was, she saw nothing. Raki. He was learning quickly, once he had realized that embracing his gifts would not turn him into some monster. Khrazhti still felt the strongest connection with Aeden, Fahtin, and Raki. It was to be expected, since they were a family, as Aeden had explained it. She had been with them the longest as well.

Marla was truly Aeden's family, though, through blood. A sister from birth, a twin. That had been explained to her, adding to the miracle of live birth that she had yet to actually witness. Shouldn't Khrazhti feel an unbreakable connection to Marla as well? She was fond of the volatile red-haired woman. Red. Before she came to this place, she did not truly know what the word meant. It was a beautiful color, the color of fire and mixed into the spectacular sunsets she had seen. A color Marla shared with Lily.

Khrazhti realized her mind was wandering. There were so many things in this new world she wanted to learn about, to experience. The water that had fallen earlier, this rain, it still amazed her. She was glad it had stopped because it seemed to irritate Marla. The others, too, but more powerfully with Marla. Khrazhti could not determine why Aeden's sister had been so prone to anger lately. She would like to help, but didn't understand or know enough to do so. Maybe she would find a way to aid her friend, if she paid close attention.

Emotions were still something Khrazhti wrestled with. She felt them, though not as strongly as her friends. Even pure animaru had emotions, though mostly they'd suppressed them over their thousands of years of life. Anger and hatred were the most common of those displayed. Usually by the most powerful and intelligent of the animaru, for some reason. Was there a relation between capacity for thought and those emotions?

Marla had gotten very angry when water had fallen on her. She looked at the ground and silently continued to lead them toward where she felt the magic she sought. Khrahzti couldn't understand why she would be annoyed at getting wet. It was logical to expect that result when water fell from the very sky. She hoped the mood would pass soon. She did not enjoy seeing Marla so distraught.

As she thought it, the woman's head snapped up and she muttered another curse. She was not as clever as Aeden, cursing in several different languages so that his companions would need extensive knowledge to understand the intricacies of the words he used. Marla's were straightforward and not as humorously unprobable as Aeden's were.

Movement near Marla's feet snatched Khrazhti's attention and she understood her friend's reaction. It appeared to be another one of those creatures from the day before, the one Raki had killed as everyone else was still trying to move quickly enough to do so. That had made Khrazhti proud of the boy, though she did feel sad it had bothered him that he accomplished with reflex what the rest of them could not do consciously.

Another grey blur from Khrazhti's other side, near Evon, arrested her attention again. Then, movement from two places at once. There were at least two of the creatures skittering around them. They almost reminded her of biuri, the type of animaru that skittered around low to the ground, fast and nimble. These creatures seemed to have a light behind their eyes, though, which no animaru did. Well, none but her.

"Ouch!" Marla shouted. "The little bastard bit me."

That meant there were at least three of the creatures around them. It also meant they were not innocently running around foraging, if they had attacked Marla. Khrazhti wondered if they would have done so if Raki hadn't killed one of them the day before. They didn't seem intelligent, but she had little information on which to base that deduction.

All around Khrazhti, her friends took out their weapons. She did not, not yet. She would observe and see if she could arrive at any conclusions about the creatures first. If they attacked *her*, she had plenty of options to defend herself from something so small without using her swords.

Marla slashed at something near the ground, Evon doing the same thing several paces away. Master Yxna was tracking something moving around her, but had not attacked yet. Raki, barely discernible within the plants, had not loosed another one of his throwing weapons, as far as she could see. He was probably still despondent about killing the one from the day before.

As she watched the others, one of the creatures boldly skittered up to her, its mouth wide to bite at her leg. It was swift, but Khrazhti's reflexes engaged and she kicked the thing before it was able to latch its teeth onto her. It squealed as she sent it skipping across the ground to slam into a tree trunk a few feet away. It shrieked again—either in pain or in anger—but skittered off to find an easier target.

The speed and erratic way in which the scraggly animals moved kept the weapons swung at them from striking, and it seemed that more of the creatures were joining in the attack by the moment. Even Evon was cursing under his breath, and Marla was shouting obscenities loud enough that Khrazhti was glad she was not standing closer to the red-haired woman.

"Gah!" Evon said. "Those little teeth hurt. They're too fast for me. It's like they can predict where my weapon will be. I can't..." He trailed off, then expelled a hissing breath as he slid his sword back into the scabbard. With a few simple gestures of his hand, he stood still, watching. Waiting.

One of the things scurried from the bushes to bite Evon

and he motioned toward it, muttering something too low to be understood. Half a dozen pellets of pure fire shot out from his hand at his attacker. The creature, to its credit, twisted in its approach and successfully dodged half the magical bullets, but not all. Three of them drilled through it, blowing chunks of it out on the other side. It shrieked and skidded as one of its legs failed. Evon didn't hesitate to stomp on the thing's head and finish it off.

Khrazhti had been wondering how the young man had been doing with his difficulties with fighting. Since she had met back up with the others after being in the highlands with Aeden, Evon had been having issues with combat and the need for it. For now, at least, it looked like he had reconciled his feelings. It was good. She knew that not all things could be fixed by violence—something she had learned since coming to Dizhelim—but there *were* times it was necessary. Like now. If there was another way of convincing the creatures to refrain from attacking, she did not know what it was.

Marla, seeing Evon's success, returned her own sword to its scabbard and started casting spells. Even Master Yxna, the Master of the School of Edged Weapons, opted for casting simple offensive spells. Khrazhti was happy to see it. Some warriors insisted on using their most powerful or skillful attacks, even if the circumstances demanded something else. That the master would use magic, even if not as skillfully as melee combat, showed Khrazhti that the master was truly insightful and not haughty.

Another creature came at Khrazhti and she decided it was time to join her friends in what they were doing. A dark bolt of magic cast from her hand took the creature before it was five feet from her and turned it into an unrecognizable piece of seared flesh.

It was easier to hit the attackers with magic. Rather, the creatures were not as adept at dodging magic thrown at them as they were with swung weapons. Still, they were quick and some spells never found their targets.

Marla, if what Khrazhti heard during the fight was any indication, was getting more and more aggravated. The others were as well, it seemed, but it was stronger with Marla. After several minutes of work, the attacks stopped, and no more of the creatures skittered through the bushes. They had either killed them all or the things had decided to call off their attack.

"Damn, stupid, scraggly little assholes," Marla spat. "I hope we killed every one of the things that live here. Bite me, will they?"

Raki appeared in the midst of them and methodically began to retrieve the spikes and throwing stars he'd killed some of the creatures with. Evon and Marla compared the wounds they'd received from multiple bites from the animals. Even Master Yxna had taken a small bite on her ankle, and she was inspecting it. Krazhti felt fortunate she had not been bitten, though part of it may have been her animaru nature. Animals, she had noticed, didn't like to bite animaru. Even dead, scavengers would leave animaru corpses to rot rather than to eat them.

"Are you...well?" Khrazhti asked them all, but she had her eyes locked on Marla when she said it.

Marla's lips were curled into a sneer and she didn't bother answering, but Master Yxna responded. "I think we'll be fine, Khrazhti. Were you bitten?"

"No. They did not appear to like my smell enough to want a taste."

The master chuckled. "Good luck for you." She turned to Marla. "We should probably heal these wounds, maybe do a delving to see if they poisoned us or gave us a disease."

"It wouldn't surprise me," Marla said. "Little bastards."

The others traded looks, but did not seem to want to say anything for fear of setting Marla off again.

Evon and Marla knew spells to detect disease and poison, and none of them had the afflictions, so in no time, the wounds were healed and the group headed out again, with no other sign they had been attacked than some blood stains on their clothes and Marla's bad mood.

The terrain took a definite dip, the land descending the way they were headed. It was not quite like going down a hill, but things were definitely sloping slightly, unlike the level ground they had been traveling on. Khrazhti could detect no real change in the trees and other vegetation around them, though she was not skilled at identifying different species like Aeden was. She followed Marla silently, as the others did, scanning their surroundings for anything that might attack them.

To Khrazhti's eyes, Marla became more and more agitated as they continued through the forest. The Academy graduate shook her head, muttered to herself, even kicked at the plants as she went. It made no sense to the animaru. They had left behind the bodies of the creatures that had attacked them and the forest. While the terrain was perhaps not any easier to traverse than before, it certainly was not significantly harder than it had been since they entered it.

Marla stopped abruptly and turned to face the others. Her right hand clenched into a fist and loosened, only to clench again. She closed her eyes for a moment, as if preparing for battle or some distasteful task.

"If you don't mind, I'd like to cut travel short today. Any

place we can find in the next hour or so that'll work for a camp for the night...I'd like to stop there."

"Marla?" Master Yxna said. "Are you okay?"

"I...need to stop. To meditate a little bit. Get centered. Please."

She turned and started back through the plants, fist still clenching and her back seeming a stone wall to any who would question her.

CHAPTER

TWENTY-SIX

hat the hell is going on? Marla thought to herself. True, she'd been having anger issues for a few weeks now, but this was ridiculous. It was almost like some cosmic power had put those little monsters on Dizhelim specifically to piss her off. It wasn't bad enough she had to deal with the forest, the strange magical pulling, and people in general. No, ugly little biting rodent-things had to be added to the mix.

She seriously wondered if Moschephis hadn't actually left Dizhelim. Maybe the God of Mischief had stayed and waited until Marla was born, grew to deal with all the bullshit in the world, and get good and ripe for him to poke her with a stick. That was as likely an explanation as she'd thought of so far.

The others no doubt thought she was crazy, wanting to stop with hours of daylight yet during which they could travel. For all any of them knew, the source of whatever was drawing her might be a few miles away.

She didn't care. The anger burning in her right that very minute was strong enough that it threatened to take over at any time. Anything else—attack by creatures, another rainstorm, stubbing her toe—could send her over the edge.

Like Ivel.

There was no arguing. She needed to stop, plunge herself deep into soothing meditation, separate herself from everything and everyone. It wasn't a matter of convenience; it was a safety thing. Safety for her friends. She'd even thought of trying to smack Master Yxna once, earlier in the day. Master Yxna! As if anyone alive *could* smack that woman, prepared or not.

As she mechanically pushed her way toward the magic she felt, not even really seeing where she was going, she clenched both her fists, digging her nails into her palms painfully to give her something to focus on. She didn't know how long after she had told the others that she wanted to stop that a voice broke into her walking trance.

"Marla?" She blinked and turned. Master Yxna was only a couple of steps from her. "I asked if this place would do. It seems as good as we're going to get."

Marla found she was standing in a slight depression. It looked like something had happened in the past and several big trees had been uprooted, maybe in a storm, tearing their roots and soil up. All the missing chunks formed the bowl, though there was no evidence of any fallen trees. How long ago would that have had to happen for there to be no trace of wreckage? Regardless, the small crater was relatively clear of trees, if not of other plants. Even those, though, seemed fewer than most other places they'd been through.

"Yes," she said. "Yes, this will work fine. Thank you." She had to work hard to force out that last part, not because she didn't appreciate it, but because when she was in a pique, gratitude came hard.

The others had been waiting for her decision and as she gave her agreement, they dropped their packs and went into motion, searching for firewood and clearing a space to build a fire.

"We'll take care of it," Master Yxna said, shifting her head and narrowing her eyes to peer into Marla's. "Go ahead and do your meditation."

Marla nodded to the master and found a nice patch of grass to sit on. She put her pack down beside her and sank into a cross-legged position Master Jusha had taught her so many years ago. It wasn't strictly necessary, of course, but once she'd developed the habit for sitting that way, it always made her more comfortable to use it. She could use every edge she could get right now.

She plunged into herself, counting on her friends to guard her and let her know if danger approached as she put herself in a completely undefended position.

It was like swimming against the current in a rushing river. Her mind, wild as the emotion welling up in her, refused to be calm. Try as she might to clear it, images of things from earlier in the day and over the last week and more inundated her. Unruly students, inconsiderate people, capture by the Arunai, attack by little creatures that shouldn't have even been able to bother her. Everything wrapped up into one big swirl of color, resolving itself into that fateful day so many years ago when she had witnessed the ultimate result of anger taking over every facet of a person's faculties.

Ivel Danson. She remembered his eyes, could see them now. Visibly clouded with rage, drilling into Sharan Kolga just before he actually attacked the fellow student.

This was doing nothing but aggravating her further. Marla clamped down on her mind, applied her powerful will to it. Gradually, step by tiny step, she wrested control of her thoughts from the images that came to her unbidden. If she could sweat within her mind, she had no doubt she would be drenched, but still she pushed on.

Master Jusha had taught her a relatively simple but powerful technique when he first introduced her to meditation. To clear her mind of things, she imagined a raging fire. It was controlled, a bonfire built and lit specifically for her benefit, so though she could feel its warmth and see its glow, she had no fear it would unleash its power on her or the world.

As she was taught, she pictured every thing that prevented her from obtaining a blank, calm mind. All emotion, distraction, and extraneous thing she laid out in a line for inspection. Those students—not the people, but an image representing their actions and annoying tendencies, sat there in front of her. Likewise, all the other things weighing on her mind, stomping on her nerves, irritating her. There were quite a few of them, and those were only the very recent—and admittedly, relatively minor—triggers to her anger and her distraction. She wasn't about to focus on thngs such as being the hero prophesied thousands of years ago or the responsibility for saving the world itself. There was only so much meditation and a strong will could mitigate.

Each of the items lined up in front of her, she picked up and casually tossed into the bonfire. As soon as each hit the flames, they flared and were incinerated instantly instead of burning slowly. She could feel her mind easing as each annoyance ceased to exist, even for a brief moment.

When she reached the end of the line, the object representing the rat creatures, she threw it with more force than necessary into the fire and sighed when it flashed out of existence.

She relaxed for what seemed the first time in ages, her mind not harboring dozens of disparate thoughts vying for her attention. Now all she had to do was to...

Some kind of energy spiked in her, shocking her enough that if she had eyes in the place within her mind, they would have snapped open. At first, she couldn't pinpoint what was wrong, but whatever it was felt dangerous.

Then she realized what it was. The fire. Her bonfire, the construct she had created to help her attain calmness and to purge the unwanted thoughts from her mind, it was jerking. Twitching. Growing.

She could sense the intent within the fire, seeking a target for its wrath. With invisible coils, it snatched her and began to squeeze, the heat that was so comforting just moments before now becoming painful.

Marla writhed, trying to get loose, but with every struggle, the flame wrapped itself tighter around her, pulling her in farther until she was actually within the fire itself.

Not sure if she had shrunk or if the fire had grown larger, Marla found herself swimming in a sea of red, orange, and yellow, swirling and spiraling toward the base of the flame. She didn't know for sure what would happen if she reached that base, but she thought it might destroy her utterly. She didn't want to find out.

With powerful strokes, she swam away from the pulling. Within seconds, her powerful arms and legs were fatigued and, though she'd managed to remain in place while fighting the current, her tired muscles were now failing and she slid downward, toward her eventual end. Another burst of energy, throwing everything she had into trying to escape, and she managed to move a few feet toward the freedom outside the flame's body, but it didn't last long.

The whirlpool within the fire, not air and not flame but some kind of liquid, turned her around and snatched her up. As she spun crazily, her vision wasn't able to keep up with the turning and she shut it off, like closing her eyes if she'd had them in this place. With a sick lurching, her body flipped through the medium surrounding her as she prepared for her own destruction.

Marla's eyes snapped open and she let out a startled cry, falling backward from her cross-legged position to flop onto the grass on her back. She blinked rapidly, trying to make sense of where she was and what was happening, but it all came too slow.

"Marla?" Master Yxna said, suddenly there beside her.

Marla recognized the master after a moment and threw her arms around the woman, holding onto her like she was a rope able to pull her out of the whirlpool she'd been in. Master Yxna patted her back gently as Marla sobbed like a beaten child, her friends watching the display from a distance.

Marla wasn't sure how long she stayed in Master Yxna's arms, but by the time she extracted herself, she was almost tired enough to fall asleep immediately. The master wasn't going for that, though, apparently.

"What happened?"

Marla slumped, trying to figure out the best way to explain it. She decided the best thing to do was to describe it completely. After she did so, with as much detail as she could muster, she looked around at her friends, half expecting looks of incredulity or rolling eyes. What she found was sincere concern.

"I've never known Master Jusha's relaxation techniques

to fail," Evon said. "I've been feeling agitated since we got here, too, but that sounded pretty extreme."

"How do you feel now, Marla?" Master Yxna asked.

"Tired."

"Yes. I mean, how do you feel insofar as your anger and irritation are concerned?"

"Better. A little. This place still grates on me, but I'm not contemplating trying to kill any of you right now."

Evon smirked at her. "Well, that's an improvement, anyway."

TWENTY-SEVEN

The next day's travel started the same way as it had since they'd arrived on the island. They packed their gear up, ate a little, and Marla led them toward their destination. Wherever that was.

This time, it was less than an hour before they ran into trouble.

Movement in the corner of Marla's vision stopped her as her hand found its way to her sword's hilt. She scanned the area—the same type of vegetation they'd been slogging through before—and couldn't pick up what she had thought she'd seen.

"Did any of you see something?"

Her question was responded to with shakes of the head.

A dozen steps more and more motion snapped her head around just in time to see something grey disappear in the foliage. It wasn't the pale grey of the rat things, but a little darker, and it was more than three feet off the ground. Definitely not the creatures they'd seen before. She waited for a few minutes, trying to catch sight of it again, but it didn't reappear.

That started a game of hide-and-seek with whatever it was. Over the next hour, she *almost* spotted it several more times, but didn't get anything more than a flash past her vision.

The whole thing was starting to piss her off.

"Isn't anyone seeing this thing? I mean, it's been several times now I've seen it. You haven't even caught any motion out of the corner of your eye? Nothing?"

"We're looking," Evon said. "You're up in front, so you'd see it before we would be able to."

Marla grumbled at that, but had to admit he had a point. It seemed that all she could do was to keep looking as they traveled and hope she wasn't hallucinating the entire thing. Even one partial sighting by the others would make her feel better.

It came when she had given up on anyone else corroborating what she'd seen.

"I just saw something," Raki said, materializing far off to the left of where Marla was. "I thought if I strayed out to the edges, I might, and I did. It was a grey streak. It looked like smoke, but it wasn't rising. It was filtering through the plants at about chest height."

"It sounds like the same thing," Marla said. "Thanks, Raki. That means I'm not going crazy."

"Or it means we both are," the boy said.

"Yeah. Or that."

As they continued, the sightings increased. Marla got a few good looks at the things—they did look like smoke traveling the wrong way—and the others spotted them, too. They couldn't tell if it was the same one or more than one, but as they continued smashing through the plants, they all kept an eye out for the things.

All at once, several of the figures rushed in on them

from the sides. At least six of them slithered forward, looking like snakes made from smoke. Because of their incorporeal appearance, Marla didn't bother with her weapons, but cast a protective shield on herself.

The smoke creature passed right through it. Not only that, but when it touched the skin on her arm, it stung like she'd been bitten.

"Ouch."

"Ow."

"Gah."

It seemed that the smoke things had bitten Evon and Raki, too, by their exclamations.

The one that had touched Marla lazily circled around and came back at her. She let her shield drop and cast Flame Wash toward it, hoping that even though the thing resembled smoke, it was susceptible to magical fire.

It wasn't. Instead of showing in any way that it took damage, the thing went at her face and stung her there. If anything, it hurt more than the previous contact.

"I can't hit it," Evon called out.

"Me, either," Raki agreed as he became visible just in time to slash one of his knives through the closest creature.

Marla noted Master Yxna, cutting through two of the things, without any evidence her weapons had done anything to them. Even Khrazhti, who casted spells that blasted out darkness in three different forms didn't do so much as change the trajectory the weird smoke-snakes were flying.

Another sting on the back of Marla's shoulder, right where she knew there was a tiny gap between her leather pauldrons and her chestpiece, fired her reflexes to slash ineffectually at the thing attacking her.

She could only describe the pain, woefully familiar to

her by now, as a cross between a low-level shock from a lightning bolt and an injection of poison. The crazy thing was that it did no visible damage, caused no bleeding, and didn't affect her limbs as a cut or blood loss would. There was the instantaneous pain, which lingered for a second or two, but no other effects she could distinguish.

Aside from driving her into a rage at being so helpless.

"This is really starting to get on my nerves," Evon said, trying to damage one of the creatures with fire missiles.

Marla almost felt better about others being angry, since she'd spent the whole time on the island fighting with that emotion, but it was no real consolation. She could see the others getting frustrated, attacking recklessly and muttering to themselves. All of them but Khrazhti, that is. The animaru still tried to attack the creatures, but she did so in a methodical and measured way. A way that was beyond Marla at the moment.

When she got stung on both arms at the same time, Marla flipped out a little bit, whirling and slashing with both blades, then sheathing both and casting Gale, which she had a good feeling would work. After all, the spell blasted a powerful force of air from her all around her and the things were made of smoke. Logic told her they'd be blown away. Not that logic was the guiding principle at the time.

Somehow, the smoke-snakes didn't move an inch. Not a ripple disturbed them, though plants were flattened nearly ten feet around her. Unfortunately, Evon and Raki were also knocked down and Master Yxna was forced backward as she twisted to keep her balance. Khrazhti, who was the farthest away, didn't appear to be affected by the spell.

"Hey!" Evon said. "Watch it."

She ignored him, having other things on her mind at

the moment. Things like unbeatable creatures attacking them at will. She growled and started casting spell after spell to find one that would affect the monsters.

As she cast, part of Marla screamed for her to stop. Nothing good came from losing control in the middle of battle. She knew this, had been taught years ago and had ingrained it into her mind. Getting carried away by rage was a good way to lose a fight...and one's life.

She didn't care, though. The frustration from not being able to kill the creatures stinging her was too much. It wasn't clear how much the things could hurt her or her friends, but she wasn't about to stand there and let them attack her at will. She redoubled her effort to find an attack that would work as she suffered the stings of the creatures that didn't seem to react at all at her attempts to kill them.

"Aaarrrrrggghhhh!" she yelled, casting and slashing at the things. She couldn't remember ever being so frustrated, so mad. She had to find a way to destroy the things attacking them.

A heavy pounding through the vegetation struck her as odd. Was it one of her friends running at her? The smoke things didn't make any noise, didn't even touch the ground. A blazing line of pain slashed across the back of her left leg and she hissed at the pain. That hadn't been a sting from one of the smoke things.

True enough. She spotted another type of monster, this one midway in color between the rat things and the smoke things. It was grey as well, but its form was so much different.

The monster that had attacked her was an abomination she'd never seen nor heard of. It ran on two legs, each with three joints. Powerful muscles and conventional knees no doubt allowed the thing to jump well. The next joint, sort of a backward knee, led to the longest section of the thing's legs, down to an ankle that allowed huge three-toed claws to pivot. A short tail that ended with a curved spike emerged from the back of the creature. A head nearly as big as the rounded body of the thing, was covered with rough hide that looked like bark. A mouth filled with needle fangs split the head nearly in half, and a long tongue dangled from it like it was an overheated dog. The creature's beady black eyes, on either side of its head, locked onto Marla. The two appendages coming off the top of the body looked like ice picks, twitching as if to promise Marla that the sharp claws on them would do more of what the one with the point stained red had already done.

"Son of a..." she said, drawing both her blades.

The slash on the back of her leg had thankfully not hamstrung her. It was painful and one glance back told her she was bleeding, but she could still move. She lunged at the monstrous thing as movement all around her resolved itself into several more of the creatures.

The thing was quick, dancing on its two legs in a hopping, skittering kind of movement. Her first slash the monster actually blocked with its ice pick appendages, the clang of Marla's sword on it hardened claw ringing out in the midst of the other sounds of battle. She caught glimpses of the others fighting more of the bipedal creatures but nowhere she looked could she see any more of the smoke things. Had they turned into these new monsters?

While the attacker she was fighting kept her swords busy with blocking her blows and lashing out at her with its spikes, it snapped its tooth-filled head at her, trying to sink all those thin fangs into her. She had to roll out of the way to keep from getting bitten.

Unfortunately, she rolled right into the path of another

one of them, heading toward Evon. She and the monster slammed into each other, but luckily for both, neither had a chance to react with a skilled attack. The thing's hide felt like it looked: like a hardened leather sack full of rocks. The collision made stars explode in Marla's vision as she did her best to regain her feet from the roll.

When she was in a stable stance again, two of the monsters faced her. They took a moment to eye each other, then both opened their horrible mouths to screech at her, spittle flying from between the dozens of crooked, narrow and very sharp looking teeth.

Marla screamed back.

It seemed that was not the correct thing to do. It was almost like the monsters sensed something in her shout. They both lunged at her instantly, teeth ready to rend her flesh.

It was her reflexes that saved her. She still wasn't thinking straight, but her body reacted without her guidance, whirling as she stepped to the right. As the pair passed by, both stretching their necks to snap at her she rammed her sword down into the top of the closest monster's head. The blade made a satisfying pop as it punctured the thick skin, went through the brain, and continued on until she could see the point inside the thing's mouth. It dropped and slid, pulling itself off her sword.

"Yes!" she shouted. "These can be killed."

As the other attacker dug its claws into the ground to turn back toward her, Marla wondered if her friends had already discovered what she just announced like a green student in their first combat class. Whatever. She was just happy she could actually do some damage. She flicked the ichor off her blade and brought it back up, crossing it with her dueling dagger in a defensive posture.

The beast lunged at her, not even hesitating to consider its companion's body on the ground nearby. It slashed viciously at her with the two ice pick appendages, then performed an acrobatic move where it leapt into the air and swung its large claws out to cut into her. Marla dropped to the ground, allowing the whirling claws to pass over her and, just as the second passed, she swung as hard as she could with her sword to cut into the abomination's leg.

It was so tough, she wasn't able to cut through, but it landed awkwardly, rolling onto its side and trying to come back up onto its feet. She must have damaged something within the leg, though, because it couldn't hold the creature's weight. It listed to the side as it snapped at her with its mouth.

Marla rammed her sword into its maw, hoping she'd hit something vital before all those teeth in its long mouth could clamp down on her. She shifted her body to bring the dagger in her left hand around and over, driving the point into the monster's little black eye. As the shorter blade penetrated the creature's head, she released her sword, which had already gone far enough that some of its teeth would definitely get her hand if she kept hold on it. She pulled it free just in time to avoid its slamming jaws.

Then it jerked three times and stopped moving.

Marla looked around and found more of the strange roundish creatures dead or dying. The last one she saw fighting was in front of Master Yxna, who danced around it and cut into it four times in the space of a breath. Both of the appendages on its upper body and half its head spun off into the blood-soaked bushes.

"Clear?" Marla called.

"Clear," Evon said, followed by Master Yxna, Raki, and

then finally Khrazhti when she figured out what they were doing.

Marla pried open the mouth of the last creature she had killed and carefully extracted her sword. It had gone down the gullet of the monster. She wasn't sure if it had hit anything vital, but she did know that the dagger through the eye was what had killed it.

"These things bleed red blood," she said, not quite sure why she was noting the fact.

"Most creatures on Dizhelim do," Master Yxna answered.

"Did anyone see what happened to those smoke-snakes? Did they turn into these?"

"I do not think so," Khrazhti said as she wiped blood from her swords using a patch of moss she'd found. "I saw the others flee before these showed up."

"Why?" Marla asked. "They could have kept at us all day, chipping away. Why leave? Were they afraid of these things?" She kicked the carcass closest to her.

"How about we move out of the area before we deconstruct our performance," Master Yxna said. The master sounded...irritated.

"Yeah. Right. We need to head this way." Marla did one last sweep of the trampled down area and headed toward the source of whatever was pulling her onward.

CHAPTER
TWENTY-EIGHT

Marla led the group another mile through the foliage before she stopped.

"What was that back there? Did anyone recognize either of those creatures? I can't think of any myths or legends that describe them."

"Me either," Evon said. "That makes three so far. Every moving thing in this place is unfamiliar. For all I know, the plants might be, too. I don't know a lot about identifying species of trees and things, so I'm not sure."

"I've noticed several that I think might be thought extinct or have never been recorded before," Master Yxna said. "Quite a place we have wandered into."

"Yeah," Marla said. "And if it's like that here, what are on the other islands farther out?"

Raki raised his hand, which he often did when he didn't want to interrupt a conversation. Marla nodded at him to speak.

"How do we know there are other islands if no one has been able to go out into the seas?"

"That's a very good question, Raki," Master Yxna said.

"The simple answer is that land has been sighted from ships off-shore up the coast, near Horizon and Squalls Landing, and also farther down southwest near the Black-pool Swamp, below Campastra. None have been able to get to them yet, as far as I know, but it's clear that there are at least two more islands or landmasses we know nothing about. For all we know, they could be bigger than Promistala, though that's doubtful. The ancient myths seem to indicate that the bigger part of the one continent stayed intact as Promistala and the other parts split up to the south."

"Oh. I wonder how many there are altogether."

"We have other stuff to talk about, though," Marla said. "If we were in doubt about those rat things attacking us, there is none as far as the smoke-snakes and those...those things with the sharp claws and spikes. I can understand more now why no one has ever seen what's on this island and returned."

"Do you suspect there is intelligence behind the attacks, and the timing?" Khrazhti asked. "I did not notice evidence that our attackers were particularly smart."

Marla hesitated, not wanting to engage in wild conjecture. She wasn't sure if the things she was thinking were logical assumptions or related to the difficulties in thinking clearly she'd been having of late, especially since coming to Iracundia. When none of the others answered, she decided she might as well. Her friends would tell her if she was fabricating explanations.

"I think you're right, Krazhti. They didn't seem all that intelligent on their own. I did notice something, though. Like the rat things, those smoke creatures harried us, irritated us. It was even worse than the rats because we couldn't damage the smoke-snakes at all. The only thing we could do was to try ineffectually while they continued to sting us or bite us or whatever it is they do. I don't think I'm alone in being antagonized and getting angry."

"You're not alone," Evon said. "The frustration kept building until I could barely think. I lost my temper and control completely. I didn't want anything else in the world more than to destroy those monsters."

"Me, too," Raki said.

Master Yxna nodded.

Marla eyed Khrazhti, but she wasn't even sure the animaru could have her emotions driven to those lengths. She was half human, but it might not be enough. The animaru woman did display emotions, but she hadn't fully embraced—or been subjected to—them yet.

"It seems too coincidental to me," Marla continued. "Almost like they were specially designed or deployed to rile us up. To stoke our anger."

"You make a good point," Master Yxna said. "If the creatures were controlled, they could be used to do what you suggest. But why?"

"That's a question we have been facing a lot lately. Why mess with our minds, why attack nature itself, why twist our sense of honor or challenge our sense of what knowledge really is?" She jerked her head toward Raki. "Why dangle the power of darkness in front of us and make things happen to indicate that it might cause our own destruction?"

Master Yxna cocked her head at Marla. "I'm not sure exactly what you're getting at."

Evon took up the conversation. "Over the last several months, we've been confronted with all these things. Each time, it ended up with us finding a Well of Power."

"You think there is a well here, on this island?"

"Maybe. Possibly. Probably. We still don't really know anything about the wells. Are they all under the control of someone—or something—else or do they actually think for themselves? It could be they were created for a specific reason, one we haven't yet discovered. Their creators may not even be around anymore."

"The gods?" Master Yxna asked.

"Who knows?" Marla said. "The point is—my point, anyway—is that it seems clear that for whatever reason, the creatures in this place are meant to increase angry feelings. Whether that's to feed something that eats such emotions or it's simply to make it easier to kill us, well, that's anyone's guess. All of this is too coincidental. The island being named wrath, the strange feelings that drive us toward annoyance, creatures that seem custom-designed to entice our rage. I'm guessing it does have something to do with a well. It's too much like other wells we've found."

"Okay," Evon said. "Let's say it is a well. Let's call it the Well of Anger, though I've never heard of anger magic before. What do we do different than what we have so far?"

Marla threw up her hands. "I have no idea. I think all we can do is to keep following whatever it is that's drawing me to it. Let's assume it's a well. Maybe by knowing the trick it's playing on us, we can think our way through it."

"That's not much to go on," Master Yxna said.

Marla barked a laugh. "Welcome to what our lives have been like the last half year. It's something our briefings and reports can't describe accurately. It's why I've been such a mess lately. 'Sure, be the Malatirsay. Save the world. Oh, and by the way, we're going to fuck with your mind and make you question your sanity at every turn.'"

Master Yxna narrowed her eyes at Marla.

"That's pretty much it," Evon said. "I've seriously considered several times whether or not I had actually lost my mind."

"Me, too," Raki said. "It's been...hard."

"Our travels have been difficult for all of us," Khrazhti admitted. "I experience the tension and I have observed it in all of my friends. Such things are not normal for you on this world?"

Marla laughed again. "Uh, no. Not like this. Are things like that on Aruzhelim?"

"They are not. Constantly, there is posturing and animaru lords scheming and engaging in combat, but the... feeling is not there. I assumed it was a natural feature of this world, as well as my struggle to reconcile with my human half."

"I'm sorry," Master Yxna said. "I never really thought about it. I sit and listen to your reports of what happened, but aside from your problems recently, Marla, I hadn't given much thought to how it all was affecting you mentally and emotionally. Feeling a little bit of it on this trip makes me understand more, enough for me to apologize that I haven't done more to help. When we return to the Academy, I will be discussing it at length with Master Qydus."

"Thank you. Before we can do that, though, we need to finish here. We need to get to the bottom of all this, especially if we're dealing with a well. There is a bright ray of sunshine in all this, though."

"There is?" Evon said.

"Of course. I have my two objectives, to find the source of the magic pulling on me and to get my anger under control. With what we just discussed, I'm thinking we'll be solving both problems at the same time. You know, either that, or the island will kill us."

No more than half an hour after they set out again, Marla stopped and put her hand up for the others to do so as well.

"Do you hear that?"

Khrazhti nodded, tilting her head to aim her ear at where Marla thought the sound was coming from.

"I don't—" Evon started.

"Shhh."

Standing still and hardly breathing, the entire group listened. Nothing further came to Marla's ears and she thought for a moment she was imagining it, then a screech floated toward them on the wind, with a few other sounds, so subliminal she knew she was only catching the spikes in the sound, not the true noise.

"Screams?" Evon said, wincing at how loud his voice sounded and probably the memory of being shushed a few minutes before.

"Sounds like it."

"Should we go see what it is?" he asked.

"No. It's probably just different types of monsters running into each other."

"Do the creatures do such a thing?" Khrazhti asked. "We saw no evidence of that. In fact, we detected no sign of any of the animals anywhere until they attacked us. Your supposition that they exist to attack outsiders and drive them to anger seems accurate to me."

"Maybe," Marla said, "but it could also be a way to lure us to them. If we go and investigate, we might walk right into a trap. Whatever intelligence is leading the wildlife has already shown it can manipulate us. I'd rather have them coming after us than to walk into an ambush."

"Yes," the animaru said. "That is wise."

Despite being convinced she was correct, Marla couldn't help but to look back toward where the sound had come from. She didn't think whatever made the sound was close, but it was hard to tell in the forest. The trees and other plants were surprisingly good at diffusing or absorbing sound. Still, she turned to lead the others toward the magic she was following.

The terrain was definitely changing, the fern-like plants being replaced with woodier bushes with few leaves. Even the trees were progressively getting smaller as they continued, and the ground was becoming less soft. That last was probably the effect of fewer plants dropping their leaves to the forest floor to make the thick blanket of decaying vegetable matter they'd grown accustomed to. Even so, it seemed to transform too abruptly for Marla's liking.

The ground still slanted downward slightly as well, making Marla wonder how difficult the climb back up would be. It was hard to judge with the varied terrain and them going downward. She mentally shrugged. It didn't really matter. The important thing was to get to where they were going. The return trip they could put off thinking about until they were ready to leave.

More suddenly than she could have expected, Marla stepped out of the trees and plants into a different kind of landscape altogether. She had to put her hand up to shield her eyes because of the brightness of the unobstructed sun. It was high in the early afternoon sky, beating down on what appeared to be the site of some type of disaster.

Evon emerged right behind her, almost running into her as he was temporarily blinded by the bright light as well. The two of them stared out over what they'd found.

They were on the edge of a great bowl, miles wide. She

thought at first it might be a remnant from a colossal meteor strike, but then the wind shifted and she caught the tang of sulphur in the air. Using both hands to shield her eyes, she looked downward to spot steam or smoke below her. It wasn't from a campfire, but apparently came from the ground itself. It reminded her of Fyrefall.

"Volcanic?" Evon asked, following her gaze as he sniffed the air.

"Seems like it."

"Great."

Master Yxna came up alongside her and whistled. "That's a big bowl. It seems likely that there was a volcano here that erupted and then collapsed in on itself."

"Do we have to...?" Evon said, trailing off as he scanned the huge bowl.

Marla pointed down into the depression. "The magic I've been following comes from there. We're going to need to figure out how to best go down."

"Wonderful," Evon said. "Based on all the other good news, it's just what I expected to hear."

"Shut it," she told him. Ostensibly, it was a joke, but there was a certain bite within it as well. "The sooner we figure it out, the sooner we can find out what all of this is about and go home."

"Do you really think the island is going to let us just leave like that?"

Now that was a good question. So far, it had only irritated them and thrown some moderately dangerous monsters at them. What would it do when they tried to be the first people ever to see it and then leave?

"We can think about that later. First things first. Figure out how to get down there, decide what we need to do when we find what's been tugging me here, then we can think about the return trip." It sounded to her like she was parroting what she'd told herself a few minutes before.

They split up and searched around the edge of the bowl. It wasn't incredibly steep, but neither was it solid rock. More than anything, it seemed to Marla to be like a sink-hole, the edge and lip made of dirt that could crumble unexpectedly, sending them for a tumble of at least fifteen or twenty feet, more in some areas. They could survive a fall like that, but it could also break bones, something they definitely didn't need at the moment.

After close to an hour of their individual explorations, they reunited where they'd started and compared their findings.

"I did not see any paths downward that would provide us with a controlled descent," Khrazhti said.

"Same with me," Evon chimed in. "It's not that far down to the next bit of level ground, but it's steep. We might be able to slide down it, but it would be more like a fall than a graceful sliding."

"My part was farther down than it is here," Raki said.

"Nothing good where I checked out the terrain," Master Yxna stated.

"I'm not sure what to do, then," Marla said. "I'm a little embarrassed to be stuck on something so simple. There are a few places near here where we could probably slide down and not be injured too badly, though we'd have dirt inside our clothes and armor for the rest of the trip. Tie a rope to one of the trees and use it to rappel down? We should have enough if we tie all we have together."

Evon ran his hand through his hair. "That would prob-ably work. I'd hate to leave all our rope tied up here, though. If an animal chews it, we'll be stranded and we—"

All eyes snapped in the direction of the foliage from

which they had come. Something was crashing through the brush—or several somethings—and whatever it was wasn't small.

Two dark-skinned men emerged, both with bows. Before Marla could react, both of them loosed arrows in their direction.

CHAPTER
TWENTY-NINE

For a fraction of a second, Marla stared at the two men—they were actually human!—who had come from the forest. One of the two arrows loosed was coming straight at her and she ducked to the side, while flicking her dagger up out of the sheath to deflect the shaft as it passed through the space she had just been in. The motion parried the projectile upward, which she realized was a very good thing, since Evon was behind where she'd been standing. It missed him, too, luckily.

A flash of blue from her other side told Marla that Khrazhti had been the target of the second arrow. She wasn't sure what happened to it, but she didn't hear any grunts or yells, so she was fairly certain it didn't strike anyone.

The two men pulled other arrows from their quivers as they stepped to the side to take more stationary shots. Meanwhile, a flood of other people, dressed similarly to the tribe she had been captured by all those days ago, stomped toward them.

"Arunai," Marla shouted, as if her friends needed the identification. It was probably enough for them to know the attackers were shooting arrows at them.

Another arrow came at Marla from one of the others, but she's already snapped a shield in place and the missile pinged off the protection and off the edge of the bowl to get lost within the expanse of the depression.

As the other Arunai charged, Marla took a quick count. An even dozen. It shouldn't be a problem. All of Marla's friends were skilled, especially Master Yxna, not to mention they had magic on their side as well. As far as she knew, most Arunai warriors did not have magical abilities.

One of the men gestured and the rest of the tribes-people moved into position to attack. She tagged him mentally as the leader. He looked the part, tall and muscled, though in the supple way of the skilled Arunai warriors and not in the bulky way of some of the barbarian tribes from the Sittingham Desert. He withdrew two small hatchets from a sheath holding several more of them at a time and rushed toward her himself, only a step behind his warriors.

Of the twelve, four held bows and were using them to soften up Marla and her friends. Those would have to go first.

Using the method Master Yxna herself had drummed into Marla over several years, she quickly assessed the forces arrayed against her and her friends. The four archers were already accounted for. In addition, there were two men with spears, another with a heavy blade that resembled a machete—but with a thicker blades than she was accustomed to seeing—a genuinely massive man with what looked like a shaped thick portion of a tree trunk with a wicked axe blade on one side and spike on the other, a guy carrying an elaborate weapon that consisted of blades in a kind of pinwheel formation, a woman with a long-handled and long-bladed weapon, and a man wielding a pole with an axe head on on end and a metal banding on the other.

She was familiar with most of the weapons, at least in theory, but Marla had not fought against some of them before. Not that it mattered. Most weapons techniques were variations of perhaps a dozen basic systems.

Besides, she had magic. It was probably time to use it.

She quickly cast one of her go-to spells, Fire Missile. Interestingly, as the little pellets of condensed fire rocketing from her hand, another similar set shot out from Evon's.

Though a simple spell—one of the reasons it was easy to cast quickly—it could not be guided once loosed to change the trajectory in the air. Still, their aim was good. Evon's target took half a dozen of the missiles in his chest, earning himself holes that went all the way through his torso. Marla's ruined her target's face, punching through and leaving the man unrecognizable as he dropped to the ground.

A sort of negative flash indicated that Khrazhti had also cast a spell, this one the dark lightning bolt Marla had seen her use before. It slammed into a third archer, actually lifting the man off his feet and throwing him several paces away to slam into the ground in the middle of some bushes. He, also, did not get up.

Marla was quicker on the draw than any of the others and fired off a second volley at the fourth man with a bow, but being forewarned, he managed to dive to the side, only taking minor damage as the pellets raked his torso before landing on the ground and being extinguished. While Marla cursed at missing her target, a puff of darkness coalesced into a slender form as Raki slashed at the dodging archer. Again, the man's reflexes served him well as he jerked to the side and received no more than a shallow cut down his other side.

The man impressed her not only in his dodging ability, but by the way he dropped his bow, drew one of the thick machete weapons from his side, and slashed out with it all in one smooth motion. Raki, leapt back awkwardly, but succeeded in getting out of the way of the weapon before he rolled and, in the middle of the motion, disappeared again.

The leader Marla recognized from when the group had been chasing her earlier threw one of the small hand axes he carried, his target apparently Master Yxna herself. The master, who had not even drawn her weapons yet, calmly flowed around the whirling weapon, spinning to snatch it out of the air, turning around to release it back toward the attackers. Her aim was perfect, taking one of the spear wielders in the face with such force that not only was the axe blade buried deep in his skull, but it actually knocked the man backward off his feet to land on his back. There would be no getting up for that one, either.

The opening salvo done, literally everyone within sight was in motion, swarming toward each other. Already, the two groups were close enough and intermingled enough that Marla didn't want to risk spellwork for fear of hitting her friends. It was convenient to train to fight in formations to keep things nice and tidy, but rarely did that happen in real combat, especially with a sneak-attack like the one she was currently in the midst of. She drew her blades—sword in the right and dueling dagger in the left—and scanned the battlefield for who she would kill next.

The remaining spear-wielder and the man with the poleaxe were already near Evon, who had been unfortunate enough to be closest to the forest. He set his shield and drew his sword, ready to meet the longer weapons. It wasn't long before they reached him.

Predictably, the spear came straight in while the axe blade of the poleaxe arrived in a more arcing fashion. Evon shifted his feet, using his entire body to pivot the shield while he swung it outward with his shoulder. It swept the spear aside and—angled effectively—deflected the axe head away. He twisted to ram his sword at the attackers, but seemed to realize halfway through that he didn't have the reach, so he reset his stance and prepared for the next attack.

The strange multi-bladed weapons a tall and somewhat lanky Arunai carried caught Marla's eye. They looked to be forged of one piece of metal, the handle consisting of leather wrappings. There were three blades on one of them, with four on the other two, and they seemed to flow in one direction. The first was no more than a curved, spike-like blade projecting from just above where the man was holding the weapon. The remaining blades were longer and set in such a way that, though they might do damage if the weapon was swung in one direction, they seemed designed to do the most harm in the opposite direction. It was almost as if they were created to...

The Arunai threw the pinwheel-like object in his right hand, flicking his wrist at the end of his throw to start the blades spinning. He snatched the other weapon off his belt as the first one flew, but Marla only noticed it out of the corner of her eye. With how he had thrown the blade, it would be a whirling collection of deadly sharp steel that would penetrate anything it hit very deeply.

Luckily, Khrazhti had put up a shield as well, it seemed. The strange weapon clanged off her magical protection and skipped off to her right, away from anyone else. In the meantime, the thrower had charged forward to engage the animaru in closer combat. Marla half-expected him to bounce off the shield as well, but Khrazhti had apparently dropped it because she met his attack with her own swords, the shorter weapons clanging off her curved blades.

The last archer had dropped his bow to try to get to Raki and now he came straight for Marla. Alongside him was a smaller man who had thick machete-like blades similar to his companion. Whereas the bowman stomped toward Marla, the other man was light on his feet, almost skimming the ground. When the two came near, he turned that into an acrobatic leap, whirling in midair to attack Marla.

For a fraction of a second, she watched him come, surprised at the unusual attack. Then her reflexes kicked in and she ducked out of the way to engage her other attacker more conventionally, with a block of his blade with her sword while she slashed at him with her dagger.

A flicker of motion off to Marla's right allowed her to move her eyes enough to see Raki becoming visible to try for the acrobatic enemy. His head snapped up and he disappeared again without attacking. Half a second later, one of the hand axes the leader carried passed through where Raki had been. The leader cursed, snatched one of the long knives off his belt, and charged Marla along with the other two already trying to kill her.

The leader's knives were not like Tere's, which were almost completely straight. Instead, these blades were angled into an elbow, both the inside and the outside of the blade sharp. She'd seen them before—almost admired the way they looked, in fact—but she wasn't thrilled to be fighting against two of them at the same time as three of the thicker, blockier blades.

Of course, Master Yxna would be the first one to tell Marla that she couldn't always have things the way she liked. Wasn't that the truth?

Her three attackers came in, a storm of sharp metal cutting from every conceivable angle. Marla sidestepped to her left, slapping the two blades from the acrobat toward the other two men. It allowed her to use the man's body to block the other weapons from reaching her.

What were those thick blades anyway? They were too long and wide, not to mention thick, to be knives, but they weren't quite swords, either. Maybe a type of falchion? She'd have to ask about what they were called. If she survived.

The tall man twisted around his companion and tried to cut Marla with two downward strikes. She thrust both her weapons up into the air, angled slightly, thankful that she had guards on both just in case what she was trying didn't work. It did, though, both of the oncoming blades skipping off her own to continue downward and outward. Marla threw a lightning-fast front kick into the man's chest, torquing her hips and stepping through the strike to knock him back into the leader.

While the other two were tangled up, the acrobat flipped over his companions and came down with both his weapons aimed at Marla's head. She threw herself backward, rolling onto her back while putting her weapons up into a cross guard position to block the blades. At the same time, she swung both feet up, contacting the man's abdomen and kicked hard while rolling backward to throw the man through the air behind her. The sound of a hard landing was almost as satisfying as the *whoof* of air leaving his body, forced from him by her feet.

She kipped up back onto her feet, both blades up and

ready, faster than her opponents thought she'd recover. Her deflection of one of the tall man's blades, allowing her to lunge in and skewer him with her sword seemed a surprise. The twist of her blade and abrupt exit to widen the hole she'd made no less so. She missed the expression on the man's face because she had to rush to respond to the leader's attack. His three quick slashes, a thrust, and an ingenious rolling technique happened in mere seconds and could easily have taken her hand off had she not defeated him with two parries. They were followed quickly by a block, a redirection, and a desperate evasion.

While Marla was scrambling to keep from getting stabbed, the only woman Arunai and the largest man in their group went after Master Yxna. The big man hefted the strangely shaped wooden weapon and, using his entire body, threw it end-over-end at the master. The thing was shaped of one solid piece of wood, curved into a slight angle, with a long axe blade on one side and a spike on the other. It flew through the air with a whomping sound, the sheer force and bulk of it audibly pushing air from its path. The master calmly sidestepped the unwieldy weapon and it passed by her and flew out into the crater.

Not deterred, the man unstrapped another identical weapon from his back and, in stride with the woman, closed the distance. Her weapon consisted of a long handle, maybe twenty inches long, with a curved blade two feet long. The entire weapon was shaped like a relaxed S and the razor-sharp steel of the blade ended in a wicked point. As the two closed, Master Yxna finally drew her twin straight swords, of the type they used traditionally in the nation of Shinyan.

Marla darted her eyes around her to track where her enemies were. The man she had cut down slumped to the ground and she doubted he'd come back to his feet. The leader, still launching flurries of strikes at her, she could handle at the moment, but she was concerned about the acrobat. The last she'd seen, he had landed hard behind her, but she couldn't see him now.

A whisper of movement behind her was all the warning she got and her reflexes took over, throwing her to the ground in a sloppy roll that almost caused her to receive a slash from the leader's knives. Where she had been, the acrobat had cut through the air with both of his blades. If he hadn't been moving slightly slower than earlier—probably because of the pain or lack of breath he was suffering from—that might have been it for her.

As if dealing with both of the men wielding two weapons each wasn't enough, she strayed too close to where Evon was with her roll. She'd barely made it back to her feet when the spear-wielder jabbed the sharpened metal tip of his weapon at her. It skittered off her armor, digging into the breastplate just before it reached a critical spot between the breastplate and her shoulder armor. She spun away in time to keep the spear from doing real damage, but as she did, the acrobat slashed out at her and ripped through the lower half of her cloak.

"Not my cloak," Marla said, recovering herself. "You're going to pay for that, you bastard."

With the enemy's attention on Marla, Evon took the opportunity to ram the spear-wielder with his shield, pushing him off-balance so he couldn't attack Marla again. At the same time, he slashed at the poleaxe guy, though the man expertly shifted the shaft of his weapon to parry the attack.

Before Marla could bemoan three people attacking her, Raki flashed into view long enough to lay a long slash down the spearman's arm. Raki struck again, cutting into the man's face with both daggers, one of them cutting deep enough to ruin his left eye. Raki wisely faded back into the shadows before he could be counterattacked.

She left Evon to deal with the injured spearman while she turned her attention back to the two she was originally fighting. That acrobat was to her right, while the leader of the group was to her left.

She chose to go to her right, to the guy who had ruined her cloak.

Marla leapt toward the man, twisting to keep out of the range of the leader's knives. When she reached the acrobat, she found him more flat-footed than he had been before. Either he was fatigued or he had cracked or broken ribs. The point was that he no longer bounced lightly on his toes, though he weapons seemed steady in their guard pose.

That didn't mean much to her, though. The man had ruined her cloak. She would pay him back for that. In spades.

Her leap took her right in front of the man and she used her descent to lend power to her strikes. She used her dagger mainly to occupy one of his weapons, while she hammered relentlessly on him with her sword. After the fourth strike, his guard broke and her blade got through to cut into his shoulder. She used her dagger to force the weapon in his right hand outward and used a powerful shift in her hips to throw a close elbow into his face. Blood spattered from his ruined nose and he staggered for the briefest of moments. It was enough for her to circle her dueling dagger around and punch into his chest.

She could feel the blade slide in, reach a little resistance in the form of cartilage, and—with a little more effort—pushed it farther into his heart. Her senses told her she couldn't wait for the end, though, so she threw her body to the side, twisting the acrobat in front of her just as the leader's knives would have reached her. Instead, they slashed the acrobat's back, but he was too far gone to scream at the new wounds. She pushed his body away, interfering even more with the leader's attacks, and Marla backed up a couple of steps to return to a stable guard position.

Interestingly, Master Yxna hadn't disposed of the two Arunai attacking her yet. The two attacked as she danced around their weapons, barely even moving her swords to peform the occasional parry. It was clear that the master was taking her time, setting the two up for instant defeat, but it seemed a strange choice for responding to an ambush.

As Raki finished off the spear-wielder, Evon shifted his focus completely to the attacker with the poleaxe. Marla wasn't concerned; she'd seen Evon defend against long weapons many times and he was skilled at the techniques necessary. While Marla reset her defense against the Arunai leader, she snatched a glimpse at her friend as he shifted his stance and transferred his sword to the hand holding his shield. She knew what was coming next.

The poleaxe blade had a common configuration, with the blade on one side, a spike opposite, and another spike thrusting out on top of it as well. The wielder came at Evon in a thrust with the spike on top of the axe head. He effortlessly angled his shield and the weapon skipped off as the attacker continued deeper into his lunge.

Then Evon threw out his empty palm and a wash of flame burst out, striking the spearman in the face. The man dropped his weapon, hands going up to protect himself while Evon grabbed his sword again and performed a picture-perfect lunge to ram the blade through the man's middle. Between the gut wound and trying to put the fire in his hair out, the Arunai succumbed and dropped to the ground.

Off to the side, Khrazhti laid into the man with the strange pinwheel weapons. He was skilled at deflecting swords, and even managed to get close to her a couple of times, but she was far too fast for him to cut with his shorter weapons. The animaru finally stabbed toward him with weapons that weren't well suited for that type of attack because of their curve, but the reason became clear a few seconds later. As the man swept aside her blade with his weapon, Khrazhti twisted her wrist and raised her elbow, allowing her sword to work its way in between two of the bladed projection of the man's weapon. With a sharp jerk in the other direction, she got her sword caught in his blade.

The man couldn't get his weapon loose and Khrazhti took the opportunity to land a blurringly fast front kick full in his face. The blow snapped his head back and loosened his grip on the trapped weapon. The one in his other hand stopped as he staggered. Khrazhti calmly flung his dropped weapon away then cut down savagely to slash through most of his neck. A look of surprise jumped onto his face as he fell away from her, no longer a threat.

The leader of the doomed tribespeople lunged forward a few steps to go after Marla with another of his flurries of strikes as Master Yxna prepared to close her trap and finish the huge man and the woman attacking her. Before anyone could strike an enemy, though, the ground beneath all of them suddenly gave way.

One moment, Marla was thinking how with only three of the attackers left, the battle was all but done, and the next moment, she was sliding down a steep slope that had been solid ground a few seconds before.

The last thing she thought as she fell was that she just couldn't seem to catch a break. Even winning a battle, the ground itself conspired to beat her.

CHAPTER
THIRTY

When Marla's head stopped spinning, she opened her eyes, which she had apparently closed. It was probably a good thing, too, so much dust and dirt was floating around her, surely some of it would have gotten in her eyes.

She was down on one knee, her legs feeling bruised but hopefully not broken. As she stumbled to her feet grit ground against her skin, having gotten down into her armor and possibly her clothes. She groaned and brought a hand up to her head, almost conking herself with the hilt of her sword. At least she seemed to have retained her weapons, the habits she'd developed over the years keeping her from releasing them even though she was falling into a great hole.

Through the cloud of dust, she could see the sunlight above her and to the side an entire section of the lip of the rim of the creater that had collapsed. Movement from next to her brought her thoughts into clarity and she raised her weapons to meet whatever was there.

It was Evon, squirming around on the ground, his

shield still in his hand covering half his body. His sword lay half-buried a few feet away. At least he'd made it without looking like he'd been seriously injured.

A quicker movement from her other side and she turned her attention there. The leader of the Arunai, his dark skin dusted with grey dust, stumbled to his feet, eyes darting about. No doubt he was looking for his weapons, which he seemed to have lost. That was good, too.

Marla stepped over and clocked him with her sword pommel. The man fell back into the dust.

By the time Marla found her friends—all of them bruised and dirty but none with wounds too serious— Master Yxna had already incapacitated the other two Arunai, the big man and the woman.

"Well, we wanted to get down here," Evon said. "Be careful what you wish for and all that." He rotated his shoulders and moaned. "As if falling down a hill and getting beat with rocks on the way down wasn't bad enough, I think I have gravel inside my clothes." He swiveled his hips a little and a pained expression came to his face. "And in my underclothes. Ugh."

Given most other circumstances, Marla may have laughed at her friend, but she wasn't in the mood. "The damn Arunai followed us across all that distance and even over the ocean? What is that about?"

"We can ask them when the one you clobbered wakes up," Master Yxna said, seeming much too calm for the situation.

"Yeah, I'll do that. For now, though, we should probably figure out what we're going to do."

Khrazhti brushed at her skin, trying to scrape the dust off. "Nothing has changed, except that we must either keep control of three prisoners or destroy them. Do you feel the magic drawing you still?"

Marla blinked at the animaru. *Destroy them?* "Uh, yeah. I still feel it. We won't be *destroying* them. They're people and they're unarmed."

"They are enemies who attacked us from hiding. If they had us bound, they would kill us."

Marla sputtered, but couldn't really argue the point.

"We'll take them along with us," Master Yxna said. "After we've had a chance to question them. If it becomes necessary, we'll end them, but only as a last resort."

The one Arunai still conscious, the huge man, blanched at the master's words, but set his jaw and didn't comment on it.

"Do you want me to try some healing on that one," Evon asked, pointing toward the leader, whose feet and hands they'd bound to keep him from causing trouble. "We can question the one that's still conscious, but I doubt he'll answer us without his leader's approval."

Marla wasn't surprised that Evon had picked up on the unconscious man being the leader. He did pretty blatantly direct the other Arunai. "No. We won't be healing any of them. They're lucky we don't kill them outright. I want him to have the headache I gave him when he wakes up. In the meantime, you and I can heal each other's injuries, and those of the rest of our group's."

"Not me, thank you," Khrazhti said. "I do not know what your healing may do to me, since it is based on life magic."

"I've seen you get healed," Evon said.

"Aeden is able to heal me with his magic from the Song of Prophecy. I do not know if the same will be true of the spells from your Academy. I would not like to take the chance it would harm me or destroy me. I am fine. My body is rugged enough not to be harmed seriously by a short fall such as we suffered. I heal quickly, as well. I do thank you for your concern, however."

"I'll take you up on it," Raki said, limping toward Evon. "I took a bad bounce and my knee is swollen."

It was only a matter of minutes before Evon and Marla used their healing spells to erase some of the painful effects of both the short battle and their fall.

"You're getting good at healing spells," Evon told Marla. "Probably already better than me. You're going to pass me right up and master that school, aren't you?"

The biting, sarcastic response that immediately came to mind didn't make it out of her mouth. She was able to grapple it into submission before she spoke. She calmed herself, then answered in a measured tone. "Eventually. It's what I do, Evon. You know that."

He blew out a breath. "Yeah, I do. Sorry, the thought just irritated me for a minute. I don't know what's wrong with me."

"It's this place," she told him. "I understand completely."

The leader came to a little while later, and the woman warrior a bit after that.

"Time to answer some questions," Marla told the man, who squinted at her. Good, it seemed that he did have the promised headache. "Why in all that is right and good would you follow me for that many miles and then cross the sea to an island that everyone knows is death itself to set foot on?"

"Do I need more reason than that you are from the cursed Academy, the one full of people who almost succeeded in erasing my entire people from the face of Dizhelim?"

Marla's hand found her sword hilt and she considered practicing her draw on the man. Master Yxna was suddenly in front of her, between her and the Arunai leader. Marla hadn't even seen her move.

"Perhaps we should take a step back," the master said. "What is your name?"

The man eyed her, then released a breath. "I am Sirak Isayu, of the Anen-Shuken tribe of the Arunai."

"Are you the chief of the Anen-Shuken tribe?"

"No, but I have some influence. Rather, my family does."

"You told the Den-Uto tribe that Marla was a criminal and that you were going to take her. What was that about?"

Sirak shook his head. "Do you not know of the history of Academy minions trying to kill my people?"

"I know of the false Malatirsay and the tragedy that he instigated. I also know that most of the Academy did not join with him."

"What do you know of it?" he spat.

"She's a master at the Academy," Marla growled. "Show some respect or I'll take it from your flesh."

Sirak Isayu spat on the ground between them. "Respect for another murdering scum?"

Master Yxna put her hand up toward Marla to keep her from doing anything rash. "You were not alive at the time of that incident, nor was Marla or myself. You blame us for things done hundreds of years ago. Would you have others blame you for the violence of your forefathers? What of all the tribe wars before Jintu Devexo gathered all of you together to fight the false Malatirsay's forces? Would you accept the slaughter and rape that occurred back then?"

"Words," Sirak said. "All words to try to cover up your guilt. The guilt of the Academy, of which you are a part."

"Fine," Master Yxna said. "Hold onto your irrational hatred. You would have us believe that because of that centuries-old event, that you challenged another tribe to secure Marla?"

"We would do anything to return some of the violence spent on us."

"How did you know she was in the Campastra?"

That surprised the man. He darted a look at his companions, but it wasn't to find an answer. "We spotted her enter."

"Then why didn't you take her."

"She...was riding a horse, moving too fast."

"That's a lie," Marla said. "I ran into warriors from the Den-Uto tribe. When I agreed to go to their village, we traveled by foot, and not at a fast pace. If you were following me, you could easily have caught us."

"All you need to know is that I will take you and return to the Campastra. My reasons are not important."

Marla laughed spitefully at him. "You're going to have a real hard time doing that with your hands and feet bound. That's even if we let you live. That hasn't been decided yet. For now, you'll come with us until we decide to slit your throats or to do something else with you."

The leader didn't have anything to say to that. Marla wasn't sure they shouldn't just go through with killing them and saving themselves the trouble of dealing with them.

"This isn't getting us any closer to where we need to go," she said. She pointed toward the center of the big bowl they were in. "It's that way. We might as well get moving."

CHAPTER
THIRTY-ONE

The bowl in which they traveled seemed to Marla to be sterilized. No plants grew there, not even small weeds. The ground was dry and cracked and the fine dust that covered it puffed up in little clouds as they stepped. Soon after they set out, they had to remove the ropes from the Arnunai's legs because they kicked up so much of the dust as they walked, it made it difficult to breathe.

"Where are you going?" Sirak Isayu asked. The man didn't answer questions, but he was good at asking them.

"None of your business."

"What are you trying to find? Some kind of treasure?"

Marla turned on him and put her nose an inch from his. "If you don't shut your mouth, I'm going to gag you. You're lucky we're letting you live after attacking us like that. It's not going to take too much more than one stupid question before I ram my sword through your eye."

The man opened his mouth, but didn't miss Marla's hand going to her hilt. He must have seen in her eyes that she was deadly serious, because he followed her instructions and went silent.

The other two prisoners were no trouble. They walked when told to do so and didn't make so much as a peep as they traveled.

Master Yxna pulled Marla aside to speak to her as the others shuffled ahead. "Does it feel like whatever is tugging on you is getting closer?"

"Yes, though it's strange. I can tell we're nearer, but it's also sort of fuzzing, becoming less distinct somehow."

"As long as we're on track, that's all that matters."

Marla took up her position at the front again and led them on.

Sometime later, she noticed what looked like strange clouds of the dust they were kicking up far ahead of them. The distance was enough that she thought maybe she wasn't seeing clearly, or it could have been something else.

"Do you see that ahead?" she asked.

Khrazhti, who had already proven her eyesight was keenest, with the possible exception of Raki, answered. "It appears to be whorls of dust several feet in the air. Perhaps there are wind currents twisting around that have caught up some of the soil?"

"They're moving erratically," Raki said. "Like the dust spirits I saw one time near the Sittingham Desert. My nani explained that they're not really spirits or monsters, but it comes from the heat making the wind move around or something."

"That could be," Marla said. "Keep an eye on them, okay? Let me know if you can see anything that's moving around to kick up the dust."

They both nodded. It wasn't until they got closer that it was clear what they were seeing. The shapes were not dust at all, but something that was the same color as the fine dirt. More correctly, what they saw were things that appeared to be made of smoke.

"Shit!" Marla said. "More of those smoke-snakes."

~

Smoke-snakes?

Sirak watched the creatures that had caught the woman's attention. The woman he had traveled all those miles to find. As interesting as she and her friends were, though, he would have to say these things they were calling smoke-snakes were a bit more so.

The only creatures he and his warriors had run into on the island had been those strange two-legged monsters with the spiked appendages. Those were bad enough. Despite there only being a handful of them, their speed had surprised him and several people had been injured before they began to coordinate to take down the unfamiliar monsters. Now he was faced with another group of dangers that he knew nothing about.

And he was still bound up, unable to defend himself effectively, even if he'd still had his weapons. He was relieved, at least, that he had decided to leave his meeting stone in the village. His captors might find where they stashed their packs and it would truly be a tragedy for the Academy to gain possession of the stone.

"Untie me," he said. "Give me a weapon. I can help to fight off those creatures."

"Shut it," the woman—Marla Shrike—told him. He couldn't really blame her. If she was his prisoner, he wouldn't give her a weapon, either. For that matter, she probably wouldn't even be his prisoner. He probably would have killed her outright, too dangerous a foe to allow even a remote chance of escape.

The Vituma was not going to be happy with him at all. It was his responsibility to bring her back to the Council, or to kill her if the first option wasn't feasible. Now here he was, hands tied and facing enemies that, if they were intelligent or efficient, would go after him, Cholu, and Ellia first. Thin the ranks, starting with the weakest. It was nature's way. It was what he would do.

In fact, it was what he had tried to do when they ambushed Marla and her companions. The problem lay in none of them being weak enough to be taken out quickly. Even outnumbered, they had far outclassed the Arunai Sirak had brought with him, as much as he hated to admit it. Considering all the warriors he brought were the most skilled of the wide number he had access to, that didn't bode well for the Council's plans.

At least he'd done one thing right. Before actually attacking the Academy minions, his group had hidden their packs so they could move unencumbered. Food, cooking supplies, and useful items aside, he had also left the message tablet in his pack. It was hard enough to convince Marla—and that master she had with her—that there was no great conspiracy going on. If they'd found the message tablet, he had no doubt they would be able to combine all the clues and discover he was with the Dark Council. Possibly that he was actually *on* the Dark Council. That would have been very bad indeed.

His mind had been on escape ever since he'd been captured, of course, though being on an island with no way off certainly put a kink in any plan he could come up with. At the moment, though, he was more concerned about being in the middle of a battle with no weapons and with his hands unavailable for any efficient use. Such was the way life some-times turned out, though. His father had told him that very few times in one's life would things be advantageous. The state-ment had become something of a core theme in Sirak's life.

"Sit there and don't draw attention to yourself," Marla said, pushing Sirak down as his thoughts distracted him. He let himself collapse into a seated position on the dusty ground as the woman drew her sword and long dagger. Her friends, arrayed around her, readied their own weapons. All but that young boy. He somehow disappeared from sight as Sirak watched him. That was interesting.

Cholu and Ellia sat nearby, apparently having been pushed down to sit as well. Ellia glanced at him, jerking her head to indicate that she wanted to hop up and attack the man with the shield near her. He shook his head. He appre-ciated her motivation, but even with her skill in using her feet and legs as weapons, it would do nothing but getting them injured. There were more of the Academy people and they all had weapons, not to mention that several of them could use magic as well. They'd have to be smart about trying to escape. This was not the time.

The creatures reached the group and Sirak understood why Marla had called them smoke-snakes. They wriggled and slithered around in the air, several feet off the ground, and they did actually look like they were made of smoke. He'd never heard of creatures like that before and had no idea what they were capable of, for defense or attack.

Three of the creatures went at Marla at once. While Sirak had been in thought, the woman had sheathed her dagger and while slashing out at the ones attacking her, she also brought up magic with her other hand. The Dark Council member paid close attention to what she did.

Anything he could tell the Council once he escaped would be valuable information for the next time they fought with her.

What looked like ice daggers flew from Marla's hand at two of the snake things. The projectiles passed right through them as one darted in and struck at her hand. Her reflexes were impressive, but even so, the snake was a bit faster and nipped at her. She cursed and mumbled to herself.

"Okay, strike off cold magic. That doesn't affect them, either."

The rest of the group wasn't having any more success damaging the creatures. They had to have fought them before, or at least seen them. The way Marla had referred to them, she was obviously familiar with the monsters. How had they destroyed them the last time they'd met? There was something Sirak didn't understand about the whole thing.

The man with the shield tried a few spells, mainly fire-based by the way they looked, but neither that, nor his sword and shield seemed to help out. He got attacked by two of the snakes and reacted as if their strike was very painful.

The blue woman—were the rumors that she was actually one of the animaru, possibly the one who led the others to this world to being with, true?—tried a combination of magic and her swords, but she couldn't seem to damage the snake things, either. Nor could the master herself, though watching her effortlessly move with those swords that seemed a part of her body, with magic cast without her breaking her smooth movements at all, made Sirak thankful he wasn't fighting the woman. He'd never seen such grace with a weapon, and that was saying something considering his upbringing.

Then the first of the monsters slipped through the others and went after Ellia. Sirak shouted to her to dodge, but it was like someone moving at half speed trying to fight someone going double fast. The thing extended its body like a true snake and snapped its jaws down on her shoulder.

Ellia shouted in rage and pain, bringing her bound hands up to try to strike the thing's body and bat it away. Her hands passed right through it.

Sirak watched in horror as the same snake decided to take a bite from Cholu. His attempts at dodging or attacking didn't do any better than Ellia's. The grunts that issued from his mouth were tantamount to a shriek of pain for anyone else. Sirak had seen the man tear a barbed arrow from his own leg in a spray of blood and flesh without making a sound.

Sirak didn't even have time to think on what kind of damage the snakes' bites had done because another of the beasts came up from his side and struck at him. He managed to throw himself to the ground, rolling out of the way so the thing missed. Once his momentum was spent, though, it simply turned itself double and struck at him again, its fangs or whatever it used to attack sinking into his chest muscles.

Even up close, he couldn't see any detail on the thing's mouth. Whatever it had struck him with burned like he was on fire, but even worse than an actual burn. He'd had run-ins with flame before and the pain that shot through him was more intense, and different. He couldn't describe it, especially since it hurt so much it dulled his senses.

Then the thing released him and moved on to attack

someone else. The pain subsided, slowly, and within a few seconds, Sirak was able to think clearly again. He looked down to the wound, expecting to be bleeding profusely, but found no evidence of the injury at all.

Somehow, even with all the pain, no physical damage had been done. There may have been internal, emotional, or magical damage, but he couldn't see anything to indicate any of it. The pain had been enough, though. So intense, he would have gladly traded it for actual damage.

He was struck three more times during the fight, each seeming to be new and more intense than anything he'd ever felt. Cholu and Ellia had been attacked again as well, their groans and grunts and screams mixing with his while their captors fought a meaningless battle against the foes even they couldn't seem to damage. Meanwhile, the curses and yells and outright tantrums of several who were involved escalated.

Sirak could feel it, the anger of not being able to do anything. He found that although he was bound and weaponless, the Academy minions seemed even more frustrated because their free movement and weapons availed them not at all.

Finally, when Sirak felt as if his own rage would cause him to break his bonds or for his heart to burst, the snake things slithered away and faded into the background, leaving the three prisoners and the five captors alone to deal with the lingering pain of their battle. Surprisingly, there was no blood and—it seemed—no permanent damage from what they'd been through.

Thundering footsteps caught Sirak's attention as he tried to regain his breath. He turned his head, a sick feeling in his stomach. Dust clouds appeared again, but this time it was actual dust and not the stuff the smoke-snakes were made of. He spotted flashes of solid bodies within the dust as they came toward him.

A group of creatures, more substantial than the snakes, charged toward the group at a speed that meant they would clash in a handful of seconds.

Somehow, Sirak knew that these monsters wouldn't simply inflict pain with no wounds.

THIRTY-TWO

"It's the same as before," Marla Shrike yelled out. "The smoke-snakes frustrated us and stoked our anger and now the real monsters attack."

Sirak Isayu didn't know what the woman was talking about. Was she trying to say that the snake things, with their powerfully painful attacks, had only attacked to make them mad? It sounded like she was a different kind of mad altogether.

"There are more of us this time, so we generated more anger," she continued. "These guys are bigger and look tougher than the last monsters we fought."

He wasn't sure what they had fought last time, but the beasts coming at them weren't ones he'd seen before. The creatures the Arunai fought in the forest had two legs. True, those legs ended in oversized claws, capable of ripping through armor, but still, they'd only had the two. They had also used their tails, equipped with a spiked end, and those other two appendages on top of their bodies, also with spikes to slash with. As the larger monsters charged them and cleared some of the dust they generated in their run, it was perfectly clear these were not the same type as before.

The new attackers were nearly the size of horses, but their form was different. The things had powerful back legs with shorter front legs. Not shorter as in useless, just not as long as the rear, giving them a profile that looked ideal for running into the wind. Or slamming into very hard objects or shields. Spikes protruded from everywhere, including the ridges on top of their sharply pointed triangular heads. To Sirak, the things looked like a cross between some kind of armored lizard and a wolf, but with a reinforced and segmented tail that was nearly as long as the rest of the creatures' bodies.

Like wolves, the monsters' muzzles split into tooth-filled mouths that looked capable of tearing both flesh and armor. Hells, he wouldn't be surprised if they could tear metal.

That wasn't all that was dangerous about the beasts. All four legs were tipped with long claws, articulated like fingers but with sharp nails at the ends. As if that wasn't enough, the back legs also had long spurs pointing backward, like the fighting cocks he'd seen when he was a boy. He had found out quickly that those unlikely weapons could tear flesh easily if used correctly. Sirak did not doubt these knew how to use their weapons effectively.

The first of the creatures came near the blue woman, bunching its muscles to leap upon her. In a blink, she slammed her swords home into their scabbards and made motions with both hands. They didn't seem coordinated and a second later, Sirak understood why. From one erupted what looked like a beam of light, but in reverse. The dark ray blasted at the creature as it left the ground to slam into her. It squealed, and its body shifted like the attack had a physical weight, but its mass was too great to be knocked away completely. It came down on top of the woman.

And bounced.

Sirak blinked, not understanding what he was seeing at first. Then he realized that she must have cast a shield of some kind at the same time as she had conjured the harmful dark ray. Two spells at the same time! He hadn't even known that was possible.

The blue woman's swords came out again and found gaps in the armored plates all around the creature. Sirak knew from standing near the woman that she was nearly seven feet tall, but the monster's bulk made her look smaller than that. How much did one of those things weigh?

The other monsters arrived and there was a chaotic melee as the beasts tried to bowl over the humans while the Academy minions tried to fend them off, with varying degrees of success.

Marla leaped straight up in the air to dodge one of the monsters that was trying to ram her. In midair, she drew her blades and swiped them at the creature as it passed beneath her. It didn't seem that she did much damage, but the monster snorted at her and skidded to a halt, its momentum arrested. When it turned, Marla brought her blades to a ready stance and scanned the area around her. There were no other beasts around her, so she charged in to fight the much bigger attacker.

The boy of the group disappeared, confusing the creature bearing down on him. Instead, it redirected its charge toward the man with the shield, joining one of its companions that was already on the way to ramming him.

Sirak generally thought shields were worthless. Too

many hid behind them, conducting their fights in a solely defensive manner. His fighting style was more aggressive. A powerful offense was better than relying on defense, as far as he was concerned. One couldn't simply defend and hope things turned out fine. The sooner a warrior attacked and injured or killed his opponent, the better. He expected to see an unfortunate demise for the shield-wielder.

The first of the monsters reached the man, dipping its head like a bull. It didn't have horns with which to gore the man, but the ridges along its skull could probably cut and do damage, not to mention that with the distinctive wedge shape of the creatures's body with its shorter front legs, the impact would probably throw the man into the air.

Sirak's eyes grew in size as the man shifted his feet, torqued his hips, and angled the shield in as precise a manner as he'd ever seen someone achieve. The first monster's head barely touched the shield as is scraped along the surface. At exactly the correct time, the man used his entire body to push at a point on the monster's body, just behind its leading shoulders, and moved what had to be many hundreds of pounds in motion so that the creature almost tripped over its own feet. More importantly, it veered enough, its own reflexes slowing it down, to slam into the other monster only a step or two behind.

The two beasts tangled and crashed to the ground in a heap, sliding for several feet in a cloud of dust before they stopped. When they did, the man was there, ramming his sword into one of the creature's eyes while guarding against the other as it climbed to its feet. The boy appeared and took out one of the eyes of the other creature, but apparently his dagger wasn't long enough to reach its brain. There was no such problem with the man's sword and as he nodded to the boy and reset his stance while pulling his sword from the other monster's head. The creature dropped to the ground, dead. It was enough for Sirak to think maybe he had misunderstood—and definitely underestimated—shields previously.

As he watched the boy disappear again, a scream from behind Sirak drew his attention. One of the monsters had gotten through the line of defenders and made it to Cholu. The big man bravely jumped in front of Ellia and the beast had taken his leg in its mouth. With a vicious shake of its head, it tore the limb from Sirak's friend in a spray of blood.

"Cholu!" he screamed, but by the time he got to his feet to help his friend, it was too late. The big warrior had fallen and with the amount of blood pumping out of his torn leg, he was already too weak to do more than stare up at the monster that had killed him. It dropped the leg and clamped its jaws onto Cholu's neck before tearing his head off with another savage jerk.

The master from the Academy leaped onto the beast's back even as it turned toward Ellia. The woman's thin swords darted in and out, somehow finding the space between the plates of the creature's armor. It roared at her as it began to bleed in several places. She flipped off the beast to pull it away from Ellia, but in a horrible twist of fate, the creature's long tail swung around, its hard plating and ridges taking the Aruna in the belly.

The force of the blow bent Ellia in half and, along with the *whoof* of air, a sound like something cracking and tearing reached Sirak's ears. The warrior wasn't even able to scream as she was thrown ten feet to land in a bloody heap, most of her midsection crushed to a pulp.

Just like that, Sirak had lost the last of his warriors, two of his oldest friends. It was only a matter of time until one of the creatures caught him as well. With no weapons, hands still bound, he wouldn't even be able to defend himself. This was the day he would die.

***

Marla roared at the monsters she and her friends were fighting. It wasn't intelligible in any way, just her expelling frustration and anger in the form of raw, primal sound.

The current creatures were the worst yet. True, they could actually be injured, even killed, but unlike the smoke-snakes, these four-legged monstrosities could do damage. As was evident by the two Arunai that were either already dead or would be shortly. It had happened so fast.

Another of the monsters circled around, wary of Marla after it had seen her kill its companions. From what she could see, there were only three left: one snapping at Evon's shield, one confronting Khrazhti, and the one in front of Marla herself. With Raki and Master Yxna able to aid the others, the battle would end soon.

If no more of the creatures came.

Her opponent twitched, hunkering down to leap. By reflex, she brought her blades up to meet the attack, though it might be better to free up one hand to cast a spell. With the armor on the beast, she had to be precise with her strikes to even injure it, let alone kill it.

It had already changed its reactions after seeing at least two of its companions go down with blades through the eye. Now, every time it tried to engage Marla, it tilted its head away at every one of her movements, taking care not to let her strike its most vulnerable spot. Marla was sure she could use the new reflex against it. She only had to work out how.

When the expected explosion of movement came, it

wasn't what Marla expected. Instead of the monster using its superior mass and armor to pummel her, it leapt to the side.

Toward the Arunai leader.

"No you don't, you bastard." With the flick of a wrist, she stuck her dagger into the ground at her feet, already speaking the words to bring forth her magic. The gestures were simple and she'd practiced them often with both hands. Just before the creature got to the Aruna, a rush of magical energy sped from Marla and struck it full on the side.

The force of the spell, accurately named Blast, knocked the monster out of the air to land hard on its side, missing the leader by several feet. When it climbed to stand, confused at what had happened, Marla was already there, both blades in motion.

She swung wide with her sword to catch the creature's attention and it worked perfectly. Its eyes locked onto the blade and it swept an armored and clawed paw out to bat it away. Marla let it, shifting around the swipe to lunge in with her dagger. The beast tilted its head at the last moment, causing her dagger to skitter of the armor around its eye.

Marla spun away before it could counterattack and barely evaded the claw that came at her. The tail coming around to hit her from the other side was more of a surprise. She twisted, trying to dodge the heavy, armored appendage, but was only half-successful. It struck a glancing blow that knocked her off her feet to spin onto the ground.

Get up! she yelled to herself in her mind. *It's going to be on top of you in a second.*

With a mighty flex of every muscle in her middle, she

arrested her spin and flipped up awkwardly to her feet. The pain that shot through her was evidence she was more than just bruised, but she had other things to worry about. Like the hundreds of pounds of vicious monster pouncing on her.

Her movement surprised the creature as it landed hard on the ground where Marla had just been. It half-turned to face her and she knew in the next few seconds death would come to one of them. She aimed for it to be the monster.

It roared at her, sending vibrations through Marla's body. As fast as she could, Marla darted in and rammed the dagger toward the beast's eye. As predicted, it tilted its head upward and slightly to the side. She twisted, generating as much force as she could through her legs, hips, abdomen, torso, and shoulders and plunged her sword directly into the monster's mouth, praying that the top of its throat didn't have armor or thick bone.

Marla's arm went numb at the force of her sword hitting something that felt like stone. For a moment, she thought her sword might break, but then something gave way and it traveled several more inches inward. The monster made a *yurg* sound and then dropped like it's legs had suddenly lost their bones. A few teeth scraped Marla's arm as she tugged her sword out, but that was a small price to pay to see the dead creature in front of her.

Despite her mind screaming that she do otherwise, Marla relied on her friends being able to finish off the other two monsters as she sat down hard on the ground, the feeling that something was definitely not right in her middle.

After a few labored and painful breaths, she looked up to find her friends coming to her. She couldn't see any of the massive creatures moving, which was good news.

Evon threw his shield down and started to immediately cast healing spells on her. She tried to protest, noticing blood on most of the others, but she didn't have the strength. Something was pulling her toward unconsciousness, a satisfying numbness filling her entire being.

The shocking cold of healing slammed into her and she gasped, pain shooting through her as she did so.

"There's a lot of damage inside you," Evon said. "As I heal it, it's going to hurt. A lot."

Through her panting breaths, she acknowledged what he said. "Right now, I'll take the pain over the alternative."

CHAPTER

THIRTY-THREE

Marla wasn't sure how many rounds of healing Evon used on her, but after an interminable period of time, she was breathing easier and nearly all the pain was gone. She was exhausted, but she'd survive.

"Give me a few minutes to recover and I'll help with healing the others," she told her friend. "And thanks. It definitely felt like something broke inside me when that tail got me."

"We're all fine," Master Yxna said. "No need for you to concern yourself with healing us."

Marla nodded, feeling more than a little ashamed she'd been hurt so badly and none of the others had.

"Why?" Sirak Isayu asked.

"What?" Marla said.

"Why did you risk yourself to keep that thing from getting me?"

"If I'd have known what would happen, I probably would have let it have you." He stared at her, waiting for an answer. "Oh, fine. I saw what those things did to your

296

friends. I couldn't help them, but I could help you, so I did. I wouldn't wish that kind of end on anyone, even someone who ambushed me and tried to kill me." She paused and thought about it. "No, that's not right. I can think of several people I wouldn't mind that happening to. I don't know. Reflex maybe. I've been hanging around too many of the hero types. It must have affected my mind. Maybe you shouldn't worry about why so much as you should be grateful and cooperate with us."

"I thank you for saving my life, though if you hadn't taken my weapons and bound my hands, I might have helped to kill the monsters."

"Yeah. Whatever. I'm sorry about your friends, but you're still our prisoner and I'll be damned if you're getting a weapon." She turned to her companions. As they'd said, none of them looked to be injured seriously. "So, same old thing. Smoke-snakes to piss us off, which drew—or maybe generated—the bigger creatures. What do you think, other than that we somehow need to keep from getting mad in this place?"

"That sounds like the most important thing to me," Evon said. "That and you finding what magic is drawing you here. I just want to find it, then get out of here."

"Yeah, you and me both," she said. "Fine. Let's gather up our stuff and get going."

Marla slapped her clothing to try to brush some of the dust off, then hitched her pack up. She faced where the magic was still pulling at her and started off.

Travel was the same boring trudge it had been since they'd entered the basin, with the obvious exception of being attacked. Honestly, she didn't care for either of the situations. At least they didn't have to bash their way through brush.

"Do you really think that us getting mad makes those monsters come to us?" Raki said from right beside her. Despite herself, she jumped. Gods, but the boy was good at being invisible and silent.

"It all fits," she said. "The whole thing seems like some mastermind created it all to trap people, to kill them, but not before playing with them. I mean, what good would those snakes do otherwise. They're not predators because what would they eat? They're made out of smoke. Each time we ran into them, they harried us, getting us into a lather, then they disappeared just in time for the other monsters to take over."

"I guess. Why, though? What's the reason?"

"I don't know. The island is named *wrath*. People some-times name things nowadays with no apparent reason, but that's not the way it was in past times. There's a reason why it was named that." She thought about how she'd felt it from the first step on the island. "Do you feel it? Does your anger want to surface here?"

Raki looked down at his hands. "I suppose. I'm not an angry kind of guy, usually. Some people get mad when they're uncomfortable. I'm more of a run and hide kind of person."

Marla chuckled. From what she'd seen, that was an accurate assessment of his personality, and the other he referred to was accurate for her. "Sure, but still, do you feel anything different here as opposed to before we got to the island?"

"Umm, I guess so. I get frustrated easier here and there have been a few times when I was pretty irritated. Not fuming mad, but not happy about how things were going, either."

"That's what I was talking about. It's not going to affect

someone like you as much as someone like me, especially since I've been angry a lot lately. It's like everything that happens to put pressure on me turns right to anger. I don't like it, and I like this place even less. I do think there's something going on magically that pricks peoples' tempers. I think your personality buffers you from it more than me, though. This place seems to use angry feelings as power."

"I've never heard of anything like that before," he said.

"Me either. We've run into so many strange things in the last few months, it doesn't surprise me, though. Which reminds me, how are you doing?"

Raki stopped and turned to her. "Me? How am I doing?"

"Yes. How's it going with the problems you had with dark magic and stuff?"

Raki started walking again, stutter-stepping to catch up to her. "Good?" It came out as a question.

"Are you asking me?"

"No...I mean, I'm good, I think. I feel a lot more comfortable with the dark magic now, after finding that well. I don't worry about it taking over my mind and turning me evil or anything."

"That *is* good. Why do I sense a but in there?"

Raki swiped hair from his face and broke into a grin. "It's not a big deal. I'm still trying to figure out all this stuff. What we're doing, what's coming up, all that. I mean, it's exciting and everything, but I don't know what tomorrow or next week or next month will bring. A few days ago, I never would have thought I'd be on an island. Across the sea!"

"It's a very short strip of water," she said. "It's not like we crossed an entire ocean or anything."

"I know, but still. If you would have told me I'd be on an actual island—not like Munsahtiz but outside of

Promistala completely—I wouldn't have believed you. What will it be like in a week or two? Will we travel to the moon?"

This time, Marla's amusement came out as a barking laugh. "Maybe."

"So it's exciting, interesting, and more than a little scary," he said. "I'm just a Gypta boy, not some great hero or traveler. Sometimes I don't know what to think of it all."

"Let me tell you a secret, Raki. That's how we all feel. I think even Tere feels it sometimes. All these things, what we're facing with the animaru and the wells and all the rest of it, none of us have dealt with it before. You've been with Aeden from the start. If someone were to write down all the adventures you've had, the tales would spread all over Promistala and people would tell them to children who would dream about what it would be like to be you. We all need to rely on each other to get through this. We all rely on you as much as you rely on us."

Raki was silent for a moment. "Then why did you run away from the rest of us?"

This time, Marla stopped walking. "How old are you again?"

"Sixteen."

"How'd you get so shrewd so young? I...was wrong to run away. It's just been so hard and I've been so wrapped up in things. Unlike you, anger is the way I deal with pressure, and there's been plenty of that lately. I'm sorry I dragged everyone into this. If it helps, I was mainly thinking of everyone else's safety. There were times there where I could have killed someone."

"That's why you need to talk to us. You can even complain and rant. We don't mind. We all want to help however we can."

Marla put her hand on the boy's shoulder and started them moving again. "I appreciate that, Raki. I really do. I'll try to remember. All of this stuff, it's hard enough without trying to deal with it on our own. Thanks."

Raki's brow drew down. "For what?"

"For reminding me. Like I said, this is new to all of us, even the masters. We need each other's strength, I think."

"That's what we're here for," he said merrily.

"It is. Now if we could only—"

For the second time that day, the ground beneath Marla's feet gave way. It started underneath her lead foot, just as she placed it on the ground, and a fracture ran beneath her and past her, toward her friends. Within seconds, she and the others tumbled into a rapidly widening hole, plunging into an unknown darkness.

THIRTY-FOUR

"You have got to be kidding me," Marla said, spitting dust from her mouth from yet another fall. "If I fall through another hole today, so help me, I'm going to—"

"Calm down," Evon said from behind her. "You're going to draw more of those creatures. We definitely don't need that."

Marla readied a scathing response to that, but clenched her teeth and breathed through her nose, containing her building rage. If barely. The dusty air tickled her nose and made her sneeze. Wonderful.

"Is anyone hurt?" Master Yxna asked. Marla couldn't see the master with all the dust around, but she sounded like she was a few paces in front and to the right of her.

"I'm fine," Raki said from beside Marla.

"I am unharmed," Khrazhti said from Marla's left somewhere.

"I'm good," Evon answered.

Marla waited. "Sirak?"

"Ugh. I'm alive, but the fall jammed my hip. If my hands

were free, I might be able to balance more effectively and—"

"Not happening. Do you need healing?"

"No."

"Raki, can you see in this mess?" The place they had landed was still too dusty to see much. The hole they had come through, nearly ten feet in diameter, was almost fifteen feet above them, the sunlight a beam piercing the fine dust floating in the air. It was as if a massive clay piple had been drilled through the top.

"Not too far. Do you want me to scout around?"

"No," she said. Let's wait until the dust settles. If anything was going to attack us, it probably would have already. We can see well enough with the sunlight for now."

They waited for several minutes until they could see each other—and more of the place they'd fallen into— better. There were still enough particles floating around to see the ray of sunlight enter into the space they were in, but it didn't obscure their vision anymore.

Their new location wasn't that impressive. It was longer than it was wide, made from volcanic rock. The rough texture of the whole thing made it clear they were not in a human-carved passage. Ceilings, walls, and floor all looked the same in the cylindrical area.

"Lava tube?" Marla said, running her hand on the stone.

"That would support the thought that the crater had been something like a volcano that had erupted and then collapsed," Evon answered.

"It's not warm in here, though," Raki pointed out.

"No, it wouldn't be," Evon said. "We're talking thousands of years ago. There may be lava moving around hundreds of feet down still, but we probably don't have to worry about that."

Marla shook her head. "Right, but what *do* we have to worry about?"

"Probably finding our way out of here."

"Thanks for that, Evon. What would we do without you?" She looked up at the hole they fell down through. With how brittle the stone was on the walls, there was no way they'd be able to climb the curved walls to get out. "Raki, we could probably use your dark vision about now. Do you want to scout around, see what you can find?"

"Sure."

"Okay, but be careful. We don't know what else is down here. Watch for holes and rifts and things like that."

Evon cast a light spell to produce a glowing ball in his hand. "While you take one side, I'll go down the other. If all the noise hasn't brought whatever might be out there to us, I don't think a little light will. Everyone else can wait here until we get a better idea of where we want to go."

"Fine," Marla said, "but the same thing goes for you. Be careful and don't go too far before coming back to get us."

"Yeah, yeah."

As the two went about their tasks, Marla picked up one of the many rocks strewn across the floor at her feet. It seemed that not all of the area that collapsed was that dusty dirt. There was some stone, too, even if it did break up. She tossed the palm-sized stone up and down. Maybe it would occupy her mind and keep her from thinking about the newest piece of bad luck that had them in some kind of cave system.

"Well, it's not any kind of cave system," Evon said less than two minutes later. "At least, there's no openings the way I went. The tube stays the same size and just ends about forty or so feet up that way."

Raki returned shortly thereafter. "Nothing up that way but a dead-end. I could hear Evon from the end and the way I went didn't go much further than his way did."

In an explosion of white-hot anger, Marla screamed and threw the rock she had been bouncing in her hand as hard as she could at a section of wall at the edge of where the sunlight illuminated thew walls. It didn't even have the decency to shatter, only struck the wall hard and bounced off.

"Did you hear that?" Evon asked.

"We all did," Master Yxna said, frowning at Marla. "Someone threw another temper tantrum."

"Oh," he said. "Yes, I mean no, I mean yes, but that's not what I'm talking about."

"Then what are you talking about," Marla snapped. "If you have something to say, say it!"

Her friend looked at her, mouth open. She didn't understand why. He knew her better than anyone. Knew her *temper* better than anyone. Maybe she had gone a bit beyond what propriety would allow, though.

"I'm sorry, Evon. I'm frustrated and—"

He waved her down. "I get it. It's not important right now. Here, everyone, watch. Listen."

He picked up a rock and threw it at the wall directly across from him. "Did everyone hear that?" Nods all around. "Good, now listen to this." He retrieved another stone and threw it to where Marla's had struck. The second sound was different than the first.

"It echoed more," Raki said. "Like the wall is hollow."

"Exactly."

That started a flurry of motion, with several people

picking up rocks and knocking against the wall with them. It took a few minutes for everyone to finish their inspection and Master Yxna said what the rest of them were thinking. "There's another cavern or lava tube or something we can get to if we can break that section of wall."

"That's what I was thinking," Evon said. "If we can hear the difference, it has to be pretty thin. At least, relative to the other solid stone walls. Maybe if we break through, we can find a way up and out of here. It's worth a shot."

Master Yxna stepped up to the wall and put her hand on it, as if she could tell by feel how thick it was. Marla had been trained in the School of Stone Magic, though she had not mastered that school yet. She could force her affinity for rock and soil to reveal such information to her, she thought. Master Yxna hadn't mastered that school, either, but it was possible she had progressed high enough in the school to sense the stone's thickness.

After a moment with her eyes closed, the master removed her hand. "I can't tell. It could be a couple of inches thick or it could be two feet thick. I can cast Water Jet, though Marla may be able to generate a stronger stream than I. What other spells might work?"

After some discussion, they had a few viable options. To start, Master Yxna cast Water Jet first to see how the spell would fare.

Marla had rarely seen the master cast spells, so she watched closely. It helped that both women had mastered the School of Water Magic, so although every high-level caster developed their own specific techniques for even the basic spells, the younger woman knew the general motions the master would use to bring forth the magic.

From Master Yxna's outstretched hand, a finger-thick

stream of water ejected and shot toward the wall a few feet away. As expected, the water split into a fine spray, bouncing back and soaking not only the master but Raki, who had strayed close to watch the process.

For several long minutes, Master Yxna directed the water stream at the same location on the wall. Frankly, it was impressive that she aimed it so efficiently, since Marla knew from experience that the water exerted a force back toward the user, definitely enough to affect aim and to fatigue muscles. When the master stopped, her arm and shoulders slumped, but she stepped forward to see what her efforts had accomplished.

"That's some rugged stone," Master Yxna said, rubbing her hand on the very clean surface of the stone wall. The section that was the target of the spell was smoothed into a little bowl, maybe as deep as the fingernail of Marla's little finger. "At that rate, it would take me many hours to get through, and that's only if the stone is a few inches thick. If it's two feet, well..."

"You've mastered water magic, too, Marla," Evon said. "Can you do better?"

She didn't like how the question sounded. It was true that the variety of skills of different people who mastered a particular school was staggering, but Marla didn't like how it sounded as if Evon was comparing the two women. She was proud of her skills and her cleverness in tweaking spells to be more powerful, but Master Yxna *was* her favorite master and she didn't like the implication that Marla was better than her.

Master Yxna must have read the thought on Marla's face, because she stepped in before an argument started. "He's only asking because each caster has their own particular spells they work on and develop into things they can cast with sublime skill. There is no comparison here, only a question about whether you've spent time and effort to do amazing things with this specific spell."

Marla's anger deflated, though she did get a little irritated that the master read her so completely. "I think I might be able to refine the stream so it's smaller, with more force, but not enough to keep it from taking hours still."

"Okay," Evon said. "My fire missiles aren't going to do anything to the rock, so I'm no help here. Khrazhti?"

"I have no spell made for attacking stone. I can try my Jagged Bolt spell. It does not do too much more damage than a well-handled blade would, but it is a concussive and powerful magic for single-point damage."

"Give it a try," Evon said.

Khrazhti stayed where she was, apparently not needing to get closer to the target. After the others—Raki first among them—took a couple of steps back, she motioned with her hand and what looked like a dark bolt of lightning sped away from her and slammed into the rock exactly where Master Yxna's water had bored the indentation. A few rock chips flew out from the point of impact, but the wall looked essentially how it had amoment before. It took closer examination for Marla to spot where the chips had come from: around the edges of the dip in the stone Master Yxna's spell had made.

"I can continue to cast the spell over and over again, but I believe I would deplete my magic and become fatigued before gaining significant headway."

"Marla?" Master Yxna said. "Now might be a good time to use youre ability to utilize spells for applications they were never intended for."

"I can try a few things," she said, stepping over to stand directly in front of the wall, but three paces back. "I'm not sure what kind of ricochet these first two will have, so you should stand back, maybe even bring up some shields."

The first spell she cast was a stone magic spell called Dig. It was meant for precisely what it sounded like, excavating soil. It could be used on stone, by those with a higher-level understanding of the magical school, but it took a lot of power and Marla wasn't sure she could do it.

Seconds later, after she completed the gestures and spoke the words of power for the spell, it was clear that spell wasn't what they were looking for. At least, not in the way she was able to cast it. A thump of concussive force attacked the wall and did nothing more than push Marla back several feet. The wall looked exactly as it had before.

The next spell she tried was also from the Stone Magic category. It was called Stone Missile, which explained sufficiently what the spell did. Unlike some of the other projectile spells like Fire Missile, Stone Missile required material in the form of stone or dirt that could be shaped by the magic as the actual missiles. There was plenty to choose from, scattered around on the floor.

"I wish there was a way to use the stone of the wall itself as the material for the missiles," she explained to the others, "but it has to be loose. I can't scoop it out to turn it into projectiles or I'd do that to make the wall thinner."

She cast the spell and a dozen pointed stone missiles flew from her hand and struck the wall. At first, with all the dust and rock chips flying around, Marla thought she'd gotten somewhere, but once the dust cleared, she saw the truth. Her projectiles had disintegrated, but the wall remained as solid as ever, with only a few little scars marring the surface that Master Yxna had smoothed out with her spell.

She tried Light Lance, Knife of Air, and even Fire Missile —just for the sake of thoroughness—but none of them did any damage to the wall.

"Do you think it's magically strengthened?" she asked.

Master Yxna inspected the location where so many spells had impacted, rubbing her finger along the indentation. "Probably. I can't see normal stone being this tough, especially since the walls are brittle enough in other places to break off with my hand."

"I have one more thing to try. After that, we might be better off trying to figure out a way to get back up to the surface through the hole we fell in through. I've got a few spells I've developed using two or more of the different categories. One, using air and water, could help. If I can get the mixture of the two types of magic correct."

"What is this spell called?" Master Yxna asked.

Marla's face got hot and she wished she had come up with an impressive name for it. Because she rarely told others about her spells, she never thought she'd have to refer to it by name when speaking with someone else. "Uh, Freeze."

Evon snorted, but cut even that short when Marla's head snapped toward him.

"You will try to freeze the wall to make it brittle?" the master asked.

"That's the plan. I'm not sure if I can put enough qozhel into it to freeze a large enough area, but it's all I can think of. There's something else, too. Ideally, I'd freeze it and then hit it with my stone missiles to try to shatter it. I can't do that, though, because normal thermodynamics don't fully apply. If I stop casting, the surrounding rock, even the air, will heat it enough to keep it from being frozen completely."

"What are your thoughts, then," Master Yxna asked.

"Well, using water probably won't work because it will throw the mixture between water and air off. Fire missiles won't be good, for obvious reasons. Khrazhti? Can you cast that bolt thing you did before? We'll have to time it so that it's as brittle as I can make it when you strike."

"I will do this. Tell me when to strike and I will cast Jagged Bolt at the center of the indentation on the wall."

"Great. Let's do this."

Marla began the complex gestures she had created from merging different spells. As she did so, she chanted the words of power. She really needed to revisit the way the spell was set up, make it more efficient. It was one task on a list of many things she wanted to do. For the moment, however, she had to use what she'd already designed.

After a handful of seconds, she felt the magic build up in her, enough to launch it toward the wall. She held both hands out and mentally willed the power to go forth. A pale blue light, resembling a freezing mist, floated sluggishly toward the target. Once it hit, she could sense the contact, as well as the severe draw on the magic she was pulling both from the surroundings and from herself. It felt like lifting a wagon using only her arms.

The temperature in the area dropped precipitously. The efficiency of the spell was in no way what she hoped it would be, but she could sense the stone's surface getting to sub-freezing temperatures from the direct contact. Her body, chilled and moving slowly, matched the glacial pace of her thoughts. She hadn't expected that. What if she froze to death before she finish the spell?

Second after slow, torturous second passed as the

surface of the wall grew a layer of rime, then of large ice crystals. Still, it wasn't enough for her to be sure of the result. She pushed more qozhel into the spell, feeling herself bottoming out. Just another second or two...

"Now!" she said, though it sounded unlike real language because of her chattering teeth and frozen lips. Thankfully, Khrazhti understood the command and blasted several of her black bolts toward the frozen wall.

The explosion of black light, ice, snow, and shards of stone knocked Marla off her feet and ended her spell instantly. She blinked, trying to remember where she was and what she was doing. When she did, she ran her hands over her body, looking for the inevitable cuts and embedded shards that had struck her. Curiously, she didn't find any.

"D-d-did you sh-sh-shield m-m-me?" she asked.

"Of course," Evon said, his mouth only a few inches from her ear. "I'm not going to let you shred yourself because of a stupid oversight. Here, let me warm you up. You're ice-cold."

A soothing warmth radiated from Evon's hands and arms, which he had wrapped around her. She thanked the gods that he'd chosen Fire Magic as the spell-casting school he mastered.

After a few minutes of him warming her, Marla could sit up and speak without her teeth chattering and without feelling like she was dying. Master Yxna handed her some dried fruit and meat to chew on.

"So tired," she said. The food helped, but she could do with some sleep. Like a week's worth of it.

"Rest for a little while longer," Master Yxna said. "Then we can get going."

Get going? Marla hadn't paid attention to it earlier, but

now she looked toward the wall she had been trying to break. A gaping hole, nearly five feet high and two across stared back at her. She'd done it?

"Good job," Evon said. "You might have found us our way out."

THIRTY-FIVE

Now that Marla was sitting still, too tired for her to dwell on little things that might spike her anger, she realized the sensation she'd been feeling for the last two weeks was still there. Tugging. It wasn't leading her directly into the hole she'd made in the wall, but it seemed likely that she could get to where she needed to be by entering the tunnel beyond.

She hauled herself to her feet. "Let's get going. I want to find whatever it is we've been looking for and get out of here." She picked up her pack and headed for the hole in that wall. Sirak Isayu, quiet all during the time they'd been trying to figure out how to get out of the lava tube, stared at her as she passed him, still sitting on the floor where he'd been the whole time. "What are you looking at?"

The man didn't answer her, but he got up without complaint when Evon nudged a leg with his foot. Damn Arunai. She still needed to figure out how to squeeze the secrets out of that one, but it would have to wait. She needed to get rid of the pesky pulling sensation in her mind.

Two steps into the new cavern and she stopped and gaped. In the light of the ball Evon's held up, it was easy to tell that this was no lava tube.

They stood in a straight, level hallway with perfectly vertical sides and an arched ceiling. The floor was the same stone the other cavern had been made from: a dull, reddish grey volcanic stone. The walls and ceiling seemed to be lined with bricks or stone blocks. It was obviously not natural.

She looked back at the hole they'd made. Some of the flat bricks—looking a lot like paving stones—were broken and scattered on the floor.

"Huh," she said. "Was this place here before and the lava tube coincidentally formed right next to it, or did someone build this without realizing they'd almost bored into the lava tube?"

No answer came, the others silently inspecting their new surroundings.

"Why do we always end up underground?" she said. "None of my training at the Academy led me to believe that I'd spend so much time going through caves and tunnels."

"Nature of the work?" Evon posited. "Most of what we've done so far involves the wells and if something is going to be hidden for thousands of years, caves seem like the obvious places."

Marla grunted at that. All she knew was that she was sick and tired of not seeing the daylight in all these *adventures* they'd been having. She started off in the direction closest to where she felt the magic coming from, Evon's light more than enough to navigate by without having to cast her own.

Several minutes later, they passed under an arched place that looked a lot like a doorway, though there was no evidence that a door had ever been attached to it. Marla stopped on the threshold and quinted at the top jamb. With a simple motion of her hand, she conjured another light ball and held it close to the frame. There was something there. She rubbed it, then scraped it with her fingernail, and could finally see what was beneath the dirt.

"I'll be..." she said, tilting her head at what she'd found.

"What is it?" Master Yxna said from just behind her.

"Cogiscro."

"What's it say?" Evon asked.

"Bilarudor. Anger's Fire. That clinches it. It's..." she trailed off when she noticed Sirak leaning in to listen and see what they were looking at. Marla stepped over to the man. "Sit."

"I am not a hound you can command to—"

Marla kicked out and hooked her foot behind his knees and swept them so they buckled. The man dropped to the ground on his butt. "Stay there." She motioned for her friends to join her farther up the corridor and whispered to them. "It's a well. It has to be. That's the only place I've ever seen Cogiscro. And the name? This must be another Well of Power. We need to be careful about what we say in front of this guy. There's no telling if he'll be able to communicate with his people. I get the feeling he's not just some Aruna."

"Sensible," Master Yxna said. "So you think what you're feeling will lead us to the well?"

"I do. What else could it be?"

"A powerful monster that drew you here because it's hungry?" Evon suggested.

"Maybe. We'll find out soon enough. Collect our prisoner and let's go." She allowed her light to dissolve, going back to relying on Evon's.

The party ghosted through the hallways, Raki and

Marla in the front. The young Gypta stayed a few paces ahead while Marla directed him toward where they needed to go to reach the magic she felt. It wasn't hard, since for the most part, it was only the one hallway. They only saw two other corridors coming off their main path, but in each case, the strong feeling was to continue on as they were.

Marla passed through another arch, this one also with the Cosgiscro wording on the frame.

"It's kind of tacky to label the name of the place on every door frame and arch we pass," she said. "It's like me scratching 'Marla's house' on every door where I live."

None of the others commented on what she said. It was just as well. Her irritation was spiking and an argument might result anyway. For that matter, the others all wore looks of dissatisfaction or annoyance on their faces. All but Khrazhti, anyway. The animaru wore her typically neutral expression.

When they passed an intersecting hallway to the right and then one up farther on the left, Marla began to wonder at the floorplan of the area they were in. It seemed like it was strangely uniform. As they reached yet another doorway—with the Cogiscro in place like all the others—she stopped and narrowed her eyes at it.

"Why are you stopping?" Evon asked in a tone that made her want to punch him in the face.

She responded as politely as she could. "Mind your own business." Something was amiss with the archway. It took tilting her head and really focusing on the frame before she realized what it was. "There are smudges in the dirt here, on the Cogiscro symbols themselves." She put her hand up to them. "They're mine. We've been traveling in circles all this time."

"No way," Raki said.

Marla generated her own ball of light again and held it near the ground by the wall. "What's this, if you're so smart? Do you see those scrapes in the dirt on the floor? Do you recognize them?"

The center of the floor was a mess of footprints overlaid one another, but the section of the floor near the wall was out of the path they were traveling. There were obvious signs of scrabbling there.

"Are those the marks from when you threw Sirak down?" Master Yxna asked.

"They are. Like I said, we've been traveling in circles somehow."

"Haven't we been following your senses of where the magic is coming from?" Evon asked.

She looked at her friend like he was a moron, mainly because he was being a moron. "Do you think magic could make it seem like we were going straight even though we were actually moving in a circle but not make it seem to me that we were being led onward?"

"If we have passed through the same archway all these times," Khrazhti said, "then how do we get out of the loop?"

"That's the question, isn't it?" Marla said.

Raki jumped "The side tunnels. Maybe we have to go through them."

Marla wanted to find fault with his assumption, but couldn't. "Let's give them a try."

To make absolutely sure about things, Marla took her dagger and scratched an M into the frame of the arch just beneath the Cosgiscro symbol, then she took her place behind Raki. When they reached the corridor veering off to the right, they took it, even though it felt to her like the magic was pulling her straight down the original hallway. Once they were fully inside the new corridor, her senses snapped into place and suddenly felt like they were pulling her straight ahead.

'Huh. The magic just switched. Now it seems like we're going the right way."

Eventually, they came to another archway. Sure enough, it had not only the Cogiscro, but also an M scratched into the frame.

"Gods damned, son of an ilyu, goat-kissing mate of an escirta," Marla shouted, her hands going to the hilts of both her blades. The urge to attack the door frame with her weapons was almost irresistible, but she managed to clasp her hands together in front of her and keep from doing what would most likely dull or seriously damange her blades.

Even Raki was frustrated, his hands balled into fists and his teeth clenched. "There's still the other hallway, the one on the left up ahead."

"Go," Marla commanded, and the boy knew better than to argue.

As expected, they came to the passage going off to the right and continued on. When they reached the hallway on the left-hand side, they followed it. Marla muttered under hear breath, solely for the reason that she did not want Master Yxna to hear the foul curses she spat. If they ended up back at that...

Marla stopped, along with the rest of them. She panted with the difficulty of keeping herself from attacking any and all of those around her. With her eyes squeezed shut, she hugged herself to keep her hands from straying to her weapons, knowing that as soon as she grabbed hold of them, she would do something she would regret. A keening, whispered moan emitted from her mouth completely independently of her own will.

The anger she felt was palpable, a living thing that writhed within her, swirling through her tissue in no way a physical object could. She knew anatomy and aside from magic, nothing could demonstrate such characteristics. It rose within her, ready to burn her and everything around her to ash.

"Fire!" Khrazhti said loudly. "It is the key. Bilarudor, anger's fire. Marla, you must channel your rage."

"*You* channel your rage," Marla spat back.

"I am not angry. It must be you."

"I'll do it," Evon said. "I can use fire magic."

"Don't you dare," Marla told her friend. "This is my well. It's been attacking and leading me around this whole time. If anyone is going to do anything, it'll be me."

"Then quit whining and do it, before you explode and kill us all."

"Do what?" She'd just about had enough of all the things that had been happening to her, and to these irritating people that called themselves her friends. Her fingers itched to cast fire, alright. Cast fire spells to burn them all up. Even as she thought it, the idea shocked and disgusted her, but her control was slipping.

"Cast fire at the Cogiscro," Khrazhti said. "It may be the well is waiting for you to cast anger's fire."

"Stupidest idea I've ever heard." *Yet, what if?* "Everyone get out of the way. If you get burned to a crisp because you're too stupid to move, it's on your own head."

Marla barely perceived her friends—and even her captive—doing what she said. She didn't wait, though. She couldn't. If she didn't expend some of the magic, some of the fire, within her, she *would* explode, just like Evon said. Without delay, she cast one of the simplest fire magic spells she was well familiar with: Fire Missile.

THIRTY-SIX

A dozen projectiles made of condensed magical fire, larger than her normal missiles, zipped from her outstretched hand toward the Cogiscro representation of the word Bilarudor. She could hardly see for the fire that was raging out from within her, yet she was aware that her projectiles struck the symbol dead-center. She expected that half the archway frame would explode from the impact.

It didn't. Instead, the magic went into the frame, sucked in through the symbol without causing any apparent damage.

For several seconds, other waves of missiles flew from her hand and were sucked into the Cogiscro symbols as well. Finally, her magic depleted, she dropped her arm. The fire within her had gone out—or had been pushed out through the spell. She stumbled and an arm caught her to keep her from falling. A half-second later, another caught her on the other side. When she turned to see who it was, she found Master Yxna and Evon, their faces worried.

"Did I say anything I'll regret?" she asked.

Evon chuckled. "Nah, just the usual thing. We're irritating, you'll kill us all, et cetera."

"Oh." Marla dropped her head toward the ground. It seemed to weigh a lot more than she ever remember it weighing.

Raki's gasp caused her to drag it upward again to look at the archway. As she did, she caught the glimmer that had prompted the response, like the area under the arch was water in a pond and had been disturbed by a tossed stone. The air rippled, the became invisible again, but the view of what was beyond it had changed.

It was similar to the corridor they'd been traveling all day, but it was cleaner, in better repair. Like what it would look like when it was new, however many thousands of years ago that was. She couldn't see a speck of dust, though where she stood, with the help of her friends, the floor was dusty, scratched, and stained.

"Did I say aloud what I was thinking when you suggested to cast the fire spell?" Marla asked Khrazhti.

"I do not know, but you were impolite."

"Ugh. I'm sorry. It was a good idea. You may have saved my life, and maybe some of yours. Thank you."

Khrazhti smiled. "You are welcome. I am glad it worked."

"Yeah, me too. Give me a moment to rest and we can keep going. I seem to be saying that a lot. I'm sorry for my bad attitude. I don't know what is wrong with me." For the first time in a long time, she wasn't angry or annoyed or irritated. She was only exhausted.

"It's the magic here," Master Yxna said. "I think we're all feeling it, but it's affecting you more strongly. You seem to be more sensitive to it, enough so that you felt it drawing you from Sitor-Kanda itself."

"Lucky me."

When Marla stood after sitting for a few minutes, she still felt weak, but they needed to start moving.

"The sensation of the magic pulling me has changed. It's stronger now. I hadn't realized it, but it seems like there was some interference earlier. Now it's gone. I'm ready to go."

Aside from the bone weariness Marla felt, she also noticed that her baseline anger was lower than it had been for some time. As she led her friends through the passage-way, she wondered at the effect.

"Are you all right?" Master Yxna asked her.

Marla hadn't even realized the master was behind her, let alone almost even with her. "I...think so. I'm tired, but it's like being tired after a day of good, hard work. It's a satisfying kind of fatigue. My mood is better than it's been for a long while."

The master nodded, humming to herself. "Most likely it's because of what we've talked about. When you were mad before, near to losing control, did you feel like you were going to explode?"

"Yes. Literally as well as figuratively. It was clear to me that if I didn't expel all that energy building up in me by attacking someone else, it would tear me apart."

"And then when you released it in a controlled way, at the Cogiscro?"

"All that fire and energy and anger flowed out of me in the form of the fire magic I used."

Master Yxna put her hand on Marla's shoulder and turned her to face the master. "So what does that tell you, Marla?"

"That I needed to blow off some steam?" she joked.

"Exactly. I know, you meant it as a joke, but in a very

real sense that was what happened. It wasn't so much that you had to relieve pressure—you did—but more importantly, you had to see what you were feeling in a way other than how you have been viewing it. You had to look at it as a source of energy, not as a power controlling you."

"A source of energy?"

"Marla, we've talked about this. It's your attitude toward your anger and your temper that causes you problems, more so than the rest of us." The master searched the ceiling as if she could find an answer there. "Let me try to explain it this way. You have mastered the school of unarmed combat, right?"

"Yes, just recently."

"I know Master Shanaera taught you the redirection of force. When you are in combat with someone or something much stronger than you, how do you deal with individual attacks?"

"I certainly don't try to block them, strength for strength. I might parry, maybe dodge, but the best thing to do is to use the opponent's force against them."

"Correct," Master Yxna said. "It's the same thing with unwanted emotions. You've been trying so hard to push away or completely ignore your anger and everything that triggers it, you build up pressure within yourself. I know you're strong, that you can take a lot of pressure without cracking, but as time goes on and that pressure builds and builds and builds, one of two things happen. You relieve some pressure, in either minor or major ways, or you explode completely. All the little tantrums and rants ranging from snapping at people to physically assaulting others are your attempt to relieve the pressure. The problem is, you're ignoring the root cause."

"That I'm getting angry to begin with?"

"No. That you see anger is something to be avoided at all costs."

Marla scratched her head. "I don't get it. I was raised, and am reminded constantly, that getting really angry is a bad thing, so I try to keep that from happening."

"It's the wrong approach. Everyone gets angry. It's part of being a person. Quit trying to keep from being a person. You'll get mad, and that's just fine. What is not is trying to ignore it until it gets so out of hand you fly into a mindless rage. Use the angry feelings, redirect the force into more positive things, whether that is confronting someone on what they're doing right away or cutting enough firewood to last the whole winter. Quit being ashamed that you get mad and flow with it. Raki learned that lesson when he was very young, as he showed when he told us about the emotional time when his family was killed."

"Get angry," Marla said, trying to confirm she understood, "and then use it as energy to do something that's not mindless and stupid."

"Yes, now you've got it."

"That will take a lot of getting used to."

"As does every habit that is beneficial for us. Think about it. Long after we resolve whatever it is that we're doing here, there will be times your anger is going to try to get away from you. You'll live a much happier life if you accept that you're not a bad person for feeling that way, and you'll be a better hero using the strong emotion to get the job done."

The master slowed down to rejoin the others behind them as Marla continued on ahead. It made sense, what Master Yxna said, but it didn't sound easy. Marla realized the master had tried to explain it to her several times recently, but with her irritated mood, she hadn't given it the thought it needed. Once she finished dealing with the magic and the well and the current circumstances, she'd think harder on the subject. She only needed to get through her current crisis and hope the annoyances didn't begin to build up again.

The hallway continued on for much longer than the one they had been using to somehow travel in circles. It was an unending tube of perfectly straight walls and floor, the stone in pristine condition, with no side passages or archways. Marla was beginning to think that they would be walking for several days when abruptly, it changed.

Ahead, the hallway looked to be ending. Marla held her light aloft and increased its intensity to illuminate the area ahead, trying to make sense of what she was seeing. At first, it looked like the corridor ended at a stone wall, like whoever had built it suddenly decided that it was deep enough and simply stopped. As she got closer, though, she realized that wasn't the case.

It was true that the perfectly placed stone tiles on the walls and floors ended, but they didn't end in a wall. They changed to carved stone walls that funneled into a narrower tunnel that would only allow one person to pass through at a time.

Marla stopped two steps in front of where the tunnel narrowed. Even holding her light out as far as her arm would stretch, she couldn't see more than five feet into the passageway. Nothing but the cold, grey walls narrowing and then running off in parallel in front of them as far as they could see.

"Well?" she said. Irritation was starting to creep back into her mind. When would the stupid well stop playing games with them and just let them get to what they needed to do?

"I can't sense any magic or traps or anything," Evon said, "though I probably wouldn't unless I was within the narrow part."

"I can still feel the magic coming from that direction," Marla said. "It's still pulling on me. Besides being the only way we can go, it's the right way if my feelings are correct."

"Perhaps we should cast magic down the tunnel," Khrazhti said. "Your fire missiles or my dark bolt or something else?"

"It may not be the best idea to release harmful magic down a long tunnel when we don't know what's down there," Master Yxna said. "What if there is some neutral entity that takes being attacked from hiding unkindly?"

"Of course," Khrazhti said. "You are correct. Pardon me."

"It was a good idea, Khrazhti," Marla said. "At least the core of it. How about I cast a ball of light down there? True, it could still be viewed as an attack if something very light-sensitive is hiding, but if a simple light spell is considered an attack, I doubt we'll have any problems with handling such a creature."

"I can go down and use my dark vision," Raki said. He started heading past Marla to explore.

Marla put her arm out and stopped him from passing by her. "No. I...don't like the feeling. I need to go first. I'll throw a ball of light and then I'll go first."

Raki didn't look happy about it, but he backed off. No one else disagreed, though they looked far from happy about stepping into a bottleneck like they were about to do. If there was an ambush farther down the corridor, they would have to fight one at a time, encumbered by the close stone walls.

Marla wasn't going to budge on taking point, though.

She conjured another light ball, keeping the existing one in her left hand, and threw it down the passage. It bounced a few times and came to rest twenty feet or so away from them. Nothing was visible but the same walls and floor as immediately in front of them.

"Nothing," she said. "I'll pick that one up and throw it again when I get up to it. Give me a few paces and be ready just in case something attacks."

Marla headed down the tunnel, watching carefully for anything that moved. With the crowded space and the light she had available, she could see every crack and crevice in the stone surrounding her. Nothing was amiss.

That is, nothing was amiss until her fifth step. She hadn't even reached the light ball she'd thrown when all of a sudden, her stomach dropped like she'd fallen off a cliff and the lighting changed completely.

CHAPTER

THIRTY-SEVEN

T he light, brighter than it had been by at least five times, shone in Marla's face. It was so radiant it actually caused her pain and she squeezed her eyelids shut and put both hands over her eyes to get rid of the accursed light.

It was several seconds before anything else in the world but the light meant anything to her, but gradually, the purple spots in her closed eyes disappeared and the pain subsided. She found that she was lying down in a bed that, while not the most comfortable she'd ever been in, was nevertheless as soft as the one in her room back at the Academy. In fact, as she bounced a little to test it out, she thought that it might very well be her bed back at the Academy, as strange as that would be. Had she dreamed the entire journey?

She removed her hands first, then over a period of a minute or two, let her eyelids relax and then finally creep open. The room she was in was definitely not her room, though it was similar. That bright beam of light that had caused her so much trouble was coming in through a window at exactly the perfect angle to sear her eyeballs as she was lying there. Coupled with her being in a dimly lit cavern—relatively speaking—just a few moments before, it did a good job of starting her grumbling at the irritating beam.

Marla swung her legs down and lurched to her feet, only to ram her big toe into something on the floor. After a spattering of curses, she looked down to see what it was that had caused what felt like a dead toenail.

It was a wooden box, the sharp corners of which were obviously the culprit. Who in Dizhelim had put such a thing right next to her bed?

She stopped and gaped. Not at the box, which was common looking, if not armed with what felt like razor sharp edges. No, it was the throbbing toe and foot that caught her attention.

"That's not my foot." She said aloud, then slapped a hand over her mouth and darted a look around the room, afraid someone else would be there to hear her talking to herself. No one else was present, so she relaxed as much as she could with her aching toe and rapidly souring mood.

The room, obviously one of the dormitory rooms in the Academy, was a mirror image of her own, but with the same type of furniture. The bed, a desk, a wardrobe, dresser, chest, and a couple of chairs were the sum total of what was there, aside from a few books lying around and more loose clothing scattered about than what was tasteful.

Banging from the next room made her jump and then glare at the wall. Who was making so much racket so early in the morning? A look out the window revealed that yes, it was early, with the sun just cresting the horizon at a perfect angle to create the beam of death that had almost blinded her.

But back to the unfamiliar foot. She reached down to soothe her toe and realized she didn't recognize the arm and hand, either. Too wiry, too hairy, and the nails were atrocious. She wasn't one of those women who expended a lot of energy to paint and pamper their nails, but she at least kept them neat and the cuticles in good shape, neither of which was the case with the ones she was controlling at the moment.

When her thinking finally kicked in, she very nearly slapped herself in the head. Turning toward her dresser, she peered into the mirror hanging above it. The image there had its mouth open and its eyes wide.

She recognized that face. A lanky young man with brown hair falling onto his unremarkable face stared back from the looking glass.

Oh, gods, no. No, no, no.

She dressed quickly, donning what seemed like the cleanest clothing available, before heading out her door. It wasn't until she ran into someone coming down the stairs and almost stumbling into another person carrying a plate of food that it occurred to her that the clothes she had put on were familiar as well. She had seen that ensemble. Several years before. The thought gave her a chill, which was erased entirely as someone opened the door from the common room of the dormitory hall to the outside and slammed the wooden plank into her shoulder.

Marla let loose with a few choice curses and pushed by the hapless woman who had rammed her. Better just to get away from all these people. The familiar burn of her anger being stoked sat in her middle, pulsing as if it were coming to life.

She wasn't sure where she was supposed to be or why she was where she was, but the area was familiar enough. She was at the Academy, heading toward the magic lycad at the moment. More specifically, the magical combat training fields. As she tilted her head at a couple of trees she could swear were smaller than they should be, her foot found something squishy on the path. She closed her eyes and shook her head as the scent of what she had just stepped in wafted up to her nose.

"Who in the hells was riding a horse on the footpaths and why didn't they clean up their mess?" she shouted at nobody. A couple of passing students took in her situation and laughed, but thankfully didn't say anything to her or stick around so she had to knock them both out.

A couple of minutes of scraping her boots in the grass got most of the goo off, but she could still smell the stench of the horse manure as she rounded a corner to go toward the practice fields. She wasn't thinking properly, so it wasn't clear why she needed to go there, but her feet brought her there nonetheless.

While she tried to figure out what was happening and her irritation was increasing by the moment, she didn't notice until the last second that someone was walking opposite her on the path. She juked to the right, then to the left as the other person matched her movements. Despite both of their best efforts, they collided in a slow-motion crash.

"Why are you doing this?" the woman said, her teeth gritted and eyes blazing. "I thought we were going to be civil. I know you don't agree with me breaking things off with you, but you're too petty and your temper is too volatile for me to deal with. Besides, Sharan has been wanting me to spend some time with him for a while. Some close, special time." She gave Marla an exaggerated wink, then pushed her hard, nearly knocking her down. "Now get out of my way and don't bother me again, you horse's ass."

Marla wasn't sure what had just happened, but something inside of her responded to what the woman had said. She had broken up with Marla—or with whoever normally occupied the body Marla was in—and jumped right into bed with this Sharan guy? The affront ratcheted up her annoyance and she stood fuming, contemplating going after the woman to kick her face in. The bitch. Break up with her and mock her, will she?

Marla shook her head. What was she thinking? No one broke up with her. Still, the anger was there. Her fists clenched and unclenched of their own volition and she had the most overpowering urge to hurt someone. A final glance at the back of the woman, who was already disappearing behind a bend in the trail, and she huffed a breath, starting off again to wherever she was supposed to go.

She reached a group of students who looked familiar, though she couldn't really place names to them. They all waited on one of the practice fields, obviously biding their time before a class started. Marla scanned the other fields, seeing a few classes doing the same thing. One group of younger students caught her eye, especially the red-haired girl standing off from the others. Something in her grew sad at the sight, though she didn't know why.

"So, Tresica finally realized she's too good for you," someone's voice said from behind her. Marla didn't respond, figuring the young man was talking to someone else. That was until a hard push on her left shoulder.

Out of reflex, she allowed her body to twist, extending

her right arm and delivering a backhand slap to the face of the one pushing her. The young man staggered from the blow, though she hadn't put too much force into it.

He was fit, with blonde hair and blue eyes, and she disliked him immediately. She also recognized him, which did two things to her. First, it spiked her already hot anger, making it cry out for her to hit him again, and again. Second, it shot an icy tendril through her entire body.

She knew where and when she was now. Knew *who* she was now.

"Struck a nerve, Ivel," the young man said, wiping a small trickle of blood off his lip. His name was Sharan Kolga, and in this situation, Marla knew things did not end well for him.

"I will tell you this once, Sharan. Now is not the time. Trust me when I say that you really don't want to push me right now."

Another young man came up to her and she could barely keep herself from punching him in the face as he grabbed her shoulder. She didn't recognize this one, an average looking student in the robes of a mage-in-training with unkempt reddish-brown hair and a slight build.

"Come on, man," he said. "Don't let Sharan get to you. You know he's just trying to get a reaction out of you. It's not worth it, Ivel, I'm telling you."

Marla understood now. This guy must have been one of her—well, one of Ivel's—friends. The way he treated her anger so casually reminded her of Evon when he attempted to cool her down when her temper rose. She shook his hand off and faced Sharan. The idiot didn't realize what he was playing with and continued to taunt her.

"What's the matter? Wittle Ivel Danson is cranky?

Maybe he needs to take a nap or someone needs to burp him. Oh, I have an idea, how about I punch you really hard in the stomach? That'll make you burp out all the things that are making your tummy upset."

It was irrational, the feelings building within Marla. She knew that. The pitiful attempt at angering her should not have done anything. Yet it did. It could have been all the little things that had piled up on her so far that morning, or maybe it was because though she really didn't feel anything inside about the situation, somehow Ivel's girlfriend ending her relationship with him and choosing the horse's ass in front of her cranked up her anger. All she knew was that the fire within her was increasing, building up to the point where her insides would boil over and explode into action she knew would have dire consequences.

She saw it clearly in her mind, as if she was standing back and watching it. Sharan kept needling her, her anger continued to build, then it would all come to a head. She'd warned him, but he paid no mind to his own safety. Fire erupted from her hands and burned the flesh off the miserable creature in front of her. She would kill him and then would have to pay the consequences for her actions. As she watched it, the scene overlaid with the feelings roiling inside her. All the annoyance and inconsideration and just plain bad luck, it swirled together into a deadly combination. A great heat that would escape with deadly intent. Anger's fire.

The two words made her shake her head and blink. Where had that thought come from. The term was appropriate for the cauldron of rage within her, to the point where she would do the unthinkable.

Marla raised her hands and started to cast a spell,

gesturing with definitive authority and barking the words of power as if they were commands. The magic built, stronger than any spell she'd ever cast before, more than adequate to do the job. With a final syllable screamed at the top of her lungs, she released the magic and directed it at her target.

CHAPTER
THIRTY-EIGHT

A huge gout of flame shot out from Marla's hands, wider even than she could reach with both arms outstretched. It roared ahead and engulfed where she had aimed it.

The trunk of a tree, more than two feet across, burst into flames in an instant. Within seconds the entire twenty-foot height of it was burning so rapidly, the smaller branches were turning instantly to ash. Embers floated downward, students underneath jumping and slapping at the burning particles as they landed on them.

Through it all, Sharan stared in horror as the flame suddenly cut off from Marla's hands. The flame had passed so close to him on its way to the tree, some of his hair was curled and blackened.

Marla put her hands on her knees and sucked in breaths. He body shook as she tried to wrestle it under control.

"If you have any intelligence in that ugly, stupid head of yours," she spat at Sharan, "you will run as fast as you can before I go into a rage. I can't promise I'll be able to miss you on purpose again."

Sharan, showing an impressive knack for self-preservation, silently turned and ran. So did everyone else, including the friend who had tried to talk her out of doing anything rash. So much for friendly advice.

For a time, Marla stood alone, fighting to rein in her anger as the tree nearby was consumed as quickly as only magical fire could accomplish. She had done it. She'd kept herself from killing the weasel Sharan as Ivel had done. She had fought back against the anger and she had come out victorious, if exhausted.

"Ivel Danson," Master Isegrith said. "Come with me."

Damn. She wasn't in the clear yet.

Marla knew where they were going long before they turned down the path to the Administration area. Her worst fears were confirmed when Master Isegrith marched her up to the headmaster's office and sat her down in front of Aletris Meslar's desk. The headmaster's secretary looked younger than she was used to.

At first, Marla thought that maybe Aletris was upset with her, disgusted with what she had done because she frowned at Marla and ignored any attempt to meet eyes with her. Then she realized that she wasn't Marla. She was in Ivel's body, so of course Aletris wouldn't give her the consoling looks she normally did when Marla sat waiting to talk to Master Qydus about her misbehavior.

Master Isegrith returned from speaking with the headmaster and motioned for Marla to follow her into the headmaster's office.

"Sit," Master Qydus said, pointing at a chair without looking up from some papers he was reading. Marla sat.

For several minutes, Master Qydus continued to read while Marla waited. Master Isegrith had taken another chair and waited patiently for the headmaster to finish. When he finally did, he turned his eyes to Marla and she wished he had kept reading. The headmaster's face was made for scowling, but she'd never seen such digust and anger in them as they were now. His brows, drawn down, created sharp cuts in his forehead, emphasized even more on his narrow features.

"You have, in the full view of more than a dozen students and at least one master, cast powerful magic at another student. How do you explain this?"

"I didn't cast it at anyone. I cast it at a tree."

Master Qydus glared at her for a moment, as if he was waiting for more. "Do you think the distinction matters?"

"Yes, Master," she said. "I do. The taunting and the baiting sparked my anger and something in me wanted to attack Sharan Kolga, but I was able to control myself enough to release my rage on the tree instead of him. I didn't harm anyone."

The hard slap of the master's hand on his desk made Marla jump. "Do you find this funny, Iven Danson? Casting dangerous magic with little or no control around other students is a very serious issue. You expect to be rewarded because your loss of control resulted in you destroying Academy property instead of killing another person?"

"No. I..."

"It is clear to me that you do not deserve the privilege to wield magic, nor to receive instruction at this school. You will first be taken to the Medica, where Masters Videric and Isegrith will remove your ability to cast. Once you have been rendered unable to cause further damage magically, you will be escorted from the Academy grounds. You are hereby expelled from Sitor-Kanda and disapproved for all time."

Marla's mouth dropped open. Expelled and made unable to cast at all? As far as she knew, that had only happened once in the entire history of the Academy. They couldn't take her magic. They couldn't kick her out. She was the Malatirsay and she wouldn't stand for it. They'd see she wouldn't give up easily. She'd fight, fight and escape.

The tingling in Marla's hands cried out for her to use her magic, to strike preemptively before several of the masters got together to render her unconscious so they could carry out their punishment. Her hand twitched, ready to burn Master Qydus to ash where he sat, just before she destroyed Master Isegrith.

The anger was building again, threatening to take over her entire body, to make her do whatever it willed. Many would lose their lives if that happened. It was even worse than what really happened with Ivel.

A voice deep inside her head shouted at her to remember who she was, what she was about. *You can't let it control you,* it said. *You must not try to dispel it, but to come in harmony with the anger.*

She growled under her breath, wanting to disregard the thought completely. But she couldn't. It was Master Yxna's voice, saying essentially the same thing she had told Marla before. Not only that, Raki's soft voice echoed in her mind as well. *I realized that those emotions are part of me and I accepted them instead of trying to fight them.*

She realized she was still sitting in the chair, Master Qydus staring at her. Her knuckles were white from her gripping the chair arms so tightly, but she hadn't done anything yet. She wouldn't.

She couldn't.

Marla closed her eyes and focused on her breathing. The anger inside her moved like a great serpent, shifting her internal organs as it slithered around, bringing heat with it as it went. It was a foreign thing, an invader, something to be fought with every bit of her strength.

But was it? Master Yxna had told her she needed to accept that all her emotions were part of her. None were truly good or bad, but the results of how she accepted them might be. It made a bit more sense now, more than it ever had. The anger—as well as sorrow, disappointment, and all her other feelings—were just part of who she was. The sooner she accepted that, the better off she'd be.

She mentally embraced the snake, taking it into her, accepting that it *was* her. The heat and pressure she'd been feeling so often lately dwindled. Not completely, but they became more familiar, more comfortable. Part of her.

She sighed out a shuddering breath and opened her eyes.

Master Yxna looked back at her from mere inches away.

"Marla? Are you...okay? What happened?"

Marla blinked and took in a deep breath. She felt oddly calm, though seconds before she felt like she'd been fighting for her life against herself. "I...yeah. I think I am. Wait, what do you mean 'what happened?' What did you see?"

Evon stepped up, crowding Master Yxna in the narrow corridor they'd been in before her...her what? Visions? Dreams? Hallucinations?

"You disappeared," he said. "Just vanished, and something blocked us from moving forward in the tunnel."

Marla tilted her head at her friend. "Vanished? For how long?"

"More than half an hour."

"Closer to an hour," Raki called from behind Evon. "Jia has been working with me on keeping an internal clock going so I can figure out the time and how long things take."

Evon frowned at the Gypta boy, but conceded. "Okay, almost an hour."

Marla thought back to whatever it was that happened to her. It could have all happened in an hour, though it seemed like longer. Now that she thought about it, there were a few pieces of time in there where it seemed she skipped the boring bits, like most of the walk to class.

"You said the passageway was blocked during that time?" she asked.

Master Yxna answered this time. "It was, but not by anything we could see. It simply would not let us pass. We tried every spell we could think of, but there wasn't anything to target. We couldn't even sense that there was a magical obstruction. Where did you go?"

"I..." she started, but decided against going into the whole story at the moment. "I'll tell you about it later. It was a vision kind of thing, though I was in it, but I wasn't me. Oh, it doesn't really matter right now. Let's continue on. While we're talking, someone may be getting an ambush ready."

She knew that the logic there was flawed, but it didn't matter. She reached down and found the comforting feel of her sword hilt on its belt where it was supposed to be, and maneuvered it so she could turn and head down the narrow tunnel she was now in. Again. The others followed after and nothing stopped them from doing so this time.

The passage didn't stay narrow for too long, a couple of turns and it suddenly widened, just as it had narrowed when they first entered it. Better yet, nothing was waiting to attack them. Marla exited the slim corridor as quickly as she could and breathed out in relief when she could no longer touch both walls at the same time, even with her arms outstretched.

The new hallway looked a lot like the one they'd been traveling in before the bottleneck. Stone covered, no dirt or dust, and no damage to any of it. Marla waited for the others to spread out in the corridor and spotted Sirak Isayu, right behind Evon, with Raki and Khrazhti behind him in case he tried to escape. He looked at her curiously, no doubt trying to figure out where she had gone and how it had happened. She wished she knew.

"Okay," Marla said. "That's a little more comfortable. Now all we need to do is follow the..." She realized as she was talking that something was amiss.

"What is it?" Evon asked, hand going to his sword.

"The magic that's been drawing me. It's gone."

"What do you mean it's gone?"

"I can't feel it. It's like it disappeared off the face of Dizhelim, or like I suddenly have lost the ability to feel it. I don't know what we need to do now."

Master Yxna stepped up even with her. "All we can do is keep exploring. There has to be something here."

Marla shrugged as the master led her down the wider corridor. It soon emptied into a larger area, one that looked like it was an auditorium or a big meeting room.

"This looks promising," Marla said, taking in the same stone façade on the walls and floor as had been in the corridor. Though large, the round room had no furniture of any kind. It also had no other corridors or any doors except the hall they entered through.

Marla opened her mouth to complain about dead ends when something unseen but powerful nonetheless slammed into her. From the grunts and moans of the others, she wasn't the only one.

CHAPTER
THIRTY-NINE

A power the strength of which she'd never felt before bathed Marla's body and diffused through it. Instantly, the familiar feeling of rage boiled up, like it had in her stint as Ivel Danson. The pressure within her head threatened to burst her skull, and the heat of it made things even worse.

Honestly, she felt like killing anything and everything around her, just to sate her anger.

Recalling not more than an hour or two before, she dove deep within herself, analyzing her feelings and the energy flowing through her. She could see it, in her mind, a glowing mass within her body. It was a source of power, ultimately, but one that was tricky to utilize. Still, she knew it *could* be used, so she worked toward accepting it, letting it fuse with her, recognizing it as truly being part of her.

The pressure decreased and the powerful urge to destroy tempered somewhat. She dug deeper, really inspecting her feelings and, more importantly, the power afflicting her that brought those feelings to life.

It was as Raki had said, and what Master Yxna had been

trying to explain to her. All this time, for so many years, Marla had tried to fight her annoyance, her anger, and all it had done was to cause an accumulation of frustrated emotions. Now, she could see that though something was irritating her, she could use the heightened awareness to decide how to utilize the extra energy and passion it gave her. She was no longer a slave to the rage, nor did she really control it like a weapon she could pick up and set down. Instead, it *was* her, and she used it as she did any other part of her, like her arms and legs.

A smile came to her face, though her mood was still what she would consider foul. She was on her way to peacefully coexisting with a mostly unwanted emotion. It would take work—and lots of it—to become even-tempered, but it was possible. Mostly, though, she realized she could get angry but not so much that she was out of control. It was a significant point she'd reached and it held so much promise for her future.

She sighed and sat on the floor of the chamber, content to wait out whatever the power was trying to do to her. She wouldn't throw a fit, wouldn't rant and rave, she would simply wait until an obvious choice confronted her.

A few minutes later, the power disappeared, the pressure on her body easing. She saw her friends, then, scattered about the room. Some were sitting, others were standing, but they all wore looks of relief. Even Sirak Isayu, seated on the floor with his knees bunched up to his chest, had an expression of welcome fatigue. Khrazhti alone looked completely unaffected by whatever had happened.

"What was that?" Evon asked. "I got so angry. Is that what you've been feeling all this time, Marla?"

"Probably," she said. "But I finally listened to my friends

and I don't think I'll be reacting as poorly anymore. I think maybe I learned my lesson."

"It's about time. Are we going to have to take a trip over the ocean to a hostile island and almost die numerous times every time you need to learn a lesson? Because if so, I need to figure out how not to be involved. You have a lot of other lessons to learn."

"Ha. Ha."

"Marla?" Khrazhti said.

"Yeah?"

When Khrazhti didn't answer, Marla looked to the animaru and saw that she was pointing to the center of the round chamber. The object there was familiar: a circular well with a low stone wall around it, an indentation on the face.

"It *was* a well," Marla said. "But...where's the gemstone? It usually appears when we defeat the guardian of the well."

Master Yxna cleared her throat to get Marla's attention, then pointed at the stone right in front of the younger woman. There, hovering three feet above the floor, was a gem a third the size of her palm.

"Oh."

Marla plucked the gemstone from the air. It was a pale red, not quite pink and not really orange, either. It looked to her like the ghost of a ruby, barely clear enough that she could see light and shadows through it, but no real shapes. For its size, the weight seemed off as she held it up. Too light, like it really was the ghost of a gemstone.

"You're up," Evon said. "This one has been yours since the beginning."

Marla nodded. She wasn't going to argue. She'd already seen a few wells activated, but hadn't had the chance to do so herself. Until now. She caught Sirak Isayu intent on her and what was going on, his eyes locked onto the gem while he did a poor job of acting like he wasn't fascinated. She wondered what he thought of the whole thing.

Marla walked up to the well and placed the stone in the indentation present in the wall surrounding it. As she had seen with the others, the socket sucked the gem out of her hand when she brought it within an inch of placing it herself.

Light blasted out of the depths of the well, spraying up toward the ceiling. This one was mostly reds, oranges and yellows. The colors of fire. It wasn't coincidental. The name of the well was Bilarudor, so it was fitting that the magic displayed itself as fire-like.

The colors, like thousand of tiny fireflies with their glows cranked up all the way, zoomed around the room, twisting and turning as they made a circuit of the ceiling. Marla counted and on the seventh lap, the swirling increased, like a tornoado of magical light, only upside down. The magic shot up toward the ceiling, but when it reached the stone it spread out as if splattering on the hard surface, at the same time phasing through it to go outside.

Marla hadn't been outside one of the well chambers when a wells magic had been released and she wondered what it looked like. She imagined it was very impressive. Maybe she'd get a chance to observe it one of these days.

She spotted the brightly lit stone falling slowly from the point of impact of the light and the ceiling and raced over to catch it. With it's slower-than-gravity fall, she easily snatched it out of the air. As expected, the symbol for Bilarudor was etched into the surface.

The lines of the Cogiscro glowed with a red light that matched the gem she had placed in the well's wall perfectly. She could also feel heat radiating from the stone. After examining it for a moment and recognizing that it was essentially the same as the others they'd collected, but with a different word on it, she pocketed the stone to add to her collection. She'd been keeping all the stones her friends had found, certain they would have a use sometime in the future. She wasn't sure what that use was, but when she figured it out, she would have all the stones safe and neatly organized.

"Another one," she said, walking back toward her friends. "Who even knew that there was such thing as anger magic?"

"I don't think there is," Evon said. "There might be a school of magical thought that deals with anger, though I've never seen reference to it. These things we're dealing with, I don't think all of them were known even in the Age of Magic. I get the sense that they had been locked away even before that time."

"That's a scary thought," Marla said. "Who knows what releasing all of this will do?"

"It will make more magic available in the world," Master Yxna said.

"Sure, but is that a good thing or a bad thing?"

"Good. Probably."

Marla laughed, the first time she had for a long time. It felt good. Which reminded her..."Hey, I'm not in a foul mood. That's something new."

"It is, and thank the gods for that," Evon told her.

"Thank the Well of Anger," she said. "I don't know about the rest of you, but I'd like to get out of here. We've still got a long way to go to get home."

"That's it, then?" Evon asked.

"I think so. I found what was drawing me, releasing the magic of the well helped me get rid of the constant anger I've been feeling lately, though you'd think with more anger in the world I'd feel more of it. I've done what I came here to do. I'm ready to go home."

"Me, too," Raki said.

They found a door that Marla swore was not there before the well appeared. Behind it was a set of simple stone stairs that led up through a trapdoor to the surface. Not the surface of the crater, but above on the rim.

"I like that much better than the way we got down there," Marla said as she headed back toward the forest they'd crossed over the previous few days.

"Do you know the way?" Evon asked her. "Some special magic you've learned that no one else knows?"

Marla shook her head at her friend and pointed. "We— and our ambushers—trampled enough plants to make it easy to see where we came from. It might not be the most direct way, though it could be, but it won't be a problem to get back to the beach. If we hurry, we might be able to get the signal sent before daylight the morning after tomorrow."

The trip back to the beach was easier than when they'd been traveling the other way. Aside from the path they'd bashed through the vegetation, they didn't have to stop to fight. They twice saw some of the denizens of the island—one small group of the smoke-snakes and a larger group of those round monsters with the spiky appendages coming out of the top of them—but though the party was in full view of the creatures, they didn't move to attack.

"Do you think the island is safe now, or is it that we're the ones who took care of the well, so the monsters won't attack us?" Raki asked.

"There's no telling," Evon said. "Not unless we separate from Marla. She's actually the one who freed the well, so if there's an approved status, she'll have it, not us."

To Marla, it didn't make any difference. The fact that the monsters didn't attack was enough for her. She wouldn't question it too thoroughly.

As they got closer and closer to the beach, Sirak Isayu began to show signs of his displeasure. Though their pace was easy, he was sweating. His whole body was tense and his eyes darted around, looking for an escape path.

"How did you get to this island," Marla asked the Aruna. "Do you have a boat you hid here?"

The man didn't answer her, of course, but after everything else that had happened, Marla didn't even let it raise her ire. They would have lots of time to interrogate the man properly later on, if it would even be worth it to do so.

They pushed through to get to the beach the second day. It had gotten dark long before they reached the beach that had been their entry point. Though they'd been on the island longer than she'd thought they'd be, Marla cast her spell and sent several up into the sky. She planned on doing it again just before dawn, and she expected the captain would see it, or at least find out about it from someone else who had. He'd fetch them sometime around late morning. Then, finally, they'd be on their way home.

FORTY

Captain Asgeir surprised them by arriving early in the morning, not more than two hours after dawn. When they were rowed back to the ship, he explained it to them.

"I saw the bigger lights you sent two days back, in the afternoon. I think everyone in the city saw them. They were bright enough in the daylight. I wondered what they'd look like in the dark. How did you create such a display?"

"That wasn't my—" Marla started.

"Different magic," Evon interrupted. "It was a much more involved spell, and more powerful. Not really something you do often. It had to be for the lights to be seen in the daytime, right?"

"Oh, that makes sense. I came yesterday, but didn't see you. When the lights appeared last night, I came back. The others that you sent up this morning went off while I was already on the way here."

"Thank you, Captain," Master Yxna said. "We appreciate you coming to get us."

"That was the arrangement. May I ask, though, who this man is? Is he a native from the island?"

"No, nothing like that. He followed us here, though we're still not sure what boat brought him and his friends here."

"Friends?" The captain looked around for other strangers.

"They didn't make it. The island is as dangerous as you've heard."

"I believe it," he said. "Well, you're all back safe and sound. Let's get you to the mainland so you can have a proper meal."

"That would be very much appreciated," the master said.

It wasn't until the ship was well under way, rapidly approaching the mainland, when Marla realized she hadn't checked the message tablet since the day before they'd found the well. She'd been so angry the entire time they'd been on the island, she hadn't taken the thing out of her pack. No doubt the others had felt the magical shift that occurred when they freed the magic of the well. She retrieved the tablet and, sure enough, there were new messages.

Was that another shift from a well being found? who found it and what happened?
—Aeden

We felt it, too. It wasn't us, though. Marla? Evon? Is everyone all right?
—Fahtin

Marla and Evon? Why aren't you answering? Is everything okay? It's been several hours since our first messages.

—Aeden

Marla read the messages out to the others, then took out the stylus and scratched her own message, reading it aloud when she was finished.

Sorry, everyone. This is Marla. We were a bit busy. Yes, it was us. We found the Well of Anger on the island of Iracundia. We released the magic and we're on the way back to the mainland. We'll fill you all in when we get back to the Academy.

It was only a few minutes until a response came.

Iracundia? You traveled to the island no person has ever visited and departed alive? Please report to my office as soon as you return. I assume Master Yxna has found you and accompanied you, though I am not sure if it is worse that she joined you in your madness or that you went off alone on such an errand. I will wait anxiously for your arrival.
—Qydus Okvius

Marla had to bark a laugh when she read the message out loud to the others. "I guess I might get in trouble, after all."

Another message came in as the details of the the city of Hirsen grew sharper. It wouldn't be long until they made it to the harbor and could get that meal the captain had referred to.

Marla, this is Fahtin. I had another vision since you left. Several, in fact, but the one I had only two days ago included something about you. I'm not sure if it makes any sense, but I saw a dark creature stalking you. It sprang, but you injured it, then took it prisoner.

Though it seemed to be made of shadow, and I couldn't even tell what form it took, I did get a feeling about it, a sensation I recognized. I've felt it before, at least twice, in visions about the Dark Council. I'm pretty sure the creature is a person. Though it might not mean anything, watch out for any attacker that ambushes you. It might have been sent by the Dark Council. It might even be part of the Dark Council.

Be safe.

Marla had been reading the message out loud as she read it for herself, but stopped speaking before the last three sentences. She snapped her head to Sirak Isayu, who had been sitting near the edge of the deck. They hadn't rebound his feet. After all, where was he going to go? She realized immediately that had been a mistake. Even as she met eyes with him, he finished loosening the ropes from his hands he had cut with some part of the ship. He smirked at her and threw himself overboard.

"Damn it!" she shouted, and rushed to the rail, searching the water for him.

Evon beat her there and cast his Fire Missile spell, spraying out the little fire pellets into the water, but by the time Marla could get a look, there was no sign of the man. She followed the rail around the side and toward the back of the boat, scrutinizing the wake behind them. After several minutes of looking, she—and the others—gave up.

Grumbling about the situation, she read the last part of the message to the others, then penned her response.

Thanks, Fahtin, but I read too slowly. While I was reading your message, our prisoner jumped overboard and we lost him in the water. Does the name Sirak Isayu seem familiar to you?

It does, though I don't know why. I'll try to focus on it the next time I have visions about the Dark Council, but I'm afraid I'll find out he's actually one of the thirteen. I'm sorry I didn't warn you in time.

She didn't blame Fahtin, and she responded to say so. Any further discussion would have to wait until she got back home. The sick feeling in her stomach that had nothing to do with the ocean was pricking her temper and she'd just as soon not have to deal with anger issues again so soon.

"A member of the Dark Council," Evon said. "If we could have gotten him back to the Academy, we would have been able to get all kinds of information out of him. It's a shame."

"It is," she said, "but there's no use dwelling on it. The ocean is safer here than in most other places, but it still has dangers. He'll have to swim in it to reach the shore. He may end up dying. There's nothing we can do about it one way or another.

"I'm satisfied with what we've accomplished. I learned valuable lessons that will help me in the future, we released more magic into the world, and I have to think that finding another well is important to our overall mission and war with the animaru. We'll deal with the Dark Council later. For now, how about that meal, a nice rest in our inn, and then we go back home? There are plenty of other things to worry about besides Sirak Isayu. For the first time in a long time, I feel like we might actually get some of those things done."

EPILOGUE

Iacci Carino presented himself to the High Itera of the Holy Church of Vanda, Lerus Costanti. It was the first time he had seen one of the top three officials of the church. He'd caught a glimpse of the leader himself, the Patr Pruma of the church, Lucio Sanctus one time, but he didn't make it a habit of associating with the very upper echelon of his god's organization.

Rather, they didn't associate with the likes of him.

Such was to be expected, of course. Who was he to them? One of the Divinely Gifted, surely, but still of humble means, a simple servant of those who actually ran Vanda's church.

High Itera Costanti held his long-fingered hand out for Iacci to kiss, as was the accepted form of greeting. Iacci was nothing if not cognizant of the ritualistic requirements of performing his service. He bent to kiss the man's hand and straightened.

Lerus Costanti was a tall man—not that he towered over Iacci sitting as he was—and he used his height to loom. Or so Iacci had heard. He had almost a decade and a half more than Iacci's forty-two years, but his long hair was still black, without grey or white in it, at least as far as Iacci could see. The blue eyes set deep in his face contrasted well with the dark hair and added to the impression of power. As if one of the three top officials of the church, directly below the Patr Pruma himself, needed anything else to lend him authority.

In truth, Iacci was glad the high itera wasn't standing. He was of a more modest height, short if one believed the taunts, and it was a subject he didn't like to discuss. Or think about. Ah, but he wasn't here for that. He was in front of High Itera Costanti for something he would take great pleasure in discussing.

"I understand that you have something important to discuss with me, Iacci?" the High Itera said.

Iacci blinked rapidly at the church official. "I do, Patr. Thank you for seeing me."

"Of course, of course. We have so few of the Divinely Gifted such as you. You and your brothers perform important work for the church. You—and they—are valued."

"It is a privilege to serve. I have been working on trying to discern methods for obtaining more powerful...ah, resources for the glory of the church. My studies have opened up to me new avenues for doing so."

"Truly?" Costanti said. "You are circumspect, I trust? Many in the church do not agree with using all available resources. It would not do for some of these others to gain knowledge of anything they might see as untoward."

"Yes, Patr. I am very careful not to reveal any of my work. It is to you alone I speak of this. Even other of the Divinely Gifted do not know where my research leads or what plans I will propose."

"As it should be. I know I can rely upon you, Iacci. Now, what part of your work do you wish to discuss with me?"

Iacci's eyelids fluttered several times as he focused his thoughts. "It is power. The main thrust of my research is about obtaining power."

"As are most activities of men, inside and outside the church."

Iacci blinked and squeezed his eyes shut for a brief moment. "Yes, Patr. I...am not explaining this correctly. What I mean to say is that tangible, real power is my goal. Not political or social, not even the power that comes from great riches. What I study is the power to make things happen, to affect things in the world."

"Iacci, all power does what you suggest. If you cannot explain it better to me, then I am afraid you have been wasting your time."

"No." Why did his eyes always feel like they were as dry as the air in the Sittingham Desert? "That is to say, what I wish to explain is important." Iacci lowered his voice. "I'm talking about *magical* power." He glanced around to make sure no one else could hear him, though he'd checked several times already since he'd entered the High Itera's audience room.

"That is a word not to be spoken within these holy walls, Iacci. You know this."

Iacci dropped to his knees. "I do, Patr. Please, forgive me. I seem unable to describe the power of which I speak acceptably."

"You have made your point clear, my son. I shall let the transgression pass. Rise, stand on your feet. Do not utter such things where others can hear them." High Itera Costanti tapped his chin with a finger. "So this *power* of which you speak, what is it you seek to do?"

"I have located a resource, one that the church can exploit for many different purposes. I have developed a method for seizing this resource, making it our own. I ask your permission—as well as some aid that might be needed—to secure it."

"This power, it will aid us in our task of increasing the church's ability to respond to the dark forces moving against the world?"

"It will, Patr. In fact, the power could be considered light itself. A most suitable weapon."

"Yes, clearly. What will you need?"

"Some loyal followers who share our...acceptance of unconventional methods, perhaps some supplies, and some monetary resources with which to secure other necessary supplies."

"There is little trouble gaining those things. Tell me, Iacci, what form does this *resource* take? What exactly to you plan on obtaining for the glory of the church and the furtherance of its mission?"

Iacci blinked five times in rapid succession and a small smile came to his face. "It is a person, Patr. A very special person."

THE STORY CONTINUES in Song of Prophecy 12: Hero's Life, which features the stunning and extraordinary archer Lily.

If you'd like to be sure not to miss anything, and to score some free books, join my newsletter **here**.

(For the paperback version of this book, you can go to my website at pepadilla.com and click on the Newsletter menu item, or use the form at the bottom of every page).

HERO'S ANGER
GLOSSARY

Following is a list of unfamiliar terms. Included are brief descriptions of the words as well as pronunciation. For the most part, pronunciation is depicted using common words or sounds in English, not IPA phonetic characters. Please note that the diphthong *ai* has the sound like the English word *Aye*. The *zh* sound, very common in the language Alaqotim, is listed as being equivalent to *sh*, but in reality, it is spoken with more of a buzz, such as *szh*. Other pronunciations should be intuitive.

Abhincstagna (*ab·HEENK·STAG·nah*) – a lake in ancient Ascesh that reportedly had magical properties. The great dragon Tero made his home near the lake.

Abyssum (*a·BIS·um*) – the world of the dead, Percipius's realm.

Acolyte – a current Hero Academy student who has mastered at least one school, but not three or more.

Adept – a Hero Academy student who has mastered at least three schools and continues to study at the Academy.

Aeden Tannoch (AY·*den* TAN·*ahkh*) – a man born to and trained by a highland clan, raised by the Gypta, and able to utilize the magic of the ancient Song of Prophecy.

Aeid Hesson (*AY·id*) – former Master of the School of prophecy at the Hero Academy. He was murdered in his office at the Academy.

Aesculus (*AY·skyoo·lus*) – the god of water and the seas.

Agypten (*a·GIP·ten*) – an ancient nation, no longer in existence. It was from this nation the Gypta originated.

Ahred Chimlain (*AH·red CHIM·lane*) – noted scholar of the first century of the third age

Aila Ven (*AI·la ven*) – a woman of small stature who joins the party and lends her skills in stealth and combat to their cause.

Ailgid (*ILE·jid*) – one of the five highland clans of the Cridheargla, the clan Greimich Tannoch's wife came from.

Ailred Kelzumin (*ILE·red kel·ZOO min*) – the Master of the School of Water Magic at the Hero Academy.

Alain (*a·LAYN*) – the god of language. The ancient language of magic, Alaqotim, is named after him.

Alaqotim (*ah·la·KOTE·eem*) – the ancient language of magic. It is not spoken currently by any but those who practice magic.

Aletris Meslar (*ah·LET·ris MES·lar*) – the personal clerk and assistant to Headmaster Qydus Okvius, of the Hero Academy.

Aliten (*AL·it·ten*) – a type of animaru that is humanoid but has wings and can fly.

Alloria Yurgen (*ah·LORE·ee·ah YURE·gen*) – the leader (Vituma) of the Dark Council. She is the 102nd leader since the Council's creation.

Alpin Trebhin (*AL·pin TREH·vin*) – the Croagh warrior who was chosen as the chief for the Trebhin clan after the previous chief was killed in the Death Oath ritual combat.

Alvaspirtu (*al·vah·SPEER·too*) – a large river that runs from the Heaven's Teeth mountains to the Kanton Sea. The Gwenore River splits from it and travels al the way down to the Aesculun Ocean.

Amatia (*ah·MAH·tee·ah*) – a member of the Dark Council, a seeress.

Ander Tosselnam – one of the three High Itera of the Church of Vanda.

Animaru (*ah·nee·MAR·oo*) – dark creatures from the world Aruzhelim. The name means "dark creatures" or "dark animals."

Aquilius Gavros (*ah·KWIL·ee·us GAV·roze*) – the Dark Prophet; he lived in the Age of Magic, during the time of the War of Magic.

Arania (*ah·RAH·nee·ah*) – a kingdom in the western part of the continent of Promistala, south and east of Shinyan. A thing of Arania is called Aranir.

Arba – an essentially extinct race of magical people whose ancestors were directly created by Mellaine out of the stuff of the forest and her magical tears. They had a special connection to nature and could use magic directly from the natural world.

Arcus (*ARK·us*) – the god of blacksmithing and devices.

Arcusheim (*AHR·coo·shime*) – a large city on the southern shore of the Kanton Sea, the capital of the nation of Sutania and the home of Erent Caahs before he left to travel the world.

Arto Deniselo (*AHR·toe day·NEE·say·low*) – a dueling master in the Aranian city of Vis Bena who taught Erent Caahs how to drastically improve his combat abilities.

Aruna (pl. Arunai) (*ah·ROON·ah; ah·roo·NIE*) – a citizen of the tribal nation of Campastra. Originally, the name was pejorative, referring to the color of their skin, but they embraced it and it became the legitimate name for the people in Campastra.

Aruzhelim (*ah·ROO·shel·eem*) – the world from which the animaru come. The name means "dark world," "dark universe," or "dark dimension." Aruzhelim is a planet physically removed from Dizhelim.

Ascesh (*AY·sesh*) – the northernmost continent in Dizhelim. Thousands of years ago, it included what is now Teroshi.

Asfrid Finndottir (ASS·*frid* *fin·DOT·teer)* – the Master of the School of Cryptology at the Hero Academy.

Asgeir Balstad (*AZ·gare BALL·stad*) – the boat captain Marla helps in Hirsen. He takes them to Iracundia and promises to pick them up.

Assector Pruma (*ah·SEC tor PROO·mah*) – roughly "first student" in Alaqotim. This is the student aid to a master in one of the schools at the Hero Academy. There can be only one per school and this person conducts research, helps to teach classes, and assists the master in any other necessary task.

Aubron Benevise (*AW·brun ben·uh·VEES*) – the Master of History and Literature at the Hero Academy.

Auxein (*awk·ZAY·in*) – an aide to the master and the First Student (Assector Pruma) at the Hero Academy. For larger schools, there may be more than one. In some schools there may not be any.

Awresea (*aw·reh·SAY·uh*) – a kingdom that no longer exists, the home of Tazi Ermenko who taunted the god Fyorio and was destroyed. The fiery, desolate location where the kingdom was is now known as Fyrefall.

Ayize Fudu (*aye·EEZ   FOO·doo*) – a Hero Academy adept, one of Quentin Duzen's associates.

Barda Sirusel (*BAR·duh   seer·oo·SELL*) – the boy who tried to bully Marla when she was a child.

Batido (*bah TEE·doe*) – what Aeden's friends call their dormitory, from the Dantogyptain words for *second home*.

Beldroth Zinrora (*BEL·droth   zin·ROR uh*) – the Master of the School of Dark Magic at the Hero Academy.

Bhagant (*bog·AHNT*) – the shortened form of the name for the Song of Prophecy, in the language Dantogyptain.

Bhavisyaganant (*bah·VIS·ya·gahn·ahnt*) – The full name for the Song of Prophecy in Dantogyptain. It means "the song of foretelling of the end," loosely translated.

Biuri (*bee·OOR·ee*) – small, quick animaru that recall the appearance and movements of rodents. They are useful as spies because of their small size and quickness.

Blennus (*blen·oos*) – Dannel Powfrey's horse.

Brace – the term used by the Falxen for a group of assassins ("blades").

Braitharlan (*brah·EE·thar·lan*) – the buddy assigned in the clan training to become a warrior. It means "blade brother" in Chorain.

Brausprech (*BROW·sprekh*) – a small town on the northwest edge of the Grundenwald forest, in the nation of Rhaltzheim. It is the hometown of Urun Chinowa.

Breath of Galendia (*gah·LEN dee·ah*) – the boat owned by Asgeir Balstad.

Brenain Kanda (*bren·AY·in KAHN·duh*) – a mythological heroine who stole magic from the god Migae.

Bridgeguard – the small community, barely more than a guardpost, on the mainland end of the northern bridge to Munsahtiz

Broken Reach – a rugged, unforgiving land to the

southeast of the Grundenwald. There are ruins of old forti-
fications there.

Campastra (cam·PAHS·trah) – a tribal nation in the
southwestern portion of the continent of Promistala

Cara Moore – a member of the Dark Council.

Catriona (Ailgid) Tannoch (CAT·ree·own·ah ILE·jid) –
the wife of Greimich Tannoch. She is originally from the
Ailgid clan, but now has taken the last name Tannoch.

Ceti *(SET·ee)* – a higher level type of animaru,
appearing aquatic with small tentacles, even though there
is no water in Aruzhelim. They are very intelligent and have
magical aptitude. Some of them are accomplished with
weapons as well.

Cholu (*CHOE·loo*) – the leader of the group of tribespeople Sirak brings with him to get Marla.

Chorain (*KHAW·rin*) – the ancestral language of the
highland clans of the Cridheargla.

Clavian Knights (*CLAY·vee·en*) – the fighting force of
the Great Enclave, the finest heavy cavalry in Dizhelim.

Codaghan (*COD·ah·ghan*) – the god of war.

Cogiscro (*coe·JEE·scroe*) – an ancient system of runic
writing that was used in magic spells. The symbols are
phonetic and are arranged in a circular pattern.

Colechna *(co·LECK·nah)* – one of the higher levels of
animaru. They appear to be at least part snake, typically
highly intelligent as well as skilled with weapons. They are
usually in the upper ranks of the command structure. Their
agility and flexibility makes them dangerous enemies in
combat. A few can use magic, but most are strictly melee
fighters.

Corcan – one of the five highland clans of the Cridheargla.

Cridheargla (*cree·ARG·la*) – the lands of the highland

clans. The word is a contraction of Crionna Crodhearg Fiacla in Chorain.

Crionna Crodhearg Fiacla (*cree·OWN·na CROW·arg FEE·cla*)) – the land of the highland clans. It means "old blood-red teeth" in Chorain, referring to the hills and mountains that abound in the area and the warlike nature of its people. The term is typically shortened to Cridheargla.

Croagh Aet Brech (*CROWGH ET BREKH*) – the name of the highland clans in Chorain. It means, roughly, "blood warriors." The clans sometimes refer to themselves simply as Croagh, from which their nickname "crows" sprang, foreigners not pronouncing their language correctly.

Daana Vaskova (*DAHN·ah   vas·COVE   ah*) – a prophetess and author who lived at the end of the Age of Magic. She wrote many children's tales, the majority of which had hidden meanings and prophecies.

Daibhidh Trebhin (*DAY·vid TREH·vin*) – the clan chief of the Trebhin clan when Aeden went to meet with the other clans of Croagh.

Dannel Powfrey – a self-proclaimed scholar from the Hero Academy who meets Aeden on his journey.

Danta (*DAHN·ta*) – the goddess of music and song. The language Dantogyptain is named after her.

Dantogyptain (*DAHN·toe·gip·TAY·in*) – the ancestral language of the Gypta people.

Daodh Gnath (*DOWGH GHRAY*) – the Croagh Ritual of Death, the cutting off of someone from the clans. The name means simply "death ceremony."

Daphne – one of the tavern maids at the Wolfen's Rest inn in Dartford.

Darkcaller – one of the Falxen sent to kill Khrazhti and her companions. A former student at Sitor-Kanda, her specialty is dark magic.

Dark Council – a mysterious group of thirteen people who are trying to manipulate events in Dizhelim.

Dartford – a small town on the mainland near the north bridge to the island of Munsahtiz.

Darun Achaya (*dah·ROON ah·CHAI·ah*) – father of Fahtin, head of the family of Gypta that adopts Aeden.

Dasyra Tannen (*dah·SIGH·rah*) – one of the young students at the Academy. Marla chooses her to help with her demonstration when Erol proves to be unmanageable.

Denore Felas (*den·OR FEHL·ahss*) – a great mage in the Age of Magic, the best friend of Tsosin Ruus.

Desid (*DAY·sid*) – a type of animaru. They're nearly mindless, only able to follow simple commands, but they are fairly strong and tireless. They are about five feet tall with thick, clawed fingers useful for digging. They have the mentality of a young child.

Dizhelim (*DEESH·ay·leem*) – the world in which the story happens. The name means "center universe" in the ancient magical language Alaqotim.

Dmirgan (*DMEER·gen*) – a town in Kruzekstan, where a young Erent Caahs killed a man he thought was a murderer

Dob – a small arba boy whose father was killed in the battle where Urun and the others first met the arba in the Mellafond.

Dreigan (*DRAY·gun*) – a mythical beast, a reptile that resembles a monstrous snake with four legs attached to its sides like a lizard. The slightly smaller cousin to the mythical dragons.

Drugancairn (*DROO·gan·cayrn*) – a small town on the southwest edge of the Grundenwald Forest.

Dubhghall Trebhin (*DOO·gall TREH·vin*) – one of the representatives of the Trebhin clan who went to fetch

Aeden to come back and talk to the clan chiefs. He is abrasive and impolite.

Ebenrau (*EBB·en·ra·oo*) – the capital city of Rhaltzheim, one of the seven great cities in Dizhelim

Ellia (*ELL·ee·ah*) – one of the tribespeople Sirak uses to try to get Marla, the only female warrior in the squad.

Emora (*ay·MORE·ah*) – the term of endearment Tsosin Ruus used for Iowyn Selen. It means *my love* in Alaqotim.

Encalo (pl. encali) (*en·CAW·lo*) – four-armed, squat, powerful humanoids. There are few in Dizhelim, mostly in the western portion of the continent Promistala.

Epradotirum (*EP·rah·doe·TEER um*) – an extremely powerful entity who lives in another plane of existence, touching the mortal plane when, every few centuries, he is hungry. Aeden and some of his friends met the Epra while running from assassins near Satta Sarak.

Erent Caahs (*AIR·ent CAWS*) – the most famous of the contemporary heroes. He disappeared twenty years before the story takes place, and is suspected to be dead, though his body was never found.

Erfinchen (*air·FEEN·chen*) – animaru that are shapeshifters. Though not intelligent and powerful enough to be leaders among the animaru, they are often at higher levels, though not in command of others. They typically perform special missions and are truly the closest thing to assassins the animaru have. A very few can use some magic.

Erol Denagian (*AIR·ole den·AG·ee·an*) – the arrogant younger student at the Academy that says Marla is not that good, only that she's a pet of the masters.

Esiyae Yellynn (*ess·SEE·yay YELL·in*) – the Master of the School of Air Magic at the Hero Academy.

Espirion (*es·PEER·ee·on*) – the god of plans and

schemes. From his name comes the terms espionage and spy.

Eutychus Naevius (*YOO·tik·us   NAY·vee us*) – a renowned mathematician in ancient times. One of his principles, the third theorem of alternating magical series, was the key Marla used to decrypt Ren Kenata's letters.

Evindia Elkien (*eh·VIN·dee ah EL·kee·en*) – a member of the Dark Council.

Evon Desconse – a graduate of the famed Hero Academy and best friend to Marla Shrike.

Exulmucri (*EX·ool·MOO·cree*) – an ancient game of strategy, thought to be the first of its kind. It was also the first game to use dice.

Fahtin Achaya (*FAH·teen ah·CHAI·ah*) – a young Gypta girl in the family that adopted Aeden. She and Aeden grew as close as brother and sister in the four years he spent with the family.

Falxen (*FAL·ksen*) – an assassin organization, twelve of whom go after Aeden and his friends. The members are commonly referred to as "Blades."

Featherblade – one of the Falxen sent to kill Khrazhti and her companions. He is the leader of the brace and his skill with a sword is supreme.

Fireshard – one of the Falxen sent to kill Khrazhti and her companions. She wields fire magic.

Forgren (*FORE·gren*) – a type of animaru that is tireless and single-minded. They are able to memorize long messages and repeat them exactly, so they make good messengers. They have no common sense and almost no problem-solving skills

Formivestu (*form·ee·VES·too*) – the insect creatures that attacked Tere's group when they were on their way to Sitor-

Kanda. They look like giant ants with human faces and were thought to be extinct.

Fyorio (*fee·YORE·ee·oh*) – the god of fire and light, from whose name comes the word *fyre*, spelled *fire* in modern times.

Fyrefall – a desolate and dangerous land in the south central part of Promistala, full of hot pools, geysers, and other signs of volcanic activity.

Gareth Briggs – a member of the Dark Council.

Gemsport – the largest port city in the Great Enclave, on the southwestern shore of the Kanton Sea.

Gentason (*jen·TAY·sun*) – an ancient nation, enemy of Salamus. It no longer exists.

Ginsa (GIN·*sah*) (G pronounced like in *begin*) – one of the tribespeople Sirak uses to try to get Marla

Gneisprumay (*gNAYS·proo·may*) – first (or most important) enemy. The name for the Malatirsay in the animaru dialect of Alaqotim.

Godan Chul (*GO·dahn CHOOL*) – an ancient mythological race of spirit beings, created accidentally from the magic of the God of Magic, Migae. The name means, roughly "spirit's whisper."

Goren Adnan – the Master of the School of Military Strategy at the Hero Academy.

Graduate (at the Hero Academy) – a student of the Hero Academy who is either an adept or a viro/vira. That is, anyone who has mastered at least three schools at the Academy and is either still studying there or has left the school.

Great Enclave – a nation to the west of the Kanton Sea and the Hero Academy.

Greimich Tannoch (*GREY·mikh TAN·ahkh*) – Aeden's

close friend, his braitharlan, during his training with the clans.

Grundenwald Forest (*GROON·den·vahld*) – the enormous forest in the northeastern part of the main continent of Promistala. It is said to be the home of magic and beasts beyond belief.

Gulra (pl. gulrae) (*GUL·rah; GUL·ray*) – an animaru that walks on four legs and resembles a large, twisted dog. These are used for tracking, using their keen sense of smell like a hound.

Gwenore River – a large river that splits off from the Alvaspirtu and travels south, through Satta Sarak and all the way to the Aesculun Ocean

Gyerju (*gyare·JOO*) – a village in southern Shinyan where Jia Toun's father was born and grew up.

Gypta (*GIP·tah*) – the traveling people, a nomadic group that lives in wagons, homes on wheels, and move about, never settling down into towns or villages.

Hamrath – a small town on the coast of the eastern part of the Kanton Sea, just north of the bridge from the mainland to Munsahtiz Island.

Hane Bryce – a member of the Dark Council.

Heaven's Teeth – the range of mountains to the east of the Kanton sea, in between that body of water and the Grundenwald Forest.

Heronorus (*hare·ON·or·us*) – the god of honor.

Honor's Peak – the mountain bordering the Shinyan capital city of Tongqi, home of the Chamber of the Trial of Honor.

Ianthra (*ee·ANTH·rah*) – the Goddess of Love and Beauty.

Ianthra's Breasts (*ee·ANTH·rah*) – a mountain range between Arcusheim in Sutania and Satta Sarak. Even though there are three peaks, the two that dominate were named for the physical attributes of the Goddess of Love and Beauty, Ianthra.

Iaurium (*ee·OUR·ee·um*) – a port city in Arania, on the western shore of the Kanton Sea.

Iowyn Selen (*EE·o·win SELL·en*) – a great mage in the Age of Magic, the love of Tsosin Ruus's life.

Iracundamel (*EER·ah·COON·dah·mel*) – the ancient name for the well of power at the center of the Mellafond swamp. The name means, roughly, *nature's wrath* or *Mellaine's wrath*.

Iryna Vorona (*ee·REEN·ah voe·rone·ah*) – Master of the School of Interrogation and Coercion at the Hero Academy.

Isbal Deyne (*ISS·bahl DANE*) – a member of the Dark Council.

Isegrith Palas (*ISS·eh·grith PAL·us*) – the Master of Fundamental Magic at the Hero Academy.

Itera (*ee·TARE·ah*) – high level functionaries in the Vandan Church. They are essentially the second level from the top, though the High Itera, the top three of their number, are above the rest, just below the Patr Pruma.

Ivel Danson (*EYE·vell DAN·sun*) – the 19 year old Academy student who flips out and ends up killing another student when Marla was younger.

Jandar Zumlee (*JAN·dahr ZUM·lee*) – an Academy graduate who is working for the animaru to open portals to Aruzhelim.

Jarnorun (*jar·NOR·un*) – an animaru lord, one of Kirraloth's two main commanders.

Jehira Sinde (*jay·HEER·ah SINDH*) – Raki's grandmother (nani) and soothsayer for the family of Gypta that adopts Aeden.

Jhanda Dalavi (*JON·dah dah·LAHV·ee*) – the Head

Scrivener at the Hero Academy. He is in charge of the small army of scribes who make copies of books and who create many of the records necessary for the functioning of the school.

Jia Toun (*JEE·ah TOON*) – an expert thief and assassin who was formerly the Falxen named Shadeglide. She uses her real name now that she has joined Aeden's group of friends and allies.

Jintu (the Render) Devexo (*JEEN·too day·VEX·oh*) – the great hero and tribe chief who united the tribes of Campastra to fight the false Malatirsay two centuries ago, becoming the high chieftain of the Arunai.

Joceus Davenson (*joe·SEE·us DAA·ven·sun*) – the current king of the Great Enclave, a direct descendent of Thomasinus, Son of Daven, who was the first king of the Great Enclave.

Josef – the owner of the Wolfen's Rest inn in Dartford, a friend of Marla Shrike.

Juinsai (*joo·een·SIE*) – a village in Arania, in the border-lands south of Shinyan, where Jia Toun grew up.

Jusha Terlix (*JOO·shah TER·liks*) – the Master of the School of Mental Magic at the Hero Academy.

Kaeso Hiberus (*KAY·sew hi·BEER·us*) – the author of the holy book of the Church of Vanda, the Vindictae. He claims to be the prophet of Vanda and that he was given the information directly from the god at the end of the Age of Magic.

Kaila (*KY·lah*) – the young encalo girl who Erent Caahs met when he was a boy, searching for his family's killer. He helped her to rescue her caravan.

Kanton Sea (*KAN·tahn*) – an inland sea in which the island of Munsahtiz, home of the Hero Academy, sits.

Kebahn Faitar (Kebahn the Wise) (*kay·BAWN FYE·-*

tahr) – the advisor and friend to Thomasinus; the one who actually came up with the idea to gather all the scattered people and make a stand at the site of what is now the Great Enclave.

Khrazhti *(KHRASH·tee)* – the former High Priestess to the dark god S'ru and former leader of the animaru forces on Dizhelim. At the discovery that her god was untrue, she has become an ally and friend to Aeden.

Kirraloth *(KEER·uh·loth)* – an animaru high lord, given the command of all animaru on Dizhelim after Suuksis failed to turn or destroy Khrazhti.

Kruzekstan *(KROO·zek·stahn)* – a small nation due south of the highland clan lands of Cridheargla.

Kryzt *(KRIZT)* – a type of animaru with spikes all over it, shaped roughly like a wolf but with a longer tail. It has sharp claws and teeth.

Leafburrow – a village in Rhaltzheim, north of Arcusheim off the River Road, the location of a bandit ambush where Erent Caahs demonstrated his special spinning arrow technique.

Leaf Talker – the historical name for an arba community's leader.

Lela Ganeva *(LEE·lah·gahn·AY·vah)* – the woman Erent Caahs fell in love with.

Lerus Costanti *(lehr·OOS coe·STAN·tee)* – one of the three High Itera of the Church of Vanda.

Lesnum *(LESS·num)* – large, hairy, beastlike animaru. These sometimes walk around on two feet, but more commonly use all four limbs. They are strong and fast and intelligent enough to be used as sergeants, commanding groups of seren and other low-level animaru.

Lex – Evon's horse, a chestnut stallion

Lilianor (Lili) Caahs *(LI·lee·ah·nore CAWS)* – Erent

Cahhs's little sister; she was murdered when she was eleven years old.

Liluth Olaxidor (*LIL·uth oh·LAX·ih·door*) – the Master of the School of Firearms at the Hero Academy.

Lily Fisher – an archer of supreme skill who was formerly the Falxen assassin named Phoenixarrow. She uses her real name now that she has joined Aeden's group of friends and allies.

Lis (*LEES*) – a minor deity who battled the sun, nearly killing it, and causing so much damage that to this day, it is weakened in the wintertime.

Lucas Stewart – a young student at the Hero Academy. He's often used by the masters as a messenger because of his strong work ethic and reliability.

Lucio Sanctus (*LOO·chee·oh SAHNK·toos*) – the Patr Pruma of the Vandan Church.

Lusnauqua (*loos·NOW·kwah*) – the rugged land surrounding Broken Reach, in the center of the eastern section of the continent of Promistala.

Malatirsay (*Mahl·ah·TEER·say*) – the hero who will defeat the animaru and save Dizhelim from the darkness, according to prophecy. The name means "chosen warrior" or "special warrior" in Alaqotim.

Manandantan (*mahn·ahn·DAHN·tahn*) – the festival to celebrate the goddess Danta, goddess of song.

Marla Shrike – a graduate of the famed Hero Academy, an experienced combatant in both martial and magical disciplines.

Marn Tiscomb – the new Master of Prophecy at the Hero Academy. He replaced Master Aeid, who was murdered.

Masseni Devexo (*mah·SEH·nee day·VEX·oh*) – the

daughter of chief Rovalu Devexo, an influential warrior princess of the Arunai.

Mellafond (*MEH·la·fond*) – a large swamp on the mainland to the east of Munsahtiz Island. The name *means pit of Mellaine.*

Mellaine (*meh·LAYN*) – goddess of nature and growing things.

Miera Tannoch (*MEERA TAN·ahkh*) – Aeden's mother, wife of Sartan.

Migae (*MEE·jay*) – the God of magic. The word "magic" comes from his name.

Mionn Bhais (*MYOON BAJH*) – the Death Oath, a tradition set forth at the beginning of the Croagh clans. It consists of a magical ritual that binds the clan chiefs to either submit to one leader or to challenge that leader in combat to the death.

Mora Davenson (*MORE·ah DAA·ven·sun*) – the queen of the Great Enclave, wife of Joceus Davenson.

Morningsilver – the horse the Academy let Jia use, a pale grey horse whose coat shone in the right light.

Moroshi Katai (*mor·ROE·shee kah·TAI*) – a mythological hero who battled the Dragon of Eternity to found the nation of Teroshi.

Moschephis (*mose·CHE·feess*) – the trickster god, from whose name comes the word mischief.

Mudertis (*moo·DARE·teez*) – the god of thievery and assassination.

Munsahtiz (*moon·SAW·teez*) – the island in the Kanton sea on which the Hero Academy Sitor-Kanda resides.

Muscade (*moos·CAWD*) – the horse the Academy let Aila use, a light reddish brown mare.

Nanris – the unofficial capital of Kruzekstan, more

important than the actual capital of Kruzeks because most of the wealth of the nation is centered in Nanris.

Nasir Kelqen (*nah·SEER KEL·ken*) – the Master of the School of Research and Investigation at the Hero Academy.

Naxon Den-Uto (*NAX·on DEN·OO·toe*) – the chief of the Den-Uto tribe of Arunai

Nessa Shua (*NESS·ah. SHOE·ah*) – one of Cara Moore's underlings, an unattractive woman who wears very tight clothing on her superbly fit body and fights with great flexibility.

Nightheart – the horse the Academy let Raki use in his travels, a black stallion.

Nobleflame – the horse the Academy let Lily use, a dark red gelding.

Noud Grissen (*NUDE*) – a mid-level criminal, a magical artifact smuggler

Nutenlo (*noo·TEN·loe*) – one of the tribespeople Sirak uses to try to get Marla.

Omnisagnitio (*OME·nees·ahg·NEE·shee·oh*) – the name of the Well of Power found in the cave system where Tsosin Ruus's cache of information was found, within the Aerie Mountains.

Omri – a fair sized city in northern Kruzekstan, one of the first of the cities to fall to the animaru.

Osulin (*AWE·soo·lin*) – goddess of nature. She is the daughter of Mellaine and the human hero Trikus Phen.

Pach (*PAHKH*) – in Dantogyptain, it means five. As a proper noun, it refers to the festival of Manandantan that occurs every fifth year, a special celebration in which the Song of Prophecy is sung in full.

Padraig Seachaid (*PAD·reg SHAW·chid*) – the clan chief of the Seachaid Croagh clan.

Patr Pruma (*POT·er PROO·mah*) – the leader of the Church of Vanda.

Pedras Shrike – Marla Shrike's adoptive father, the groundskeeper for the administrative area of the Hero Academy.

Percipius (*pare·CHIP·ee·us*) – god of the dead and of the underworld.

Phoenixarrow – one of the Falxen sent to kill Khrazhti and her companions. A statuesque red-haired archer who had a penchant for using fire arrows.

Pilae (*PEEL·lay*) – a type of animaru that looks like a ball of shadow.

Pofel Dessin (*POE·fell DESS·in*) – a traveling scholar who meets Marla and Evon on their journeys.

Pouran (*PORE·an*) – roundish, heavy humanoids with piggish faces and tusks like a boar

Praesturi (*prayz·TURE·ee*) – the town and former military outpost on the southeastern tip of the island of Munsahtiz. The south bridge from the mainland to the island ends within Praesturi.

Preshim (*PRAY·sheem*) – title of the leader of a family of Gypta

Promistala (*prome·ees·TAHL·ah*) – the main continent in Dizhelim. In Alaqotim, the name means "first (or most important) land."

Qozhel (*KOE·shell*) – the energy that pervades the universe and that is usable as magic.

Qydus Okvius (*KIE·duss OCK·vee·us*) – the headmaster of the Hero Academy, Sitor-Kanda.

Raibrech (*RAI·brekh*) – the clan magic of the highland clans. In Chorain, it means "bloodfire."

Raimund Bainer (*RAY·mund BANE·er*) – one of the three High Itera of the Church of Vanda.

Rainstorm – the horse the Acaedmy let Urun use, a grey mare with black speckles.

Raisor Tannoch (*RAI·sore   TAN·ahkh*) – a famous warrior of Clan Tannoch, companion of the hero Erent Caahs.

Raki Sinde (*ROCK·ee   SINDH*) – grandson of Jehira Sinde, friend and training partner of Aeden.

Ren Kenata (*REN   ke·NAH·tah*) – a Hero Academy adept who was is not only one of Quentin Duzen's associates, but also a member of the Dark Council.

Rhaltzheim (*RALTZ·haim*) – the nation to the north-east of the Grundenwald Forest. The people of the land are called Rhaltzen or sometimes Rhaltza. The term Rhaltzheim is often used to refer to the rugged land within the national borders (e.g., "traverse the Rhaltzheim")

Ritma Achaya (*REET·mah   ah·CHAI·ah*) – Fahtin's mother, wife of the Gypta family leader Darun.

Roneus Lomos (*ROE·nee·us LOE·mose*) – the Master of the School of Stealth at the Hero Academy.

Rougang (*roo·GAHNG*) – one of the major cities in modern Shinyan, in former Xin tribe territory. In ancient Shinyan, it was a town, the headquarters for the rebel forces of Xin Tai Rong.

Rovalu Devexo (*roe·VAH·loo   day·VEX·oh*) – the current high chief of all the Arunai. He resides in Devexo, within in the territory of the Devex-Numantu tribe)

Ruthrin (*ROOTH·rin*) – the common tongue of Dizhe-lim, the language virtually everyone in the world speaks in addition to their own national languages.

S'ru (*SROO*) – the dark god of the animaru, supreme power in Aruzhelim.

Saelihn Valdove (*SAY·lin VAHL·doe·vay*) – the Master of the School of Life Magic at the Hero Academy.

Saevel (*SAY·vell*) – the arba huntress who guided Urun's group through the Mellafond swamp.

Salamus (*sah·lah·MOOS*) – an ancient nation in which the legendary hero Trikus Phen resided. It no longer exists. Things of Salamus were called Salaman.

Samten (*SAM·ten*) – one of the tribespeople Sirak uses to try to get Marla.

Saria Gilwenys (*SAW·ree ah gill·WEN·is*) (gill is pronounced like a fish's *gill*) – an Academy graduate who has been out in the world working as an operative for Sitor-Kanda. She is half astri.

Sartan Tannoch (*SAR·tan TAN·ahkh*) – Aeden's father, clan chief of the Tannoch clan of Craogh.

Sastiroz (*SASS·teer·oz*) – an animaru lord, one of Kirraloth's two main commanders.

Satta Sarak (*SAH·tah SARE·ack*) – a city in the south-eastern part of the continent of Promistala, part of the Saraki Principality.

Scrapper – the name Aila gave the small trebaxel they found in Sintrovis

Seachaid (*SHAW·chid*) – one of the five highland clans of the Cridheargla.

Semhominus (*sem·HOM·in·us*) – one of the highest level of animaru. They are humanoid, larger than a typical human, and use weapons. Many of them can also use magic. Most animaru lords are of this type.

Senna Shrike – Marla Shrike's adoptive mother.

Seoras Corcan (*SORE·us*) – the clan chief of the Corcan clan of Croagh.

Seren (*SARE·en*) – the most common type of animaru, with sharp teeth and claws. They are similar in shape and size to humans.

Shadeglide – one of the Falxen sent to kill Khrazhti and her companions. She is small of stature but extremely skilled as a thief and assassin.

Shadowed Pinnacles – the long mountain range essentially splitting the western part of Promistala into two parts. It was formerly known as the Wall of Salamus because it separated that kingdom from Gentason.

Shaku (*SHOCK·oo*) – a class of Teroshimi assassins.

Shanaera Eilren (*shah·NARE·ah ALE·ren*) – the Master of Unarmed Combat at the Hero Academy.

Sharan Kolga (*shah·RAHN COLE·gah*) – the student at the Academy who bullied Ivel and ended up being killed by him.

Shinyan (*SHEEN·yahn*) – a nation on the northern tip of the western part of Promistala, bordering the Kanton Sea and the Cattilan Sea. Things of Shinyan (such as people) are referred to as Shinyin.

Shu root/Shu's Bite (*SHOO*) – a root that only grows in Shinyan, the key ingredient to the poison Shu's Bite.

Sike (*SEEK·ay*) – a class of Shinyin assassins

Sintrovis (*seen·TROE·vees*) – an area of high magical power on which the Great Enclave was built. In Alaqotim, it means *center of strength*.

Sirak Isayu (*SEER·ack ee·SAI·yoo*) – a member of the Dark Council. He comes from the southern part of the continent of Promistala, near the Sittingham Desert.

Sitor-Kanda (*SEE·tor KAN·dah*) – the Hero Academy, the institution created by the great prophet Tsosin Ruus to train the Malatirsay. The name means roughly "home of magic" in Alaqotim.

Sittingham Desert – a large desert in the southwestern part of Promistala.

Skril Tossin – best friend of Marla Shrike and Evon Desconce, a Hero Academy adept.

384

Snowmane – the horse the Academy lent to Aeden, a chestnut stallion with a white mane

Solon (*SEW·lahn*) – one of the masters in Clan Tannoch, responsible for training young warriors how to use the clan magic, the Raibrech.

Souvenia (*soo·VEN·ee·ah*) – an empire that was one of the world powers before the War of Magic, and one of the major players in that war. It no longer exists.

Srantorna (*sran·TORN·ah*) – the abode of the gods, a place where humans cannot go.

Sudepta Sinde (*soo·DEP·tan SINDH*) – one of Raki's older brothers, the one whose birthday it was when Raki's family went out to get him a present and were attacked and killed.

Surefoot – Marla Shrike's horse.

Surus (*SOO·roos*) – king of the gods.

Sutania (*soo·TAN·ee·ah*) – the nation south of the Kanton Sea, the capital of which is the city of Arcusheim.

Suuksis (*SOOK·sis*) – an animaru lord; Khrazhti's father.

Szestithan (*ZESS·tih·than*) (the th is pronounced like in *thousand*) – the highest of the animaru, the only one who deals directly with S'ru after Khrazhti defected. He's called S'ru's Shadow.

Tamo (*tah·MOE*) – the name given the carved wooden masks the Shinyin Imperial Guard wear. They were named after the rebel Jee Ta Mo, who wore a similar mask in his service to Xin Tai Rong.

Tannoch (*TAN·ahkh*) – one of the five highland clans of the Cridheargla, the one to which Aeden was born into.

Tarshuk (*TAR·shuk*) – a semi-desert-like area to the southwest of the Heaven's Teeth range that has stunted trees and scrub.

Tazi Ermengo (*TAH·zee air·MANE·go*) – the king of the doomed kingdom of Awresea. He taunted the god Fyorio and was destroyed along with his entire kingdom, which was renamed Fyrefall.

Tere Chizzit (*TEER CHIZ·it*) – a blind archer and tracker with the ability to see despite having no working eyes. He is Aeden's companion in the story.

Tero (*TAY·roe*) – the Dragon of Eternity, one of the mightiest of all dragons who had ever lived and whose plummet to his death created the Astugi Sea.

Teroshi (*tare·OH·shee*) – an island nation in the northern part of Dizhelim. Things of Teroshi, including people, are referred to as Teroshimi.

Thalia Fendove (*THA·lee·uh FEN·doe·vay*) – a member of the Dark Council.

Thomasinus, son of Daven (*toe·mah·SINE·us*) – the hero who banded the remnants of the troops of Gentason together to create the Great Enclave. Once they elected him king, he changed his last name to Davenson.

Thomlin Byrch (*TOM·lin BIRCH*) – a member of the Dark Council.

Thritur Nyhus (*THRY·tur NY·hus*) – a member of the Dark Council.

Thunderlight – the horse the Academy let Tere use, a black stallion with white markings that look like slashes.

Tide's Blessing – the inn Marla and the others stayed at in Hirsen.

Toan Broos (*TOE·aan*) – traveling companion of Erent Caahs and Raisor Tannoch.

Tongqi (*TOHNG·chee*) – the capital city of Shinyan, nestled in the bowl created by the mountains near Honor's Peak.

Toras Geint (*TOR·ahs GAYNT*) – an old tracker and

scout who befriended Erent Caahs when he was a boy and who mentored the young hero, training him to track and hunt, among other things.

Toross Iardisith (*TORE·oss ee·ARD·ih·sith*) – an Academy graduate who is working for the animaru to open portals to Aruzhelim

Touhas Ailgid (*TOO·ahs ILE·jid*) – the elder of the Ailgid clan of Croagh who was named their clan chief after much of their clan was destroyed by the animaru.

Trebaxel (*tre·BAX·el*) – ape like creatures that are rumored to exist in Sintrovis, in the Great Enclave.

Trebhin (*TREH·vin*) – one of the five highland clans of the Cridheargla.

Tresica (*TREH·sih cah*) – Ivel's girlfriend who dumped him and cheated on him with Sharan Kolga.

Trikus Phen (*TRY·kus FEN*) – a legendary hero who battled Codaghan, the god of war, himself, and sired Osulin by the goddess Mellaine.

Tsosin Ruus (*TSO·sin ROOS*) – the Prophet, the seer and archmage who penned the Song of Prophecy and founded Sitor-Kanda, the Hero Academy.

Tuach (*TOO·akh*) – one of the masters in Clan Tannoch, responsible for teaching the young warriors the art of physical combat.

Tufa Shao (*TOO·fah SHA·oh*) – the Master of the School of Body Mechanics and Movement at the Hero Academy.

Tunin Ferrol (*TOO·nen. FARE·all*) – one of Cara Moore's underlings. He is obsessed with food.

Twilight – the horse the Academy let Khrazhti use, a grey mare.

Urtumbrus (*oor·TOOM·brus*) – a type of animaru that are essentially living shadows.

Urun Chinowa (*OO·run CHIN·oh·wah*) – the High Priest of the goddess Osulin, a nature priest.

Utrix (*OO·trix*) – a colechna (snake-type) animaru who looks for the hidden cache Tsosin Ruus left for Aeden and Marla. He is a mage and obsessed with study to gain knowledge of the new world he has come to.

Vadim Plesca (*VAH·deem PLES·kah*) – a mage during the Age of Magic, a close associate to Aquilius Gavros.

Vaeril Faequin (*VARE·ill FAY·kwin*) – the Master of the School of Mechanista Artifice at the Hero Academy.

Valcordinae (*val·COR·di·nay*) – a series of extremely ancient tunnels with a well of magical power at its core. The word is ancient Alaqotim for *strong minds*.

Vanda (*VAHN·dah*) – a modern god, claimed by his followers to be the only true god. It is said he is many gods in one, having different manifestations. The Church of Vanda is very large and very powerful in Dizhelim.

Vandictae (*vahn·DIC·tay*) – the book of holy writings of the Church of Vanda.

Vandictatorum (*vahn·DIC·tah·TOR·um*) – the massive domed structure in Vandomus, the center of learning about the Vandictae. Essentially a university of the church's holy writings.

Vater (*VAH·ter*) – one of the tribespeople Sirak uses to try to get Marla.

Vatheca (*VATH·ay·kuh*) – the headquarters and training center of the Falxen. It is a mixture of two Alaqotim words, both meaning "sheath."

Veraugun (*vare·ow·GOON*) – the name of the Well of Power found in Shinyan. It means true honor in ancient Alaqotim.

Vesta – a huge mythological beast that was too large to come down from the heavens to Dizhelim. Surus did battle with the monster to prevent it from destroying the world.

Videric Dewitte (*VEE·dare·ic   deh·VIT*) – the Master of the School of Magical Healing at the Hero Academy.

Vincus (pl. vinci) (*VEEN·cuss; VEEN·chee*) – Aila's chain blade weapons.

Viro/Vira (pl viri) (*VEER·oh / VEER·ah / VEER·ee*) – a former Hero Academy student who has graduated with a mastery in at least three schools and no longer lives at the Academy or participates in its function.

Vituma (*vi·TOO·mah*) – the leader of the Dark Council. The name derives from the ancient Alaqotim term for *prophet's shadow*.

Voordim (*VOOR·deem*) – the pantheon of gods in Dizhelim. It does not include the modern god Vanda.

Vora (*VORE·ah*) – the Leaf Talker of the tribe of arba in the Mellafond swamp.

Vulmer Liadin (*VUL·mer   LEE·uh·din*) – the first head-master of the Hero Academy, appointed by Tsosin Ruus himself to run the school for the Prophet.

Wolfen – large intelligent wolves that roam desolate areas in the Rhaltzheim.

Wolfen's Rest – the inn in Dartford, on the mainland not too far east from the bridge to the island of Munsahtiz.

Xaviera Contanko (*zaw·vee·AIR·ah   cone TAHNK·oe*) – the Master of Artifice: Items of Power at the Hero Academy. She journeyed to the Dark Pinnacles with Raki, Jia, and Urun.

Xin Su Jun (*SHEEN SOO JOON*) – the current Shinyin emperor, son of the former emperor.

Xin Tai Rong (*SHEEN TIE ROHNG*) – the rebel leader who eventually defeated Chao He Ling's forces and became the first emperor of Shinyan.

Yezras Farlingian (*YEZ·rass   far LIN·gee·an*) – the Master of the School of Conjuration and Invocation at the Hero Academy.

Yoniko Takesi (*YOE·nee·koe tah·KAY·see*) – a member of the Dark Council.

Yralissa Zinphinal (*eer·ah·LISS ah   ZIN·fin·all*) – the Master of the School of Illusion at the Hero Academy.

Yxna Hagenai (*IX·nah   HAG·en·eye*) – the Master of Edged Weapons at the Hero Academy.

Zejo Troufal (*ZAY·joe   TROO·fahl*) – a hero who lived at the end of the Age of Magic. He was Erent Cahhs's idol when he was a boy, before he himself became a hero.

Zhadril (*ZHAD·reel*) – an animaru mage—former high priest of S'ru—who was defeated in battle by Khrazhti to lose his position. In Dizhelim, he was given permission to study corrupted magic in a swamp area.

AUTHOR NOTES

Thank you for reading Hero's Anger!

What did you think about Marla's little anger management problem? Sure, it wasn't any great revelation. After all, the first time she met Aeden, she tried to beat him to a pulp. Still, when I read back over the story after some time away from it, it surprised me a little bit just how much things were affecting her. Not just the stress, but the magic as well.

We're well on our way to building the story to a peak and then getting some of the stuff that's going on resolved. The next book, Hero's Life, is already written, as is the one after that, Hero's Light. There's editing to be done and it may be a few months until I tackle writing the next book, but the long delays should be done. Until the next book, I hope your life has much less anger in it than poor Marla did in this part of the series.

If you enjoyed the book, **could you please leave a review?** It's no secret that authors like me need reviews from readers like you to increase the number of people who get their eyes on my books. Reviews and ratings are so important in creating word of mouth so other readers will try my stories. I would appreciate it immensely if you could help.

I appreciate you sharing my stories with me and hope to see you in Dizhelim—and other worlds in upcoming series—again.

P.E. Padilla

The Great Prophet predicted you would want to read his story

Tsosin Ruus, the most renowned mage during the Age of Magic, wrote the Song of Prophecy to aid the world of Dizhelim as it would exist thousands of years after his life ended. But who was the Great Prophet, and how did he come to be the most important person in history...up until the present time?

And what of Erent Caahs, the most famous of contemporary heroes?

Get these two full-length companion novels to the Song of Prophecy and Hero Academy series for free and find out the fascinating stories that transformed ordinary boys into figures idolized by millions.

To get your free books and find out about upcoming books, please visit my website at https://pepadilla.com (Newsletter menu item or the bottom of every page). Thank you!

ABOUT THE AUTHOR

A chemical engineer by degree and at various times an air quality engineer, a process control engineer, and a regulatory specialist by vocation, USA Today bestselling author P.E. Padilla learned long ago that crunching numbers and designing solutions was not enough to satisfy his creative urges. Weaned on classic science fiction and fantasy stories from authors as diverse as Heinlein, Tolkien, and Jordan, and affected by his love of role playing games such as Dungeons and Dragons (analog) and Final Fantasy (digital), he sometimes has trouble distinguishing reality from fantasy. While not ideal for a person who needs to function in modern society, it's the perfect state of mind for a writer. He is a recent transplant from Southern California to Northern Washington, where he lives surrounded by trees.

pepadilla.com/
pep@pepadilla.com

ALSO BY P.E. PADILLA

Adventures in Gythe:

Vibrations: Harmonic Magic Book 1 (audiobook also)

Harmonics: Harmonic Magic Book 2 (audiobook also)

Resonance: Harmonic Magic Book 3

Tales of Gythe: Gray Man Rising (audiobook also available)

Tales of Gythe: Ix: Legacy of Honor

Harmonic Magic Series Boxed Set

The Unlikely Hero Series (under pen name Eric Padilla):

Unfurled: Heroing is a Tough Gig (Unlikely Hero Series Book 1)
(also available as an audiobook)

Unmasked (Unlikely Hero Series Book 2)

Undaunted (Unlikely Hero Series Book 3)

Unlikely Hero Series Boxed Set

The Shadowling Chronicles (under pen name Eric Padilla):

Shadowling

Witches of the Elements Series :

Water & Flame

Song of Prophecy Series :

SoP1 - Wanderer's Song (available as an audiobook also)

SoP2 - Warrior's Song

SoP3 - Heroes' Song

SoP4 - Hero Dawning

SoP5 - Hero's Mind

SoP6 - Hero's Nature

SoP7 - Hero's Honor

SoP8 - Hero's Knowledge

SoP9 - Hero's Darkness

SoP10 - Hero's Strength

SoP11 - Hero's Anger (this book)

SoP12 - Hero's Life (coming October 2024)

Song of Prophecy Omnibus/Box Sets:

Song of Prophecy Series Omnibus 1

Song of Prophecy Series Omnibus 2

Tales of Dizhelim (companion stories to the SoP Series):

Arrow's Flight

Song's Prophet

Order of the Fire Series:

Call of Fire

Hero of Fire

Legacy of Fire

Order of the Fire Boxed Set

www.ingramcontent.com/pod-product-compliance
Lightning Source LLC
Chambersburg PA
CBHW020013120726
47903CB00004B/1258